FIGHTS

THE FIGHT GAME BOOK TWO
NIKKI CASTLE

Cover Design: Haya in Designs

Formatting: Books and Moods

Editing: NiceGirlNaughtyEdits

To the women who recognize their worth and get the fuck away from anyone who treats them as anything less than the queens they are

Playlist

Fuck Steve – GODS OF ROD
This Love – Camila Cabello
Fuck You – Silent Child
Best Days – Alessia Cara
Blood // Water – grandson
Hard 2 Face Reality – Poo Bear, Justin Bieber, Jay Electronica
I Feel Like I'm Drowning – Two Feet
abcdefu – GAYLE
You Can Count On Me – Ansel Elgort, Logic
Love Myself – Olivia O'Brien
Woman – Doja Cat
Dance to Deny – Al Zamora
Good Days – SZA
Whoopty – CJ
that way – Tate McRae, Jeremy Zucker
Power Over Me – Dermot Kennedy
Crawl Outta Love – ILLENIUM, Annika Wells
Better – Khalid
Enta – DJ KABOO
Desert Rose – Lolo Zouai
Praying – Kesha
If You Love Her – Forest Blakk
I Don't Want to Lose You – Luca Fogale
It'll Be Okay – Shawn Mendes
see you later (ten years) – Jenna Raine
Lost Without You – Freya Ridings
everything – John K

AUTHOR'S NOTE

2 Fights is a love story first and foremost, but it's also a story of healing. The synopsis gives you exactly the information you need to go into this book but I wanted to write an extra note to those who are affected a little more personally by this story.

The unfortunate fact of the matter is many of us have known a Steve: dated him, had a parent like him, seen a friend get lost in him. He's everywhere. People often think of domestic violence as physical abuse but it can be so much more than that. It can be emotional, mental, or psychological abuse by a person close to you. It's incredibly difficult to realize the truth of the situation and even harder to get away from it, as you'll see in Hailey's story. But it is possible.

My hope for everyone who's ever dealt with this kind of situation is that you find the kind of strength that Hailey did. You deserve to be loved, and you deserve to be happy. It would be nice if we all had the support of a Jax but the truth is sometimes we need to be our own savior. That's my wish for everyone who's ever experienced something like this.

If you ever need someone to turn to, there are many organizations that can help with counseling, creating a safety plan, or even just to talk to.

Safe Horizon Hotline: 1-800-621-HOPE

FIGHT ONE

CHAPTER ONE
Hailey

THIS IS IT. Today is the day I go to jail for proving the customer is not, in fact, always right.

"Ma'am, if you can't keep your voice down, I'm going to have to ask you to leave. Yelling at my employee is doing nothing to resolve this situation."

Oof. Karen does *not* like that.

"You're going to kick me out?!" she shouts, her voice not even a fraction of a decibel lower. "After everything that stupid hostess did, your solution is to kick *me* out?"

My nostrils flare with mounting annoyance. Nobody ever said managing a café in Philadelphia was going to be easy—or without our share of typical Philadelphia attitude—but this is just ridiculous.

"Ma'am, I'm asking you again to please lower your voice," I say through gritted teeth. "And if you insult my employee one more time, I will immediately escort you off the premises." I cut off her squeak of outrage by talking over whatever spluttering comeback her Karen-brain is currently trying to come up with. "If you'd like to be put on the waitlist, I'll be happy to get you seated in ten-to-fifteen minutes. But that is the only way you're going to be served today."

Her mouth drops open in outrage. "Waitlist? But we were already seated!"

I take a breath to calm myself down before my employees see me freak out for the first time in the history of my surprisingly long restaurant career.

"You were not seated," I say tightly. "You tried to make a reservation and failed, seeing as we don't take reservations, and when you walked in here, you decided you didn't want to wait and seated yourself. In an area that's not open because we don't have enough servers at this point in the day. Which is why you haven't been served. So you can either wait in the entryway like everyone else, or you can take your business elsewhere. It's up to you."

Karen continues to gawk and stutter in outrage, bits of *well, I've never* and *this is extremely unprofessional* being thrown in every once in a while.

She and her mousey husband begin to stand up and gather their things. "You've officially lost a customer, congratulations," she finally snaps. "I hope you learn your lesson when I leave a horrible review and tell all my friends to stay clear of this place."

I nod and gesture toward the exit. "That is entirely your right. Have a wonderful day, ma'am. Sir."

Her eyes are practically bugging out of her head by the time she reaches the front door. We've successfully attracted the attention of the entire restaurant—packed as our small café is on a Thursday brunch—and it takes everything in me not to shoo her out of the building.

Karen is still muttering and unmoving. "This is what happens when you let children manage establishments. Where is the owner? I'd like to speak with him."

"He's not here today. You're welcome to send him an email, though. Our contact information can be found on our website."

"I'm not sending an *email*," she splutters. "Just give me his phone number. I'm sure he wants to know about his staff mistreating his customers."

"Yeah, I'm not giving you the owner's number," I scoff, the Philly girl in me finally making an appearance. Once again, I gesture her toward the door.

"I have *never* been treated like this in all my—"

"Ma'am, get out of my restaurant before I call the cops and have you physically removed."

Her mouth drops open as she's finally stunned into silence. I aim one more not-very-customer-friendly smile at her before she officially gives up and exits in a huff, her husband skulking behind her.

I close the door with a heavy sigh. *And to think, I still have five more hours today and three more days before I get a break.*

But when I turn back to the restaurant, readying myself to apologize to the customers for the interruption to their meals, I'm met with applause.

The table of male college students is grinning and cheering, their whoops of appreciation sounding through the restaurant and causing other tables to quickly join in.

I can feel the blush light my cheeks at the attention and can't help trying to wave it off. Despite what just happened, customer service is actually very important to me—and I happen to be very good at it—so the last thing I need is for my restaurant to be cheering against a customer.

Even if she did deserve it and more.

I smile as I look around the seating areas. "I apologize for the interruption, please go back to your meals. My servers will be around shortly to bring every table a complimentary fruit bowl."

As everyone quiets down, I walk over to Rebecca at the hostess stand. She's one of my newer employees, though her energy and willingness to learn have made her a great hire. Of course she gets the worst Karen in all the lands on only her second week.

"Are you okay?" I ask quietly. "I'm sorry about what she said. You did nothing wrong and handled it perfectly. She had no right to speak to you like that."

She still looks a little shell-shocked, but she shakes her head quickly. "I'm fine. I've had customers yell at me before, so it's nothing new. She just caught me off-guard."

"You did great. I'll make sure you get tipped out well today."

I hear a chuckle sound from behind me and I turn to see one of my most tenured waiters walking over to us. He comes around to lean on the stand itself, his glee over this entire situation apparent.

"God, I love seeing you get all alpha bitch in here," he says with a big grin. "It will never not surprise me that you're the nicest, quietest person in real life, yet the most professional, cutthroat bitch when you're in this building. You're like Dr. Jekyll and Miss Hyde. It's uncanny."

I glare at him but don't disagree. I *am* a nice person in real life. I prefer to be kind to people because God knows there's enough negativity in this world already. I'll be the first person to give you the shirt off my back or my last hundred dollars. I don't gossip, I rarely curse, and I actually prefer not to talk at all unless I'm saying something positive or necessary. So yes, I'm *nice.*

But I also know that I have a job to do, and the restaurant industry is not always a place where you can be nice. There are times when you have to be direct and some people will see that as being mean, but it's all part of the job. And despite my young age, I am *very* good at my job.

"I am not cutthroat," I grumble. "I'm just... effective."

He laughs, and even Rebecca smiles with amusement. *Okay, maybe I can be a little cutthroat at work.*

"I'd pay good money to see how your alpha personality clashes with your demeanor outside of here," he continues, shaking his head. "I mean, what are you like as a girlfriend? Sweet but *effective?* I bet that guy follows you around like a puppy dog and does whatever you want. I can only imagine how little shit you put up with." His eyes twinkle as he grins at me. "In a nice way, of course. Your victims kind of remind me of deer when they get caught in the headlights. The only difference is, you're so nice that the deer never *actually* feels like their life is in danger. They're just... captured and killed with kindness."

I roll my eyes at the ridiculous comparison, though I don't want to admit that I kind of like the sound of it—even if it feels really far from the truth. Being both kind and powerful seems like a good balance to me, one I've always strived for but never quite felt like I've reached.

"Let's get you back to work, Mr. Dramatic," I scold as a smile twitches my lips. "I'm not paying you to psychoanalyze me *or* my relationship."

He huffs a laugh and heads back into the kitchen.

"How *is* Steve doing?" Rebecca asks me. "I forgot to ask how your date was last week at that new restaurant."

I smile, both at the memory of that night and at the fact that she remembered and is kind enough to ask. "It was great. Italian is my favorite, and this place was authentic. I'm pretty sure the owner's grandmother was the one cooking in the back."

I rarely share my personal life with my employees, but Rebecca had stayed late that day and happened to see Steve picking me up for our date. Dressed in a suit with his typical swagger and a bouquet of flowers in his hand, it's no wonder he made an impression on her.

"God, you're so lucky," she gushes. "Steve is seriously so swoon-worthy. My boyfriend hasn't taken me out on a date in who knows how long, and yours actually shows up with *flowers*. Can he please give mine a lesson on how to woo the girl even after you've been with her for a year?"

She's right, I am really lucky. Steve has definitely never had an issue wooing me with dates or flowers.

"Sometimes they just need to be reminded of what they have right in front of them," I tell her.

For the rest of the day, my thoughts are consumed by Steve.

We've been together for more than two years, ever since I ran into him—literally—at a grocery store when I first moved to the city. I was eighteen and fresh out of high school, living with my big sister and foregoing college while I figured out what I wanted to do with my life. Steve, decked out in a suit that day, too, noticed the ingredients in my cart and complimented me on being able to cook when there didn't seem to be many women anymore that enjoyed taking on that task. I had blushed, caught up in the compliment and the attention of this older, very attractive man, and didn't even hesitate to give him my number when he asked for it.

He spent weeks "courting" me, as he called it. He appreciated the build-up of a relationship, choosing not to fall right into bed with someone on the first night. And I was so smitten with the idea of this kind of chivalrous gentleman that I fell in love with him quicker than I would've imagined possible.

After only a year, we decided to move in together. He wanted me close, he said, because he was madly in love with me and couldn't stand to be apart from me for even a night. Now, we live in a quaint, one-bedroom apartment together in the historical part of Philadelphia.

He works in finance in the world of corporate America while I manage a tiny café in South Philly. He's ambitious and successful, and when he convinced me I should go to college to get a degree, it seemed like the most obvious thing in the world. So now I work at the restaurant by day, and study for my business degree at night.

That's my plan for tonight too. As I lock up the café and start my walk home, I review the homework I have to do tonight as I mentally prepare the dinner I'm going to cook. It became a natural rhythm to fall into once we moved in together: we both worked during the day, but in exchange for Steve covering a majority of the apartment costs, I would keep our home clean and cook dinner every night.

It's a comfortable pattern. I love cooking and baking and anything that gets me playing in the kitchen, which made the arrangement was an easy one to fall into. Not to mention, my life goal has always been to open up a café, so the extra practice is also beneficial.

Humming happily as I enter our apartment, I turn on Steve's favorite Mumford and Sons playlist and set aside the ingredients for Chicken Florentine, his favorite meal. My smile grows when I think about his reaction when he sees what's for dinner.

Sure enough, when he walks in an hour later and sees what I'm making, a huge grin splits his handsome face.

"Hey, beautiful. Is that Chicken Florentine? You're amazing, I love when you cook for me." He sweeps across the kitchen, stopping only to drop the bouquet of flowers in his hands onto the counter before he gathers me in his arms and presses a kiss to my hair. He holds me, rocking slightly, as if content just to have his arms around me. I sigh and tighten my arms around his neck.

"I love you so much," he whispers. "You're the best thing that's ever happened to me. All day I kept thinking about how happy I am to come home to you every night. How lucky I am to have this life with you."

I pull back to see his face as I smile at him. He's only a few inches taller than me, about 5'7, so it's easy to feel close to him when he holds me like this. I take a moment to study him, to breathe in his beauty, and once again remind myself that he's mine.

He always looks in his element when he comes directly from the office, with his dark gray dress pants and white dress shirt. Today, he's added a light blue tie, and even though he's not at work anymore, he still hasn't loosened it—it's yet another detail showcasing Steve's unwavering poise. It's just as unlikely to see him with a hair out of place as it is seeing him lose his temper. It just doesn't happen. I've always thought that he's a perfectionist, both with his physical appearance and his general attitude and emotional control.

I run his tie between my fingers, knowing he'll still my hands before long. But he's not always so forthcoming with his vows of love anymore, so I want to appreciate this moment while I have it. Placing my hand on the side of his face when he starts to reach for his tie, I brush my thumb over his beautiful cheekbones, studying his open and honest expression.

"I love you," I say softly. "I love our life. I love that I get to live with my best friend and hang out with you every night." Leaning forward, I press a sweet kiss to his lips, sighing when he gently cups my face and kisses me back.

He stays close even after he ends the kiss. Instead of pulling away, he closes his eyes and leans his forehead against mine with a sated smile.

Steve's always needed more affection than I do. Early in our relationship, it caused a little bit of a rift between us because he didn't understand how a girl couldn't want to be touching all the time. He thought my not wanting to hold his hand in public was a reflection of my feelings for him. In reality, I grew up in a family where physical affection wasn't common or needed to feel loved. Neither my parents nor my sister are huggers and we never said 'I love you' growing up. There was nothing wrong with my family or my childhood, we just weren't touchy people.

It took a while for Steve to come to terms with that. Secretly, I think he still feels there's something wrong with us, but he's gotten to the point where he doesn't bring it up anymore. Or at least, not often.

So, I stand there and wait for him to drink up as much of my closeness as he needs. Eventually, he sighs and pulls away.

"When will dinner be done?" he asks as he looks over at the chicken on the stovetop. He reaches to unknot his tie.

"About twenty minutes." Then I notice the flowers on the counter again and grin. "You got me flowers?"

He turns toward me as he drapes his tie around his neck. "I did. I told you, I missed you today, so I wanted to show you how much. Do you like them?"

I lift the colorful bouquet off the counter and close my eyes, inhaling their scent. "I love them," I sigh. I lean toward him to kiss his cheek. "Thank you, that was sweet."

Steve hands me the vase from one of the cabinets. As he walks down the hallway to our bedroom, he calls over his shoulder, "I'm going to get changed and then play a little bit of Call of Duty with the guys. Let me know when dinner is ready."

"Okay," I respond as I begin to trim the flower stems. I've never understood his fascination with video games, but I know better now than to ask. His usual argument is that it's his outlet, like mine is reading, saying that both are stress relievers and make for a good escape from the day-to-day. Which I can't really argue with. But on top of that, his friends are so "busy" that they don't get together very often. This is their way of staying in touch once a week.

It's not like Steve is constantly gaming or ignoring me when he shouldn't be, so I don't really have a good argument against it. Even if I do think it's odd that a 29-year-old, successful financial advisor enjoys shooting CGI characters in his spare time.

I sauté the spinach as the chicken finishes cooking, stripping my sweater off when I start to get hot. Then I set the little table in the corner of our kitchen and crack a beer for Steve, because after six months of living together, I know he likes to wind down at the end of the day—even if he doesn't like it when *I* drink. After I've fixed us each a plate, I call into the living room, "Dinner's ready."

"Thanks, babe. I'll be there in a minute," he calls back.

When he walks into the kitchen ten minutes later, he presses a quick kiss to my cheek. "This looks great."

I smile in answer. We're quiet as we dig into our meal, both of us too distracted by the delicious food to start chatting about our day.

"Is it good?" I eventually ask Steve after he's silent for several minutes. His mouth full, he simply nods.

I try again to get him to engage with me. "How was your day?"

At that, he finally pulls his gaze away from his near-empty

plate to focus it on me. "It was good. Long. I worked this account with Tony today, so of course the day dragged. I'm all for detailed research before a client meeting, but his level is over the top, even for me. I can't tell if he thinks I'm an idiot, or if he's just used to working with idiots." He rolls his eyes, and I know what's going to come out of his mouth before he even says it. "Although, most of these people are. I don't know how half of them do their jobs."

I awkwardly push the spinach around on my plate. Along with Steve's poise comes a general sense of superiority, at a level that's always made me a touch uncomfortable. God knows as a woman, I understand venting about people, but I'm also of the firm belief that if it's constant, then it's probably you.

I don't tell him that, though. Instead, I let him continue to vent about his day while I stand up to pour a glass of wine for myself.

"I still don't understand how Tony got hired," he continues. "He barely gets through the prep work, and half the time, he doesn't even handle the client's finances right. There's no way he got the job without pulling someone's strings."

Steve pauses his rant when I sit down and take a sip of my wine. His eyes narrow at the glass in my hand. He doesn't say anything, but I see his lip curl in distaste before he turns back to eating his dinner.

I feel a flush rise in my cheeks, then push the drink away from me. In an attempt to get him talking again, I ask, "So did you get the client squared away today, then? How'd the meeting with them go?"

He pushes the remaining chicken around on his plate,

letting my questions hang in the air before eventually answering simply, "It went fine. It was just me today."

I squirm in my seat at the clear tone change in our conversation. I hate that most of our dinner conversations go like this, with me trying to pull him out of his shell to talk to me, and him all but ignoring me. It's rare that the joy he typically walks in with lasts throughout our dinner. And I can never figure out *why*.

In a last-ditch effort to get him to talk to me about something positive, I plaster a smile on my face and say, "So Maggie and her boyfriend got back from that all-inclusive resort in Mexico yesterday that we were looking at. She said it was amazing. We should definitely think about booking a few days down there this winter. You've been working so hard, you deserve a nice vacation."

Steve chugs half of his beer before responding. He shoots another glare at my drink before focusing back on me. "Didn't you say you've been to Mexico already?"

The smile freezes on my face. I hesitate with my answer, knowing in my gut that he's taking this conversation in the wrong direction.

"Yes, I've been to Mexico. Maggie said this resort was the best she's ever been to. But we don't have to go to Mexico, we can go somewhere else..."

He frowns at me. "So were you and Maggie exchanging Mexico stories today? Comparing trip notes?"

I blink quickly, unable to tear myself away from Steve's gaze. "A little, but—"

"Didn't you go on that trip with Tommy?" he interrupts.

I close my eyes with a hard swallow when he confirms the unfortunate direction of the conversation. I rack my brain for some way to answer this question that won't set him off.

I open my eyes and lock onto his with a pleading look. "Yes, but—"

Steve scoffs and shakes his head, the look of disdain unmistakable on his face. "Unbelievable." He laughs coldly. "So while I'm out buying you flowers, thinking about how much I love you, you're walking around thinking about your ex?"

"Steve, it wasn't like that," I say hurriedly, trying to reel back his thoughts before they completely derail the evening. "Maggie was telling me about her trip, and I thought you would love a tropical vacation since you've been working so hard—"

"Just stop," Steve cuts me off again. I open my mouth to defend myself, but when I see his jaw clench, I close my mouth and shrink back into my seat. My hands fidget in my lap as I wait for him to say what he's clearly thinking.

But he just continues glaring, his grip on his fork becoming more and more white-knuckled, until finally he tosses it onto his plate and shoves the whole thing away from himself. With another shake of his head, he stands and walks out of the kitchen, at the same time yelling over his shoulder, "And put some fucking clothes on. You look like a stripper."

I glance down at the crop top I'm wearing and immediately cross my arms over my chest, curling forward in an effort to cover myself. I stay seated, feeling shell-shocked at how quickly tonight went downhill. I hear the TV come on in the living room and exhale a shaky breath that I hadn't been able to let out, finally feeling like I can relax my nerves now that he's left the room. I'm relieved enough that I don't even care that he didn't ask how my day went.

I pick at the rest of my dinner, feeling a sudden loss of appetite. I know Steve hates any mention of my ex, so I always try my hardest to steer any conversations away from him. I should've known better than to bring up Mexico. I should've known he'd make the connection and misunderstand my thought process.

When I realize that Steve isn't going to come back, I sigh and begin clearing off the table. His distance and silence make me think he needs some space to cool down. And since I was the one that set him off, I can at least grant him that much.

The strong Philly girl in me would rather deal with a problem head-on and clear it up rationally, but Steve's never been like that. He's always balanced out my preference for bluntness by forcing us to take some time apart. I've even wondered lately if my method of confrontation does more harm than good, since the worst fights we've ever had were when I tried to vocalize—probably too loudly—my opinion in the heat of the fight. I've stopped trying to force the argument, and instead let him lead the time and pace.

I take my time cleaning the kitchen and then eventually settle in for the night. By 9:00, I'm sitting in bed with my laptop, working on homework and wishing Steve would come to bed so we could put this fight to rest.

But at 10:30, I can still hear the sounds of the TV, so I shut my laptop and turn off the light on my side of the bed. I fall asleep with the thought that I wish my boyfriend was a little less emotional and a little more rational.

I've just started falling asleep when I feel the bed dip. A small smile forms on my lips, even in my sleepy state, and I turn over to press myself against Steve's arm, nuzzling into his neck with a contented hum .

Only the contentment immediately evaporates because Steve immediately turns away from me and rolls over. I pull myself onto my elbow and try to blink away my groggy surprise. But the fact still remains that my boyfriend is quite literally giving me the cold shoulder.

I try to ignore the way my stomach drops at the clear snub. Instead, I drop onto my back and stare up at the ceiling, knowing it will be a long while before I can still my thoughts and fall back to sleep.

CHAPTER TWO
Hailey

THE BED IS empty when I wake to my alarm the next morning. I exhale a heavy breath and try to listen for sounds that might tell me Steve is still in the apartment.

Sure enough, I hear the clink of dishes in the kitchen. I make a silent wish that this morning's interaction is better than last night's, since Steve is the king of giving the silent treatment and because I never know how long he's going to stay angry after a jealous episode.

Once I've showered and gotten ready for work, I cautiously make my way to the kitchen. When I step into the room, Steve is sitting at our little dining table, drinking his coffee and reading something on his phone. He doesn't acknowledge my presence in any way.

"Morning," I greet softly, hoping to start this day on a pleasant note.

He shoots me a quick glance. "Hey," he responds, his expression devoid of emotion, then returns to his phone.

I stifle the exasperated huff that almost escapes and make my way over to the coffee machine.

And the entire time that I eat my toasted bagel, drink my coffee, and pack my lunch, Steve continues to sip his coffee and ignore me for his phone. It's like I'm not even in the room right now.

I drop my dishes into the sink with a little more force than necessary. But I can't help it, I'm getting frustrated that we can't talk through a silly little problem. I'm frustrated that it's even an issue at all. It's not like I brought up my ex-boyfriend and started raving about how well he used to fuck me.

I grab my purse from the coatrack and slip my shoes on. "I guess I'll see you tonight," I mutter as I reach to open the door.

But then freeze when his words cut through the air.

"So we're not even going to talk about last night?"

I turn, my hand still on the doorknob and an incredulous look on my face. He still has his phone in one hand and his coffee in the other, but he's now looking at me with a blank stare.

"Talk?" I squeak. "*Now* you want to talk?"

He stares at me for another moment, and I have no idea what he's feeling.. "Well, I wanted to talk last night, but that clearly wasn't happening."

My lips part in surprise, and my hand drops from the door so I can face him completely. "You ended the conversation by walking into another room and staying there for hours. If the living room had a door, you would have shut it in my face. How was I supposed to know you wanted to talk?"

He holds my gaze, still rigid and still unforgiving. "You should've known," he finally answers. "We've been together for long enough. You should've known that I wanted you to follow me so we could talk about it."

I think my jaw actually pops open at that. I try to form a response but I can't think of a single one. *Is he really expecting me to be psychic? How am I expected to know what he wants when he doesn't ask for it?*

I have a fleeting thought that it's a quality I would expect only a teenage girl to have. Not a grown ass man.

"I… I didn't know," I eventually stutter. "Do… umm, do you want to talk about it now?"

He lets out a heavy sigh, like I'm inconveniencing him, as he lifts the coffee mug to his lips.

"We'll talk about it later. Have a good day at work." And then he's already back to reading whatever article he has opened on his phone. As if my presence is no longer needed.

I bite my tongue to keep from snapping at him that I'm not a child to be dismissed. But I know that would only set him off again and restart the cold shoulder clock, so instead I mumble the same goodbye back to him as I walk out the door. I'm seething the entire way to the bus stop.

Steve was never like this before we moved in together. He was the nicest, most charming guy I'd ever met when we first started dating, and it didn't take long for me to fall for his Prince Charming personality. He was kind, and thoughtful, and he absolutely *worshipped* me. He seemed so mesmerized by me, like he wanted nothing more than to be in my life. And that kind of attention—coming from a man who's so handsome and seems so perfect—the kind of man every woman wants to bring home to her mother, is nearly impossible to resist. We started dating not long after we met.

It wasn't until we moved in together that he seemed to change.

It wasn't anything specific, meaning he didn't exactly become a whole new person or show his "true colors," but everything just became... less. He became *less* interested in my desire to start up dance classes again, until slowly that lack of interest became silent disapproval. I preferred hip-hop dancing but I also did modern and lyrical, all of which were somehow too provocative for him—whether from the outfits or the movements themselves, I was never sure. Even my love for electronic music became frowned upon, to the point that sometimes even listening to the music in his presence would win me a look. And going to EDM festivals was out of the question. Between the "whorish" outfits, as he so kindly referred to them, and the variety of drugs that always accompany those types of shows, there wasn't a chance in Hell I could ever bring up the idea of going to see even a low-key trance artist.

My career path didn't please him anymore, either. He didn't approve of my being a waitress in general—because "it should never be a career goal"—but he downright *hated* the fact that I had an occasional part-time job working as a bartender. The nights that I would work at the bar were the nights we got into our biggest fights. Until one day, the extra money just wasn't worth it, and I quit to work solely at the café. Not long after that, I ended up enrolled in college, even though I grew up in a home where we were told college isn't necessary to be successful. Even my dream of owning a café was beneath him. The only thing he approved of was my ability to cook *for him*.

He became less interested in my friends and family. He no

longer tried to impress my parents, and he stopped encouraging me to hang out with my friends. I barely even text my friends anymore because I have no more excuses to give about why I can't see them—and admitting that it's because I feel guilty spending any time away from Steve is out of the question. My sister is the only one I ever really hang out with anymore.

My sister doesn't understand why I'm still with Steve. If things aren't as good as they used to be, then why would I stay in a less-than-perfect relationship?

What she doesn't understand is that even with these bouts of *less*, our relationship is still amazing. I still love Steve. And every relationship suffers the loss of the honeymoon phase at some point, which is what happened when we moved in together and began spending twice as much time together. Everyone is bound to find things they don't like about the other person when they intertwine their lives by moving into a shared space.

And on top of all of that, I still get the same Steve—the Steve that I fell in love with—the majority of the time. Things are great 85% of the time. It's only that 15% that things are subpar. And subpar is not bad. It's not *get out of this horrible relationship* bad.

So what if he's not as obsessed with me as he was in the beginning? It's completely normal to feel infatuated in the first year of a relationship, and then have those intense emotions fizzle after an extended period of time together. It seems impossible for any couple to continue living with the same level of interest as when they first met. It's hardly worth throwing away a decent relationship over.

The only times I actually question that theory is when

Steve makes me question my *worth*.

When he goes from simply not worshipping me, to making me feel less-than.

When he makes me feel like a whore.

When he glares at my outfits, even if they're not provocative, or when he rejects my idea of a tattoo because he says they're trashy. When he gives me a look of repulsion any time that I try to encourage him to be a little less vanilla in bed. Sometimes I even get the look just for being the one to *initiate* sex.

I don't think he realizes he does it. I think it's a form of his insane insecurities that he never learned to cope with after his college fiancée cheated on him. Add to that the very traditional values that he was raised with, and it makes sense that he's a little sensitive.

That thought manages to calm me down by the time I step off the bus and begin walking toward the café. I need to remember that Steve didn't freak out over my mention of Tommy because he loves me less, but because he loves me *more*. It's a defensive reaction. He doesn't really think I was mentally cheating on him, he's just conditioned to jump to that conclusion because of his own ex. He panicked because he loves me and doesn't want to lose me.

By the time I reach the café doors, my inner turmoil has gone from boiling to simmering. My thoughts haven't exactly concluded how I'm going to deal with Steve when I get home tonight, but for now, I'm at least back to being sure that he loves me. That we'll be okay.

So I put away all thoughts of last night and instead launch my energy into my day job.

It ends up being a crazy busy day. Even though it's still a weekday, the café has a constant stream of people from the very moment we open. I deal with needy customers, brand new servers, a shipment delivery, and a cook in the middle of a heartbreak-induced meltdown. I'd like to say it's an uncharacteristically chaotic day, but I'd be lying.

I lock the front doors with a big sigh, leaning my forehead against the dark wood for a moment while I collect myself.

My phone rings, and I dig it out of my back pocket. Without glancing at the caller ID, I answer, "Hi, this is Hailey."

"Hi," comes Steve's voice through the line.

I immediately stiffen as all my nervous energy comes back from our interaction this morning. I can never tell how long he's going to be angry with me or when he's going to just magically forgive me and go back to being the man who loves me.

"Hi," I say hesitantly.

"Are you done at work?"

I turn back to the empty café as I answer. "Yeah, I just locked up. I'm leaving in a minute."

"Okay, I was just calling to see if you wanted me to pick you up. I'm leaving the office now."

I nibble on my lip, unable to decipher how he's feeling right now. There have been plenty of times where he's done something thoughtful or kind, even though we were fighting.

"Yeah, that would be nice," I answer with caution. "I'll come outside in fifteen minutes."

"Okay, I'll see you then."

The phone call ends without any kind of goodbye. For the next fifteen minutes, I alternate between nervously pacing the café and occupying my hands with unnecessary busy work.

I hate feeling like I'm in limbo like this. I find myself wishing for the hundredth time that we could've just talked about our fight last night—or even this morning—so that neither of us had to stress about it for an extra second. I'd rather just deal with it and move on.

I feel like a fizzing soda bottle by the time I see Steve's car pull up. I'm so restless that I trip on the sidewalk as I make my way around the car to the passenger side.

Sliding into the seat while clutching my bag to my stomach, I shoot a nervous glance at Steve, then turn my focus to my lap. I open my mouth to say something, but nothing actually gets the chance to come out.

I feel Steve's fingers curl around my chin, pulling gently so that I'm now facing him. I stare at his warm smile, his happy expression, with amazement. But I only get to look for a moment because he then tugs me toward him so he can capture my lips with his.

The kiss feels impossibly sweet, seeming to convey his love for me. I don't know if I kiss him back, because that sensation is currently a shock to my system after everything that's happened. But when the kiss becomes passionate, when I suddenly feel Steve's hunger for me, I let a moan slip out as I open my mouth to him and surrender completely.

We're both breathing heavily when we break apart. "I missed you so much," he groans against my lips, leaning his forehead against mine. "Let's go on a date tonight. I want to take you out."

I pull away with a look of surprise. "Tonight? Where?"

He pulls me back, as if he can't bear to be any farther away from me than is absolutely necessary. "I don't care, you pick the restaurant. I just want to be with you. I want us to spend time together."

A small smile tugs at the corners of my lips. I love when he gets all needy for my company. "Umm, okay. Let's try that new tapas restaurant on East Passyunk."

He smiles and presses a light kiss to my lips. "Okay," he agrees, taking my hand in his as he turns back to the road.

The entire drive home, he doesn't let go of my hand and the smile doesn't leave his face. But even with the happy butterflies erupting in my stomach, there's a nagging feeling in my subconscious that's trying to remind me that he didn't actually apologize for freaking out over nothing. That we're—yet again—riding what feels like a wave of constant highs and lows, of love and conflict.

But he's so happy and so eager to touch me, to kiss me, while I get ready for our date, that those feelings quickly fly out the window.

The weekend passes by in a blur of smiles, kisses, and laughter. Even though he often works on weekends, Steve made it a point to put his laptop away and sweep me into the bedroom as soon as he got home on Friday afternoon. And after licking me to orgasm, he announced that we were going to spend the weekend together in our apartment.

It reminds me of when we first started dating. We talk, we

joke, we order takeout, we watch crime shows. My heart sings from the closeness because I can't remember the last time we spent time like this, just enjoying each other's company.

"If I went to jail, what would it be for?" I ask with a grin, reaching for another churro from our Mexican takeout.

Steve acts like he's thinking about it for a moment. Then, without any kind of facial expression to give away his teasing, he replies, "Probably theft."

My jaw drops open. "What?! What would I steal?"

Still expressionless, he answers, "My heart."

I gape at him for another moment before kicking him with my foot where he's sitting at the end of the couch. "That was cheesy, even for you," I mumble.

He grins and moves my feet to his lap again. "You love it," he teases.

I only roll my eyes in response. I… don't *hate* it.

"What about me? What would I go to jail for?"

I tap my finger to my lips, mimicking his previous thoughtful expression. Then, in all seriousness, I answer, "Not paying your parking tickets."

His brow furrows, likely not expecting that response. "Why that?"

I shrug. "I don't know, you probably wouldn't pay your parking tickets and then end up with a warrant out for your arrest." I meet his gaze, forcing my expression to stay neutral. "You just… you look like that kind of guy."

"Oh, really?" he says, raising a skeptical brow. "I look like the kind of guy that couldn't pay a $30 parking ticket?"

I bite my bottom lip in an effort to stifle my smile. But

still, I nod.

He grabs my ankles with a growl and yanks me toward him. I squeal in surprise as I'm pulled down the length of the couch, and my legs are spread to make room for him. "You are such a smartass," he says.

A hungry look appears in his eyes as he crawls up my body. By the time he settles in between my legs, I can feel the hard ridge of his erection pressing against me. I moan at the feel of it, which elicits another growl from Steve as he starts kissing my neck.

"You're so sexy," he groans into my skin. "I know we've already had sex this weekend, but I already want you again."

I cup his face and bring his lips to mine, nodding eagerly. "Yes," I breathe. "Yes, please. Fuck me."

I feel him freeze briefly at my dirty words, before he's back to kissing me. When I slide my tongue in his mouth, he shivers in defeat and settles his weight on top of me.

I wrap my legs around him and grind my hips, desperate for more friction, desperate to feel *more*. I try to meet his eyes in an effort to feel some kind of closeness, but he's too focused on my body. I can only watch as his eager gaze roves over me, his hand reaching down to cup himself. And when he starts kneading my breast with his other hand, I moan at the barest of contact and arch into his touch.

Far too quickly, he pulls his hand away and straightens to stand next to the couch. When he starts removing his clothes, I take that as my cue to remove mine. I wiggle out of my shirt, bra, and leggings, with Steve standing naked and watching impatiently as I slide my panties down my legs.

For a moment, I think he's going to go down on me—that's how hard he's staring at my cunt. I even spread my legs slightly and let my fingers drift down my stomach in temptation.

But the moment passes, and he presses my thigh down as he settles between my legs again.

I smother the disappointed sigh that wants to escape. It's not often that Steve puts his mouth on me, which is unfortunate because it's the only sure-fire way that he can get me off. It's hit or miss whether I come from penetration alone, so I always have a moment of irritation when he skips right to the main event.

But then he's kissing me and squeezing my breasts again, and I find myself pulled right back to that feeling of wanting him. I start grinding myself against the length of his erection.

Steve swiftly reaches down and guides himself inside me. I feel the groan that rumbles through his chest at the sensation, and he drops his head into my neck as his hips slowly start to thrust.

I wish I could feel the same satisfaction that he does at that first entry. Steve's not small, but he's also not very big. And where I've always felt like there were darker desires lurking inside me, Steve has always preferred vanilla, missionary sex. So as much as I want him to use me, to throw me down and mount me and fuck me as hard as he can, our sexual chemistry has never been like that. It's not exactly sweet or gentle, but it's not nearly as rough as I think I would like it. There's just enough friction and pounding to make one, or sometimes both of us, come.

Maybe Steve senses my need for more because he starts

to pick up his pace and intensify his thrusts. With his arms tucked under my shoulders and his face still buried in my neck, his body is angled low against mine, making a delicious spark of pleasure shoot through my body when the fuzzy hair around his shaft scratches against my clit. I gasp in surprise at the sensation. And when it happens again, I moan and start eagerly rocking against him for more.

The sound of my moan seems to affect Steve. I hear a muttered "*shit*" in my ear, and then his pace becomes frenzied.

"Damn, baby, you feel so good," he groans against my skin. "You like that, don't you?"

My eyes are squeezed shut as I nod quickly, and as a sense of desperation overtakes me. I feel like I'm running out of time to capitalize on this small feeling of bliss.

All too soon, Steve's hips lose their rhythm as he comes with a long, low groan. He buries himself deep inside me one last time before slumping onto my chest. I can feel him panting, trying to catch his breath.

I can only stare at the ceiling in regret, annoyance, and exasperation.

He must notice that I'm not breathing heavily or saying anything, so he pushes up onto an elbow to look at me. His other hand reaches up to gently brush a stray hair out of my face, and I smile warmly at the contact.

"Did you come?" he asks bluntly as he gives me a hopeful look.

I debate telling him the truth, because I *am* an independent woman, after all, and why can't I demand my own orgasms? I should feel comfortable telling my partner that, unfortunately, today's sex just didn't do it for me, but maybe he could try with his fingers or his mouth.

But then I remember how well we've been getting along this week, and how great it's been not having any conflicts between us. I remember that he gets mildly annoyed whenever I admit that I didn't come, even though he'll deny ever feeling like that. And even though he'll go down on me and get me off if I ask, we're always left in an awkward cloud afterwards—instead of post-sex bliss.

That combined with the always present, nagging worry that it's *my* fault I can't come... that there's something wrong with me...

It's easier than it should be to make a split-second decision to lie and tell him what he wants to hear. I just don't want to deal with the annoyance or awkwardness today. So what if I didn't come? He already got me off yesterday. I'll just finish myself off in the shower later, no big deal.

"Yeah, baby, I came," I tell him with a smile.

CHAPTER THREE
Hailey

"HAPPY BIRTHDAY, BITCH!!"

I wince and jerk the phone away from my ear.

"Jesus, you're loud this morning," I mumble into the phone once my sister, Remy, has stopped screaming. "Why are you awake so early?"

"I have an early meeting with Cassandra to get ready for, and I need all the coffee in the world to deal with the bitch. Plus, it's your 21ST BIRTHDAY!! What're we doing tonight?!"

I pull my phone back again and glare at it. "Firstly, we're going to calm down because you're insane right now. That's first on the agenda." I can practically hear my sister rolling her eyes at that. "Secondly, I can't do anything tonight because Steve is taking me out for a nice dinner. He already made a reservation because we're going to that new place in Old City that fills up really quick. But maybe we can do something this weekend?"

Remy lets out an exaggerated sigh. "So I don't get to see you at all today? I really can't take you out to a bar tonight to get legally shitfaced?"

"I can't," I say with a wince. "Steve wants to spend my

birthday together. And he doesn't like the party scene, so a bar probably wouldn't be a good idea."

She doesn't respond for a few seconds, so I glance at my phone to make sure the call hasn't dropped. I barely hear her growl under her breath *"fucking narcissist just wants to prove he owns you"* but so much anger coats her tone that I can't be sure that's what she said. Just as I'm about to ask if she's okay, she says, "Hailey, it's *your* fucking birthday. Steve's likes and dislikes shouldn't even play into it. Why can't you do what you want to do? You know you would have more fun if Jax and I took you out."

I wince and pinch the bridge of my nose. I know she's right, so why am I so steadfast in my decision to stick by Steve's plan? Why does the idea of going against him make me feel anxiety down to my bones?

I know I should be spending today doing whatever I want; birthdays are the one day where everyone can make their demands and the people around them have to comply. But how do I explain to my sister that I wouldn't enjoy doing what I want to do because the entire time I'd be completely keyed in to the fact that Steve is at home and pissed? And unless I spring it on him after dinner, his sour mood would probably ruin our date too.

A fun night out just isn't worth it.

"I'm just not feeling a big night out," I lie. It's the easiest way to end this conversation right now. "You know me, I'm not a big drinker. The cliché 21st birthday shitfest just doesn't sound appealing to me."

I hear Remy exhale another heavy sigh, and I know she's

given up on the argument. She won't push me to do anything I don't want to do—it's one of the things I love about my sister. She encourages me to step out of my comfort zone, but she always knows when to stop.

"At least let me take you out for lunch," she begs. "I can't *not* see you today. Just find out when you can leave work for an hour, and I'll meet you wherever you want."

A hesitant smile stretches across my face. That does sound like a good compromise. "Okay," I agree. "I'll text you when I get to work and figure out when I can take an hour."

"Perfect," Remy chirps. "I'll get Jax too. We'll make a party of it whether you like it or not."

A quiet laugh escapes me. "Okay, nutjob. I'll see you in a little bit."

When I get to the restaurant, I smile when I see Remy and Jax are already here. Walking up to their table, I watch in amusement as Jax pointedly ignores my sister's fiery attention, and instead grins into his beer before downing the whole thing.

"Why are you yelling at Jax?" I ask bluntly when I reach them, then shake my head with a chuckle when Jax winks at me.

My sister rolls her eyes at that. "It doesn't matter," she concedes with a huff. Turning her attention to me, her irritation slowly morphs into an excited smile. "Happy birthday, little sister." Never one for the show of hugs and kisses, she just gives me a nod.

Jax, on the other hand, is all about hugs. It's always amazed me that his affection doesn't bother me, since physical touch has never been my love language. But there's something about his love, and the pure intent with how he shows it, that has always had the opposite effect on me. I've always craved his hugs. And when he unfolds his massive, Viking-esque stature from the chair and stands to his full 6'4 height, I am nothing but eager for him to wrap me up in his arms.

I met Jax when I was ten years old, when my family moved to a new neighborhood, and Remy, being the tomboy that she was, immediately befriended the athletic boy next door. For the next four years, they were practically glued at the hip—Jax was over our house more than even Remy's high school boyfriends. People used to tease them about dating, but their relationship became one more of tight-knit siblings than anything else.

Our relationship, on the other hand, is something entirely different. Being five years younger than Jax, I was just the pesky little sister that wanted to hang out with the teenagers. And while Remy was never as mean to me as a lot of older siblings would be to my friends, she wasn't exactly itching to include me in things.

Jax was the only one that would give me the time of day. Even as a sixteen-year-old boy, he would go out of his way to make sure I was okay and help me with anything I needed. He could often be found in the kitchen, helping me with my math homework, or driving me to dance classes if no one else could. I definitely had a crush on him in the beginning—how could I not when he was the cutest boy I'd ever seen *and* nice to me? But after a while, my schoolgirl crush faded to a different, and deeper, kind of bond.

I was never sure if it happened because I was sick of feeling hurt when he would get a new girlfriend every month, or if I just wised up. Eventually, I stopped fantasizing about the day where he would realize I was the girl he was looking for, and instead started appreciating that I owned his heart in a different capacity. He might not be interested in me romantically, but I was undeniably the one person that he would drop everything for if I asked. Even Remy didn't have his love the way that I did. I could never decide if he was protective of me because I was small and quiet, or if it just went without saying that we'd look out for each other.

Either way, we've been close for over a decade. Even though we rarely saw each other after he and Remy left for college, and even though we don't see each other too often now, that bond stretches tight and glows every time we're in the same room together.

When he stands up from his seat, he smiles and wraps me in a tight hug. "Happy birthday, baby girl," he murmurs into my hair. I squeeze his waist and bury my face into his chest, enjoying the smell and feel of him wrapped around me.

He squeezes me once before letting go and dropping back into his seat. I take the one next to him and turn back to my sister. "Did you guys order already?"

She glares at Jax. "Yeah, this bastard already chugged his. If he's under the table by the end of lunch, we'll know why." Jax rolls his eyes at the jab that he's a lightweight despite his size. She turns her attention back to me, a grin stretching across her face. "So, what's your first legal drink going to be? And what kind of shot are we doing?"

I scrunch my nose at the mention of a shot. I was never a big drinker even before Steve, so straight liquor has never appealed to me.

"Oh, come on, you *have* to do a shot!" Remy practically whines.

I sigh in defeat at the same time that our waiter walks up to the table.

"Hi, guys, how are we doing today?" he asks, his attitude friendly and welcoming, as he places a glass of water in front of each of us.

"We're great," Remy chirps. "It's my sister's 21st birthday today."

The waiter turns his attention to me, a smile on his face. I feel Jax stiffen beside me when the waiter's eyes quickly glance over my body.

"Happy birthday!" he says too enthusiastically. "First drink is on me today, beautiful. What can I get you?"

I give him a small smile. "Thanks. I'm going to have a house margarita, please. And three shots of tequila for the table." Remy rubs her hands together, looking way too happy about this.

The waiter smiles again. "You got it, sweetheart." He turns to Remy, completely oblivious to the daggers Jax is glaring at the side of his head. "What about you? What can I get you?"

"I'll do a margarita, as well," Remy answers with a smile.

"I'll take a Corona," Jax barks. The waiter startles, as if he didn't realize that there was a man at the table. Which is comical in itself, since Jax is a giant. I can't stop the giggle that slips out of me at Jax's overprotective attitude. He aims his glare at me with narrowed eyes, daring me to tell him to stop. I just pat his arm placatingly to brush it off.

"I'll be right back with those drinks," the waiter mumbles once he composes himself. Jax watches him until he reaches the bar.

"You don't have to be such a bear, Jax," I can't help laughing. "It was harmless flirting."

Frown lines continue to crease Jax's face. "It was shitty customer service," he growls in response.

I huff a louder laugh and shake my head, eliciting a grin and a wink from Jax as he concedes. I turn my attention to my sister and ask, "Speaking of bears, why were you so grouchy when I walked up? Something happen at the gym?"

Now it's Remy's turn to glare at me. "Not exactly. I was pissed because Jax felt the need to do something without consulting the class first."

I raise an eyebrow in question. "What'd he do?"

Remy opens her mouth to answer but seems to spot something over my shoulder because she freezes. I don't know how it's possible, but her irritation multiplies tenfold.

"You're about to find out," she grits out, turning the force of her anger on Jax.

Jax just sits there, looking like the cat that caught the canary. Before I can even look behind us to see what caught her attention, Jax's roommate Tristan appears next to our table.

"Hey, guys," he greets happily. I've only met him a handful of times, but even from our limited interactions, I can tell he's not a cheerful man. Stoic or arrogant, yes, but not happy. So,

I'm confused about why he looks that way now.

My question is answered when he turns toward my sister, his grin immediately growing. "Remy baby," he drawls.

If looks could kill, Tristan would be a pile of ash on the ground right now.

"Fuck off, Tristan," Remy says through clenched teeth. "I don't care if Jax invited you, you're not welcome here."

Ignoring her completely, Tristan takes the seat next to her. And despite a murderous glare being aimed at the side of his head, his expression softens when he looks at me.

"Happy birthday," he says to me with a smile, his affection genuine.

"Thanks," I respond with a blush.

"I hope you don't mind if I crash for a few minutes—" he starts.

"We mind," Remy snaps. Jax and I both smother our grins.

Once again ignoring her, Tristan continues, "I'm just picking up a takeout order. Jax mentioned you'd be here, so I thought I'd buy you a shot. Waiter hasn't brought your drinks yet?"

Said waiter appears at that exact moment. He slides our drinks to us before placing the three shots in the center of the table. His eyes widen as they jump from Jax to Tristan, who's not quite as big as Jax but who is an equally intimidating athlete. His gaze never touches me, which means the increased testosterone has successfully scared him away from making any more advances.

"Uh, can I get you something to drink?" he asks Tristan.

"I'm good, thanks, I'm heading back to the gym in a

minute anyway." He glares at the beer in front of Jax. "And you're teaching tonight," he adds pointedly.

Jax just rolls his eyes and throws his arm along the back of my chair. "It's Hailey's birthday, I'm sure I can handle a beer seven hours before I have to teach something I can do in my sleep."

I giggle at the visual, and before I can think better of the comment, I muse, "Can you imagine? Jiu-jitsu in your sleep? I pity the person in bed with you, Superman."

The boys grin at each other. I realize then that I've now made it a sexual innuendo, since jiu-jitsu is like wrestling. And wrestling would only be needed in your sleep if there was a partner involved—and very minimal wrestling attire.

Before I can wince and say *never mind*, Remy jumps in for me. "Don't even grace us with an answer, assholes."

Tristan turns his smirk on her. "Why? Not getting a lot of jiu-jitsu in your sleep lately, Remy baby?"

"I swear to God, you're going to die because of that nickname one day," she growls.

The waiter coughs, and all four of our gazes snap to him in surprise. I guess I'm not the only one that completely forgot he was standing there.

"Are you ready to order food?" he asks, clearly uncomfortable. "Or should I give you a few minutes?"

"We need a few minutes," Jax tells him dismissively.

Once the waiter's gone, Jax slides one of the shots over to me before picking up his own. Remy grabs hers and Tristan just lifts her water, once again ignoring her glare.

I'm starting to think that's his superpower.

"Happy 21st, baby girl," Jax says with a warm smile.

"Happy 21st," Remy and Tristan echo with raised glasses.

Contentment floods my chest. I look between Jax and my sister, taking a second to appreciate how much I love these people, and how much they love me. And even though there's no birthday candle in front of me to blow out, and even though the tradition is to make a wish, I do what I do every year: I put my gratitude into the world instead.

"Thank you," I say simply, expressing the full force of that sentiment with a big smile. Then I raise my glass in a cheers.

I hear the shower running when I walk into the apartment. I hang up my bag at the door, then make my way into the bathroom and strip off my clothes.

When I open the shower door and step into the small enclosure, Steve aims a smile at me over his shoulder.

"Hey, babe," he greets me, continuing to rub the loofah over his chest. "How was work?"

I touch my fingers to his waist as I flatten my body against his back. I press a wet kiss to his shoulder, pushing my breasts into him as I get closer. "It was good," I mumble.

My hands start to wander up and down his ribs. I'm realizing now that the tequila is still running through my body, so I'm slightly tipsy and very horny. I continue leaving kisses along his shoulder.

"Babe," Steve admonishes, stopping my hand before it can venture too far south. "We're going to be late for dinner."

I rub my breasts against his back, aching for the friction on my nipples. "Nuh uh, we're already saving time by showering together," I reason innocently.

He sighs and turns around. I smile and wrap my arms around his neck, my lips lightly brushing his. His hands grip my hips.

"Hi," I whisper. My smile widens, and I'm certain it looks like a drunk one, but I just really want him to kiss me right now.

He rubs his nose against mine in an eskimo kiss, but he still doesn't give me what I want. Since I have the more voracious sexual appetite, Steve is rarely the one to initiate sex. I often have to come on to him if I want to have sex at all. And even though I expect it by now, it doesn't make me any less annoyed when I have to do it.

I stifle my huff of frustration and instead press my lips against his. I continue kissing him, nibbling on his lips, until he relaxes against me and kisses me back. I shiver when I feel his grip on my hips tighten. And when his lips finally open to mine, I moan and slide my tongue into his mouth.

He freezes, as if he's been shocked. When his fingers dig painfully into my skin, I pull back with a frown.

"What's wrong?" I ask him.

With my arms still wrapped around his neck, there's only a little bit of space between us. And from here, I can very clearly see the fury that's flashing through his eyes. That I swear I can feel down to my very bones.

"Were you drinking?" he asks coldly. His fingers dig into me so hard now that I feel the skin break under his nails.

"*Ow!* Steve!" I shove at his hands and he lets go without any further struggle.

"Answer the question," he grits out, clenching his fists at his sides and ignoring the cooling water from the showerhead.

I resist the urge to rub my hips where he grabbed me and instead glare at him in answer, my arms crossing over my chest in a very useless attempt at hiding. "I had a drink at lunch. I wasn't *drinking*."

He shakes his head, the disapproval clear on his face as he rinses the rest of his body. Neither of us says a word as he steps out of the shower. I reach for my own bodywash, scrubbing my body and silently wishing I could wash the alcohol from my scent and the shame from my skin.

When I can't hide in the shower any longer, I wrap a towel around my body and walk through the doorway of our bedroom. I don't even step inside, feeling like I need the space between us right now. Steve's rummaging in the closet, looking for clothes and blatantly ignoring my presence.

He seems to lose his patience in an instant when he very suddenly turns to me and demands, "Who did you have lunch with? Why didn't you text me that you were going out with someone?"

"Steve, I was out with *Remy*." I answer, then sigh in exasperation as my arms drop to my side. I pointedly leave Jax's name out of it, knowing that my drinking with Remy is enough of a trigger for Steve as it is. Jax would make this situation so much worse. Because no matter what I or anyone else says, Steve still doesn't understand how a man and woman could be friends without romantic feelings. He doesn't understand my relationship with Jax, which means he's still very much threatened by it.

I've never handled his jealousy very well, for the sole reason that I've never seen the point of the emotion. It's hard to wrap my head around Steve's mindset when he gets like this.

"You still could've told me."

Could've, not *should've*. He's always so sneaky and intentional. He knows exactly what words to use where his tone implies an order, but his word choice can never be said to be domineering.

"They took me out for lunch on my birthday," I explain incredulously. "We weren't exactly bar hopping, Steve."

At that, the flames of fury reignite in his eyes. "And you thought you would just have your birthday drink without me," he summarizes in a deceptively-flat tone. "And I wouldn't care. In fact, you thought I'd be grateful, didn't you? To have a drunk, horny girlfriend begging to be fucked like a whore? Is that what you were hoping for?"

I flinch at the derogatory words like I've been struck and grip my towel like a physical shield.

He frowns. "Wait a minute. *They?* Who else were you with?"

Everything in me freezes when I realize my slip-up. *Fuck.*

He doesn't even wait for me to confirm his suspicions. He just sneers at me and says, "I knew you had a thing for that oversized moron that hangs out with your sister. So now you're cheating on me with him? You must love him more if you're lying to me about it and wanting to spend your birthday with *him* instead of me." He cuts off my stuttered defense by giving me another disgusted once-over. "Go ahead, then. Go get drunk with your sister and her friends. Clearly, you'd rather spend the day with them."

I would normally do everything in my power to squash this tension so as to avoid the shitty feeling of a fight—especially on my *birthday*—and the two day silent treatment that follows it. But today, instead of trying to play peacemaker, I just feel angry.

Angry that I'm constantly walking on eggshells around his feelings.

Angry that I'm made to feel guilty *every time* I have a drink.

Angry that I'm being asked to bend my will *on my birthday*.

Yet somehow, I still can't bring myself to throw my anger in his face. Even though he has no problem shredding me to ribbons with his fury, I can't manage anything more aggressive than a furious glare.

I finally step into the bedroom, forcing myself to crush some of the distance between us. "I'm allowed to have a drink with family," I manage to spit. "The first legal drink doesn't have anyone's name on it, so it shouldn't matter who I was with. It was just Remy and Jax. It's not like I was out with random guys."

"*I* was the one you made plans with for your birthday. *I* should've been the one you had your first drink with." He's still angry, but he's not yelling. He never yells. Sometimes I wish he would, just so we could get into a screaming match and I could get everything out in the open.

"I didn't realize it was such a big deal." And even though I hate myself for saying it, there's a need ingrained in me to appease him that forces me to say, "I didn't know it was so important to you. I'm sorry."

It does the trick. I watch as some of his anger deflates and he lets out a heavy exhale.

"I just hate when you drink," he says through clenched teeth. "I hate when you drink, and I especially hate when I'm not around when you do it."

I stiffen. I've heard this spiel so many times, and it's baffling every single time. Yet, I've never quite worked up the nerve to face it head on.

"It was one drink," I force out. "On my 21st birthday. I'm hardly shitfaced right now."

"You weren't shitfaced that night in high school that you decided to act like a whore, either," he snaps.

My eyes widen and I actually take a step back in the suddenly too-small bedroom. Steve shakes his head with a look of pure disgust before turning back to the closet and pulling his clothes on.

I feel my blood begin to boil in my veins. That's the second time he's called me that in a matter of minutes, which is a personal best for him. He usually waits to drop it as a singular conversation-finisher, since he throws that fucking word around like it's my main descriptor and the worst thing a person could be. Thank God I figured out early on that he only uses it because it's the easiest way he knows to make me feel like shit, and it's not actually something I should feel bad about. His go-to of name-calling says more about him than it does about me.

Of course, that doesn't mean that his obvious attempt to

lash out at me doesn't hurt and piss me off at the same time. But even with the fury simmering under my skin, I still can't bring myself to defend myself.

He must feel the moment my anger deflates because he lets out a sigh and takes a seat at the end of the bed, dropping his head into his hands. But annoyance still laces my voice when I ask, "So, what, we're just going to ruin tonight because I had a drink with my sister on my *21st birthday?* Is that really what we're doing right now?"

His head snaps up, fury glittering in his eyes. "Don't act like I'm being unreasonable. You know exactly why your drinking bothers me. And I would've thought you'd be smarter than to glorify the cliché 21st birthday bullshit."

My eyes widen. "You didn't expect me to have a legal drink today? Seriously?"

His glare darkens. "I expected you to have it with *me*. I'm the one that's been there for you. I'm the one you should be celebrating your birthday with. I don't even feel like going out now. You ruined it by celebrating without me."

"We're not going out anymore? I ask incredulously.

He sighs again and drops his head into his hands to rub his temples. "We'll still go out," he concedes. "Even if it's not the same, I still want to celebrate you tonight. I'll do that for you." When he looks up at me, I can clearly see the hurt in his eyes. "I just wanted to be the one you want to celebrate with."

Something inside of me cracks. I walk over to where he's sitting on the bed, gently pushing his hands out of the way so I can straddle his hips. He continues looking at me with that same pained expression, making my heart twist.

"Of course, I want to celebrate with you," I whisper, brushing his hair out of his face. "I love you. You're the one I want to spend tonight with." I wince and drop my hands into my lap. "I'm sorry, I went out today. I didn't think about how it would make you feel to be left out."

Steve wraps his arms around my waist, burrowing his face into my neck. "It's okay," he mumbles against my skin. "Let's just forget it happened and spend tonight the way we planned." He pulls away and gives my ass a light smack, aiming a small but genuine smile at me. "Go get dressed. Wear that red dress I love so much."

I nod eagerly, relieved to be back on firm ground with him. I hate the tension that arguing with him brings, and it's always a huge breath of relief when we come out on the other side. I climb off of him so I can go grab my red dress and finish getting ready.

Dinner that night is wonderful. Our conversation is easy and fun, and Steve laughs more than he has in a few weeks. He's in such a good mood that he doesn't even aim his usual sour glance at my mojito when the waiter sets it on the table in front of me. We're happy and everything is perfect, like it used to be when we first started dating.

Like I want it to be again.

Our earlier fight is completely forgotten.

CHAPTER FOUR
Hailey

"How LATE IS this thing going to go? It better not go past midnight. You know I hate being out in the city that late."

I roll my eyes as I finish buttoning my jeans. Then I turn to check out my appearance in the floor-length mirror, as I tell Steve, "It won't go that late. They're usually over by 10pm, so stop worrying."

I can feel his glare on my back. "Don't act like I'm being unreasonable. How organized can these fights actually be? They're basically run by meatheads."

At that, I turn to glare at him. "That's a stupid stereotype. Why do you put them down? You don't even know them. Some of my best friends are fighters and they're plenty intelligent."

Jax and Tristan are both smarter than you.

I don't say it, but I'm definitely thinking it right now. I hate when he gets in these *holier than thou* moods.

"If that were true, they wouldn't willingly be going into a fist fight," he mumbles, adjusting the collar on his polo shirt.

He looks like a stereotypical rich kid douchebag. He's going to stick out like a sore thumb in an arena full of red-blooded men.

"You know, you don't have to come tonight," I seethe. "You're more than welcome to stay home and play video games with your friends. I'm sure killing zombies is more fun than watching real men beat each other bloody."

His eyes narrow at the subtle dig that I didn't anticipate slipping out. I hold my breath and wait for his response, sensing he's not going to let that slide.

"You're pitting primitive idiots who only know pain against a successful adult who enjoys a harmless, creative pastime? Nice, Hailey. You're not exactly proving the case of your own intelligence." My nostrils flare and my jaw tightens, but he ignores me and continues talking. "I'm coming tonight. Some people actually like to make time for their partners."

My jaw drops open at that. He's acting like *I* never make time for *him?* That's insane. And false. I prioritize most of my life around him.

Steve stays oblivious to all the thoughts I'll never work up the courage to say out loud. "So even if I have to endure this insanity to be with you tonight, I'll do it. Because I love you and that's what people who love each other do." And before I can flounder around with a non-response, he aims a look my way that has the power to instantly make me feel guilty and then leaves the room.

"Let's just go," he calls from the kitchen.

I exhale a tired breath and give my appearance one last look before grabbing my purse.

"Well, tonight's off to a great start," I grit through clenched teeth.

The arena is loud when we finally get there. The beer is flowing, and the fights have already started, so fans are cheering loud enough to wake the dead, especially when one of the fighters in the cage lands a devastating blow to the temple that knocks his opponent to the mat.

And while the familiar environment makes me grin at the feeling of being *home*, it just makes Steve cringe. He actually lifts the hand that's not holding mine to his ear and looks around disapprovingly.

"How long before your friend's fight? This is not my idea of an ideal Friday night."

I fight the urge to roll my eyes. "We have to find out what fight this is. Jax is number seven, I think. Let's go find Remy, and then we'll figure it out."

I glance at the number written on my wristband and start to make my way toward our section, politely pushing people out of my path as I pull Steve behind me.

"Hailey!" I hear from my left. I turn to see Remy and the rest of the gym gang clustered in a section and hurriedly make our way over to them.

"I was just about to text you to see if you were still coming," she says by way of greeting. She glances at Steve, and if I didn't know my sister as well as I do, I would've missed the slight sneer curling her lips when she takes him in. "Hey, Steve. Nice of you to join the lowly fighting crowd for an evening."

Steve's nostrils flare, but he doesn't taunt her back. I've

always had a feeling he's scared of my sister, which in all honesty, doesn't surprise me at all. Remy has a very intimidating, take-no-shit attitude about her, and on top of it, she's deceivingly cunning. She's not one you want to go up against.

So instead, Steve forces a smile on his face as he wraps an arm around my waist. "I just wanted to come support my girl's friend."

Remy's eyes narrow perceptibly as she studies him for any implied insults. She's just as protective of Jax as she is of me, so taunts against him won't be tolerated either.

To break the awkward tension before it can escalate, I blurt out, "How many fights until Jax is up?"

Remy finally tears her gaze away from Steve. "Four more. They're on fight number three right now."

I can practically feel the groan rolling through Steve. He's not saying anything, but I can tell in the way his body tenses against mine that he's not happy about being here for that long.

I nervously nibble on my bottom lip as my gaze whips to him. I hate when he's annoyed or unhappy. His emotions always feel like they settle directly onto my skin, forcing me to find the source of his unhappiness and figure out how to banish it. I don't know when it happened, but the urge is entirely engrained in me now.

"We'll go right after his fight is over," I whisper so only he can hear me. "It means a lot to me that we're here. Thank you for coming with me."

Immediately, the tension seeps out of him. His shoulders relax, and he turns his gaze to me with a sigh. "Of course. It makes me happy to make you happy."

I shine a shaky smile at him and kiss his cheek. Out of the corner of my eye, I see Remy stiffen, but I ignore her, more focused on making Steve feel comfortable while we wait for Jax's fight to start.

I spend the next hour and a half glued to Steve's side, feeling him become more and more tense, even as I try to talk to Remy and the other fighters. The male fighters ignore me, save for the initial awkward hello—whether it's from Steve standing next to me or the fear of God that Jax put into everyone in the gym to scare them away from pursuing me, I'm not sure. The only people to approach me are Remy and our friend Lucy.

I sneak glances at the other fighters as they laugh and tease each other between bouts. There's something to be said about friendships formed doing hobbies. I've always thought that the kind of bond that comes from common interests is one of the best ones, since it's completely centered around an activity that everyone enjoys. It's also where you meet the most interesting friends because every person has a different background, job, and reason for being there.

I used to have a hobby of my own. I danced when I was in high school, and I was damn good at it. It made me happy. It became my outlet, just like training became Remy's. The place I would go to express myself on both good days and bad. And I loved it.

When I moved to the city with Remy after high school, my plan had been to find a job first, and then a dance studio. Philly has some great ones, so I was looking forward to a new environment where I could really challenge myself.

But I became so immersed in Philly after I moved here

that it never ended up happening. I was constantly working at the bar, and when I wasn't there, I was discovering a new home that wasn't a small town whose only entertainment was a Dunkin' Donuts. I became obsessed with seeing all that Philly had to offer. And it's *a lot.*

By the time I was ready to get back into dancing, I had started dating Steve. And he was less than thrilled about the idea. It didn't matter that there weren't any men in the classes, or that I wasn't performing anywhere. In his eyes, it was unacceptable to move in a way that simulates sex outside of the bedroom. So I never ended up finding a studio.

Instead, I threw myself into something he deemed more worthwhile: college. Because how could I have a hobby—any hobby—if I didn't have a career plan? And working at the bar was hardly a job to aspire to. God knows I heard that line often enough.

School trumped everything and everything trumped dance. And soon all I knew was school and work and Steve, without any friends to speak of.

So, looking at the fighters around me, at the men and women that spend most of their free time training and hanging out together, I realize I'm jealous. Jealous of their friendships, and of the fact that they have this hobby that brings them happiness instead of a bitter boyfriend.

I snap out of the dangerous spiral my thoughts have begun pulling me into when the lights dim for the start of Fight #7. Our section cheers the loudest.

I forget all about Steve and his comfort as soon as the announcer calls out Jax's name. I even let go of his hand so I can clap manically and scream as loud as the rest of our group, completely immersed in my friend's success as everything else fades into the background.

The smoke machine starts up and Jax's walkout song "Blood // Water" starts to sound through the speakers, the lights in the arena going crazy. The music builds up until finally the beat drops and Jax appears through the smoke.

He jogs up to the cage, his expression all business. He quickly strips his shirt off and faces the referee for the pre-fight checks.

Watching him, the nerves seep in—like they always do when I watch him fight—but I take a deep breath and remind myself that Jax is very good at what he does. That he's won plenty of fights and never been seriously hurt. I just need to trust and support him.

In the blink of an eye, Jax's opponent is in the cage and the announcer is introducing the fighters. I can't help holding my hands to my mouth and squeezing in worry, even as I take in my friend's serious expression and battle-ready body. Nothing else exists but Jax and this victory right now.

"Fighters, are you ready? Let's *FIGHT!*"

I'm so wound up that I jump at the sound of the bell. But Jax strides forward, confident and unhurried in his movements. The second they touch gloves, it's like he's been shot out of a cannon.

It's a flurry of punches and kicks, all power and forward pressure. Being the aggressor has always been Jax's style, and even though I'm sure his opponent knew that going into this fight, it's still a style that works. He overwhelms the red corner so quickly that in less than thirty seconds, he's landed a cross to the face and a hook to the body, the effects of which are a stunned and backpedaling Red.

"Stay on him, Jax, he doesn't know what to do with it!" I hear shouted from Jax's corner. I glance to the cage and see Tristan coaching his best friend, just barely managing to keep his ass in the chair.

Jax heeds his corner's advice and increases his forward attack. It doesn't take long for him to push his opponent back into the cage, where they wrestle for an advantageous position. Jax seems to be the bigger fighter, but Red looks like he's recovered from the initial onslaught and is now putting up a good fight. In a surprising turn of events, he hooks Jax's leg and takes him down to the ground.

I gasp at the sound of them crashing to the mat. They each probably weigh close to 215 pounds—if not more—so the impact is a very loud, very painful-sounding one.

"Damn." I hear Steve chuckle next to me.

I'm too focused on the massive man raining blows on Jax to pay him any mind. From the corner, I hear Tristan yelling, "Control the body, bring him down and go for that sweep!"

I've always been fascinated by the moments in fights that feel like a video game. Because that's what happens now. As if controlled by a joystick, Jax follows Tristan's instructions to the letter and grips Red's head and so he can't sit up to throw his punches. And when he tilts him off balance just enough, he scissors his legs in a way that flips their positions and ends with Jax on top.

The crowd cheers at the action, and grows even louder

when Jax starts to drop punches of his own. Our section is *screaming*, but all I can do is press my fingers to my mouth and wait with bated breath for the finish.

Sure enough, after several calls to defend himself and even more unanswered punches, the ref steps in to end the fight. Jax stands up with raised arms and a victorious grin on his face.

Screams echo throughout the entire arena. Fans love finishes more than anything else, so victories like this one always earn a lot of praise, as evidenced by the volume of the arena right now. And for the first time, I'm able to drag my hands away my face and let out a loud cheer.

I'm overjoyed when I turn to an equally excited Remy, who's holding onto Lucy with a white-knuckled grip and screaming, "*That's what I'm talking about!*"

I can't help but smile even bigger at the sight of Jax pulling Tristan in for a hug. Clearly, Tristan is so excited about his friend's victory that he forgets all about his usual comfort levels and returns Jax's hug with equal amounts of enthusiasm. And when the ref pulls the fighters back to the center of the cage, so he can raise the victor's hand, his grin stretches from ear-to-ear.

When our screams and cheers finally die down and Jax is led out of the cage, I hear Steve sigh and murmur, "That was fun. So can we go now?"

I look at him in surprise. I completely forgot he was even here. I nibble on my lip, torn about what to do. On the one hand, I know Steve doesn't like fighting and only came here because of me. But on the other hand, it's an unspoken rule that you wait for the winner to come out into the arena after he gets cleaned up.

"You're not coming out with us?" Lucy asks when she overhears Steve's question. "We were going to head over to Frankie's as soon as the next fight is over. You guys should come for a drink!"

The corner of Steve's lip twitches in distaste, though he tries to hide it. "That sounds fun, but I think I'd rather get Hailey home." He wraps an arm around my shoulders and says, "You know she can't really handle her liquor. It's better if we just call it a night. Isn't that right, babe?"

I'd much rather stay and hang out with my friends, but I know there's no chance of that with Steve here. So I just smile and nod.

"Raincheck," I tell Lucy. "We should get you, me, and Remy together one of these nights anyway. We could hang at Remy's place, and I could make those margaritas you guys love so much."

I feel Steve stiffen next to me, and I'm immediately reminded that I should never blurt out that kind of plan without talking to him first. I press against his side in silent apology.

"We should get going," he interjects in a flat voice.

I smile at him and nod. "Okay, babe. Let me just use the bathroom before we go."

He gives a stiff nod goodbye to Remy and Lucy, and then he's turning me toward the exit. I toss a silent, apologetic glance over my shoulder at my sister and friend, trying to block out how much I hate the pitying looks on their faces.

Well, Lucy's is pitying. Remy's is furious.

I push both out of my head and follow Steve to the

bathroom. But right after I pull away from his side to cut off to the ladies' room, who else but Jax steps out of the men's.

His eyes light up when he sees me. It's only been a few minutes since he's gotten out of the cage, so he's still shirtless and drenched in sweat, a red mark starting to appear on his ribs where he got hit.

"Hailey," he says in surprise. "I didn't know if you were going to come."

I can't help the smile that stretches across my face. "Of course, I was going to come. I'll never miss one of your fights. Congrats on the win, Superman."

Happiness overtakes his entire expression. He steps forward to give me a hug but then glances over my shoulder and freezes.

I hear Steve's voice next to my ear just as he steps up beside me and slides his arm around my waist. "Yeah, man. Congrats on beating another man into a bloody pulp."

I wince at the not-so-veiled mocking in his tone. It's no secret he's not a fan of fighting, but he's rarely this obvious about it. I can feel the embarrassed blush flame across my skin.

Jax just stares at Steve. If I didn't know him as well as I do, I wouldn't be able to see the hate behind his expression. But I do know him, and my blush intensifies from the knowledge that all my friends hate my boyfriend.

I remind myself yet again that they just don't know him like I do, that they don't see the sides of him that I know and love.

"Thanks, man," Jax says tightly. "Yeah, it's pretty fucking satisfying knowing I could kill a man with my bare hands."

My eyes widen. Jax is the nicest guy I know, so it's shocking to hear him say something like that. If I didn't know better, it would almost sound like a threat.

Steve must interpret it as one because I feel him stiffen next to me. But this must be some kind of dick-measuring contest that I don't understand because he responds with, "I didn't realize we've reverted to the times where we solve conflicts by physical means."

"Steve," I scold quietly.

He turns to me with a frown, as if he's surprised I spoke up against him. I can see him mentally roll his eyes when he drops his arm from around my waist at my expression.

"I'm just going to pull the car around. Try not to make me wait."

Despite the borderline-order he just gave me, I'm glad he's leaving. I'm mortified at his behavior and the fact that Jax was the one to see it.

"I'm sorry," I tell Jax as soon as Steve is out of earshot. "I don't know why he said that, he's not usually so... confrontational."

Jax just looks at me, frozen in place. I have no idea what's going through his mind right now.

I nervously fidget with the fabric of my shirt as I try to steer the conversation away from the awkwardness it's now taken on. "Did he land anything? Are you hurt at all?"

I see his jaw flex, but he answers in a tight voice. "No, he didn't land anything."

When he doesn't say anything else, I try again. "Are you going out to Frankie's with everyone? They all sound like they want to celebrate with you. You love Frankie's, don't you?"

"Why aren't you coming?" he asks suddenly. "You love Frankie's, too. Or at least, you did."

The unspoken jab is hard to miss. *Until him.*

I swallow the lump in my throat. I hate fighting with Jax more than anything in the world. "I'm just not really a big drinker anymore. Neither is Steve, so I just thought we'd call it an early night and go home. I'll come out with you guys another time—"

"You should leave him at home next time, then," Jax snaps. "Or better yet, just leave him entirely."

I flinch at the force of his words. I can tell he immediately regrets his tone because his entire expression softens and becomes pained.

"Fuck, Hailey, I'm sorry," he mutters. "I don't want to snap at you. I just—" He swallows and looks away from me, the pain in his expression multiplying. "Forget it, it doesn't matter. I just miss you, that's all. I wish you were coming with us tonight."

The tension eases from my shoulders and a small smile appears on my face. "I miss you too," I say softly.

But then I realize that's probably an inappropriate thing to say, even though Jax and I have been friends for over a decade. I glance around nervously to make sure Steve didn't somehow reappear next to me.

"I should probably get going," I murmur. "I don't want to keep him waiting." I smile at Jax, even though there's a tight feeling in my chest that I can't name and that I somehow know I won't be able to shake. "Congrats again on the win. You were amazing, you should be proud."

His still-taped hands squeeze into fists, and it looks like he wants to reach for me, but instead he just gives a stiff nod and says, "Thanks. And thanks for coming."

And as I turn away from one of my oldest and best friends, I can't help but feel like I'm making the wrong choice tonight.

CHAPTER FIVE
Hailey

THREE WEEKS LATER, I'm waking Steve up on his birthday by throwing a leg over his sleeping body and straddling his hips. When he only groans in his sleep, I lean down to press a kiss to his neck. I still don't get a response, so I start to kiss my way down his naked chest, pulling the sheets down as I go.

It isn't until I reach the edge of his boxers that I feel him fully wake up—when he fists my hair in a brutal grip and yanks.

I stare up at him in shock. Steve has never once been aggressive in the bedroom. He's generally the opposite, mostly sweet and gentle and a perfect gentleman. He's always treated me like I'm fragile.

Which, ironically, is the exact opposite of what I've always wanted. But it doesn't matter how many times I've begged him to be rough, or a little dirty, he can never bring himself to do it. And he doesn't understand how I could possibly want that, so it's an argument that I've accepted I have no way of winning.

Only now, he's being as aggressive as I've only ever hoped for.

My eager, lust-filled wish dies as quickly as it came.

Because as soon as I look at him in shock, he interprets it as horror and immediately lets go of my hair. His own eyes widen, as if he didn't even realize what he'd done.

"Sorry, I—I think I was still asleep," he stammers. "You scared me. I didn't mean to hurt you. Are you okay?"

I barely stop my eyes from rolling before I answer. "You didn't hurt me, Steve." I let my gaze shroud over with desire as I bring my hand to his morning wood, letting him see my intentions. "Do it again," I whisper as I reach for his boxers.

But he stops me by grabbing my hand. His jaw clenches, and I can tell he's annoyed by my silent ask for roughness. "I'm not in the mood, Hailey."

I sigh and pull away from him, straightening to a sitting position where I'm still straddling his hips. "I just wanted to wish you a happy birthday," I say quietly.

When the hard expression doesn't leave his face, I lie down next to him, curling up under his arm and pressing myself against his side.

"Should I make you breakfast instead? What would make you happy? We can do whatever you want today." I punctuate my offer with a kiss to his cheek.

He finally sighs, and the tension drains from his limbs. "Breakfast sounds good," he mutters.

I prop myself up on my elbow so I can shine a smile down at him. He's not annoyed anymore, but he still doesn't look happy, so I lean down to kiss him on the lips this time.

"Happy birthday," I whisper against his mouth. When he doesn't say anything, I try to deepen the kiss. "I love you," I try again.

He finally returns the kiss as he buries a hand in my hair and opens his mouth so I can slide my tongue in.

It isn't until I'm trying to slide my leg across his waist to straddle him again that Steve pulls away. He grips my hip as if holding me in place, then looks at me and asks, "Breakfast?"

I swallow my disappointment, reminding myself that today is about him, not about my base sexual needs. But we've only had sex twice in the past three weeks, and I'm getting a little hard up.

Normally, I would think a lack of sex signals that something is wrong in a relationship, but Steve's never been a horndog in the first place. I just have to deal with the fact that I need it more than he does.

Steve and I are in a comfortable place now with our relationship. We haven't had any more arguments since my birthday, and he's still sweet to me, taking me out to dinner and bringing home flowers every so often, so I don't have much to complain about. The overwhelming happiness that we shared the night of my birthday dinner didn't last past that evening, but I'm chalking that up to that level of joy being hard to maintain. Things aren't *bad*, just different. I need to stop expecting perfection.

I'm in the kitchen making Steve's favorite omelet when he wanders in, wearing his usual suit and tie. I took the morning off work so I could wake up with him on his birthday, but I knew he would still want to go to work. He's nothing if not a dedicated employee.

Even if his only goal is to make enough money to retire.

"So what do you want to do tonight?" I ask with a smile as

I shake the pan over the stove. I want to ask if he wants to go to a bar to celebrate, but I'm not sure what kind of reaction that will be met with, so I stay silent.

"I don't care, we can just do dinner or something," he says nonchalantly as he pours himself coffee. "The big celebration will be this weekend anyway."

I freeze. A frown mars my face as I turn to him in confusion. "What do you mean? What's this weekend?"

He leans back against the counter and gives me a blank stare. "I'm going down to Atlantic City with the boys."

My frown deepens. "You're what? Why didn't you tell me that?"

He just shrugs, taking a sip of his black coffee. "We were originally going to invite girlfriends, but we decided to make it guys only. You wouldn't want to hang out with a bunch of drunk idiots anyway."

My head continues to alternate between shock, hurt, and fury. "What happened to not doing the cliché drunk party bus birthday thing?" I manage to grit through clenched teeth.

Again, he just shrugs. "I want to see what all the fuss is about."

Anger starts to overpower every other feeling raging inside me. "So you get to drink and gamble and be a total glutton on your birthday, but I can't have a drink with my sister *on my 21st birthday?*"

He turns his stare back to me, and for the first time it occurs to me that he may have been planning this as my punishment since the night of my birthday. He's never been one to let a transgression go, and I should've realized he let me off too easily that night.

He continues to stare at me, and for a moment, I think he's not going to answer. But then he says, "I just want to have a nice night out with my friends, you don't have to make such a big deal out of it. You can come if you really want to."

I actually take a step back in shock. And in this moment, in my kitchen at 8am on a Wednesday, understanding dawns.

I suddenly realize how badly I've been manipulated. I think back to the night of my birthday, to our angry conversation, and realize with a start that *I* was the one to apologize. I didn't do anything wrong, yet I was the one to come crawling back to Steve. *On my birthday.*

But even that wasn't enough for him. He has to punish me with something else, too. He wants me to suffer for that night, wants me to wait at home while he has the birthday celebration that he knows I wanted. That I tried to steal a piece of when I met Remy without his permission.

It feels like I'm a completely third-party observer watching not just this interaction, but every questionable moment we've ever had as a couple. The reality of the last year flashes in front of me, and suddenly, I'm experiencing every cutting insult, every forced apology, every bit of silent treatment all over again.

I stare at Steve with a newfound perception.

Unfortunately, perception is not the same as action.

Despite realizing the web that Steve has tangled me in, I'm still smothered by the pressure of the tension between us. I still feel the weight of his disapproving stare. I still feel the overwhelming need to make him happy.

I still can't bring myself to call him out on it.

I finally break away from his gaze that's challenging me to fight him on this. He knows how badly he's beaten me down. He knows I don't have it in me to push this.

"No, that's okay," I mumble, turning back to the now burnt omelet. I busy my hands by dumping it in the trash and reaching in the fridge for ingredients to start over again, for some reason driven by a deep-rooted need to make Steve quality meals—even though the stress of the past few weeks has ruined my appetite enough that I've barely been eating. "You have fun with the guys this weekend. I'm just going to catch up on schoolwork."

He doesn't even smirk in victory. He's already accepted that I'm going to acquiesce, so it doesn't even warrant celebration. He walks over to me and kisses my cheek.

"I have to get going. Don't worry about breakfast, I'll pick up something on the way." He takes a few more gulps of his coffee, then sets it down next to the bowl filled with eggs I've just broken. Without another word, he grabs his laptop bag and leaves the apartment.

I slump into a seat at our kitchen table. I debate calling my sister to talk through the mess of thoughts in my head, but I don't think I'm actually ready to hear what she has to say. She's been plenty vocal about not liking Steve, even implying a few times that he's controlling and bad for me, but I always brushed it off as her having a tendency to dump guys at the first sign of a problem. She's never found anyone that she felt was worth working on a relationship with. Anytime I would try to talk about some of the not-so-perfect sides of Steve, I could always tell she was waiting for the right moment to tell me to dump him instead of actually listening.

I debate calling our friend Lucy, who I've been more open with. But she's only a friend through Remy, and I don't exactly talk to her outside of fight nights. Plus, she's never been in *this* situation. I've only ever talked to her about what it's like when the honeymoon phase ends once you've been with someone for a while. I leaned on her to understand what changes are considered normal and what should be a red flag about partners becoming too complacent.

But this is something entirely different. And I realize that I don't have anyone to call because I don't know of a single person who's ever dated a borderline-narcissist.

I frown at that thought. The word tickles something in my memory, something I overheard Remy say recently about Steve wanting to prove that he owns me.

Does he? Is all of this just to flex his power over me?

Is he a narcissist?

I reach for my phone without conscious thought. Then I take a deep breath and google: *What is a narcissist?*

Several pages immediately pop up, including the WebMD definition of Narcissistic Personality Disorder. I scroll through the symptoms.

Inflated sense of importance.

A need for attention and admiration.

Unable to take criticism.

Lack of empathy.

There's even an article titled *6 Signs You're Dating a Narcissist.* I click on it and skim the paragraphs.

1. They were charming... at first.

I frown, knowing that describes Steve but also recognizing that applies to plenty of long-term relationships.

2. They lack empathy. "*Narcissists lack the skill to make you feel seen, validated, understood, or accepted, because they don't grasp the concept of feelings. Translation: they don't do emotion that belongs to others.*

Okay, also somewhat true. Even this morning is a perfect example. I was vocal about it bothering me that Steve was celebrating his birthday in the way that I wasn't allowed to, yet it didn't affect him whatsoever.

3. They don't have any (or many) long-term friends.

That one's not true. Steve has plenty of friends from high school that he still keeps in touch with.

4. They pick on you constantly.

At that one, my eyebrows shoot up. That one's the definition of Steve, especially since we moved in together. He's careful not to say anything that's outright hurtful, but my self-confidence has taken a serious dive in the past few months. He knows exactly what kind of little comments he can slip into our conversations that will have me second-guessing myself—or even make me feel like complete shit.

5. They think they're right about everything... and they never apologize.

My mouth drops open when I realize just how much that applies to Steve. I can't remember the last time I heard him apologize, and I'm not exactly the one to start any of our fights. And there have been so many times when we've moved past a fight, but then I was left thinking that it's odd he never actually apologized. Every disagreement has ended with either me apologizing just to get rid of the overwhelming tension, or him manipulating his way out of it without having to say the words 'I'm sorry.'

I stare in shock at my phone, scared to even look at the last number.

6. They gaslight you.

Number six makes me frown again. I've heard the term *gaslighting* thrown around a lot in the past few years, but it's so common now that I've started to think people are too lenient with its use.

Signs of gaslighting include:

You feel more anxious and less confident than you used to

You often wonder if you're being too sensitive

You feel like everything you do is wrong

You apologize often

You make excuses for your partner's behavior

You have a sense that something's wrong, but aren't able to identify what it is

I slap my phone facedown onto the table, shaking my head as if trying to clear the newfound information from it.

This is ridiculous. Steve does not have a personality disorder— he's just a little bit of an asshole.

But between what happened this morning and the things I just read, I can't stop twirling the idea around in my head. I can't stop thinking about how manipulative Steve is, how selfish and cruel he can be. How he's perfect on paper but oftentimes the complete opposite behind closed doors.

How my 85/15 rule is starting to look…

…like a 15/85 rule instead.

I start to pace around the kitchen as I turn these thoughts over and over again in my head.

Realizing the truth about Steve is one thing, but doing something about it is something entirely different. Because now I'm stuck asking the questions: *What do I do now? Do I confront him? Can he even change? Should I just leave him?*

I pause and let out a heavy exhale as I think about what a confrontation would even look like. It's not hard to take a guess. Anything I would point out would be immediately shut down, either by being swept under the rug or by somehow being twisted to be my fault. That's just who he is. That's just the gaslighting asshole that he is.

I can't lie to myself that I think he's capable of change. He's not. This isn't a singular quality that someone can work on, it's an entire personality type. It's literally called a *personality* disorder. So if that's the case, is it even worth trying to argue about it? What good would it do me to confront him if 1) it wouldn't even be acknowledged, and 2) it's not something that he could change?

The answer is… none. It wouldn't do any good.

I drop my head into my hands on another heavy exhale. The only option left is to just… end it. Break up with him and get out of the relationship.

But *fuck*… the idea of walking up to him and saying "I want to break up" is terrifying. Because his next question would be to ask why, to which I wouldn't have a good enough answer—by his standards, at least. Telling him that he's a certifiable narcissist that makes me feel like shit about myself would get me… I have no idea what it would get me. Laughed out of the room, probably. Because he definitely wouldn't accept a breakup.

I raise my head, anger roiling in my gut and a frustrated scream getting trapped in my throat. I want to *rage* at the unfairness of it all, at the fact that I not only ended up with a fraud but also that it took me this long to realize it.

And I *still* can't bring myself to leave. Because even knowing everything, knowing all that he is, I still feel like I need a better out. Like I need a true excuse before I end it.

And I fucking *hate* that I feel that way.

Because I know I'm a coward for thinking like that.

I give up on my internal argument, swallow my scream, and turn to the kitchen for a distraction. I set to cleaning up the pointless breakfast mess, every swipe of the sponge an attempt at clearing my mind the way I'm clearing the dishes. It doesn't help, though. I'm just as confused by the time I'm done.

Just as confused by the time I get home from work.

Just as confused by the time Steve crawls into bed that night, giving me a chaste peck and acting like nothing even happened this morning.

And when he comes home from his weekend in Atlantic City, looking just as smug as he is hungover, I can't stop thinking about what all of this means for my future.

"BABE, CAN YOU drive me to the airport on Monday morning? I have a flight to Chicago at 8am."

I frown at the chiffon shawl in my hands, trying to remember what I have going on Monday morning.

It finally dawns on me. "I can't on Monday. I have a yoga session with Remy in the morning."

There's a pause that I don't think anything of until he walks into the bedroom and crosses his arms over his chest. He's dressed in a three-piece dark blue suit and, just as it always is when he's dressed up like this, his confidence is palpable. "A yoga class? Since when?"

I turn to study my reflection in the mirror. I'm wearing a floor-length dress, the blue color bringing out the brightness in my blue eyes, and the thin straps leaving nothing to be desired of my shoulders and back. I wrap the shawl around my shoulders in an attempt to cover myself a little more. "We saw a flyer for it at the café and thought it looked fun. We're actually taking the morning off work so we can get brunch afterwards."

When he's quiet again, I finally recognize the stillness in

the room. I look at his reflection through the mirror, and sure enough, there's fury flashing like lightning in his eyes.

I grip the shawl tighter and quirk my head in confusion. "Why? What's wrong with that? Can't you just take an Uber to the airport? I thought the company paid for stuff like that."

I see his fists clench where he's still standing in the doorway. He's not looking at me, which is not a good sign.

He's not used to me pushing back on him. In the past year, I've fallen so deep into the yes-woman hole that even asking an innocent question like that is enough to inject palpable tension into the room. But lately… it's almost like that part of me that's always tried to keep from angering him isn't automatically snapping into gear. Or maybe I care less. Because this is now the second time this week I haven't jumped to do something he's asked of me—even as I feel his anger grow.

"Were you even going to invite me?" he asks through clenched teeth. "Or did I not even cross your mind?"

I swallow nervously and turn around so I can give him my full attention.

"I—I wasn't going to invite you," I admit quietly. "You hate yoga, and you hate mornings. I assumed a 7am yoga class was the last thing you would want to do."

He lets out a rough laugh and shakes his head, still not looking at me.

"You really don't ever think of me anymore, do you?" he asks with a cruel laugh. "While I'm out here buying you flowers and planning dinner dates, trying to make you happy, I don't even cross your mind. Unbelievable."

I feel a pang in my chest at his accusation. I *know* his logic is flawed, and I *know* he's manipulating me, but his tone and control over my emotions don't stop his words from hitting their mark. I can't escape the bone-deep need to make him happy.

Even if I really, *really* want to.

Because despite my epiphany three weeks ago on the morning of his birthday, I *still* can't bring myself to stand up to him in the way I need to. I still feel like I'm chained to his well-being, like no matter what he does or says, if he's wrong and being an asshole, I *still* need to do what I can to placate him.

"That's not true," I say quietly but firmly. "I think about you all the time, Steve. Not inviting you to something I know you'll hate doesn't mean I've stopped caring about you."

His nostrils flare as he finally turns to me and tries to incinerate me with his stare. "Is that true? So then why would you agree to brunch if you give a shit about me?"

I give him a quizzical look. "What's wrong with brunch?" Suddenly, it occurs to me that he might be protesting me leaving the house—*at all*—without his knowledge. I narrow my eyes at him as rage starts to boil in my veins. "Are you seriously telling me you expect me to *consult* with you before I make any plans that involve leaving the house? Have we really progressed that far?"

If it's possible, his fury intensifies tenfold. He doesn't like that I'm standing up to him. And I want to feel proud, but instead I feel nervous. Steve's not the type to take a lashing. He's the type to give them out, whether they're deserved or not, just so he can hold the power in the dynamic.

I shrink into myself, bracing for whatever verbal beating

he's about to cut me with.

He stares at me with a darkness in his eyes that I've never seen before. "Don't be a fucking idiot. I'm not a tyrant. But it *does* involve me when your plans include being a worthless drunk in public."

My eyes widen. "A drunk? Because I'm getting brunch? What the *fuck*, Steve!"

"*Don't* use that language with me," he snaps.

By now, I'm sure I'm gaping. "*You* cursed at *me!*"

He finally shakes his head and drops his gaze to the floor in front of him. As if in total disbelief, he shakes his head again with a rough laugh.

"Whatever," he says flatly. "Do whatever you want, Hailey. Get as drunk as you want. Fuck as many guys as you want. I'm sure you and your whore sister can pick up plenty of guys for a little orgy."

My blood freezes at the words. Everything around us stops, and I'm not even sure I'm breathing anymore. This can't be real life. That did not just happen. He did not just say that.

I *know* he gets jealous when something or someone other than him holds my attention. I've heard plenty of stories about his horrible ex-fiancée who cheated on him, and I've seen him take his insecurities out on me just as often. It's not the first time he's talked down to me by implying I should go cheat on him; it's not even the second.

But he has *never* involved Remy in his insults. It's always been an unspoken thing between us, a clear line that's been drawn without saying it out loud that I won't tolerate any hate against my sister. I might have trouble standing up to Steve to defend myself, but there's not a bone in my body that will stand to hear him talk badly about Remy, regardless of his issues.

He's testing me, I realize as I stare at him in disbelief, in outrage, in shock. He's looking at me with a *what are you going to do about it?* expression. He's waiting for my retaliation, knowing it's never going to come because he's spent too much time cutting me down, making me completely dependent on him. He doesn't think I have it in me to say a bad word against him because he knows exactly how important he's made his comfort mean to me.

But now... now he's going after Remy. This is just a new boundary that he's pushing, trying to stretch the line farther and farther until there isn't a single thing he couldn't get away with.

How far will he take this? What else will he go after? First it was my self-esteem, my happiness, my independence. Now it's my love for my family and friends, whom he's already begun to alienate. He's just going from indirect to direct right now.

What's next? Blatant, even more vicious insults? He's been subtle with them so far, digging them in like a splinter so they're annoying but not exactly overwhelming. Or will it be physical abuse? Would he ever hit me? Lately, I've actually found myself wishing he would actually hit me, just once, just so I'd have a clear sign of his abuse that I can point to and say, *There! That's why he's a bad guy. That's why I broke up with him.*

Up until this point, I haven't had anything specific to point to. No good enough reason to break up with him that he would accept. I've just been waiting for something to break me out of my daze so I can finally walk away.

And he just gave it to me.

With that one comment about my sister, it feels like the rest of his mask has been lifted. Suddenly, I see him clearly for every ugly thing he's ever said to me. I feel every dig at my mind, my clothes, my career choice, my hobbies, my personality—everything that was meant to cut down my self-esteem. I see how he's alienated me from my family and friends. I see how he's *changed* me, both physically and emotionally.

I am a shadow of the woman that I once was. And I'm done. Officially done being made to feel this way.

"You're an asshole," I say in a stunned voice. "You're... you're just an asshole, Steve."

He raises an eyebrow in disbelief. "That's it? That's all you have to defend your precious sister?" He scoffs and straightens from where he's leaning on the doorway, looking completely at ease. "You're pathetic."

At least I was right about his insults getting worse. In the span of an hour, we've gone from subtle digs to outright condescension.

"No," I say quietly. "That's not all."

He turns to me with a cocked eyebrow, looking visibly smug as he waits.

I feel like I've finally woken up. I feel like I'm finally seeing my past, present, and future for what it was, is, and will be if I continue down this path. I might not magically snap back to my pre-Steve personality, but at least now I'm aware of what's happened to me and why.

At least now I feel like I'm capable of doing something about it.

I straighten to my full height and lift my chin in the air with a deep breath. "We're over, Steve. I'm done."

He scoffs and shakes his head. "You're not leaving over this. You'll get over it; it's not like I said anything untrue."

"You just called my sister a whore!" I shout in disbelief. "After you've treated *me* like one for our entire relationship."

"Shouldn't act like one if you don't want to be called out for being one," he sneers at me. "If you're going to beg me to treat you like a whore when I fuck you, then you should be prepared for me to call you what you are, sweetheart. Can't have it both ways."

I can only gape at him in shock. "Are you kidding me right now? Those two things are *not* the same. Just because I want more than just vanilla sex does not mean you get to kink shame me. Especially outside of the bedroom!"

A look of disgust rolls over his face. "So now you have *kinks?* What's next? Are you going to ask me to fuck you in public? Or maybe you want me to piss on you? Huh? Just how depraved *are* you, Hailey?"

I flinch at the crude words, each question hitting like an individual blow. I always knew Steve thought I was dirty for wanting more than just slow and sweet lovemaking, but he's never actually said it out loud. So far, I've only ever gotten judgmental looks and implied comments.

Is this what we've come to now? Openly shaming me? Since the birthday incident three weeks ago, Steve has clearly become more comfortable doing what he wants and not caring about how it affects me. He has less of a filter now and his comments aren't nearly as subtle as they used to be.

It's almost like he watched me that day and noticed that I was finally seeing him for what he is—as well as that I wasn't doing anything about it. It felt like my final approval for him to step into his true personality and devastate everything in our relationship.

Any good things that have happened since then were only to reel me back in and taunt me with the possibility of what we had in the beginning.

"Go get your things, we're already running late to this party that I'm not sure why we're going to," he orders, gesturing at my shawl and purse.

"What?" I ask in disbelief. "I just told you I'm breaking up with you, we're not going anywhere."

He gives me a look that should be reserved for parents looking at their whiny teenagers. "We're not breaking up. You can throw your temper tantrum in the car. Let's go."

I steel my spine and repeat myself with harsh clarity. "Steve, I'm serious. I don't want to be with you anymore. We're over."

Another look like he's dealing with an insolent child flashes my way. "You're not leaving me. Where would you go? You can't afford anything on the money you make at your shitty job."

Something inside of me begins to roil and grow even stronger. It's frustration and outrage and resentment, and it's going to explode out of my chest at any second. I can feel it. I want to tell him to go fuck himself. I want to scream and cry and tell him he's the worst kind of asshole and that he doesn't deserve me.

But… I can't.

Because next to that anger is also a sense of helplessness that is keeping me chained. Even though I want to unleash on him, he still has enough control over me that I can't actually bring myself to do it.

The most I can do is harden my resolve and get through the breakup.

"I'm tired of being shit on by my own boyfriend," I choke out. "I don't deserve this."

He laughs, and the sound is cold and cruel. "Yes, you do. I give you exactly what you deserve. You'd be an idiot to leave me because you'd never be able to do better."

I grit my teeth, the rage growing even as the helplessness smothers the emotion at the same time.

"You're wrong," I whisper. "And even if you're not, I'd rather be alone than spend another minute with you."

For the first time, his expression becomes serious. His brow furrows as he stares at me, the animosity radiating from his body.

"Fine," he snaps. "Leave me. I give you two days before you come crying back to me."

I shake my head, frustrated tears pooling in my eyes that I refuse to ever let fall in front of him again. "I will never come back to you," I say quietly. "I'm *done*, Steve."

He must finally sense how serious I am because he straightens, his jaw clenching.

"Fine," he spits. "I don't need this shit. You're not worth it anyway."

And in typical Steve fashion, he makes sure he has the last

word by turning on his heel and walking out of the apartment, slamming the door on his way out.

For a moment, I just stand in the quiet that's the aftermath of our fight.

Of our breakup.

A breath stutters out of me. There are so many emotions running through me right now that I don't know which one to deal with first. I'm not surprised that I'm not sad but I am a little in shock that I'm not some mix of relieved and raving mad. I've been with Steve for two years and have been unhappy for months, so the fact that we just broke up is more than a little surreal. And the fact that *I* was the one to break up with him is insane.

I look around the apartment in a daze. My life has revolved around another person for so long that I'm a little lost on what to do next. *Do I call my girlfriends? Do I go out and get laid? Do I get drunk?*

At that last thought, I straighten. *I can drink now. I can do anything I want now. He's not around to judge me or tell me I can't.*

I immediately stride into the kitchen to grab the bottle of tequila. And even though I'm more of a cocktail girl than a shot girl, I forego the glass and tip the bottle directly into my mouth.

I cough from the burn, but even still, a grin stretches across my face.

I feel fucking *free.*

I twirl in place, looking around for more things that I haven't been "allowed" to do. My gaze lands on the Bluetooth speaker next to the oven. *Perfect.*

I rip my shawl off and place the tequila bottle back, instead grabbing a Corona from the fridge—just because I can drink now doesn't mean I'm going to ignore my limits and drink myself into the toilet. I crack the beer and flounce across the kitchen, then press play on my favorite EDM playlist.

And crank the volume up, my smile growing bigger with each beat.

FIGHT TWO

CHAPTER SEVEN
Jax

"ARE YOU STILL coming to my parents' anniversary party tonight?" I ask Tristan. "I know you said you would, but you've been so focused on training lately that I wasn't sure."

I leave out the unspoken part of my question that's something like, *Are you going to come or bail because Remy will be there tonight?*

He just continues to push around the steak on his plate that I know he won't eat. The past few weeks I've basically had to force food down his throat; that's how messed up the bastard's been over Remy. Apparently, leaving these two together in our apartment for ten days while I was traveling, and Remy needing a place to stay resulted in both of them leaving with broken hearts. God only knows what happened during that time, because neither of them will admit their feelings to each other, let alone to me. So, I just play the clueless best friend, offering comfort with meals and vague words.

"I'll be there," he says in a gruff voice. "I promised your parents I'd go, plus I'm hoping..." He looks away and swallows his words, even though I know the end of that was going to be,

I'm hoping Remy will be there.

I nod and steal a bite of steak off his plate. "Eat the rest. You sucked in training this week because your strength has been shit lately." I climb off the barstool and start to clean up my own plate. "I'm leaving in a little bit. I'd offer you a ride but I have family stuff before and after and I figured you wouldn't want to deal with that." I don't bother telling him I'm driving Remy to the party and that's why I can't take him. "So I'll just see you there, yeah?"

He nods and continues pushing his last bite around. With a sigh, I step up to him and clap him on the back. "Everything works out in the end. If it hasn't worked out, it's not the end."

He looks up at me, and in his eyes I see so much pain, so much desperation, that I'm almost tempted to blurt out that I know Remy's in love with him. The two idiots have their wires crossed and don't know that they have the same feelings for each other, so they're both just sitting around, miserable and heartbroken.

He just nods an unspoken *thank you*, to which I nod in return before walking upstairs to get ready for the party.

But as I shower and get dressed in one of my suits, it's not Tristan and Remy that I'm thinking about with concern. It's Remy's sister, Hailey.

Although Remy's been the one closest to my family for over a decade, Hailey's been a big part of it too. While Remy was my best friend growing up, inseparable and always by my side, Hailey was the little sister who I couldn't help but take under my wing. Being five years younger than me meant I was the responsible adult figure between us, even at the age of fifteen. And she was mesmerized by me.

Everyone knew she had a kid's crush on me when we were younger. No one was surprised. What ten-year-old girl wouldn't crush on the fifteen-year-old boy always hanging around her house? I never treated her any differently because of it, except maybe making sure I didn't do anything to further her crush or give her false hope. And when I started seriously dating at seventeen, her crush seemed to lose its steam and settle comfortably into friendship. By the time she became a teenager, and I left for college, we had a friendship that's bond was so strong that no distance could test it and no words could hurt it.

Even seeing me bring home my college girlfriend didn't affect how close we were. Her welcoming smile was just as warm, just as *Hailey* as I could've hoped for. It became an unspoken thing that she would always be *baby girl*, my friend through relationships, school troubles, family drama, all of it. I was the boy who drove her to dance classes and helped her with her math homework, and she was the girl whose sunshine could melt any storm clouds in my life in a heartbeat. She was so happy, so wholesome, that it never surprised me that our bond was as pure as it was. It always felt like this living, breathing, ironclad thing that became apparent every time the two of us were in a room together. I would've done anything for that girl.

I never thought of her as anything but a friend. In fact, I got more comments about dating her sister than I ever did about Hailey. A big part of that was obviously her being so young—an actual minor for the majority of the time we spent together during our childhood—but even after she turned eighteen, it never really occurred to me to pursue anything more. I knew she was gorgeous, but I never felt like I wanted to change what felt like a perfect friendship. I liked being her friend and protector, the guy she always knew she could count on. I almost felt like I didn't want to mess with perfection.

Even when she moved into the city with Remy after high school, I liked the comfort of those nights I spent with the two of them, reminiscing about our hometown and talking about whatever happened during our days in the city. We lived such different lives—me in Corporate America by day and the gym by night, and her, an 18-year-old waitress, working in the restaurant industry—and it was fun sharing over our different experiences. I even kept my reactions to only slightly-feral when she started dating. I would always be protective of Hailey, but I only ever wanted her to be happy.

Which is why, as I finish buttoning my shirt, I can't stop stressing over tonight. Because Hailey's not happy anymore, and the piece of shit that she's bringing to my parents' party is the reason why.

I finish the last button and remind myself once again that I need to keep my fucking cool. Too often I want to strangle Steve for snuffing out the sparkle in Hailey's eyes, and I had to make a vow to myself a long time ago that I wouldn't physically hurt him for it.

I've tried talking to her about it, but I've seen how she reacts to Remy's attempts, and the fact of the matter is, I have even less of a right to tell her what to do than her sister. At the end of the day, it's her choice how to live her life and as long as he's not physically or mentally hurting her, I don't really have a good reason to step in.

I just hate the fact that he's so much less than she deserves. Even Tommy, her high school boyfriend, was good to her despite being a bit of an airhead. It never shredded me to see them together the way it does to see her with Steve, who I can see is killing her self-esteem. But she swears that she's happy, so between that and not having the right to step in in the first place, I just watch from afar and grind my teeth in my fury.

I never know if today is going to be the day that I finally snap, but as I slide my suit jacket on and grab my car keys, I remind myself that it would only hurt my relationship with Hailey if I did.

"Jaxon, darling, I haven't seen Remy yet. Don't tell me you didn't bring my favorite future granddaughter-in-law tonight."

I swallow my sigh as I take a big gulp of the beer in my hand and turn to face my grandmother.

"Hi, Grandma Birdie," I greet her with a smile. "How are you enjoying the party?"

She returns my smile, but its shine pales in comparison to the obnoxious bird pin in her hair.

"Don't change the subject," she says with a knowing look. "Did you bring her tonight or not?"

This time I don't contain my sigh. "Yes, I brought her. I was just talking to Mom and Dad with her. But, Grandma, you know we're not dating. We'll never date. It's too weird, I've known her too long."

She flaps her hands as if all my reasons are bullshit. "Nonsense, you can always move from friendship to relationship. I knew your grandfather when we were both in diapers and look how we turned out. You're just being a pussy about pursuing her."

I choke on my beer. She doesn't even blink, just gives me a few hard pats on the back and waits for me to respond with God knows what kind of answer.

"Jesus Christ, Grandma, how did you—why did—I don't even know what to say to you right now. Other than no, I'm not." Suddenly, I remember the point of her comment, so I straighten and glare at her. "I'm not a pussy. We just don't mesh well. We're better as friends. Plus, I'm pretty sure she's in love with my roommate."

She seems to deflate at my response. Everyone knows that she's always been smitten with Remy—feisty women unite—so she never takes it well when we inevitably reach this point in the conversation.

She sighs as she concedes. "I'm not sure anyone would be better than you, but if she's happy, then I guess that's okay."

I just smile and press a kiss to her weathered cheek. That seems to brighten her back up because she smiles up at me, a sparkle in her eye. "What about her sister? She's beautiful and mature, from what I remember. And you've never treated her as someone that you couldn't be more than friends with." She rolls her eyes and puts air quotes around that last part, causing me to aim a glare at her that definitely reads *careful*.

She ignores the warning. "What's your excuse for her? Too

101

pretty? Too smart? Or something else ridiculous?"

I sigh, knowing I'll never win this argument. She has too much spunk and gives too little fucks for her own good.

"She has a boyfriend, Grandma. They're actually coming tonight. Would you like me to introduce you?"

She huffs in frustration and waves me off. "No. No one could be a better catch than you, so I don't want to meet someone that she's clearly wasting her time with."

I wrap an arm around her and squeeze her in a hug. "I love you, Birdie. You'll always be my biggest cheerleader."

Her smile grows at my proclamation. "Of course. Always. I just want the best for you, you know that."

"I know. I would never change a thing."

But the sudden mention of Hailey is like a splinter in my mind, a nagging reminder that she still isn't here. She's never late—it's practically a joke between Remy and I that Hailey's more punctual than someone in the military. I look around at my parent's decked out, lit-up backyard, scanning the crowd for the sunlight, silky blonde hair I know so well.

"I actually need to go look for Remy and her sister. I'll come find you later, okay?"

She pats my cheek with a smile and says, "Of course. Enjoy your evening, darling."

I make my way through the party, searching for either Remy or Hailey but not finding either of them. I even stop to ask my parents if they've seen them, but no one has.

I manage to keep my impatience under control for another hour, glancing at the time on my phone and debating just sending Hailey a text.

By the fifth glance at my phone, I decide *fuck it, I'm just going to call her.*

I almost don't think she's going to pick up, it rings so many times, but then I hear the call connect. For a moment, all I hear is heavy breathing.

"Hello?" I ask tentatively. "Hailey? Are you there?"

The breathing gets closer, and then I hear, "Jax!"

I pull the phone away from my ear to stare at it in confusion. When I bring it back to my ear, all I can do is repeat myself. "Hailey? Are you there?"

A giggle rings out through the line. "I'm here. Where are you?"

A frown creases my face as I start to pace around the backyard—as I try to figure out what the fuck is happening right now. "I'm at my parents' house. Did you forget about their anniversary party?"

"Of course not. I love your parents. Unfortunately, Steven and I will be unable to attend this evening. Please send them our regards." She says it with an exaggerated formal lilt, and even though it pretty much proves my thoughts, I ask the question anyway.

"Are you drunk?"

Another giggle. "Yesssir. Very drunk."

My frown deepens. I can't remember the last time I've seen Hailey really drunk—if ever. She prefers to be in control, so the most she'll ever do is get buzzed. Although now that I think about it, I've barely seen any drinks in her hand at all the past few months.

"Are you... okay? Did something happen?"

She sighs heavily on the other end of the line. "Nothing important. I just wanted to relax for once."

"Are you at home? Where's Steve?"

Now the sigh is angry. "I don't give a shit. He can go fuck himself."

My eyes widen at her hostile tone. Hailey is one of the kindest, most easygoing people I know, so to hear her curse is somewhat shocking. It takes me a few seconds to decide which question I want to ask first.

"Uh, that kinda makes it sound like something happened. Hailey, what's going on?"

She groans loudly. She doesn't say anything for a while, so I give her space to sort through her own thoughts. Eventually, I hear her sigh again, softly this time.

"Steve and I broke up," she mumbles.

I almost trip over my own feet at the admission. For a moment I can't think of anything to say, I can only gape in shock and try to process this news that Remy and I have been holding our breath for but were worried would never happen.

"What?" I finally choke out. "When? How?"

"We got in a fight, and I ended it. He left, and I don't know where he went. But I figured a breakup is a good excuse to get shitfaced, right?"

I wince and pinch the bridge of my nose. "Just… please tell me you're at home and not out by yourself somewhere."

She snorts—another un-Hailey-like sound. "Jax, I'm not an idiot. I'm not out wandering around Philly by myself."

My sigh of relief morphs into one of exasperation. "Hailey, why didn't you call me? Or Remy?"

"Because I'm perfectly capable of taking care of myself, *thankyouverymuch*. I don't need a babysitter."

I shake my head, even though I know she can't see me. "Not a babysitter, just… you shouldn't be alone right now. Plus, what are you going to do when he comes home?"

She hesitates, and I can tell that hadn't occurred to her yet. "I don't know, I'll figure that out when it happens," she mumbles.

"Let me come get you," I say hurriedly. "He might be drinking right now, too. I don't want you drunk in that house by yourself when he comes home."

She groans again. Then eventually, she concedes with a sigh. "Fine. I'll take an Uber over to your house."

"Don't you dare," I growl into the phone. "You keep your pretty little ass in that apartment, and I'll call you when I'm outside. Don't move, I'll be there in twenty minutes. I mean it, Hailey."

She grumbles a few choice words but agrees to stay where she is. By the time I go to hang up, I can hear she's cracked another beer in the background. I groan and pick up my pace through the house toward the backyard.

It's not hard to spot my parents, but it is hard to wait for people to stop talking to them long enough to get my own words in. I lose all my patience far too quickly and interrupt my mom's conversation with one of my aunts, flashing an apologetic smile.

"Sorry to interrupt, but I need to leave, Mom. Hailey needs some help, so I have to go pick her up."

Mom's eyes widen in alarm, and I'm once again reminded

how much a part of our lives Remy and Hailey have become over the years. I swear my mom loves the girls just as much as she loves me—sometimes probably even more.

"Is she alright?" she asks with a worried frown. "What's going on?"

I lean forward to kiss my mom's cheek. "She's fine, I promise," I say softly. "She just needs a ride. I'll call you tomorrow."

She relaxes with a smile. "Okay, honey, drive safe. I love you."

"I love you too. And if I didn't say it before, you look absolutely beautiful tonight."

She waves me off with a blush. By the time she turns back to the next person to catch her attention, I've already made my way through the house to the driveway.

Twenty minutes later, I'm parked illegally in front of Hailey and Steve's apartment. I grab my cell phone to call her so she can let me in.

She doesn't answer the first time.

Or the second.

By the third missed call, I'm starting to panic, my fingers tapping the wheel in rising agitation. Visions of a drunk Steve coming home and finding a back-talking ex-girlfriend flash through my mind. By the time two more calls go unanswered, I'm damn near convinced I need to break the door down to get to her.

At the last minute, before I do just that, I remember that Remy once gave me a key in the case of an emergency. We never thought Steve had it in him to be violent toward Hailey, but we definitely never trusted the guy. So she made a copy of the spare key that Hailey gave her and snuck it to me in case I ever needed to help her when she couldn't.

Now is one of those times.

I quickly work through the keys on my keychain until I find the one that unlocks the front door, and then the door to their apartment. I push it open with a sigh of relief, one that immediately gets caught in my throat when I realize I have no idea what I'm walking into.

There's no sign of Hailey in the kitchen, so I make my way down the hallway toward the living room, following the sounds of electronic music. As soon as I walk through the doorway, I see her sprawled out on her stomach on the couch, snoring softly.

My breath catches at the sight of her. She's wearing a long blue dress, the thin straps crossing in a pattern across her back in a way that shows off her beautiful pale skin. Her blonde hair is hanging in a curtain in front of her face, and when I finally bring myself to crouch down beside her and brush her hair out of the way, I smile when I see some drool on the corner of her lip.

My gaze trails down her arm that's hanging off the couch to where a beer bottle is placed on the floor at her fingertips. It's barely halfway empty. I only see one other beer bottle around me, and although it's empty, from where I'm sitting, it looks like Hailey barely had a beer and a half—a Corona, no less, so hardly a beer with high alcohol content.

I place my hand on her back and rub gently. "Hailey. Hailey, wake up. Let me take you home."

She mumbles something in her sleep but doesn't wake up. I try again, harder this time, but it's no use. She's out cold.

There's zero chance of me leaving her here, so I realize I'm going to need to carry her outside. Carefully, I roll her over so I can reach under her back and knees to lift and cradle her to my chest. I swear under my breath when I realize how light she is. She's always been tiny, but it's easy to tell that she's too small right now. I don't know what's been going on with her the past few weeks, but she definitely hasn't been eating enough.

I make a silent vow to stuff her full of greasy, hearty food in the morning.

With Hailey tucked against my chest, I make my way back down the hallway. Somewhere between the front door and my car, a breeze ruffles her hair and she curls in tighter against my chest. A small whimper escapes her lips, and I hug her even closer to me.

When I finally have her curled up in my passenger seat, I buckle her in and cover her with my suit jacket. Then I quickly hurry around to the driver's seat so I can pull away from this godforsaken place. I hope Steve enjoys coming home to an empty apartment tonight.

Hailey starts to stir as I park in front of my house. By the time I've walked around to open her door and crouched down beside her, she's sleepily blinking her eyes open. She lifts her head from where it was resting on the seatbelt and looks around in confusion before her gaze finally settles on me.

"Jax?" she says with a sleep-heavy voice. "Where am I?"

"We're at my house," I answer softly. "I picked you up after you told me you and Steve broke up, remember?"

At the reminder, she frowns. I'm wondering if she'll yell at me for breaking into her apartment when she finally huffs and glares at me.

"I hate that fucking guy," she growls.

I bark a laugh at hearing her curse again. She continues to glare at me, so I just straighten up with a grin and hold my hand out to her. "I agree. Let's get you inside, so you don't have to deal with that fucking guy anymore."

She mutters something under her breath but grabs my hand. She doesn't let go until we reach my front stoop and I'm ushering her inside with a hand on her lower back. And she's talking the entire time.

"Do you know that I actually wrote a *Fuck Steve List* not long ago?" she babbles as she tosses my suit jacket on the couch and heads straight for the fridge to grab two beers. I open my mouth to ask if that's a good idea, but the words never make it past my lips because Hailey quirks an angry eyebrow at me. The car nap seems to have dropped her from drunk to buzzed, so I raise my hands in mock surrender and crack the beer she's slid across the kitchen island to me.

"It was basically just a list of shit that I *wanted* to do but couldn't because Steve was a pussy. Want to know what was on it? You'll never believe how boring this stupid list was." She starts counting off on her fingers. "Get drunk, get a tattoo, smoke weed, smoke *hookah* even, kiss a girl, travel someplace by myself. I literally created a bucket list for when I break up with my boyfriend." She spreads her hands out wide in victory. "Well, joke's on him because I'm already checking my first thing off the list."

It doesn't seem like she's really expecting an answer, so I don't say anything. But while I'm debating if I want to ask her if she wants to talk about what happened tonight, Hailey jumps up to sit on the counter and then chugs half her drink, making me stare at her in awe. Not just because she's a sight, drinking like a frat boy while looking like a goddess in that dress, but because she's actually opening up to me. She's never been vocal with me about her relationships, so I've never really understood that side of her. Part of me is frustrated that it took booze and a breakup for us to have this conversation, but the other part of me is thankful that it's happening at all.

"Let me ask you a question," she starts angrily. "Does everyone know Steve is a piece of shit? Was I the only one completely blind to this fact?"

I wince and look down, which she immediately notices and correctly reads. She lets out a harsh laugh and drops her head back against the cabinets.

"God, I'm so fucking stupid," she sighs. "For the past few hours, I've been trying to figure out how that's even possible. I mean, I get that he's perfect on paper, but I like to think I'm not a total idiot. How did I not see him for what he really is?"

"You are not an idiot," I say forcefully. "No one thinks that about you. You just saw other sides of him that we… couldn't necessarily see. That's all."

She jerks her head up to glare at me. "The other sides of him are even worse. Don't you get it? That's what makes this so annoying. There is *nothing* decent about him."

At her words, my heartrate speeds up. A mixture of fear and anger that I've never felt before starts to churn in my gut, and I'm trying to figure out how to fight the temptation of shredding Steve apart for long enough to ask the question that's always burned in my brain.

"Hailey," I say with a tremor in my voice, "did he hurt you?"

Completely oblivious to the chaos currently holding me hostage, she waves me off as if it's nothing. "Of course not," she replies as she swallows another few mouthfuls of her beer. "He's way too big of a pussy to ever lay a hand on me."

The anger in me abates just enough for me to take a deep breath. But I'm still not sure what could be worse than what we already know about Steve, so I'm not exactly at ease yet. I finally manage to ask, "So... then what happened? Why tonight?"

A flash of pain crosses Hailey's face, and I almost jump out of my seat to move around the island to her. But I don't. I give her space to process this how she needs to.

With a sigh, she drops her head against the cabinets behind her again. "He called Remy a whore," she finally mumbles.

My brow furrows in confusion. Remy has had a handful of boyfriends over the years, but she's not exactly the type to sleep around or juggle multiple guys at once. I'm also convinced she's in love with my roommate, so I doubt she's spending her time hooking up with a bunch of guys. She's as far from a whore as a normal 25-year-old can get.

"I mean, I can understand why he would call me a whore, but Remy? That girl has never fucked a stranger in her life. She's practically only ever fucked boyfriends. How does liking sex make someone a whore in his eyes?"

At the admission that he's used that word as a derogatory term describing *Hailey*, I really am jumping out of my seat and rushing around to stand in front of her. I grip the counter on either side of her legs with white knuckles, searching for the last shred of patience inside of me.

"He called you a whore?" I manage to grit out. "When?"

She blushes and looks down at the can beside her where she's fiddling with the beer top. "All the time," she mumbles. "It was practically a theme in our relationship."

I stare at her, trying—and failing—to process that statement. My brain fumbles through what I know about Hailey and her sexual history in order to try and understand what on earth Steve could be talking about. All I manage to get out is a weak, "Why?"

She looks up at me with a hesitant gaze. I can tell she's drunk because her eyes are slightly bloodshot—on top of the fact that she would never normally have a conversation with anyone that is this aggressive or blunt—so I wonder what her alcohol-muddled brain is stumbling over right now.

"You can't judge me," she starts defensively. "It was a long time ago, and I was drunk. I wouldn't normally tell you this since you and I have hardly had the kind of relationship where we talk about sex, but I'm drunk and pissed off. And you asked."

Speechless and confused, I just nod.

She sighs in defeat. "I had a threesome with Tommy and one of his friends in high school."

For a moment, all I can do is blink at her.

Fuck, that's hot.

But then I think about it in the context of this conversation, and my brow furrows in confusion. "Okay… So?"

She purses her lips and narrows her eyes at my response,

like I'm just not getting it. "So? Jax, I had a threesome with two guys. That's pretty slutty."

The frown on my face deepens as I think about how this could be used to insult her. "Did you do it so you could brag about doing it?" She shakes her head in confusion. "Did you cheat on anyone?" Another shake, this time angrier.

"Of course not! I had just started dating Tommy and realized I liked sex, and then one night his friend came over and we started drinking and... it just kind of happened. It wasn't even anything crazy, we were too young to do any more than fumble around."

I exhale a heavy sigh. "Did you regret it? Or did you enjoy it?"

Her eyes widen, and I can practically see the memory wheels turning in her brain. "I... I liked it," she answers quietly. "I doubt I would ever do it again, but... it was fun."

I sigh again as I step closer to Hailey and cup her face in my hands. She's still looking at me with a face of such pure innocence that it damn near shreds my heartstrings. My thumbs start to caress her cheeks as I stare into her big blue eyes.

"Hailes," I whisper quietly. "You are so far from a whore that it's laughable. I want to kill Steve just for putting the idea in your head. And to know that he's been treating you like one for so long... well, let's just say I'm trying really fucking hard to convince myself that I shouldn't leave you here and go hunt him down so I can rip his tongue out for ever talking to you like that."

A tipsy giggle escapes her lips. I smile, my heart jumping

a little bit at the sound.

"I don't ever want you to think of yourself like that again, do you hear me? If I find out there is a single self-deprecating thought running around in that pretty little head, I'm going to start switching out your sugar and salt just like you *loved* to do when you were a little troublemaker. We'll see how your customers like your food after that."

Another giggle. But she nods, and I drop my hands with a sigh. I don't realize they've landed on her waist until she takes a shaky breath, and her ribs expand under my big hands. I'm only now realizing how close we are.

She stares into my eyes, her lips parting as our gazes lock. My breath hitches, but I don't dare to look away. I have no idea what's going through her head right now, so all I can do is sit in this moment with her, heavy with alcohol and a tangle of emotions.

The moment breaks when she throws her arms around me. She burrows her face into my neck, and I barely hear her mumble, "Thanks, Jax."

My heart and lungs somehow start to function again. Tentatively, I reach up to wrap my arms around Hailey, marveling at the curves of her body that the skin-hugging dress allows me a moment to appreciate. The coconut scent of her hair invades my senses, and I automatically take a deep breath to try to envelop her in as many ways as I can.

Her arms tighten around my neck, and I suddenly become very aware of the fact that my best friend's drunk, post-breakup little sister is currently wrapped around me. I drop my hands to her hips and step away with an awkward cough.

"Do you... do you want to watch a movie or something? Or if you want to go to bed, you can take my room. I'll sleep on the couch. I should've offered you a change of clothes, too, you're probably freezing in that."

She shakes her head and jumps off the counter. I'm yet again reminded how tiny she is when I realize the top of her head barely reaches my shoulder now that we're on even ground. She chugs the rest of the beer and then walks over to the recycling bin to toss the empty can.

"Let's just watch Seinfeld, or something," she says as she plops onto the couch. She pulls her floor-length dress up to her thighs so she can rearrange herself to sit cross-legged. "And I don't want to get changed yet. I bought this dress for tonight, so I'm going to get my money's worth. Even if we're just sitting on the couch and laughing about Jerry's atrocious acting like we used to when we were younger."

The edge of my mouth quirks in amusement at her TV show choice. Everyone in our friend group always forgets that Hailey's only twenty-one—between her general life wisdom and her mature habits, half the time she acts even older than we do. She was the youngest out of all of us when she got her first job, she always made sure her homework was done, and she's been eating balanced meals since she first started cooking at thirteen. Even with the one "young person" hobby she has— going to raves—she still never did drugs or participated in anything remotely rebellious.

"Yes, ma'am. Seinfeld, it is," I concede with a grin. I grab another beer for myself—purposely not offering the already-drunk girl another one—before dropping onto the couch next to her. I turn the TV on, glaring at her when she takes the beer from my hand but staying silent. She rolls her eyes as she takes a big swig before giving it back when I press play.

We stay like that through a couple of episodes, laughing at the show but otherwise not talking to each other. I can tell when the booze starts really hitting Hailey because her laugh gets progressively louder. And then I can tell when her drunk energy starts to fizzle because she quiets down again and drops her head onto my shoulder.

I somehow manage to grab the blanket from the back of the couch without jostling her and gently wrap it around her shoulders. I enjoy the closeness for a few minutes, relishing the fact that she seems happy and not dwelling on everything that's happened tonight. I always knew she'd see Steve for what he really is one day—that she would realize her self-worth and leave the bastard in the dirt. A weight has lifted off my chest that I didn't even realize was there.

When Hailey's breathing steadies, and she stops laughing, I notice she's fallen asleep. I nudge her softly in an attempt to wake her up.

"Hailey," I say quietly. "Let's get you to bed. You're falling asleep."

She mumbles something and nuzzles into my neck. I sigh, realizing I'm probably going to have to carry her again.

I turn to try to slide my arms under her, but she straightens as soon as her head drops off my shoulder. She looks at me with bloodshot eyes, sleep-drunk and confused.

"Let's get you to bed. Can you walk?"

She rubs her eye with a closed fist, and I can't help but

grin at the adorable gesture. But then she nods and stands up, making her way toward the steps.

I follow her upstairs and head into my room, pulling the comforter back on my bed and fluffing the pillows while I wait for Hailey to finish using the bathroom next door. But when I turn around to grab her some clothes to change into, I damn near choke on my breath.

Hailey has stumbled into my room with half-lidded eyes and a big yawn, the alcohol clearly catching up to her. But what makes my eyes widen and my jaw drop is the fact that she's unzipped her dress and peeled off the straps, so the material is pooled at her waist.

"Hailes, maybe you should—" I start, but it doesn't seem like she can even hear me. She pushes the dress down over her hips, and I almost lose another lung when she steps out of it completely and walks past me toward the bed.

She's practically naked, wearing only a matching white lace bra and panty set, neither of which covers much. And I'm the idiot that can't do anything other than stare at her in open fascination.

I've always known that Hailey is drop dead gorgeous. Even when she was little, she was the most photogenic kid in both our families, which was further proven when she never went through an awkward puberty phase. She was just always known as the pretty one. Between her big blue eyes, silky blonde hair, and angelic smile, she's been turning heads since she was a teenager. Couple that with the perfect model-thin body that she grew into, and it's really fucking hard to find something unappealing about her physical appearance.

But she's never flaunted it, and I've never really thought about it past the general knowledge that she's obviously attractive—and when making the occasional threat to the guys at the gym to stop ogling her. She's also never been one to wear anything super revealing, so she doesn't exactly exude sexuality. She's simply… beautiful.

But right now, I feel like I'm receiving a crash course on just how sexy she is. Her tits are perfect orbs in her lacy bra, small because Hailey is small but still entirely too enticing. Her stomach is flat and her trim waist widens into womanly hips and a very grabbable, round ass. Everything about her is petite, yet still perfectly shaped and proportioned to the rest of her body. She is mouth-wateringly sexy.

I can't stop staring at her. I'm probably gaping like a fish, trying to pick my jaw up off the floor. It isn't until she reaches for the clasp on the back of her bra that I'm shaken out of my reverie and hurriedly look away. I turn my back as I try to mumble through a coherent response.

"I—uh, I'll grab you some, uh—some clothes to wear," I stutter. Then I rip my closet door open and grab the first T-shirt I can find, trying really hard not to look behind me as I practically launch it at where Hailey is sitting on the bed.

I keep my back turned as I give her time to put the shirt on. But I'm not a strong enough man to resist glancing over to see if she's dressed. I turn slightly, and I'm not sure if I really don't want to see anything or if I really do, but either way, I find Hailey sitting on my bed with her back to me, bare of a bra and fumbling to orient the shirt the right way.

At the sight of her bare back and smooth, ivory skin, I

whip my head back toward my closet again with a silent curse. I close my eyes and begin begging for whatever patience and strength any gods can offer me. My brain is spinning, bouncing between shock at Hailey's beautiful, womanly body, to male arousal that it feels like I have no control over right now, to disgust—and more shock—at myself for having these kinds of thoughts about my best friend's little sister. Who I've also known since she was ten.

I mumble a few more choice words under my breath. I've just made my decision to face the closet for the rest of the night instead of chancing another glance back when I hear Hailey's tiny voice.

"Jax?" she whispers. I look to the heavens and mumble another prayer for strength before hesitantly turning around.

Thankfully, Hailey's got the shirt on and is already under the covers. She has the comforter pulled up to her chin and she's snuggled so deep into the pillows that I can see more of her hair fanned around her than her actual head. I slowly walk over to the bed and, after a second's hesitation, reach down to tuck the comforter around her body. She smiles sleepily at the feeling, and a bolt of joy rushes through me at the sight of her like this.

"Night, Hailes," I say quietly.

Her eyes are already closed by the time I straighten to walk quietly out of the room. But I'm stopped by the feeling of Hailey's slim fingers wrapping around my wrist just as I start to turn.

"Thank you," she whispers. "For… everything. For being someone I can count on." Her hand drops from mine as her eyes close again, and I can tell she's already asleep.

I look down at her and smile, and the thought pops into my brain that I can't fathom how anyone could possibly think she's anything less than perfect. I reach down to brush her hair away from her face, momentarily caught up in the sight, the scent, the essence of Hailey. Instinctually, I lean down and place a gentle kiss on her forehead.

CHAPTER EIGHT
Hailey

I WAKE UP to the familiar sound of Jax yelling about something, though it takes me a second to remember that he hasn't bulldozed his way into my apartment building to kill Steve the way I secretly suspected he might one day. I realize I'm in Jax's bedroom, and suddenly all the events of last night come rushing back: the breakup, drinking myself into a stupor, waking up to Jax, him putting me to sleep.

I blink up at the ceiling, mentally taking stock of my emotions now that I'm not in shock. I'm definitely not sad, like I might be after a normal breakup. I might be a little hungover, though, a little frustrated, still, but no worse for wear after breaking up with a long-term, live-in boyfriend. I actually feel... *lighter.*

A hesitant smile spreads across my face. I know I still have a lot to figure out when it comes to Steve and the breakup, but I decide I want to spend it guilt-free with the people I miss most in my life. Starting with Jax.

I jump out of bed and notice the only thing I'm wearing is an oversized T-shirt. And just like that, the memory of me stripping in front of Jax comes flooding back, and a flush spreads across my skin. I don't remember him seeing anything, but it's still more of me than he's ever seen; and now I'm wearing his shirt.

Sighing, I brush off the embarrassment my head wants me to feel because I don't want anything to ruin this *lightness* flowing through me, at least for the day. I'll deal with everything else later.

I open the door and follow the sound of Jax's voice down the stairs. Before I've even reached the bottom, I see my sister and Tristan standing together in the entryway, staring at a shell-shocked Jax.

"Why is Jax screaming at 8:00 in the morning?" I ask with a sleepy smile. I stop on the last step and lean on the banister, waiting expectantly.

They all just look at each other, waiting for someone else to speak, until Tristan clears his throat and replies, "I got a fight in the UFC."

At first, I can only blink at him in surprise. Then...

"HOLY SHIT!" I scream. "Are you *serious?!* That's insane, congratulations!"

"Thanks," Tristan says with a grin. Then he turns to Remy with a skeptical look. "You know, I'm starting to feel a little hurt that my own girlfriend didn't react by screaming. Everyone else seems to think it's screech-worthy news."

Remy just glares at him and swats his arm, at the same time that I gasp, "*Girlfriend?* What the hell happened last night?"

Remy looks up at me with a hesitant gaze. "I think I need to ask you the same thing," she responds softly. I swallow nervously but nod in answer. She turns back to the boys. "So... gym? I'll stay here with Hailey. And you should call Coach."

Her words snap the boys into action. Tristan squeezes past me so he can get upstairs, but Jax stops next to me on the first step. He looks thoughtful for a moment, as if he wants to say something, but in the end, he settles on kissing my temple. "I'll be back later, don't go anywhere," he says quietly.

I look up at him with wide eyes, remembering how it felt to have him carry me out of my apartment and spend the night taking care of me here. I remember that he listened, and how good his proximity felt. Even now, with him standing so close to me, I just want to hug him even closer.

I give him a small nod, letting him know I'll stay here today. Some tension seems to ease from his body at that.

When I look back at Remy, she mutters, "It sounds like we have a lot to talk about." I let out a nervous laugh.

By the time the guys have gotten ready and left the house, I've already made myself at home in the kitchen and made breakfast for Remy and I.

"So... you and Tristan, huh?" I eventually ask with a grin. Even though Remy and Tristan have been at each other's throats for years, a few of us have suspected that they were secretly compatible. They were recently forced to live together in Jax's house, and to no one's surprise, they fell in love with each other. Still, they were too stubborn to admit their feelings, and because of some miscommunication, had been dancing around each other for weeks. I knew it was only a matter of time before they swallowed their pride and fixed things, so it makes me happy to see that's finally happened.

Remy starts picking at the omelet on her plate. "We're not talking about me," she says with a blush. "Stop trying to distract me. What happened with Steve last night? You broke up with him?"

The smile slips from my face. I push my plate away from me so I can cross my arms and lean on the granite countertop.

"I just... lost it last night," I start quietly. "It was like all of a sudden I could see him for everything that he really is." I aim a mock-glare at her. "Why didn't anyone tell me Steve was a piece of shit?"

My teasing tone falls flat as she winces. "That's not an easy thing to tell your sister. We—" She winces again and glances away. "We all knew it, but you were so happy at first, and we didn't want to hurt you. Then later, we tried to tell you, but I don't think you wanted to hear it. Especially from me, since I have a track record of running at the first sign of trouble."

I sigh and nod in understanding. "I know. There's probably nothing you could've said that I would've believed. I had to figure it out on my own. Which you knew." I lift an eyebrow in question, and she nods once, confirming what I subconsciously suspected weeks ago.

"So what happened last night?" she asks again with a subtle nudge.

I take a deep breath, not wanting to rehash the whole thing but knowing I need to give her an answer. "He said some things that opened my eyes. It wasn't even anything notable, it was just enough to finally cross the line. Because for the past few weeks, I feel like things have been shifting, and I've been noticing more and more about him, about the way he treats me and talks to me. And he's been pushing the line more and more each day. Until finally..." I mime an explosion with my hands. "...kaboom."

The tension visibly leaves Remy's shoulders. I never really thought about how my relationship might affect my friends and family, but looking at her now, I realize both she and Jax have been genuinely worried about me. Even now, I can remember the look of relief on Jax's face after he picked me up from my apartment.

"Well, I'm glad you're finally out of there," she says on a breath. But then something must occur to her because she shoots me a hesitant look and asks, "Do you regret breaking it off? Do you think you'd ever go back to him?"

I snort in a way that's so unlike me lately that it makes Remy's eyebrows rise in surprise.

I blame the newfound freedom for my restored personality.

"Fuck no. I will never go back to that man. Porters don't second-guess relationships, you know that."

She finally allows herself to relax and aim a grin at me. "Damn right, we don't."

I return the grin and pull my omelet back to me, stabbing a big bite onto my fork. It almost reaches my mouth when I hear Remy ask, "So then what happened with Jax last night?"

Immediately, my face flushes at the memory of drunkenly stripping in front of Jax.

At which Remy's eyes widen.

"Did you—did he—what—" is the only thing she manages to sputter.

"Nothing happened," I blurt out quickly.

I don't bother mentioning that he would never touch me. I never talked to Remy about my kid crush, but I'm sure it was obvious to a teenage girl four years older than me what was happening, and how Jax felt about it. It's always been clear that he looks at me like a friend he needs to protect, nothing more. But I never talked to Remy about how I had to get over my crush and watch Jax be perpetually uninterested in me.

I could never explain just how unlikely what she's suggesting really is.

"Oh, thank God," she says on an exhale. "I don't think I could handle that much news in one morning." She gives me a quizzical look. "So then why were both of you so weird this morning? What happened last night?"

I groan, too tired to be embarrassed about it. "I... may or may not have drunkenly stripped in front of him last night."

Her eyes widen. "You... you *what?*"

I roll my eyes at my sister. "Oh, hush. I just said nothing happened. I was just too drunk and too impatient to wait for him to leave the room before I got changed. It was a minor oversight."

She snorts. "I had no idea you were a get-naked type of drunk. Noted for future reference."

I just roll my eyes again and huff a laugh. "Very funny. Like I'm going to be getting shitfaced every weekend now that I'm single." My eyes narrow when something occurs to me. "Speaking of interesting nights, what happened with *you* last night? Since we're on the topic of being drunk and naked."

I can probably count on one hand the amount of times I've seen my sure-of-herself sister blush, but as of this morning, I'd count one more finger. Because she is *red*.

"Wow, that good? I always knew that man was a freak," I tease with a grin.

My comment snaps her out of her embarrassed state because she lifts her gaze to glare at me. "I doubt you want to hear details about my sex life, Hailes."

I cringe. "No, I don't. Especially since I'm sitting in Tristan's house, who will be back soon, and who I'll have to look in the eye. Just give me the CliffsNotes version of what happened last night pre-sexy time."

She bursts out laughing. "Sexy time? We need to update your game now that you're back on the market. No guy is going to want to sleep with you if you call it sexy time."

I wave her off. "I'm not exactly the sleep-around type, despite what—" I cut myself off and swallow roughly before I can finish that thought. Remy's too protective as it is, so she doesn't need to know the details of how Steve treated me. "Stop deflecting. What happened last night?"

Her laughter dies down, to be replaced by a content smile. "We... ran into each other at the party last night. He may or may not have cornered me in the study so we could talk through a few things. And then we may or may not have spent the entire night naked in my apartment..."

I smile, feeling so genuinely happy for her that I don't even cringe at the last comment. "I knew you guys would figure it out. You're perfectly matched; it would've been insane if you two didn't end up together."

Her head drops back to the couch with a happy sigh. She looks like the definition of lovestruck—or maybe *dick*struck, if her previous comment held any weight.

I head to the kitchen to make Jax's favorite Bloody Marys, and we spend the next few hours talking and laughing, barely paying attention to the movies that we put on in the background. The smile never leaves my face, my cheeks physically aching. I haven't spent time like this with my sister in far too long, and I know I'd normally feel a lot of guilt over that, but today, it's overpowered by the freedom I feel instead.

We're slightly tipsy and very giggly by the time the guys walk in the door. Tristan takes one look at his drunk girlfriend and mutters a curse. Jax just seems relieved to find me still here.

"How was the gym?" Remy asks from beside me.

Tristan strides over to her and leans down to press a hungry kiss to her lips. "Good. I can't wait to get you back in the gym with me."

I've never seen a smile like the one that stretches across Remy's face at that, and even the sight of it makes my heart flip over in my chest. I've never experienced love like that, no matter how much I tried to convince myself otherwise.

It makes me happy for my sister but sad for my own reality.

Suddenly, Jax appears next to me and takes a seat on the armrest of the loveseat. I smile up at him when he tugs a loose strand of my hair gently.

"Hi," he murmurs with a smile.

"Hi," I whisper back.

"How was your day?"

"Good. We've just been hanging out here since you two left. How was the gym?"

"Good. It's always fun beating Tristan around a little bit."

I hear a snort from my right and turn to see Tristan has dragged Remy into his lap and is currently twirling her hair around his finger. "It's been a while since you've 'beaten me around,' brother," he drawls.

Jax raises an eyebrow. "Oh yeah? Then how'd you get that shiner on your eye?"

"Remy," Tristan quips without even a pause.

Remy's jaw drops in shock. "You did not!" she exclaims. "I've *never* hit you!" And when we all look at her in disbelief, she mumbles, "Not hard enough to leave a bruise, at least."

"You can make it up to me tonight," Tristan says with a smug smile.

"Nuh-uh, you're in fight mode," Remy admonishes, pulling out of his lap and sitting beside him. "I already told you: no distractions."

Tristan actually *pouts*.

"Fucking children," Jax mumbles. "Can we please just get through dinner? You two can do whatever you want—and *talk about* whatever you want—after dinner."

I bite my lip to hide my smile when Tristan just continues to glare at his girlfriend.

"Are you staying here tonight?" Jax asks, turning his attention to me. Then something occurs to him, and he frowns. "Please tell me you're not going back to that piece of shit's apartment."

I chance a nervous glance at Remy. "Umm, I hadn't really thought about it. I need to get my stuff, so maybe I should just stay there while I find an apartment—"

"Like hell you will," she growls. "I don't want you anywhere

129

near that asshole. No, you're staying with me. My couch turns into a decent pull-out bed, so you can sleep there for as long as you need. I can even turn it into a studio type room, since I still have those dividers I kept from my old studio apartment. We'll set you up with your own space, so you don't feel like you're sleeping on the couch. Alright?"

Still I hesitate, but I ask her, "Are you sure? I don't want to invade your space, you *just* moved in there. I can always push Steve out of the apartmentor just find a place to sublet."

"No," I hear growled above me. I look up to see Jax tense with frustration. "I don't want you alone or anywhere near him," he says through gritted teeth. "Can you just stay with Remy until you find a new apartment?"

I breathe a sigh of relief. "Okay. I can do that."

It's Jax's turn to relax at my concession. A relieved smile appears on his face, and I realize just how worried he's been about me. I reach for his hand and squeeze it, the unspoken communication clear between us.

"I'm going to make dinner," he says, standing from the couch. "Are you both staying? Tristan gets chicken because he's officially in weight-cut mode, but I can make some steak if you would rather eat that."

I share a look with Remy before we answer at the same time, "Steak."

Jax just chuckles and makes his way into the kitchen. And when Remy turns back to a very grabby Tristan, I decide to follow him.

"I can make the sides," I offer when he raises an eyebrow at me. "What were you thinking of making?"

He's already digging around in the fridge for ingredients when he says, "Tristan gets greens, so just grab some of the frozen vegetables that we keep specifically for last-minute weight cuts. And I think we have potatoes if you want to chop some up and roast them while I do the steak."

I nod and finish off the rest of my drink before pulling off Jax's sweatshirt that I stole earlier. But when I turn to the fridge to grab my own ingredients, I find Jax staring at me with a look I can't decipher.

"What?" I ask in confusion.

He just shakes his head, a small smile on his face. He steps up to me and gives me a quick kiss on the top of my head. "I'm glad you're here," is all he says.

And the only thing I can do is smile up at him, conveying with my gaze that I'm glad too. I'm glad I'm away from a toxic environment, and I'm glad I'm back with my family. I'm glad I have people like Jax to look out for me.

"I don't think you two have ever cooked together, have you?" comes Remy's voice from the kitchen island where she takes a seat. "You two are both so good. Have you ever made something together?"

I share a glance with Jax and then we both shake our heads. "No, I guess not," I answer. "It's usually just one of us cooking." I make my way over to the fridge for my ingredients at the same time that Jax starts with the steak

"Well, in that case, I am very excited about this dinner," Remy says with a grin.

"You know, you should probably learn to cook too." I hear Tristan's arrogant drawl. "You were so proud of being the ideal female partner, but how is that possible if you burn everything?"

I chuckle as I reach into the freezer, not even having to look at my sister to know that she's glaring.

"You didn't seem to have any issues when I was choking on your dick last night," she snaps.

The pan in Jax's hand drops to the stove with a clatter. We both turn to Remy with equally stunned expressions.

She's grinning smugly at Tristan, but when she sees that we're just gawking at her, the smile immediately slides from her face. I'm fairly certain it's the first time I've seen her look it, but she actually looks bashful when she realizes what she's said. A blush flames her cheeks as she looks down and mutters, "Sorry," looking properly chastised.

Jax shakes his head, mumbling something under his breath about *never should've given my blessing*. I just laugh and go back to my ingredients.

The rest of the night is spent enjoying each other's company. Not once do I think about Steve or heartbreak or anything else that breakups usually come with.

My family and friends replaced it all with laughter and joy.

Two days later I'm packing up my office to leave for the day when I finally decide to call Hailey. She and Remy left after dinner on Sunday night, and I've managed to hold off until now on checking in with her. I know Remy is as protective of her sister as I am, so I know she's probably fine, but there's something in me that can't go another minute without hearing her voice and making sure she's okay.

She picks up on the second ring with a frazzled, "Hello?"

"Hey, baby girl," I croon into the phone in an effort to calm her down. "Busy day?"

She laughs, the sound breathless. "Something like that." I hear dishes clattering in the background.

I frown. "You're still at work?"

"Yeah, it's been... an interesting day." I know there's more to that story, but she doesn't give me a chance to ask because she says, "Nothing big, I'll tell you about it later. What's up?"

I force myself to not push her on the subject, despite wanting to know what's upsetting her. "I just wanted to see if you needed help moving out tomorrow. Remy said you're going in the morning?"

"Yeah, I figured it'd be best if I moved out while he's at work. But I know that's when you work too, so I didn't want to ask you. Remy will be there, so don't worry about helping out. I don't have that much to move anyway. I should be able to fit everything into her car with two trips."

"I'd rather be with you when you go back," I admit in a tight voice. "I don't want him showing up and catching you by yourself. Even Remy isn't enough of a threat to him."

She giggles, and the sound immediately calms me down. Infinitesimally. "Don't let Remy hear you say that."

I sigh. "I don't think he would do anything, but... I just hate the idea of you being around him. I know that makes me a Neanderthal. Can I come with you anyway?"

There's a pause on the other end of the line and then her sweet voice sounds and soothes the jagged edges of my angry heart. "Of course, you can come. I would never hold your caveman instincts against you, you know I love them." Another laugh. "Plus, I'd be an idiot to turn away a massive amount of muscle and another car. You'll probably cut our time by half."

I chuckle. "That's true. So what time are you going over? I assume you managed to take the day off."

"Yup. I want to be over there at 10am so we can get everything out quickly. Can you meet us there then? I could probably even have you done by lunch, so you don't have to take a full day off."

"Don't worry about that. We'll take as long as you need."

I can hear the smile in her voice. "Thanks, Jax. I appreciate it."

My chest warms at her words.

"Anytime, baby girl."

When I pull up in front of Hailey's old apartment, I see Remy already walking down the stairs with a big box in her hands.

"You get here early?" I ask as she loads it into the back of her car.

She drops it with a grunt, then turns to me as she says, "Not really. I just lit a fire under her ass because I want to get her the fuck out of here."

I nod my agreement. I want to distance her from Steve as much as humanly possible after this.

"Hi, Jax," comes floating down the steps like a song on the wind, and when I turn to face Hailey, she's got a smile on her face rivaling sunshine itself.

I return the smile and wrap an arm around her shoulders when she finally reaches me. "Hi, baby girl," I murmur, pressing a kiss to her temple.

"Thanks for helping," she says as she squeezes my waist. "We already started packing, so I think we'll actually be done with this pretty quickly. If you could do the kitchen, then Remy and I will finish up in the bedroom and bathroom. Sound good?"

I nod. "Whatever you need. Let's get you out of here."

She sobers at my intensity and gives a quick nod.

Once we're upstairs, she directs me to the kitchen, where

everything but the plates and utensils are hers to take. And as I pack the boxes, I realize just how invested Hailey is in her dream of owning a restaurant.

It's not that she has every appliance or cooking tool, it's that the ones she does have are well-used. She clearly loves spending time in the kitchen. I've always known she likes cooking for her loved ones, but by the looks of every item here, she seems to spend a lot of time experimenting, possibly even using it as a form of self-care.

I've always known her ultimate dream is to own a restaurant or café, and as I stand in the kitchen and pack everything into boxes, I suddenly find myself wondering why we don't encourage her more. I've eaten her food and know she has the talent for it, so why haven't we pushed her into culinary school or to open her own place? Clearly she has the skills and drive for it.

When Remy walks out of the bedroom an hour later, with two boxes in her hands and pushing another with her feet, I hurriedly finish wrapping the last mug and stride over to her to help.

"Just grab the top one," she says through gritted teeth.

"A little too ambitious?" I chuckle as I easily pluck it from her hands.

"Fuck you," she mutters. "I am an independent woman; I could carry it if I wanted to. You're just easy labor."

I just laugh again and follow her out the door.

Except when I accidentally bump the doorframe on the way out, the bottom flap of the box gets caught and the entire bottom falls open.

Including all the underwear and lingerie in said box.

I let out a muttered curse. Remy's already down the hallway and heading out, so she doesn't even notice I'm not behind her anymore. All I can do is drop to my knees and begin hurriedly stuffing it back in the box, trying desperately not to touch anything more than I have to because it feels wrong, even deviant, to touch something like this of *Hailey's*.

So I just continue piling everything back into the box as fast as I can. All of the silk thongs and matching bra sets and thigh high stockings that I never knew Hailey was capable of wearing. And it's all I can picture now... Hailey leaning against the bedroom doorframe in a midnight blue thong and bra set, her breasts pushed up into perfect handfuls, her garters swaying tantalizingly as she cocks her hip and beckons me closer—

"Oh my God." I hear said on a breath behind me. I turn to look just as Hailey drops to her knees next to me and immediately starts grabbing the clothes from my hands and stuffing them into the box. Her cheeks are flushed bright red, the embarrassment clear in her expression.

"I'm sorry, the bottom opened up," I mumble awkwardly, continuing to kneel there with my hands in my lap because I don't want to make her any more uncomfortable by touching her underwear.

The sudden awkwardness has me scrambling to say something, anything to distract from her embarrassment, and for some reason, I settle on, "Why don't you talk more about wanting to open up a restaurant?"

Her head snaps up in surprise. "What?"

"I just mean, you clearly love the kitchen, and we all know you're really good at it, so why don't you talk about it more? I don't even know if you know what kind of place you'd want to run."

Her gaze drops back to her clothes, and she continues to hurriedly stuff them in the box. "It's just a hobby. I don't know if I'll ever actually do anything about it," she mumbles.

"But you could make a career of it," I blurt, the tension of the entire situation making me more honest than usual. "Why not pursue what you love?"

"It's just not realistic," she babbles. "Being an entrepreneur is too risky, and in an industry like this, especially at my age, it doesn't make sense to make it my whole goal. Even working in a restaurant right now is just temporary until I can get something more stable. Better to work a salaried job." She shines a tight smile at me. "Like you."

My brow furrows in confusion and anger. I do work a 9-5 in Corporate America, but I happen to love my job. The stability of the salary and benefits is obviously great, but I love it because I believe in the technology, and I enjoy the social aspect of selling it. It just works for me. But I also recognize that corporate jobs are not for everyone, and that there are plenty of very different—and incredible—benefits of being an entrepreneur. And I know Hailey knows of them because we used to talk about them when she was in high school and she dreamed of being a world-famous baker.

Right now, she just sounds like she's regurgitating some bullshit she heard from some Corporate Asshole.

My jaw clenches when I realize who that particular asshole

is.

"You would hate my job," I tell her. "You'd hate the rigidity and lack of creativity in a cubicle. Not to mention, you've always enjoyed physical jobs more. Who told you corporate is the way to go?"

When she doesn't answer my question or look me in the eyes, I know I've guessed right.

But before I can continue this conversation, Remy appears at the end of the hallway.

"Well, that's awkward," she blurts when she sees what we're doing on the ground.

I just glare at her. "Helpful as always, Remy baby."

A quiet growl sounds from her throat at the nickname I know she despises. But I just throw a smirk at her and pull Hailey to her feet, the clothes finally all picked up from the floor.

"Grab the other boxes from the bedroom. I'll bring the kitchen ones down," I order. "What else do you need to pack, Hailes?"

She glances at the clock in the kitchen before looking around the apartment. "Umm, just the bathroom, I think. We made way better time than I thought we would."

I nod. "Good. Let's finish what we need to, then."

Within only another half an hour, we've packed up the rest of Hailey's stuff and have stuffed Remy's car as full of boxes as it will go.

"Why don't you drive home and we'll meet you there?" I suggest. "I just want to load the rest of these boxes into my car and then Hailey and I will head over.

"Sounds good," Remy agrees, dropping a nightstand and table lamp onto her passenger seat.

"Thanks," Hailey tells her with a smile. She glances at the clock on her phone. "This went way quicker with the two of you here."

Remy returns her smile with a light punch to her shoulder. "You got it, little sister. I'm glad you're finally out of this hellhole."

A light blush appears on Hailey's face as she nods her agreement, and I glare at Remy over Hailey's head. It seems like she gets embarrassed by these kinds of negative comments, likely because people can sometimes feel like "idiots"—as she stated last night—for staying with or even dating people like Steve. I *never* want her to feel like that.

I mentally set a reminder to talk to Remy about how we should be speaking about him in front of Hailey.

"Come on, baby girl, let's finish up." She flashes me a graceful smile before turning to walk back into the building.

"I'm sorry she's not more sensitive about Steve," I tell Hailey as we do a last sweep of the apartment. I grab a box and finish packing any other miscellaneous items around the living room. "I don't think she realizes she's doing it."

She sighs and starts folding the throw blanket in her hand. "I know. She's never really understood what it was like with him, or why I stayed with him for so long. I know she means well and is trying to understand, so I just have to remind myself of that when she says those things." She smiles at me. "You don't have to apologize for her. But thank you for caring enough to do it."

I just grunt in response. "Of course I care. I know this is hard on you. I know this whole last year was hard. You don't need anyone else making it worse for you."

"You and Lucy are the only ones that understand any of it," she says quietly. Thoughtfully. "Lucy, because she knows how long-term relationships can change—how they can change people—and you, because... well, I'm not sure why you understand what I'm going through. Or at least, you understand that it's hard and complicated and confusing."

I nod. "I know who you are as a person. I know your heart and your dreams and your mind, and I know who you were— who you were growing into—when you met Steve." I swallow my bubbling anger on a harsh swallow. "And I know that it must've taken a lot for him to hurt and confuse you, enough that you seemed to lose your Hailey sparkle."

She doesn't respond, just nods her head sadly.

I straighten nervously where I'm taping up a box. "You know you can come to me about anything, right? I'll listen whenever you want to talk."

She smiles at me, but again, it's just sad. "I know. Thank you for being there for me. I'll tell you everything, I promise. I just want to work through it in my head a little first. There are a lot of things I feel like I need to completely reevaluate in hindsight."

I nod my agreement. "I can only imagine." But then something occurs to me and I take the folded up blanket from her hands so I can lay it on the couch and grip her chin in my hand. She doesn't say anything, just blinks at me in surprise.

I stare at her, taking a few seconds just to appreciate the

fact that she's here and whole and happy—that I can stand here with her and even have this conversation.

"You take all the time you need, baby girl," I murmur, my thumb gently stroking her jaw. "Work through whatever you need to work through. I just want to make sure that you understand you're perfect the way you are—a queen in her own right. And I'm sorry he didn't treat you that way. He didn't deserve you. He didn't deserve your kindness and your beauty and your heart. And it kills me that he didn't treat you the way you deserve. Because you're worth so much more than he ever gave you, and I just want you to know that that's on him, not you. And one day, someone *will* be worthy of you, and they'll love you the way you deserve to be loved. I promise you."

For a moment, I think I've said too much, she's frozen that still. Her eyes are glassy, and her chest visibly rises with her shallow breaths. It hits me that no one's ever told her that—no one's ever bothered to tell her that she's worthy.

But then a breath whooshes out of her chest, and she whispers, "Do you really believe that?"

"Wholeheartedly," I respond without missing a beat.

She stares at me for a moment longer, unblinking, and then she nods.

There's nothing left to say, so I smile and press my lips to her forehead. Something about it makes me feel like I'm sealing my promise with a kiss, and that thought is enough for me to linger for a little longer than is probably appropriate.

And when I pull away, her gaze is locked on mine in a way that literally takes my breath away. My breath catches at the sight of her standing before me like this. And it feels like something between us moves, shifts, sparks in a way I don't understand, yet—

I'm snapped out of my Hailey-driven haze when I hear the front door open. Part of me hopes it's just Remy coming back, but the smarter part of me knows I'm not that lucky.

Instead, Steve is standing in the doorway.

He stops just inside the apartment, shell-shocked and staring at us with unblinking eyes.

"What're you doing here?" he blurts out, never taking his gaze off of Hailey.

"I came to pick my stuff up," she says in a quiet voice.

And it's that nervousness, that voice of self-doubt, that snaps me to attention and makes my hackles rise.

"We're just leaving," I say with a bite, putting every bit of frustration, rage, and helplessness that this man has made me feel into my tone. I grab the blanket Hailey just folded and shove it into her arms in an effort to get her moving. I want her out of here, *now*. I don't want her spending another second around this toxic motherfucker.

"Wait," Steve blurts out. "Can we talk? You haven't answered my calls."

"There's nothing to talk about," Hailey responds without looking at him. She just continues walking toward the last box in front of her bedroom, setting the blanket on it before picking it all up.

"You don't think a two-year relationship is worth talking about before we chuck the whole thing out the window?" he asks incredulously. Like he's genuinely shocked that Hailey doesn't want to talk to him.

I almost laugh at the absurdity of it. At his insane mentality.

"No, I don't," she replies immediately. And even though she can't bring herself to make eye contact with him, I'm still proud of her for sticking to her guns. God knows I've seen plenty of couples break up and get back together because one look at their ex and they get sucked right back into whatever environment they were in with their relationship.

"Hailey, come on," he almost-whines. "I said I was sorry about what I said. I was just angry, I didn't mean it. Can't you just forgive me? I forgave you."

At that, her gaze finally snaps to his, fury licking like flames in her eyes. My mouth drops at the sight. I've never actually seen her angry like this. It's mesmerizing to see the passion in her expression.

"Forgiveness isn't a bargaining chip, Steve," she spits. "You don't get to compare your fuck-ups to mine and then use that as a get-out-of-jail-free card. We deal with each thing on its own, and we decide whether or not we want to forgive the other. *I've* decided your fuck-up was unforgivable. One of many. There's no changing it or apologizing for it or using it as a stepping stone. So no, we don't need to talk."

I want to roar with pride at the sight of Hailey handing Steve his ass. Even he looks surprised at the fact that she's standing up to him, which makes me think he's probably been the alpha for way too long.

That thought reignites the anger inside me. Now that Hailey's said her piece, I feel better about pushing her out of here.

"Sounds like she knows what she wants," I say coldly,

scooping up the last two boxes from the kitchen. "I don't think there's anything left to talk about. So if you'll excuse us, I'm getting her the fuck out of here and away from you."

It seems like Steve is only just noticing that I'm here, which would be laughable if this whole situation didn't enrage me. He glares at me with a hate I've only ever seen from men when they're locked in a cage with me, and I can practically taste the insecurity, the beta energy, radiating from where he's still standing frozen in the hallway.

"Let's go, Jax," Hailey commands. She turns to Steve with a cold glare. "Don't call me again."

Steve just stares at her, expressionless. But when we finally pass him and make it through the front door, his quiet voice carries out to the hallway.

"You're going to realize you made a mistake. And I'll be waiting when you do, because I love you. And we're perfect together. You just need some time to see that."

I see the second his words crawl beneath her skin, just as he intended. It's like I can see the doubt take shape in Hailey's mind, can see it in the way her shoulders slump, and she bites her lip in uncertainty.

And the sight of that just earned him some extra time with me.

"Go down to the car, Hailey. Wait for me there."

She turns to face me completely, her eyes widening. "Jax, don't—"

"It's okay, I'll only be a minute behind you," I reassure her. "I just want to talk to him."

She chews on her lip with indecision, but ultimately when

I give her a *Trust me* look, she nods and continues down the hallway.

I watch her until she reaches the door to the steps.

"She'll never go for you, you know," Steve snarls. "She's too good for you—"

I don't hear the end of his sentence, because the second Hailey is through the stairwell door and out of sight, I'm dropping the box and grabbing Steve by the lapels of his shitty suit and slamming him up against the wall. I could just as easily lift him up by the throat so he's dangling in the air, but I happen to prefer looking down on the piece of shit and watching his eyes widen in shock.

"I'm only going to say this once, so you better listen," I snarl. "You two are done. Don't ever contact her, look for her, even look *at* her, ever again. God knows I'll never understand why she started with you in the first place, but now that she's decided it's over, I want you out of her life for good."

"You can't make that decision for her—" he starts.

"I didn't. She did. I'm just enforcing it," I growl, pressing him harder into the wall. I feel a pang of satisfaction from the wince on his face. "That girl is worth her weight in gold, and you squandered your chance with her for your bullshit mind games. And to be honest, just knowing you put her through that shit makes me want to put your head through this wall. So you don't get to pursue her anymore. You're done."

To his credit, Steve doesn't look scared. Even in this position of inferiority, of being totally dominated, he's still trying for the upper hand. Still trying to manipulate his way to victory when he says, "She'll never want you. You lost that battle when she had to get over her childhood crush because you were too busy fucking other women. So I might not have a chance anymore, but neither do you."

My lip curls in a sneer as I shove away from him. "You're an idiot. As long as that girl is happy, I don't care what I am to her. Wanting someone to be happy shouldn't be dependent on whether or not you're getting your dick wet, you piece of shit." I hammer the final nail in the coffin when I glance at his crotch with a raised eyebrow. "Although from what I hear, your dick was the only thing getting wet."

It's a total guess—I don't think I could stomach listening to Hailey talk about sex with Steve—but it's not a hard one. I know my comment lands on the mark when his face flames with embarrassment, his mouth opening to snap back with something but nothing coming out.

I shake my head as I bend down to grab the moving box again. And when I turn my back on him in a power move meant to show that I'm not afraid of him, I end the conversation with, "Stay the fuck away from her."

Hailey's waiting for me by the car when I walk outside. She jumps up from where she's leaning against it, biting her thumb in clear worry.

"Did you hurt him?" she asks immediately.

My steps falter, caught off guard by her question. I can't help the small frown that tugs the corners of my lips down at the knowledge that not only is she still worried about him, but that she thinks I would physically beat someone outside of the gym.

She must see all of that on my face because her eyes

widen, and she says hurriedly, "Not because I care about him, I just don't trust him not to call the cops or take it out on you somehow if you hurt him. Even now, I wouldn't put it past him to punch himself in the face just so he could say you did it."

My eyebrows rise in surprise. *What the fuck? I knew Steve was an asshole, but I didn't realize he was this kind of fucked up.*

But then I process what Hailey said and a relieved breath whooshes through my chest. *She's asking because of me, not him.* "No, I didn't hurt him," I reassure her. "We just... had some words."

Her eyebrow quirks in disbelief. "Just words?"

I shrug, turning to load the last box in the car. "Just words. Although there may or may not be an imprint of his back on your wall now. So maybe don't be surprised if you don't get your security deposit back." At that, something occurs to me for the first time. I turn to face her. "By the way, what are you doing with the lease? If you're worried about him retaliating for the breakup, then what about the lease?"

For the first time in weeks, I see a sparkle of the old Hailey. The corner of her mouth curls with a small smirk, which just makes me raise an eyebrow in curiosity.

"I'm not on the lease," she grins. "We both paid rent, but something told me to make sure my name wasn't on the papers. His loss." But then her smile drops into a small frown as she considers something. "I think maybe I've known since then that something was wrong. I've had a nagging feeling ever since he suggested we move in together, which I now know were my instincts because that's when he really changed." She winces and looks down at her feet. "That's when he started to alienate me from everything and make me dependent on him. He used the apartment as a tactic."

I step forward and touch a finger under her chin so I can raise her eyes to meet mine. "It didn't work," I tell her softly. "You got out, and you're back with your family, and you're your own person again. It didn't work." I smirk and chuck her chin. "Plus, now he's stuck with the repercussions of using that very tactic. And a very large rent payment."

My reminder brings the smile back to her face, and suddenly all the nerves, frustration, and anger from this morning disintegrate into nothing.

CHAPTER TEN
Hailey

"ARE YOU READY?" Remy calls from the bathroom.

"Yeah, I'm all done," I answer as I swipe another layer of lip gloss on. I lean back to take a final look at myself in Jax's full-length mirror, fluffing my hair one more time.

I decided to wear a bodycon dress that hasn't seen the outside of my closet since before Steve, for the sole reason that it completely hugs my every curve. The dress' blue color brings out the blue in my eyes, and combined with my blonde hair that I've left naturally straight, even I can admit I look like a Barbie doll. The only difference between us is my height—at a whopping 5'2, I rarely go out without some kind of heel on. Tonight is no exception.

I... look good. I look like a woman. I've never liked flaunting my body, but I've always known I feel best when I look good, so I enjoy putting effort into my appearance. But it's been a while since I've dressed up to the extent that I like to dress up.

I think about the last time I dressed like this.

It's been longer than I want to admit.

I inhale a shaky breath when I think about how much my

appearance has changed in the last year. Steve never liked it when I wore anything tight because he said I was "showing off my body" and that I should have respect for my boyfriend by not wearing anything too revealing. I got way too comfortable wearing pants and flowy tops instead of the dresses that I love to wear.

I never even realized that I was doing it. In hindsight, he had me so wrapped up in his manipulation that it never even occurred to me that it was an unreasonable request. At the time, I just thought I was making a compromise and being respectful to my boyfriend. I never realized how much of Steve's bullshit I had internalized.

Now, I feel like I have to recalibrate my brain to remember that a boyfriend shouldn't control how you dress. A boyfriend *should* be your cheerleader and should support any outfit that makes you feel good about yourself.

The knowledge that I can now wear anything I want is surprisingly daunting. I take a deep breath and spin in front of the mirror, smiling, reminding myself yet again that I have nothing to feel guilty about. Reminding myself that it's okay to be beautiful, to look sexy, that I should feel happy to express myself in whatever way makes me feel good.

"Okay, the Uber is ten minutes away so—holy *fuck*."

I turn to see Remy in the doorway, gaping at me.

I smooth my dress down, shuffling nervously in my sky high heels. "Do I look okay?"

Her eyes snap to mine. "Do you look *okay*?" she asks incredulously. "Dude, you look like a fucking Victoria's Secret model. Lucy is going to *kill* you. She was all excited to be the center of attention tonight with some new side-boob outfit she bought."

That makes me laugh. "I'm sure she'll still get plenty of action."

"Not if you're anywhere within twenty feet of her," Remy scoffs. Her gaze becomes thoughtful. "I feel like it's been forever since I've seen you dressed up like this." She softens as our eyes meet. "It's good to have you back."

I smile, and in a moment of uncharacteristic affection, I walk over to my sister and give her a hug. She stiffens for a second but then softens and squeezes me back.

She pushes me away, not quite able to tamp down on her smile. "Yeah, yeah, enough with the mushy shit," she mumbles. "Let's get out of here. You ready?"

I smile and nod, already feeling lighter than I have in months. I grab my purse and follow Remy down the stairs.

Tristan is sitting on the living room couch; he lets out a loud whistle when he sees his girlfriend.

"Goddamn, baby, you look hot." She smirks and twirls in place, showing off the leather pants and red backless top that she picked out for tonight. I can practically see the lust darken Tristan's eyes as he stands up and pulls her flush against his body.

"You're lucky you're going to a gay bar, or I wouldn't let you out of my sight," he growls against her neck. She giggles when he nips at her ear.

"What if we weren't?" The question bursts out of me before I can think to stop it.

Tristan pulls away from Remy with a surprised look.

"What?"

I swallow roughly and decide to commit to the question. "Would you let her out like that if we were going clubbing? Like, not to a gay bar?"

Tristan's brow furrows, but before he can reply, Remy opens her mouth to express some kind of outrage, if the flashing in her eyes is any indication.

Tristan clamps his hand over her mouth before she can get a word out. "The question wasn't which limb you would cut off if I ever tried to tell you that you *couldn't* do something," he says dryly, giving her a knowing look. She relaxes in his arms, but her eyebrow quirks at him anyway.

He just shakes his head and turns back to me, his hand dropping from Remy's mouth. He gives me that trademark, dead-serious look of his before he answers.

"I would never tell her what she could or couldn't wear," he answers honestly. "I would never tell her what she could or couldn't do. Remy can make her own decisions. If she asks for my opinion, I'll give it, or if I think she's doing something that's putting her in danger, I'll voice my concerns, but ultimately, Remy is her own person. I have no right to dictate any part of her life."

I can only nod. I have no response to such an honest answer.

My brain recalibrates a little more.

After studying me for a moment, Tristan turns back to Remy. "Did you call an Uber already?"

She nods as she glances down at her phone. "It'll be here in three minutes. I figured we could all do a shot before—"

Suddenly, something shatters behind me. I jump at the

loud sound and turn toward the kitchen.

I see Jax standing next to the fridge, his shell-shocked gaze jumping back and forth between me and the shattered beer bottle at his feet. He swallows roughly when he meets my eyes.

"Dude, what the hell?" Tristan laughs. "Since when are you clumsy? You were just bragging about how it's impossible to sweep you in the gym."

That seems to snap Jax out of whatever weird daze he's in. He glares at Tristan, then reaches for the broom to clean up the broken beer bottle at his feet.

"Here, let me help," I offer, walking around the kitchen island and reaching for the mop behind Jax.

"No, don't, there's glass everywhere," he says hurriedly, reaching out to stop me from getting any closer. His hand lands on my hip only long enough to stop my forward steps, then he pulls away as if burned. His glare remains fixed on the glass scattered across the floor, and he begins sweeping up the mess in a hurry.

"So what're you guys doing tonight?" I ask, my attention still focused on Jax.

"We're just watching the fights," he answers. He seems to think of something, and he looks up with a frown. "Where are you guys going again?"

"Woody's," Remy chirps happily. "Lucy's going to meet us there. For as long as it takes her to pick up some chick." She rolls her eyes, but it just makes me chuckle.

Jax glances between Remy and I, looking like he wants to say something, until finally he sighs heavily and says, "Just be careful, okay? I know it's a gay bar, but there might still be assholes in there trying to hit on you."

I cock my head and stare at him thoughtfully. "Would you ever tell me how to dress? Or tell me I couldn't go somewhere?"

His eyebrows rise, and he looks directly at me, as if he's searching for something, and it takes him a moment to answer. "Never," he blurts. But then his look becomes almost sheepish, and he looks back down at the glass on the floor. "I just want to make sure you guys are safe," he mumbles defensively.

A warmth blossoms in my chest, and a smile spreads across my face, growing bigger and bigger until it feels like my cheeks are going to split. I step forward and lift up on my toes so I can kiss his cheek, my happiness feeling like it wants to bubble out of my every pore.

Jax gives me a confused look, his eyes darting over my face as he tries to figure out where that came from.

I want to tell him that he's a good man. That he just proved there's a difference between protective and controlling. That between his answer and Tristan's, I have a slightly better understanding today of acceptable male behavior.

But I don't get the chance, because Remy's phone beeps.

"Uber's here," she says. "We gotta go." She turns and gives Tristan a quick kiss, but before she can pull away, he grabs her by the throat and pulls her back for another more intense kiss. I hear Jax grumble next to me, but I just smile and shake my head as I look away.

"Okay, let's go," I hear Remy say a moment later. She sounds just as breathless as she looks flushed. She shoves Tristan away from her before he can grab her again.

"Call me if you need anything," I hear Jax say. I turn back

to him to see a grin on his face. "And have fun."

Before I can stop myself, I press another happy kiss to Jax's cheek. This time he just smiles, and I swear it's because he can understand the change that came over me.

It's late enough that when we get to the club, the line outside is already stretching down the street. Thank goodness it's only September, the weather cool enough to still be comfortable as we move to the end of the line.

"Have you ever been to Woody's?" Lucy asks me, pulling her coat tighter around her body. For the first time since I've known her, she's actually wearing a dress. It's black with leather banding around her breasts to match the combat boots on her feet, but it's a dress nonetheless. Combined with her blonde hair pulled back into a ponytail to show off the lines shaved into the side of her head, and she looks like a total lesbian badass.

I shake my head. "I've been to a few bars near the one I used to work at that would let me in before I turned twenty-one, but I've never been clubbing."

Her red-painted lips stretch into a grin. "Well then, you're in for a treat. Woody's is the best club for dancing. It has two dancefloors upstairs, so you can pick the type of music you want to dance to, and because it's a gay bar, you're less likely to get hit on by douchebag frat boys."

But just then, a catcall sounds from across the street.

"Less likely, not impossible," I hear Remy mutter from next to me.

Sure enough, a group of three guys starts crossing the street, clearly heading in our direction. They look like your typical Saturday night bar-goers, just out to get drunk and laid. They're already on their way to being one of those, and by the predatory glint in their eyes, it looks like they're working on the other one.

"Ladies," the leader of the pack slurs. "How we doin' tonight?"

"We were fine up until about ten seconds ago," Remy snaps. "Get lost, we're not interested."

He holds his hands up in a gesture of surrender. "Whoa, whoa, whoa. There's no need to be so aggressive, I haven't even said anything yet." His eyes trail the length of my body, taking in my short dress and non-RBF expression, and he smirks when his gaze settles on my face. "How's your night going, beautiful?"

I shuffle awkwardly, not used to drunk guys hitting on me so blatantly. Or at least, it's been a while since I've been in this kind of situation. Working at the bar when I first moved to the city was different, since I was eighteen and not really the partying type. And I already looked so much younger than I was, so between my overprotective coworkers and the fact that I looked like jailbait, most people stayed far away from me. Then once I started dating Steve, I never went out anyway, so the situation just never came up.

Now, I'm forced face to face with it.

I want to tell him to fuck off *so. badly.* The take-no-shit Philly bitch in me that's been hiding for the past year is practically demanding it.

But all I hear is Steve's voice in the back of my head telling me *no one wants a loud-mouthed, aggressive woman. And he's only complimenting you—you should be thankful for the attention.*

"It's going okay," I manage to mumble.

"Take a hint, assholes, we're standing in front of a gay bar," Lucy snorts.

Captain Dickhead never takes his eyes off me. "She doesn't look gay to me." He grins.

"And what exactly does gay look like to you?" Lucy snaps, now clearly irritated.

He breaks my stare for the first time to turn to her with a grin. "Like you. Although, I'm sure you're just one good dick away from reevaluating that choice. I bet my buddy here could prove it to you."

On cue, said buddy sidles up to Lucy with a sleazy grin, growling, "Sure could, baby."

Remy starts to laugh. It's loud and raucous, and it catches the guys off-guard.

"Oh my God, I cannot believe you just said that," she chokes out. "You really think your dick is so good that you could get a lesbian to change teams? You're insane. I bet she eats pussy ten times better than you do."

Her crude language and obvious distaste cause Captain Dickhead to frown, his brow furrowing in anger. He turns his attention back to me, the sleazy grin returning.

"I'd love to show your friend here just how well I could eat her pussy," he says. "I bet I could have her screaming my name in less than five minutes."

Remy reaches her breaking point when she grabs my arm

at the same time that Lucy lets out a loud, mocking laugh. "Five minutes? Fucking amateur."

I'm still frozen in shock over the whole encounter as Remy starts to pull me away, but my arm jerks when I feel Captain Dickhead latch onto it.

"Come on, baby, gimme a chance," he purrs. "I promise I can show you a good time."

Finally, fucking *finally*, a little bit of my inner bitch overpowers Steve's voice. The second he makes aggressive physical contact, I feel justified in striking back.

I yank my arm from his grip. "I'm good, thanks. You should get lost."

Thankfully, we've reached the front of the line during the interaction, so by the time we turn away from the guys, the bouncer is standing in front of us, waiting for our IDs.

The very tall, very *large* bouncer aims a glare at the guys. "You wouldn't be bothering this nice group of ladies in front of me now, would you?"

Sensing his defeat, Captain Dickhead just huffs his frustration and walks away without responding.

The bouncer checks our IDs without another word, but as he waves us in, he says, "If for some reason those assholes come back, I won't let them in. Have a good night, ladies."

I smile my gratitude before following Remy and Lucy into the bar. They immediately push their way up to the bartender, ordering for us without asking me what I want. Yet when they return to where I've claimed a high-top, my eyes light up at the beautiful cotton candy-colored drink in my sister's hand, complete with an umbrella.

"They make the best fruity drinks, pun intended," she says with a laugh, handing me one of the cocktails. And sure enough, at the first sip through the straw, my taste buds explode with the fruity, slightly sweet, barely-there alcohol taste.

"Good, right?" Lucy asks with a grin, sucking down some of her own drink.

I nod eagerly and take another sip.

Remy's the one that finally acknowledges the elephant in the room. "Hailes, you have to get better at dealing with assholes. If we weren't there, would you have told him no?"

I immediately sober as the reality of our situation ten minutes ago washes over me. "I did tell him no," I defend weakly.

She shakes her head. "Only when he grabbed you. Would you have let him sweet talk you in the beginning?"

"I didn't want to be rude," I say weakly.

Remy sighs. "Hailey, you're single now. And hot as fuck. That's going to happen more often now, and I don't want you to get hurt just because you can't say no to men."

I take another sip of my drink, staying quiet instead of responding to her comment. I don't mention that I didn't feel like I *could* say no to him. That it was only when he blatantly crossed the line that I was able to push back on him. If he had been subtle with his advances, like in the beginning, I would have continued to be polite. I would have done what I'm used to when it comes to men.

Suddenly, I get flashbacks of Steve's quiet manipulation, of my subconscious wishes for him to, just once, be obvious about his abuse so I could finally point to it and say *okay, there, that's why I was right to push back.* Because without the over-the-line behavior, I'm stuck in the trap of man-pleasing that Steve buried me in.

Remy sighs again when she sees that I'm not miraculously going to start cursing at every man who dares look at me. She just nudges my shoulder and says, "You know I'll rip apart every douchebag that tries to hurt you. But I want you to be comfortable with putting up boundaries on your own, you know?"

Instead of answering, I just nod. I don't bother explaining my thought process, because I know no matter what I say, she'll never understand what it's like to not be willing to shit on a man without fear of consequences.

"Alright, enough about shitty men," Lucy interrupts with a grin. "It's girls' night, and we're at a gay bar. Let's get drunk and dance."

And for the next two hours, we do just that. We switch between the bar downstairs and the pop and rap/hip hop dancefloors upstairs, downing several cotton candy drinks and laughing way more than I can remember doing in the past few months. Lucy's the hilarious party girl of the friend group, so between her energy and Remy's constant encouragement, my face hurts from laughing at these two. And when I think about the fact that I've been missing this in my life, I'm only sad for a moment.

Because it hits me that even though I could've been doing this the whole time I've lived in the city, my *now* is the only thing that matters. *Now* I am free—free to spend time with whoever I want, free to do whatever I want. No person in your life that cares about you should be holding you back from doing anything that's safe and that makes you happy.

And right now, I'm doing something I love with people I love, and I'm enjoying myself while I do it. And right now, I am happy.

"I'm going to go to the bathroom, want to come with me?" Remy yells in my ear.

We're currently on the hip hop dancefloor, singing out loud to Doja Cat and shaking our asses to the beat of the music. I'm so swept up in the movement and in finally being able to dance again that I just shake my head in answer.

"I'm good here, I'll stay with Lucy," I shout back. She nods and heads toward the bathrooms, leaving me with a fairly intoxicated and very-horny Lucy, who is completely lost in the sensuality of the music right now.

In fact, less than thirty seconds later, she manages to catch the attention of a very attractive Asian girl, who wastes no time immediately sidling up to Lucy so she can grind against her.

I chuckle when I see the obvious lust in Lucy's eyes and know that we've officially lost her for the night. But I don't mind dancing by myself, so I just close my eyes and let my hips sway to the beat. I let the music guide my body, my hips rotating as I raise my hands above my head, a smile stretching across my face.

I don't even really mind it when hands land on my hips from behind. They're not aggressive, not pulling me into an unwanted hard-on, they're just holding me as my body moves.

"You're gorgeous," a male voice says in my ear. "You move like you were meant to dance."

I smile again, but keep my eyes closed. I just continue moving my body the way it's dying to do.

He must take my not pushing him away as acceptance because he pulls me flush against his body. It's still not quite aggressive—despite being able to feel his dick now—which is why I don't pull away. He seems to have a decent sense of rhythm so I just let our bodies flow together.

Again, he takes my non-resistance as acceptance because a pleased rumble sounds in my ear, and one of his hands slides from my hip to my stomach. He presses me harder against him, which still doesn't feel like the worst thing, but then his hand starts to trail lower.

I grab it to stop its descent. "Too much," I tell him in a tight voice.

He nuzzles into my neck, just barely running his lips over my skin. "What's your name, gorgeous?"

I shake my head, the spell of the music broken, leaving me instantly cold and nervous. "It doesn't matter," I respond tightly.

"You're not going to give me your name?" His words make it sound like he's offended, but the tone in which he says them sounds almost smug, like he's enjoying that I'm playing hard-to-get.

"No," I state firmly, even as it makes me nauseous to do so. This guy hasn't done anything wrong; he's just pushing the boundaries further than I want to go.

Is that really enough of a reason to be a bitch to him? What if he's a nice guy who just wants to get to know you? It's pretty rude to shut him down like this.

I try to ignore the tiny voice in my subconscious, but it's louder than even the music. I can't shake it from my head.

"Well, what am I supposed to call you when you're grinding so sweetly on my cock?" he purrs in my ear. And when he tries to push his hand down again, I finally decide to fully pull away.

I yank his hands off my body and spin out of his arms to face him. "I said no," I say in what I hope is a firm voice. Except it seems to come off *too* firm because his face crinkles in disgust.

"Jesus, you don't have to be such a bitch about it," he sneers. "You could've just said you weren't interested. You didn't have to freak the fuck out."

My face pales when I realize I've offended him. "I'm sorry, I wasn't trying to be rude, I just—"

"She might not want to be rude, but I don't have that problem," a voice says from behind me.

Remy steps around me and gets right in the guy's face, looking almost as intimidating as any bouncer in this place, despite the fact that she's barely taller than five feet.

"She said no, jackass, so get the fuck out of here," she spits. "How you choose to accept the *L* is nobody's problem but your own. Get lost before I rearrange your face."

His eyes widen in surprise. He almost seems too shocked by Remy's aggression to actually react to her words, which is why he falls back a step and subconsciously admits defeat. Remy smirks in victory and turns to grab my hand.

"Lucy?" she asks me, looking around for her friend.

"Preoccupied," I answer on autopilot. When Remy finds Lucy making out with the Asian girl on the edge of the dancefloor, she just shakes her head with a sigh and tugs me out of the room.

"Home?" she asks me.

I nod mutely. I'm still in shock from the encounter, still embarrassed and confused about how it ended.

Remy nods her agreement and leads us downstairs toward the exit.

"I'm glad you said no to the bastard," she muses simply.

And when I'm lying on my makeshift bed in Remy's apartment later that night, trying to figure out what I did wrong, I don't come any closer to an answer.

I just continue wishing I could be as strong as Remy is—as strong as I want to be. As strong as I was before a man came along and eroded my confidence and ability to speak my mind.

When I close my eyes and finally drift off to sleep, I do it with the promise to search harder for that old-Hailey tomorrow.

CHAPTER ELEVEN
Jax

"When was the last time the three of us hung out just us?" Remy asks as we grab our drinks and walk over to one of the high-tops in our favorite dive bar.

"I think it was that night that Max fought," Hailey muses. "That night he won by knockout and we went to Frankie's afterwards. When Jax ended it by attempting to shotgun a beer bottle?"

Remy glares at me, even as I grin at the memory. "I swear, you're the worst drunk," she grumbles.

"Bullshit, you love babysitting me." I wave her off. "God knows I've done it for you enough times."

She glares at me. "When have you ever had to stop me from doing something idiotic when I'm drunk?"

I give her a pointed look. "How about last month when you wanted to get in a fight with the 6'5" Olympic weightlifter because he didn't know the words to *Benny and the Jets*?"

For a moment, she only blinks at me. Then she breaks my stare and turns away, mumbling, "Okay, fair enough."

Hailey chuckles from beside me, so I turn to wink at her.

"What about you, baby girl? Ever do anything really stupid when drunk?"

Too late, I realize my poor choice of words. She just told me not long ago about how she's been judged every time she's had a drink in her hands, so the last thing I need to do right now is be another person that sounds like they're judging her for doing something reckless under the influence.

She blushes and looks down at the beer in her hands.

"Hailey's never really been a drinker," Remy says, oblivious to the tension in her sister's shoulders. "Although, it was fun seeing you let loose the other night with Lucy. Why'd you drink then but not before?"

Hailey's smile is tight, and I wonder how Remy can't see it for what it is. "You know me, I act older than I am. The belligerently drunk and stupid phase never appealed to me."

Remy just shrugs and takes another swig of her beer. "I always thought those stupid days were fun."

"How *was* the other night?" I ask instead, trying to move us to a safer topic. "Did you have fun?"

Hailey shines a grateful smile at me. "It was a lot of fun. Drinks were good, music was good, and Lucy was fun too, until she found her booty for the night."

I chuckle, knowing the crazy game Lucy has with women. I'm not surprised at all that she ditched girls' night for some action.

"Speak of the devil," Remy mutters, fixated on her phone. She looks up at us with an apology already written in her eyes. "I have to go. Lucy's got some kind of lady crisis. Can we raincheck? I really do want to have a night with just the three of us."

I wave her away and reach for my beer. "Just go. We'll do it another time."

She shoots her sister a guilty look, but Hailey smiles and tells her, "We're fine. Go."

Remy sighs but eventually gives us a nod and walks out of the bar.

I turn to Hailey, a grin slowly stretching across my face. "So," I start, "it's just you and me, baby girl. What're we doing tonight?"

She gives me a smile that I haven't seen in so long. *God*, I missed her smile. I missed seeing her happy.

"I have an idea," she says with a mischievous sparkle in her eye.

"Okay, at this point, I feel like I should get a Mulligan or something," I grumble, glaring at the pool table that has yet to give me a win against this math genius of a woman.

Hailey's tinkling laugh rings across the bar. Several men turn to look at her, but it only takes one glare from me before they know to stop looking. She's too damn pretty for her own good. And the worst part is, she doesn't even realize the effect she has on people.

"Just admit you suck at pool." She chuckles, leaning forward onto the pool stick.

I shake my head in defiance. "I do not. You just... keep getting lucky." I shake my head again, this time in confusion.

"Okay, seriously, how did you get so good? You were the one that sucked the last time we played."

"After you and Remy left for college, I spent all my time at the Bensons', playing pool with Katie. It was the only thing that made me feel better about missing you guys. And at least then I actually got a turn." She glares pointedly at me, at which I chuckle and hold my hands up in surrender.

"That was your sister's fault, not mine. I'll bet she was competitive even as a toddler, taking all the toys from the kids and keeping them for her own evil games. Blame her for never getting a turn. I had nothing to do with it." I look around the bar for a game I might actually have a shot at winning. I might not be as competitive as Remy, but I'm not exactly happy about losing four straight games of pool.

My eyes land on the dart board. "Let's play a game of darts. Surely, they didn't remind you of us?" I tease with a grin.

Hailey shudders and finishes the rest of her beer. "Not unless you almost take my toes out like Remy that one year. I don't think I've played since."

I nod. "Good. Darts it is, then."

Hailey rolls her eyes, but I see a smile teasing her lips. A feeling of satisfaction washes over me at the sight. She looks so much better now than she did even two weeks ago. She seems... like herself. It feels like I'm watching her come into her own again.

I wave our waitress down and order two more beers, then make my way over to the dart board. Thankfully, there's no one around us because Hailey's right: we're all notorious for sucking at this game.

I hand her the red darts as I line up for a practice throw. "So how is everything?" I ask casually. Though I know she knows exactly what I'm gearing up for.

She sighs, but I think even that is a happy sigh. "Things are great," she answers. "I feel bad moving in on Remy's space, but it's nice to be living with her again. I feel like I can finally breathe. Even school is going better lately."

"I'm glad to hear that," I comment, eyeing the three blue darts that are on opposite ends of the board and as far away from the bull's-eye as can be. *At least they made it on the board?* "I know you were worried about this semester because of that statistics class. Let me know if you need any help; either Tristan or I could go over it with you."

She shakes her head with a small smile. "It's still so weird to think of Tristan as a brainiac. I never would've guessed."

I turn my attention to her and quirk an eyebrow. "Is it more likely to guess that I'm a brainiac? I'm the one that Remy loves to swear looks like a Viking."

"Who said you were a brainiac?" She grins with a teasing glint in her eyes.

I poke her side, which makes her giggle and swat my hands away. "Watch it, woman," I growl. She laughs again, and the sound has an even bigger smile spreading over my face. I swear seeing her happy makes me fucking happy.

The waitress arrives with our beers, so I take mine and walk over to the board to retrieve my darts. "But you're good?" I ask again, needing to make sure she's okay for my own peace of mind. I study her out of the corner of my eye.

She sighs, her expression becoming serious. "Yes, Jax, I'm

good. I promise. I don't feel heartbroken or anything like that, so you don't have to worry that I'm internalizing anything. I'm just over the whole thing and happy to be past it." She lines up to throw her darts but seems to get lost in her thoughts because it's almost like she's looking beyond the board.

Her eyes still unfocused, she lazily lobs a dart. It hits the edge of the bull's-eye.

I don't even have time to be shocked or call her out for playing me because her next words capture every bit of my attention.

"I think I'm just trying to figure out what the truth was," she says, more to herself than anyone else. "I feel like my memories from the last year are totally different from what the reality was. I have to look at them through a new lens and almost re-remember them." She shakes her head and looks down, appearing suddenly tired. She continues in a quiet voice, "I will never understand how I got sucked into believing I was the problem. I never thought I'd be the girl who would let a boy destroy her self-confidence so thoroughly that some days she would walk around thinking she was the dirtiest whore in the city."

The reminder of that particular fact makes my blood boil the same way it did the first time I heard it. If I didn't know that Hailey would yell at me, I'd gladly find Steve and pound him into the pavement. To make *any* girl feel like that is disgusting, but with Hailey, it's equal parts unforgivable and blatantly false.

Despite the fact that she's lining up for another shot at the board, I step in front of her and cup her face in my hand.

I gently tilt her head up, so I have her full attention when I growl, "The fact that he made you feel like anything less than a fucking queen makes me murderous." Her eyes widen at the intensity of my tone. *Good. Let her see how serious I am.* "I hope you know that. I hope you know what you're worth, Hailey. But if you don't, I'm happy to remind you every single day until you wake up with it as inherent knowledge. I have no problem shouting it from the rooftops, or buying you a crown, or bowing at your feet like a fucking servant. Whatever it takes to get it through your head."

She giggles at my imagery and tries to look away, but I gently guide her back to me so she can see my dead-serious expression.

She sobers when she realizes I'm not kidding, the smile sliding from her face. "I don't ever want to hear you talk about yourself like that again, understood?" I ask softly but firmly. This time she nods without hesitation.

I sigh and pull her in for a hug. I automatically relax when she winds her arms around my waist, the scent of her coconut shampoo enveloping me like a hug in and of itself.

She squeezes me once before stepping back. The serious moment broken, I grab my beer again and lean against the high-top in our area. I watch as Hailey lines up for her second throw.

"You know what the funniest part about the whole thing was?" she asks with a laugh. The red dart lands in the bull's-eye. She lines up again for her last shot. "He treated me like a whore everywhere except where I wanted him to."

The last dart lands square in the bull's-eye, right next to

the other, so Hailey turns around with a smile.

A smile that freezes when she meets my eyes.

He treated me like a whore everywhere except where I wanted him to...

I can only think of one place a girl would want to be treated like a whore, and it's not a place I ever visualized Hailey in.

But despite the space between us, as the air heats and our eyes never break contact, I can *feel* the truth in her words. I can sense the desperation in her statement, can sense how badly she wants exactly that.

And now, she knows that I know.

I'm not sure if she meant to say that out loud, or if she understood what it implied when she said it, but I watch as she looks away and starts fidgeting nervously with the edge of her shirt.

Hailey and I have never really talked about sex. It's not just that she was too young when we were growing up together, but by the time we were both adults and living in the same city, it became an unspoken thing that we didn't talk about sex beyond who we were having it with. Remy was too much of a sister for me to want to hear about her history, and Hailey was a quiet, private person in general. The extent of my knowledge of her dating history was what I heard from Remy while they were living together, plus the drunken confession the night she and Steve broke up.

I never really thought to wonder about Hailey's sexual preferences.

Now, I can't *stop* thinking about Hailey's sexual preferences.

I swallow roughly and look away, the vision of Hailey on

her knees, with tears running down her cheeks as she looks up at me and chokes on my cock, looking every bit the obedient whore, is suddenly fresh in my mind.

I try to clear my throat, but when that doesn't help the dryness, I chug half the drink in my hand. I force myself to avoid looking at Hailey, willing my erection to settle the fuck down before this gets awkward. She probably didn't mean to tell me that, and is probably embarrassed trying not to look at me.

I attempt to put her out of her misery by changing the subject. "So are you going to tell me when you got good at darts, too?"

The tension in her shoulders disappears, and she gives me a grateful smile. She looks back at where all three darts landed in or very close to the red bull's-eye. "I wasn't lying about not playing since Remy almost took my toes out. But I was good before that too. You guys just never let me play." She aims a smug grin my way, and I'm immediately relieved to feel like we're back to normal. The last thing I want to do is make her feel uncomfortable when my goal has only ever been to get her to smile more.

"Always full of surprises," I sigh.

She bites her lip to stifle a smile, my gaze automatically dropping to her mouth to watch it happen. But then she hops up onto her seat at the high-top and gestures for me to take my turn at the board.

I shake my head and line up to lose again. "You're trouble," I mumble.

I let loose one dart—that goes so wide it's a miracle it even hits the board—when Hailey pipes up behind me. "So how have you been? What's going on with you lately?"

I line up for another shot. "Nothing very exciting." I shrug. "All I do is work and train, per usual. Work is good. The company hired some new developers a few months ago, so we launched a new software product that's doing well. The money is good right now, which always makes life a lot easier. So I can't complain."

I let the last two darts fly as she says, "That's always good. And you still like the company? The industry? You think you're going to stay?"

I shrug as I walk back to stand next to the high-top to grab my beer. "I like technology. And I like selling it because it makes good money. Maybe one day I'll go over to the engineering side to be more hands-on with the products, but I'm content where I am right now. And Corporate America suits me."

She chuckles at that. "Who would've thought. Just once I'd love to be in the room when you meet a new client and their eyes go wide when the very large and insanely hot, blonde-haired, blue-eyed Scandinavian model walks in to start talking shop with them."

It takes her a moment to realize what she just let slip but when she does, she sucks in a startled breath. When she sees my lips twitch in an attempt to smother my grin, she tries to cover her tracks by gesturing at me and saying, "I mean, you're—you know—you're huge. Do they look surprised you know your stuff?"

I reach forward to affectionately flick her nose, which makes her laugh again. "Smartass," I murmur. But there's a smile on my face.

"What about fighting?" she asks, the dartboard momentarily forgotten. "I know you've been… less than enthusiastic lately. Do you know what you're going to do?"

I sigh, the smile dropping from my face. "I don't think my heart is in it anymore. I love training but I don't feel the same hunger to fight that I did before. The last fight was the hardest training camp to date because there were more bad days than good ones—I barely pushed through it, even though it ended with a win." I start to pick at the label on the beer bottle, unable to keep from fidgeting as I try to describe my inner turmoil. "I feel ridiculous saying I want to retire for a corporate job. But lately… it just feels like I want to move on. Like I'd rather settle for a steady, easy job, with a nice hobby, and actually get to relax with my family and friends. The stress of fighting just doesn't even out with the payoff anymore." I shake my head and take a swig of my beer. "That probably sounds ridiculous."

Hailey places a hand on my arm, a serious and fiery look in her eyes. With me standing and her sitting at the high-top, she's almost at the right height to stare directly into my eyes. "Of course that doesn't sound ridiculous," she says firmly. "It sounds like your priorities have changed, and different things make you happy now. That's not a bad thing, Jax, or anything you need to be ashamed of."

I push my beer bottle around again, still unable to make eye contact. "It doesn't sound like I'm giving up? Like I'm settling because I'm lazy?"

"No, of *course* not," she huffs in frustration. "Nobody would ever think that, especially of you." She tugs on my arm to force me to meet her gaze. "*Nobody* would think that, Jax. Nobody would judge you for it."

When I'm still not convinced, she says, "Fine, then look at it this way. Fighting is 90% mental, right? That's what I always hear." She waits for my nod before she continues. "Then how could you even keep fighting if your head isn't in it anymore? This isn't a sport you can fake your way through. Fighting when you don't want to fight sounds really dangerous."

I finally meet her eyes of my own volition. "Okay, that makes sense."

She nods, looking pleased with my answer. "You can always go back if you miss it. But it doesn't sound like a good idea to do it just because you feel like you need to." Her expression turns worried. "That sounds like a good way to get hurt. And watching you fight is hard enough."

I sigh. "Okay, you're right. I think I already knew all of that, I just didn't want to admit it to myself. I haven't talked to anyone else about it."

She smiles, the brightness of it immediately lightening the weight on my chest. She's so fucking *pretty*. "Remy and Tristan would both understand, but I'm glad you feel like you can talk to me about it."

I smile back at her; if she were closer to me and standing, I'd pull her into a hug. "Always so wise," I murmur, settling for squeezing her hand that's still on my arm.

The light in her eyes fades the slightest bit. And when she speaks, I know why. "I missed you," she says quietly. "I missed talking to you and hanging out with you. I'm sorry, I fell off the face of the earth for such a stupid reason."

At that, I really do pull her into a hug. I tug her off her seat and immediately wrap my arms around her, reveling in the fact that she tucks under my chin and fits perfectly in my arms. "Don't you dare apologize for something like that," I murmur. "It's completely natural to get caught up in a relationship and see your friends less. You did nothing wrong."

Her arms wrap around me, and I squeeze her tighter to my body. "I missed you too, though," I murmur into her hair. "I'm happy I have you back."

Her head tips back and she looks up at me with a smile. "I'm happy too. I don't like not being around you."

I press a kiss to her forehead, my lips lingering for a moment. It feels so natural to hold her like this. And I'm effortlessly swept up in the essence of *Hailey*, of her sweetness and beauty and genuine kindness, and for a moment, the knowledge that she's here in my arms is enough to steal the breath from my lungs.

Hailey breaks our connection by pulling away, and I reluctantly let her go. But there's a smile beginning to form on her face as she asks, "Wanna keep being around me?"

My brow furrows in confusion, but I nod.

Her smile grows. "Good. Then let's go get drunk."

CHAPTER TWELVE
Hailey

Two HOURS LATER, we're at the third bar when Jax and I slam down our shot glasses at the same time. Shockingly, both of us are lightweights, so we've paced ourselves by ordering mostly mixed shots and light beer. I can't tell how far gone Jax is, but I'm comfortably drunk and feeling happier than I have in a long time.

"Do you remember that time in high school when you and Remy were drinking in the basement and our parents came home early?" I ask with a giggle. Jax groans and drops his head between his shoulders.

"How could I forget? I had to somehow muster all the brain power in the world just to get through a conversation with your dad about his company's new merger. All while knowing that if he found out I was drunk, he would literally chase me off the property and into the snow while I was only wearing shorts and a T-shirt."

My giggle turns into laughter. "You were so weirdly focused on his eyes, I have no idea how he couldn't tell that you were shitfaced."

"I count it as one of the few miracles I've experienced in my lifetime," he says on a sigh, motioning to the bartender for two more beers.

Once he's ordered, I watch as Jax gets a thoughtful, almost hesitant look on his face. After a few moments, he finally asks, "Why did you never drink before?"

I sigh as my good mood evaporates. I realize now that I probably should've known the question was coming. I steel myself for anger, disappointment, confusion, whatever cocktail of emotions Jax is going to experience once I tell him the truth. I begin tracing a nonexistent pattern on the bar top so as to avoid making eye contact with him.

"Do you remember when I told you about that threesome I had in high school?" I ask bluntly, diving right into the heart of the explanation.

I sense, more than see, Jax's surprise. "Uh, yeah," he answers, confused.

"It was the first time I ever drank. I got drunk that night, though it's not the reason I initiated everything." I wince and look up at the shelf of liquor across from me so I can focus on something that's not Jax. "I told you Steve judged me for that night. It was the whole reason he treated me like I was dirty. I told him the story early on when we were first sharing fun dating stories, but later I figured out the reason he didn't say it was a problem was because he was trying to come off as easygoing. Sometimes I wonder if he was even looking for things to hold over me so he'd always hold the power in the relationship."

My voice has gone quiet by the end, lost in the painful

memory. I shake my head in an effort to clear it. "Anyway," I continue, "he could never get over the fact that I did something like that. I think he tried so hard to explain it away that he latched onto the fact that I was drunk. He still blamed me for getting drunk enough to make a bad decision, but it was easier for him to believe that his girlfriend's mistake was drinking too much, versus the mistake of wanting two men to take her to bed. He somehow started to associate drinking with threesomes. Every time I had a drink in my hand, he would give me a judgmental look or make a snarky comment. It was his way of reminding me that he still held what happened before he even knew me over my head. It became easier to just not drink."

"Jesus Christ," I hear Jax mutter. "What a fucking psycho." He turns toward me, and I notice how many emotions are warring for space on his face. Anger wins out when he asks, "I still can't believe he judged you for a consensual sex act. Like what year is it? That's such an archaic standard to hold your girlfriend to. It's like the equivalent of judging you for having sex before marriage."

I give him a sad smile. "It didn't help that his ex-fiancée cheated on him too. He was messed up over everything that had to do with sex, I think because sex is about power. Between my past, his past, and—" I feel my cheeks pinken, but I push forward anyway, "—and my sexual preferences, it was the one place he never felt like he had any."

I feel Jax freeze at my acknowledgement of my earlier admission. But I don't give him a chance to respond, I just continue talking. "I think that's why sex became the core issue in the relationship. Because if there's this big thing that you can't get over, something that causes you to not respect your partner, how can you possibly have a healthy relationship?" I shake my head. "You can't. Without respect, you're not equals. And in hindsight, I think that was his whole goal. I think the reason he never let it go is because he needed the upper hand."

Jax shakes his head in disbelief, which seems to be the only acceptable reaction to recapping anything Steve did. "You have no idea how badly I want to hunt down that piece of shit and put my fist down his throat every time you tell me something that he did or said while you guys were together. He's not worthy of even breathing the same air as you, Hailey. I hope you know that."

I turn to Jax with a smile, my heart warming at his words. He's always been vocal about how highly he thinks of me, but his words hit a little bit harder now. I'm fully aware my self-esteem is at an all-time low lately, so hearing Jax say things like that—hearing him respect me and care about me and want to protect me—it lifts a massive weight off my chest.

And I love him for that.

"I know," I answer him. "I realize that now. I couldn't see it at the time because he had me all screwed up with his mind games, but I understand it now. A man shouldn't revel in having power over his partner; he shouldn't shame her repeatedly for a"—I make air quotes with my fingers—"'mistake.' He shouldn't… well, there's a lot he shouldn't do. Let's just agree Steve was a shit boyfriend and a shit person."

Jax laughs at that. I wish I could bottle up the sound of his rumbling laughter and get drunk on *that*. It brings me the same sense of peace that the sound of a rainstorm does.

Just then, the bartender appears in front of us. She slides two shots of tequila across the bar, and a second later, she's walking away with Jax's card in hand.

I raise an eyebrow at Jax. "Shots?" I ask in an amused tone.

He just shrugs. "If we're gonna drink, we're gonna *drink*. Take the shot, baby girl."

I shake my head, but a smile is playing across my lips. I grab the shot of tequila and lift it in the air. "Okay, what are we cheersing to?"

He looks me square in the eye as he raises his shot glass and says, "Cheers to recognizing your worth and getting the fuck away from anyone that treats you as anything less than the queen you are."

A shiver runs through me at the intent in his words.

We both down our shots and then Jax is signing the tab and turning to me with a smile. And even though the tequila only went down my throat a few seconds ago, I feel something start to simmer low in my belly at his heated gaze. *Have we been this close the entire time?*

"Alright, baby girl, where to next?"

I squirm in my seat, feeling suddenly breathless from the alcohol, the conversation, Jax's presence... I want to keep hanging out, but it's been a long time since I've been drunk with another person, and I don't know if I can trust myself to keep my head about me with these strange feelings roiling inside me. Jax would never make me nervous, but my not knowing if these reactions are from the alcohol or something else definitely does.

"I should probably go home,," I murmur. "I don't want to be the annoying drunk girl that needs to be babysat, and that's probably where I'm heading."

Jax just grins, the alcohol making him happier than normal. "I don't think you could be annoying even if you tried," he says as we climb off the barstools and start to head toward the front of the bar.

"Your sister, on the other hand…"

I let out a loud laugh at that, but it's cut off when I see a familiar annoyed expression out of the corner of my eye.

"Fuck," I gasp, feeling my heart freefall into my stomach. I look around for a quick exit, but we're too far back in the bar, and any path to a door has me getting way closer to Steve than I'm comfortable with. Despite knowing Jax would have my back, I really just don't want to deal with Steve right now. It's been hard enough ignoring his texts.

"What happened?" I hear Jax ask, and I notice he's looking around for the source of my sudden distress. I know he spots Steve when his jaw clenches hard enough to pop, and he takes a step forward.

I block his path and fist my hands in his shirt in an effort to stop him. "No, please don't," I plead, hoping my eyes convey my desperation. "I just—I don't want to deal with him right now. Please. Just… not now."

Jax looks down at me, fury still sparking in his eyes, but I can tell he's weighing my feelings right now. After a tense moment, he gives a stiff nod.

I only have enough time for a relieved exhale before I see Steve coming closer in my periphery. He hasn't spotted me yet, but it's only a matter of time before he does. Without thinking, I push Jax into an employee hallway.

I don't even realize I've flattened my body against his until I hear my name growled into my ear, and my eyes snap up to his in surprise.

Despite the height difference, we're so close that I can see every fleck of silver in his gorgeous blue eyes—it reminds me of a lightning-filled sky, especially with the way they're flashing as they look down at me right now. The sight literally takes my breath away.

And as I suck in a startled breath, my breasts press even closer to Jax's chest. He must realize it too, because I feel his fingers dig into my hips as his grip tightens.

My gaze drops to his lips. I've never thought about how nice they are for a guy's lips, even though they've laid plenty of kisses on my cheeks and my hair. But they've also never been this close to my own. I've never been so tempted to find out what it feels like to press mine against them.

"Hailey," he growls again, and I realize his gaze is jumping between my eyes and my lips too. And now I can't remember anything that's ever happened before this moment. There is only Jax and I, in these shadows, staring at each other as the alcohol and proximity winds the tension higher and higher until the air feels suffocating.

I don't know if one of us would've made the shift forward. And we'll never know because the door at the end of the hallway is yanked open to reveal an angry bar employee coming in from the street, reeking of cigarette smoke.

I jump back from Jax, likely looking as flustered as I feel.

The guy just glares at us before he pushes past to go back to work.

I look nervously between the street exit and Jax. "Um, maybe we should..." I manage to mumble.

My words seem to snap Jax out of whatever stupor he's in. "Yeah, let's get out of here," he agrees. He hesitates for only a moment, then grabs my hand and pulls me out of the bar with him.

"I'll grab an Uber," I mutter once we've put some distance between us and my ex-boyfriend. Jax nods stiffly, dropping my hand and jamming his into his pockets. He doesn't look at me as I take my phone out and pull up the app.

We don't talk while waiting the few minutes for my driver to pull up. I shuffle nervously the whole time, unsure of how to break the tension and cursing myself for putting us in an awkward position with my clumsiness.

I sigh when the car finally arrives, resigned to the fact that I've now made things weird between us. All because I couldn't get far enough away from fucking Steve.

Another sigh.

But just as I start to mumble some kind of half-assed goodbye, I feel Jax grab my wrist in order to stop me before I can reach for the car door. I turn back to him in surprise.

He gives me a small smile before saying, "Text me when you get home, baby girl."

I couldn't help the smile that takes over my face even if I wanted to.

He visibly relaxes at that. When he opens the car door and guides me inside with a hand on my lower back, his smile is back to its normal shine.

The entire car ride home, I can't stop thinking about what just happened. What it felt like. I've been close to Jax before—since God knows he's an affectionate person, especially with me—but something about today felt different. The way he looked at me, the way it felt to be pressed against him... it almost felt like he was looking at me like more than just Hailey, Remy's little sister.

But... that doesn't make sense. Jax and I have been friends for so long, if something was going to happen it would've happened already. But it never did. I know he knows that I had a crush on him when we were younger. I was so obvious, even strangers could tell that I had a thing for my big sister's best friend. And even though I was too young for him then and knew he wouldn't reciprocate my feelings, he also never acknowledged them or returned them once I was old enough. It just became a childhood crush that we never dealt with.

I drop my head back against the seat with a groan, feeling the beginning of a headache coming on. Deep down, I know Jax doesn't like me like that, since he's had plenty of time to develop feelings and opportunities to broach the subject. It wouldn't even be a big risk for him, since I've already had feelings for him. It's not a stretch to think I would again.

I sigh and press my forehead against the cool glass of the car window. I make a vow in this moment to not make a bigger deal out of today than it really was, to shove away any remnants of my schoolgirl crush to keep it from rearing its ugly head. It was simply a tense moment brought on by accidental proximity, nothing else. The last thing I need is to complicate my relationship with one of the most important people in my life, who also happens to be a big crutch for me right now.

By the time I climb the steps to Remy's apartment, I've forced myself to forget about anything that may or may not have happened between Jax and I.

I'm making coffee for a very grumpy-looking Remy the next morning when my phone alerts me that I have a text.

"Who the fuck is texting you at 7:30 in the morning," she grumbles.

I scowl at her, even though I'm just as confused as she is. Remy and Jax are the only people to really text me, and Jax isn't exactly a morning person either.

"Just drink your coffee and try to become a decent human being again," I tell my sister with a pointed glare. "I have no idea how you used to work a 9-5, you've become useless before 10:00am since you started writing."

She scowls at me but doesn't disagree. I shake my head and turn back to my phone.

7:22AM STEVE

> Forget it. You were only good for one thing anyway.

My hands tremble slightly as I grip the phone in my hand. Scrolling up, I realize I missed about half a dozen texts from Steve yesterday.

"Who is it?" Remy asks gruffly.

I startle and look up at her, but then immediately shake my head and answer, "It's nothing. Just an Instagram notification."

When she grunts her acceptance and goes back to her coffee, I look back at my phone and begin scrolling through the texts. With each one, my anger grows.

8:02PM STEVE

Hey. I thought I saw you near Rittenhouse Square earlier. Made me miss you.

8:19PM STEVE

I think we should talk. Can we talk? Let's meet for coffee somewhere.

8:44PM STEVE

Hailey, please... Give us another chance. I'm sorry about being jealous. I just get crazy at the thought of not having you to myself.

9:32PM STEVE

You know I don't mean the things I say. Don't make a big deal out of them. I love you.

9:42PM STEVE

You know why drinking is such a trigger for me. It's not my fault, I can't help it.

11:03PM STEVE

I've forgiven you so many times for high school, why can't you forgive me for this?

7:22AM STEVE

> Forget it. You were only good for one thing anyway.

When I reread this morning's text, I slam my phone on the counter, fury boiling in my veins. Remy looks up at me with raised eyebrows.

"Everything okay?"

I nod quickly. "Yeah, I just need to get to work. I'll see you later."

She doesn't look convinced, but she stays quiet anyway. Within a few minutes, I'm dressed and walking to work.

I'm distracted the entire day, Steve's texts rolling on a loop in my head.

No part of me wants to take Steve back, or even hear him out. I know that. I *know* Steve is a manipulative piece of shit that doesn't deserve me. There hasn't been a single moment where I've felt sad about the breakup—only relieved. The texts are infuriating because even through a phone, it feels like he has a hold on me.

I told him we were over. I *told* him how I felt about the way he treated me, and that I wanted nothing to do with him anymore. Why is he contacting me to try to get back together? Is he really that desperate to regain his power over me? How dare he try to pull me back into his toxic bullshit?

My anger grows, more and more throughout the day, my confused thoughts getting tangled in the rage. *Why does he still have a hold of me? Why am I so weak? Why do a few texts from him make me feel like shit and ruin my whole day?*

Because they do. They ruin my whole day. I'm curt with my customers, I snap at my employees, I freak out when one of my cooks questions me. I feel so on edge, so *defensive*, that I am admittedly a royal bitch all day long. It's like any conversation with Steve immediately makes me question my self-worth. And the fact that he still has a hold on me like that makes me *angry*.

I end up asking one of the managers to close up, and I can practically hear the sigh of relief from the café employees. I mutter a gruff thank you and then grab my bag to go... I don't know where. Somewhere that's not in my head.

The fresh air—as fresh as it gets in the heart of any city—does seem to help. I feel Steve's metaphorical grip on my heart loosen, and my inner confident woman is able to take her first real breath of the day. I still can't shake the crushing sensation completely, but at least now I don't feel like curling up under the covers for the rest of the day. I keep walking, hoping the cool October air will continue to lift this weight off my chest.

I don't even realize where I've ended up until I'm standing in front of the doors, staring at the words "Bulldog MMA" that I know so well. I glance at the building in surprise, but only hesitate a moment before walking up the steps.

It's Saturday afternoon, and it looks like people are finishing up their workouts for the day. There are still a few people doing jiu-jitsu on the mats, but for the most part, people are sitting on the mat drinking water and talking. The mascot himself is snoring loudly on the couch in the reception area, his scrunched face tucked between his giant paws and his owner sitting beside him with his phone in his hand. Coach glances up at me as I walk past, giving me only a nod for a greeting.

From behind me I hear, "Little Porter, long time no see. What's up?"

I turn to see Aiden grinning at me. He's drenched in sweat, his dirty blonde hair thoroughly tousled, and his shirt long gone as he lounges comfortably on the mat, like the picture of male arrogance. He's got your typical welterweight body—six feet tall and 170 pounds of dangerous muscle—but he barely cuts weight for his fights, which means he walks around already shredded. A fact he loves to show off at the gym. Couple the swimsuit model body with the mischievous eyes and the dimples in his cheeks, and you have a man that will flirt any girl right into bed. If I thought I could handle the charmer type, I'd probably melt at his feet, but as it stands, I just can't take him seriously. He makes me smile and roll my eyes more than anything else.

"Um, I don't actually know why I—" I start, but he cuts me off.

"Jax is in the bag room in the back, teaching one of the new guys. You can go in." The devilish grin never leaves his face.

I narrow my eyes at him. "Why do you think I'm here for Jax? Maybe I'm looking for Remy."

He just shrugs and says, "Just a hunch. Am I wrong?"

At that, I frown. *Who did I want to see when I walked in here?*

I love my sister, but she doesn't understand any of this. She's been headstrong since she came out of the womb, having no problem voicing her opinions or making it clear what she wants. No one has ever tried to make her feel like she's not good enough. I know she tries to understand what I'm dealing with and how it feels, but she just can't.

Jax might not have gone through what I did, but he understands enough. And he's definitely the best at making me feel good about myself.

So, Jax it is.

I glare at Aiden when I realize he's spot on. The mischievous twinkle glows even brighter in his eyes. "He's in the back," he grins.

I huff in annoyance but trudge to the bag room anyway.

When I walk through the doorway, I see Jax standing next to one of the heavy bags, instructing a young guy on how to throw some kind of punch-kick combo. I lean against the railing overlooking the space, watching the two of them work together.

The kid is staring at the bag, hands up and brows furrowed, as he listens to Jax's instructions and tries to follow them. He throws the combo a few times, Jax offering minor suggestions each time, until finally Jax yells, "Yes! That's it! Now do it again."

I smile at the pride in his voice. He's always been a great coach, to the point that I've always wondered why he keeps fighting when he clearly enjoys teaching far more. He has a way with the amateur fighters, especially the teenagers, and he has the patience of a saint. Both of which are proven by him standing by and watching the fighter execute the same move over and over again until finally, it clicks.

After a few more reps, he finally notices me standing at the top of the stairs. His eyes light with the kind of smile that warms my chest and makes me smile right back. And any of the awkwardness left over from yesterday immediately dissolves, leaving us with the same pure connection that's stretched between us for years. The kind that nothing can disrupt.

"Hailey. I didn't know you were coming over. What's up? Everything okay?" Concern mars his smile slightly, so I quickly reassure him.

"Everything's great. Sorry to barge in, I was in the area and thought I'd see if you wanted to get something to eat. But if you're busy, it's no big deal. I'll just—"

"No, no, that sounds great. Just let me finish up with Pete. We'll just be a few more minutes."

I smile and nod, watching them start back up again. Jax has Pete go through some more reps, tweaking a few details and adding something onto the end of the combo. By the time they're done, both guys have a huge grin on their face.

Jax slaps Pete on the back and says, "Alright, kid, you're done for the day. Enjoy your weekend. We'll get back to working that into sparring next week."

Pete nods and says, "Thanks, man. That was really helpful." He glances at me as he makes his way up the steps and out of the bag room. And even though I shine a smile at him, he barely gives me a sliver of one in return before he's rushing past me.

I scowl at Jax, who doesn't even try to hide his grin. "You don't have to scare them away from me, you know," I scold. "I'm a big girl, I can take care of myself."

The smile doesn't leave his face as he practically bounds up the steps to me. "I know, but it's them I don't trust. Too much testosterone in here, and you're too pretty." He presses a kiss to my blushing cheek, and any fear I have left that he's going to treat me differently after yesterday's tension is officially gone. I exhale a sigh of relief as I aim a shy smile up at him.

He cocks his head as if something just occurred to him. "Speaking of, why don't we change plans a little? Before we go grab food?"

I aim a suspicious look at him. "What do you want to do?"

A grin splits his face. "Let's teach you how to fight."

CHAPTER THIRTEEN
Jax

HER EYES WIDEN. "Teach me how to fight?" she squeaks.

I nod, my grin still firmly in place. "Yes, baby girl. You're overdue for a lesson with me anyway. Why not now?"

She looks down at her clothes. I'm assuming she came from work because she's wearing leggings and a polo shirt, and I can see the thoughts swirling in her head that she's not dressed for a workout.

"We'll just do fifteen minutes of technique, no sweaty workout clothes required. Then we'll go eat." When she continues to hesitate, I tug on a strand of hair that's escaped her messy bun. "It would make me feel better if you knew a little bit of self-defense. Especially now that you're single."

And even though my comment makes something flash in her eyes, it also deflates any argument she might have. She makes her decision and nods. "Okay. Are we staying in here?"

I press my hand to the small of her back and usher her down the steps. "Yup. Right here. Drop your bag, we're starting with bitch slaps."

She laughs but does as I say. And before I realize what

she's doing, she's pulled her shirt over her head and dropped it on top of her bag. She's left in only a thin white tank top, through which I can definitely see the grey bra she's wearing underneath.

I swallow roughly and try to avert my eyes, immediately regretting this plan. She's not indecent in any way, but she's definitely less clothed than my focus can handle after what happened last night. Being that close to her…

My self-control seriously needs to get its shit together.

I clear my throat and force myself to turn back to her. She has a hint of a smile on her lips, which immediately makes my apprehension disappear. Self-defense really would be good for her, and I'm not going to be the asshole horndog that fucks something up for her just because my attention goes to the curve of her neck, or the sliver of skin exposed between her tank top and tight leggings, or the perfect ass whose shape I want to trace with my…

I wrench myself away from the vision that is Hailey. The *unassuming* vision, since she clearly has no idea that she looks completely edible and is wreaking havoc on my focus. She's staring at me with those beautiful blue eyes that melt me every time I see them.

"Okay, what are we starting with?" she asks, a hint of eagerness in her voice.

I clear my throat again. "I told you, we're starting with bitch slaps."

Her smile morphs into a confused frown. "Seriously? That's a thing?"

I nod, holding my hand out to show her my palm. "Punching

someone is actually pretty dangerous if you don't know how to do it—or even if you *do* know how to do it—because you run the risk of breaking your knuckles. So it's actually better to do an open-palm slap." I touch the heel of my palm. "This is what you want to slap with. Not the fingers, but the heel. It's harder and stronger, and if you do it right, you can actually knock someone out with it." I grin. "Although if you're going to punch someone, remember your focus should be on driving your first two knuckles into your target's face."

I get in my fighting stance, legs shoulder-width apart and my right leg back, as Hailey just looks on in wonder. I don't know how much Remy has taught her, but I do know she's at least done a few lessons with her sister to learn the basic weapons: punches, kicks, knees and elbows. "You already know how to stand," I tell Hailey. "So get in your stance for me."

She does as I say without question, bringing her fists up to her face without my instruction.

"Good. Remy's shown you how to punch, so keep some of the same things in mind when it comes to slapping. The power comes from your body, not just from your arm. You want to put your whole hips and ass into a strike. So when you slap, you start with your hand down by your side and then you whip your whole body and arm around when you want to throw it. Twist your hips when you do it."

I watch as she tries to follow my instructions, but her slap looks more like a mosquito is irritating her than a self-defense technique. She's still only using her arm instead of her whole body. I can feel myself start to sweat when I realize I'm going to have to touch her to correct her form.

I exhale a stuttering breath and step up behind her to place my hands gently on her hips. She freezes at the sensation but doesn't push me away, just twists to look over her shoulder and peek up at me from under her lashes.

"You have to put your hip into it," I mumble. "Throw it again."

This time when she does it, I twist her hips at the same time. Her palm whooshes through the air, and even I can feel the power difference between the strikes.

"Oh," she breathes. I quickly step away from her and gesture for her to do it again, this time on her own.

Her next rep is better. She's starting to put her body into the strike, instead of just swatting with her hand. I'm nodding my approval when Aiden pokes his head in the room.

"Hey, man, everyone's heading out. You good to close up?"

I rip my attention away from Hailey so I can give Aiden a nod. "Yeah, I'm good. See you Monday."

"You got it, boss. Have fun with Little Porter." I aim a murderous glare in his direction, but the massive grin on his face stays right where it is. I can hear his chuckle as he leaves the room.

I turn back to Hailey. "Okay, that looks good. Has Remy shown you how to throw a knee? That's the other important self-defense move I always teach. Go right for the balls."

She grins and nods. "Yeah, we've done both knees and elbows. I like throwing elbows, they're fun."

I chuckle at her enthusiasm. "Okay, those are the only strikes I was going to go over. Has she done anything on the ground with you? Any of the jiu-jitsu moves?"

When she shakes her head, I rub my chin in thought. "Every street fight will probably end up on the ground at some point, so jiu-jitsu is arguably the most important type of self-defense," I start to explain. "A few basic moves can help you to push an attacker off, stand up, and even get out of the worst possible position of someone sitting completely on top of you with their hands around your neck. So that's probably what we should work on."

The only problem is, there are only two of us here right now. *Which means I would have to be the attacker that's on top of Hailey.*

I shuffle nervously, once again regretting this idea. I try to offer us a way out of the situation. "Do you want to do more striking? I could get you a pair of gloves, we could do some kickboxing on the heavy bags..."

She's shaking her head before I've even finished. "No, I've already done that. I want to do some jiu-jitsu. That's the piece I'm missing. And I know that's the best self-defense, so I want to do that."

I inhale a shaky breath but give her a tight nod. I lead her over to the small mat at the back of the room, away from all the heavy bags. I sit down and pat the mat next to me, gesturing for her to sit down.

"Okay, we'll go over how to stand up first. Believe it or not, people don't stand up right. There's a way to brace yourself and make sure you're always balanced and ready when you're standing up."

I go over the technique with her, and although it's not the cleanest move I've ever seen, she seems to understand the gist of it. She's graceful but looks like I could knock her over with a heavy exhale if I really tried.

I move onto the next move before she can get too frustrated with this one.

Fuck, this is the one that's going to kill me.

I gesture for her to sit down, and then I drop to my knees in front of her. I clear my suddenly-dry throat. "Uh, do you know what full guard position is? When I'm on top and you're on bottom?"

I hear her breath catch, but she nods quickly. I know her sister loves MMA enough to both explain the basics of the sport, and to instill a respect for it. Even though certain jiu-jitsu positions could be seen as sexual simply because of their closeness, anyone that understands the sport even a little bit knows not to treat it that way. It's a martial *art*, and an important one, at that. Nothing about it should be treated with anything less than 100% focus and respect.

But despite being a professional with years of practice, none of that computes right now. The only thing I'm focused on is the fact that I'm about to get on top of Hailey.

And she knows it.

I hold my hands up in a gesture of surrender, so as to make the objective clear and to ensure I don't spook her. Although at this point, that might be more for my benefit than hers. "I'm going to be on top in your full guard, simulating someone choking you from on top. Is that okay?"

Her breathing is still erratic, and I swear I see a slight color in her cheeks, but she nods and lies down. Slowly, so fucking slowly, I shuffle forward on my knees until I can nudge her knees apart. I slide between her legs, moving forward far enough that I can reach her throat with my hands, but not close enough that my increasingly growing, and completely inappropriate, erection actually presses against her.

I don't even lie to myself about the fact that I would 100% combust in front of her if that happened. Typically, you want to be as close to your opponent as possible in jiu-jitsu, but right now, distance is the only thing keeping me sane.

I gently wrap my hands around her throat, and this time I couldn't miss her tight inhale even if I wanted to. There's definitely color in her cheeks now, and she's looking up at me with a gaze that there's no mistaking the meaning of.

She's turned on.

I tell myself it's a natural reaction to the close proximity, that anyone who hasn't done this sport before has this same reaction. It's undoubtedly weird the first time you try it because everything looks sexual. You're rolling around on the ground with another person, your legs wrapped around each other... of course people are going to have inappropriate thoughts. It's only natural.

That doesn't stop my dick from hardening even more from the look in her eye. That knowledge doesn't help one bit.

And when I suddenly remember Hailey's comment the other night about the particular *flavor* of sex that she enjoys, I have to swallow the groan that wants so badly to roll across my tongue.

This was officially the worst idea I've ever had.

But I can't exactly stand up and walk out right now, so I take a deep breath and start talking.

"Okay, you're going to twist onto one hip, so you're on your side, and then slide your shin across my chest and stomach as a sort of block, so I can't push forward. That's it." I'm not sure how much of this heat Hailey feels—although based on the pink that's flushed across her porcelain skin, my guess is a decent amount—but it's not stopping her from doing the move. That knowledge helps me swallow back a little more of that urge to grab her and pull her under me for *real*.

"Good, now I want you to get up on your elbow with one hand and brace on my shoulder with the other to keep me away from you. Now, simulate slapping or kicking me in order to get me off of you. Like that. Good girl." She does as I say, lashing out at me and forcing me to fall back so I don't get caught with one of her strikes. "Now that you've created distance between us, stand up with the move we did right before this. Keep your balance and don't ever take your eyes off of me."

She stands, but it's just as shaky as the first few times she did it. Being unsure of the movements doesn't help either; she's one shove away from falling over, and based on the frustrated look on her face, she knows it.

Before I can even encourage her to try again, she lies down and gestures for me to do it again. I'm not entirely sure why she's so frustrated, but it does seem to distract us from the tension of our close proximity. We barely hitch a breath when I wrap my hands around her neck this time.

She goes through the steps again, blocking my body with her shin and then striking out at me with a slap. But the block is a flimsy one and we both know I could easily overpower it. By the time she manages to get to her feet, she's visibly even more frustrated than she was with her first rep.

"Again," she snaps. Without a word, we go through it again. It's slightly better this time, but not by much. And I can tell it's really starting to get to her.

"Hailey, it's okay," I try to appease her. I step closer to where she's standing with her hands on her hips, willing my gentle words to break through her mental block. "Not everyone is going to get it on the first try. It takes dozens of repetitions to get the hang of it so don't worry if—"

"Let's just do it again," she interrupts as she drops back to the mat, her frustration visibly morphing into anger. I'm starting to wonder if there's something else going on that has nothing to do with our self-defense lesson.

I swallow the words that want to come out and climb over her to repeat the move.

Again, it's better, but not great.

"Try to slow it down. If you focus on each step as a move, you can nail each one before putting it all together. Just try—"

She ignores me completely and tries to fly through the move, inevitably making it worse. By the time she gets to her feet, she's practically sparking with her anger.

"God, I *suck* at this," she exclaims. "I suck at *everything!*"

I frown and step closer to her, being careful not to touch her. "Hailey..." I start.

"No, Jax, just admit it! I'm terrible at this. I bet even the kids class can get this damn move, yet I'm fumbling around like I just learned how to walk. God, what is *wrong* with me?"

By now, her anger has morphed back into frustration, this time accompanied by teary eyes. It confirms my suspicion that something else happened today. I just don't know what.

I grip her hand in an effort to get her to focus on me. Her eyes don't turn to me but I feel her shiver at my touch.

"Hailey, what's going on?" I ask softly. I rub gentle circles on her wrist in an effort to soothe her. "Did something happen?"

She won't meet my eyes as she answers. "I suck at everything today," she whispers. "I feel like I keep screwing everything up." She wipes a tear away and then lets out a cold laugh, shaking her head. "Steve's right. It's a good thing I'm pretty because I can't do anything else. I'm only good for one thing... so maybe I am just a whore."

The name of that bastard on her lips—and the knowledge that he's still fucking with her head and making her feel like this—makes all rational thoughts fly out of my head. All I see is red.

Without thinking about what I'm doing—or whether this is a terrible idea—I shove forward until I have Hailey caged between my arms at the wall. I'm not touching her, but I might as well be with the tension radiating from both of us. I see her teary-eyed, beautifully broken gaze snap up to my face as I vibrate with rage.

"I told you before I never want to hear you talk about yourself like that ever again," I say through gritted teeth.

She jerks her attention away from me, a blush staining her cheeks as she avoids my eyes and mumbles a *sorry*.

"No, don't do that," I say firmly but gently, tipping her chin back up with a finger. "I don't want your sorries." I study her eyes, willing her to see what I see. "What's wrong with being a whore, baby girl?"

Something passes through her gaze at that, and she starts to stutter through some kind of non-answer. But I don't want to hear it. I'm sick of that fucking word having any power over her.

"He's making you feel like shit by calling you a word that should mean nothing to you," I say softly. "Unless it's used in the bedroom by a man whose sole purpose is to break you apart with hunger and stitch you back together with pleasure, it should mean *nothing*. He was supposed to use that word to love you and instead he used it to hurt you. Don't let him do that. Don't let it be a negative thing. You said it yourself, you wanted to be treated like a whore in the bedroom. And that's not a bad thing, baby girl. So, take the power back. Because if you say things like that again, I'll have no choice but to show you how."

Her lips part in surprise, and it takes everything in me not to lower my head and bite into her perfectly pink lips. "How...?" she whispers in disbelief. Her eyes show me she's scared, but also desperate to be stronger than this. To be more than what Steve made her.

Fuck it, I'm already too deep into this.

I drop my head so my mouth is pressed against her ear. "That's up to you, Hailey. What kind of whore do you want to be? On your knees with my cock in your pretty mouth? Or on all fours with my handprint on your ass as punishment for thinking you're anything but perfect?"

I hear her sharp intake of breath at the same time that she starts to tremble. I know I should feel guilty about crossing so many boundaries, but I can't bring myself to make light of the situation.

I pull back just far enough that I can look down and see her expression, keeping her caged between my arms. There's no chance I'm letting her go before we finish this conversation.

I come face to face with a Hailey I've never seen before. Her face is flushed, her breathing erratic, and her pupils are so blown out that her usually-blue eyes are almost black. She's so turned on that she can't even speak, her mouth opening and closing but no words are coming out.

Eventually, she manages a whisper. "Jax..."

All I can think about is how badly I want to take her home. How badly I want to see her on her knees, and then show her what I look like on mine. How badly I want to worship her body and erase every self-deprecating thought she's ever had about herself. I want to take her to bed and show her how a man *should* treat a woman.

But as quickly as those thoughts come, so does the knowledge that I'm fantasizing about fucking my best friend's little sister. A woman that I've known since she was ten years old. A woman that just got out of an emotionally abusive relationship and is looking for me to be a friend.

A woman that I have no business telling I want to fuck her, let alone admitting to wanting to fuck her *like that.*

The realization immediately shocks the lust out of my system. My eyes widen, and I stumble back a few steps.

Hailey must see the panic in my eyes because she steps forward, reaching for me. "Jax..." This time it sounds more like a plea.

I shake my head, as if I can rid myself of the damning thoughts that way. "Fuck, Hailey, I—" I take another step away from her before she can touch me. "I'm sorry, I shouldn't have said that. I don't—I don't know what came over me. Fuck—"

"Jax," Hailey says, her tone now sounding more like a warning. Like she can see me freaking out and is trying to scold me into holding myself together.

"No, Hailey, I'm supposed to be helping you," I blurt out, trying to make her understand. "I'm supposed to be your friend right now. I shouldn't be—I mean, we shouldn't—fuck, Hailey, I'm so sorry."

She finally gets close enough to take my hand. I look down at her with pleading eyes, hoping I didn't just damage her or our relationship.

"Jax, it's okay," she says softly. I wait for her to say something else, but she just smiles at me—that warm, trusting smile—and repeats, "It's my fault for even making that comment yesterday, and for insisting on a jiu-jitsu lesson today. It's okay, I swear."

"No," I say forcefully. "You have nothing to apologize for. *I'm* the one that made this inappropriate, not you. Never you. I'm the one that started this whole lesson. And I never should've—fuck, Hailey, I never should've said…"

I squeeze my eyes shut as the shame of my words rolls through me. *God, what the fuck is wrong with me? She needs a friend right now, not* this.

"Jax, it's okay," she says quietly, squeezing my hand in an effort to bring my attention back to her. "I promise."

I search her face for any dishonesty, any lie she might be telling me because she doesn't want to hurt my feelings by telling me I just fucked everything up. But there's none. She's telling the truth.

Some of the tension eases from my shoulders. I squeeze her hand in a silent thank you.

"Do you still want to grab something to eat?" I ask hopefully. "Or I can take you home if you'd rather do that. Whatever you want."

She smiles at me again, squeezing my hand. "Let's get you fed, Superman," she says. "Maybe we can grab a drink, too. I'm kind of enjoying this drinking thing without a cloak of disapproval, and it's even more fun doing it with you."

The reminder of Steve is like a shower of ice cold water. Not only does it make my teeth clench in fury that he would ever treat Hailey with less respect because of a drink, but it also solidifies my resolve to be a good friend to her. The last thing she needs is more drama or headaches from a man, so I definitely shouldn't be coming on to her—in *any* capacity. There are so many reasons why that isn't a good idea, but at the top of the fucking list: Hailey deserves a friend right now.

"Then let's get you that drink, baby girl. Your wish is my command."

THE REST OF the night passes comfortably. We make our way to my favorite local pub and spend the next couple hours eating, drinking, laughing, and enjoying each other's company like we always do when we're together. Anyone that takes a look at us probably thinks we're just two friends catching up on a Saturday afternoon.

But I know Jax well enough to recognize that there's still a tiny hint of tension in the air. Not enough to make it awkward between us, but enough to recognize that something happened.

Something's changed between us.

I glance at Jax, letting myself admire his good looks for the first time. I've always known he grew into a handsome man, but I never really let myself appreciate it before this. Out of the corner of my eye, I look over the dark jeans and black T-shirt that he changed into at the gym, both of which cling tightly to his muscles. His jeans must be stretchy because I can see his quads clearly, and his shirt is *definitely* stretchy because I can see every dip, and every ridge of his defined shoulders and huge chest. I wonder briefly how I could have possibly ignored the stunning specimen that is Jax Turner.

Because right now, it's all I can focus on.

His bright blue eyes are a given, and the only thing I could never overlook. I've held Jax's gaze through too many silent conversations, watched as his eyes lit up when he smiled, for far too long to not notice how mesmerizing they are. Between that and his dirty blonde hair, he's looked like a Men's Health magazine cover model since he was a teenager, ever since the summer in high school he shot up to 6'4 and went from a scrawny kid to a built young man.

His height and massive, muscular stature have always been a running joke between us because it highlights the huge size difference between us, but right now, all I can think about is how easily he could dominate me physically. That moment in the gym only emphasized that. I think back to Jax crowding me against the wall, saying things that I've always wanted to hear but never *ever* expected to hear from Jax, and I can imagine everything he described so clearly, every spank, every push to get me in the position he wants, every—

"Can I get you guys anything else?" the bartender interrupts my spiraling thoughts, and I clear my throat with a forced cough.

"We're good for now, thanks," Jax answers, oblivious to the filthy thoughts currently occupying my mind.

I toss my napkin onto my empty plate and reach for the Corona in front of me. We've been sitting at the bar for about two hours now, much to the bartender's annoyance. Jax isn't a big drinker outside of his corporate sales job and I'm still a total lightweight, which means we've only managed to order two beers each. It wasn't until Jax ordered enough food to feed an army that the bartender's permanent scowl softened slightly.

I down the last few sips of my beer and push both bottle and plate away from me. Next to me, Jax does the same.

"God, that burger was good," he groans. "Want another beer?"

I look at the shelf of liquor behind the bar, suddenly desperate to distract myself from the day's events and my current traitorous thoughts. "I think I want some kind of liquor. I've always liked tequila the best, but it's been a while since I've worked at the bar. I'm not sure if there are any new cocktails they're making with it nowadays."

Jax studies the mixers along the bar. "Tequila sunrise is still the go-to, I think." I shake my head, not liking the idea of orange juice right now. "I don't know if they do margaritas here, and our bartender might frown us into the ground if we ask him for one." He tilts his head for a moment as he contemplates something. Then he snaps his fingers and says, "I got it. I have the perfect drink for you."

He waves the bartender over, who, once again, has a massive scowl on his face. Jax says something to him in a low whisper, after which the guy turns around to grab us two Coronas and then two shots of Patron.

When he slides the drinks over to us on the bar, I just look at Jax in confusion. "Um, the whole point of a cocktail is so I don't have to do a shot. You know I can't swallow those things."

Something flashes in his eyes at that, and I'm once again reminded of the tension floating between us. It's in the hesitation, in the glance at my lips, the unknown emotion in his eyes. It has me automatically clenching my thighs and sucking in a breath, even before I can think about what it means.

When he speaks, his voice sounds completely normal and all trace of the unknown has vanished. "It's a loaded Corona," he explains. He grabs the Corona and takes a few gulps. I watch, mesmerized, as his Adam's apple bobs up and down, and I don't even have time to process the thought before it's flying through my brain.

Why is that so erotic?

Ignoring my admiring gaze, he grabs the shot of tequila and pours it into the beer bottle that now has room for the liquid. Finally, he takes the lime and drops it into the beer before plugging the top and flipping it upside down to mix it.

"Loaded Corona," he gestures with a grin. "It's good, and so easy. You won't even taste the tequila. Try it." He slides the drink he just concocted across the bar to me, which I grab and—after sniffing the bottleneck suspiciously—take a curious sip. My eyes widen when I turn to Jax.

An explosive, happy laugh bursts from his chest at my expression. "I told you. It tastes just like a Corona with a hint of that tequila aftertaste, right?" I nod, taking another, bigger swig from the bottle. "We can throw another shot in if you want to make it a party," he says with a grin.

I debate for a moment, but ultimately decide against it. I can already feel the afternoon's beers buzzing comfortably in my veins, so a shot of tequila will be more than enough to put me at ease. I'm not entirely sure I want to be shitfaced in front of Jax right now, so I just shake my head.

"One is enough," I tell him. Then, I reach forward and

make his drink the same way he made mine. Once I'm done, I slide it over to him, at which point he grabs it and holds it up for a cheers. I hold my glass up and wait for whatever he wants to say.

"Cheers to good drinks with good people." He clinks his bottle against mine before downing a fourth his drink in one go.

We're both quiet for a few moments, sipping our drinks and staring at nothing in particular. Even without looking at him I can see Jax hesitating, trying to figure out how he can say whatever it is he wants to say.

I know exactly what he wants to say, so I don't rush the conversation.

"Do you want to talk about whatever happened today that upset you?" he finally asks me.

I sigh, twirling the beer bottle on the bar. "It's not even worth repeating. I got a few texts from Steve this morning that set a bad tone for my day. That's it." I sneak a sideways glance at him and see that he's got a tight jaw and he's glaring daggers at his beer. "I'm sorry I freaked out. It was a momentary lapse in sanity, it had nothing to do with you or the lesson."

His knuckles whiten where he's gripping the bottle. "I told you I don't want your sorries, Hailey. There's nothing to apologize for."

I nod immediately in agreement. "You're right, I'm s—I mean, I won't do it again. I just had a bad morning. But I shouldn't have let it get to me, and I definitely shouldn't have taken it out on you."

I see the tension in his shoulders ease. He sighs and says,

"I meant what I said, though, Hailey. The negativity needs to stop."

I focus my attention back on the bartop in front of me, feeling a blush stain my cheeks. I'm mortified that I exploded the way I did in front of Jax. It's not like me to publicize my self-confidence issues, or take it out on others. The fact that I freaked out on Jax means I let Steve's comments hit more of a bull's-eye than I realized.

"I know," I whisper. "I didn't mean to, it just slipped out." I take a deep, stuttering breath. "I don't know why it bothered me so much today."

I hear Jax let out a heavy sigh, then I feel his big hand on the back of my neck, gently massaging my neck and shoulders.

His touch instantly soothes me. My body relaxes the second he makes contact with my skin, a relieved exhale escaping my lips. I close my eyes to enjoy the touch and before long, the day's stress has completely left my body.

When I aim a grateful smile at Jax, our eyes meet—and the air instantly charges. I'm instantly flashing back to the moment in the gym where he had me pressed against the wall, whispering the filthiest thing I've never imagined ever coming out of his mouth.

My heart pounds at the memory.

I don't think I ever could've imagined that Jax would enjoy... *that* kind of sex. He's such a nice guy, I just assumed he enjoyed the normal, good guy kind of sex.

What kind of whore do you want to be? On your knees with my cock in your pretty mouth? Or on all fours with my handprint on your ass as punishment for thinking you're anything but perfect?

A shiver runs through me. I meant what I said to Jax last week about hating the fact that Steve never gave me what I asked for in the bedroom. I've always known I wasn't a vanilla-sex kind of person, but I've never had partners that would give me what I want. Even my threesome in high school was as PG as a threesome can get, a sloppy night with two teenage boys that didn't know what they were doing. I've always wanted it to be a little filthy, a little rough, a little degrading.

I want exactly what Jax described. I would love to be forced onto my knees. To be spanked until my ass is pink and then fucked until I can't remember what it feels like to be empty.

But the thought of Jax being the one to do it... is not something I've ever imagined.

Now I can't *stop* imagining it.

Jax back at the gym, pressing me against the wall, taunting me with his dirty words before grabbing me by the throat and pushing me down—

My breath catches at the fantasy that my memory just built. He must be remembering the same thing because as soon as we make eye contact, his hand pauses on my neck, and I swear I see a tinge of pink bloom on his cheeks.

Jax pulls his hand away and clears his throat. He doesn't look at me as he says, "So, uh, you should probably block his number, right? I mean, if his messages bother you this much you should probably just block them entirely."

I laugh nervously. "Yeah, probably." But for a reason I can't yet make sense of, I can't actually bring myself to do that.

I twirl the beer in front of me before taking another long drink. "Have you ever had a bad breakup?" I ask, trying to mask the sudden—and entirely unexpected—strain between us.

He chuckles, just as nervously. "I mean, the Kara one sucked, but that one was on me. I got too sucked into fighting and didn't treat her the way she deserved to be treated." He quiets for a moment, looking thoughtful and sad. "I hated that breakup because I regretted my part in it. I probably should've fought harder for her afterwards, but I knew she was right to break up with me. She deserved better."

If this is what I sound like when I'm talking badly about myself then I completely understand why Jax gets frustrated with me. This sucks to listen to.

"Jax, you didn't do it on purpose," I admonish quietly. "You had just gone pro, you were looking for jobs... you just had a lot on your plate. And you were young. It's not your fault you two matched at the wrong time."

He shines a grateful smile at me, then reaches over to playfully tug on my hair. "Always so wise," he mutters.

I smile, exhaling a grateful breath that the air has lightened and no longer feels tense between us. I take a long swallow of my drink, welcoming the comfortable buzz of the alcohol. Then I turn my body and full attention toward Jax. "So. I knew your type then, what about now? What are you looking for?"

His eyes light with something I can't decipher as he contemplates my question. Then he turns back to his beer with a sigh. "I don't know what I want. It's not like anything I'm doing is actually working, I'm basically just finding women that want to sleep with me."

I roll my eyes. "Such a hardship," I tease.

He gives me a playful grin. "Don't get me wrong, it's fun, but... it gets boring after a while. Either they don't want to pursue something or I don't, and then it's over. So what was the point?"

I study him thoughtfully. "So, you want a girlfriend but don't know what you're looking for?"

He winces at that. "I mean, I don't *need* a girlfriend. I'm fine with just sex, I just wish it didn't feel as meaningless, you know?"

I nod in understanding, even as the thought of sex with Jax starts taking over my brain again. Jax above me, whispering dirty things in my ear, Jax behind me, pulling my hair as he drives into me, Jax below me—

Jesus Christ, I need to get a grip on myself. You'd think I haven't gotten laid in months.

"I totally get it," I manage to squeak. I clear my throat and chug half my drink in an effort to cover my weird tone.

I can feel Jax studying me, so I avoid looking at him. God forbid he figure out the very inappropriate, not-friendly direction my thoughts have taken.

He looks at my almost-empty beer bottle. "Do you want another one?"

I hurriedly shake my head. If I keep drinking, I'm just going to end up admitting something I shouldn't.

Like how I can't stop thinking about how much I want to sleep with my best friend.

"No, I'm okay. I should actually get going. I'm not used to drinking as much as I have been lately so I'm trying to slow it down a little, especially with Vegas next week."

Jax gives me a quizzical look as I climb off the barstool. "Vegas?"

I quirk an eyebrow. "I guess Remy didn't tell you, then. We're flying out for Tristan's fight next week. Just for the day but we managed to snag cheap last-minute flights. So we're coming out on Saturday."

His jaw drops. "You're coming to Vegas?" he repeats in shock.

I chuckle and shake my head. "You process this however you need to process this. I'll wait."

He shakes his head as if to clear the cobwebs in his brain. "I can't believe you're coming out to watch him. That's amazing. Does Tristan know?"

I nod. "Remy's been trying to give him space with the fight coming up but she told him last night that she'll be there to cheer for him. He seemed excited about it."

"He should be, it's way better when you're not there alone. Especially for a big fight like this." Suddenly the shock clears, and a grin stretches across his face. "You think you're ready for Vegas?"

My eyes narrow. "I don't know, am I? You sound suspiciously excited. Are you planning to get me drunk and married?"

Something flashes in his eyes, but it's gone before I can make any sense of it. "Not exactly the way my thoughts were heading, but we can get you married if you want, I guess? I'm sure we can find an agreeable bastard somewhere and make it the luckiest day of his life…"

I give his arm a playful smack, but there's a smile tugging at the corner of my lips. "You're hilarious. What do you *actually* do when you're there?"

He sighs and turns back to his beer. "Nothing. I hate Vegas. It's where most of Tristan's fights are going to be so I guess I have to get used to it but I'm not a big fan of it anymore. Might just be that I'm over the partying thing."

I gesture to myself, and the fact that I'm leaving. "Clearly I am, too. But I'm sure we can find something enjoyable to do after his fight anyway."

Jax smiles at me, and in this moment, it hits me how easily we sink back into our friendship, even when something goes wrong—or when something goes weird and sexual.

"I'll find you some edibles and a great club for dancing, how about that," he offers.

I roll my eyes and pull my jacket on. "I guess that doesn't sound like the worst thing," I agree with a smile. And at his answering grin, I can't help but lean forward and press a kiss to his cheek. Jax happy is one of my favorite sights ever.

"Thanks for today," I tell him. "I'm sure we'll talk before Saturday, but if I don't see you before you leave, safe travels and good luck."

He smiles again as he nods. "See you soon, baby girl."

CHAPTER FIFTEEN
Jax

I WATCH TRISTAN shadowbox in the center of the mat, his nerves a palpable energy in the tiny locker room.

I chance a look at Coach sitting next to me. He's got the same expression on that he wears when he's watching a technique class at the gym—he's attentive, watching everything, but entirely at ease. I should've guessed he wouldn't be rattled, God knows that man has been in more locker rooms than anyone else.

Tristan, on the other hand, is nervous as fuck. I know my best friend better than anyone else and even though he's trying to hide it, I can see the tension in his shoulders and the tightness of his jaw.

We've always agreed that the hour before a fight is the worst. It's the time when you have nothing else to focus on but the fight, and no other thoughts to consume you but the ones where you acknowledge that you're about to be locked in a cage with a very large man that is going to try everything in his power to hurt you.

It's slightly unsettling.

It's also the thought that every single fighter has, but that only the realest fighters face head on and step into the cage anyway.

Out of the corner of my eye, I see our striking coach step into the locker room.

"It's time," is all he says.

Tristan just gives a stiff nod and immediately starts walking toward the exit. Without a word, Coach and I stand up to follow.

As we start down the hall and into the tunnel, I hear *Voodoo Chile* by Jimi Hendrix start to play through the arena. It's always surprised me that Tristan doesn't need "hype" music—he's too intense for that. He probably doesn't even hear the song, that's how focused he is right now. He doesn't look back at us once during the entire walk down to the cage.

On the other end of the spectrum, I'm shaking in my fucking boots and trying to keep myself together for the sake of my teammate.

When we reach the steps to the cage, Tristan wastes no time pulling off his shirt and shoes. The referee steps up to check his equipment—his gloves, his cup, his mouthpiece—and then he begins slathering Vaseline on Tristan's face and eyebrows. Tristan stands still, his eyes closed, even when I see goosebumps pimple his flesh as the nerves rush through him.

Finally, the ref's prep is done. He steps back to allow Tristan a moment to say goodbye to his corner.

Both coaches give him a quick hug, neither being one for big speeches. When he gets to me, I see a flash of vulnerability in his eyes, and I know I'm the only one he's let see it.

Instead of a hug, I grab him by the nape of his neck and pull his forehead to mine.

I don't say anything as he takes a deep breath. I give him a moment to collect himself, to soak up this moment and do what he needs to do to mentally prepare himself. But I can't let him go without some kind of encouragement.

"This is your time, brother," I say quietly. "You were born for this. Every run, every training session, every fight has prepared you for this exact moment. You've been better than every guy in this division since you were a teenager. You know it, I know it, now everyone else needs to know it. Show them why the fuck you deserve to be here."

A heavy exhale escapes his lips. He gives a stiff nod, after which I see determination blaze in his eyes.

He gives me a quick hug and then turns to jog up the steps to enter the cage.

I circle the cage with the two coaches and settle into our respective seats, keeping one eye on the very large, very intense fighter that's currently eyeing Tristan from across the octagon. Tristan just paces around his space, keeping loose and completely ignoring his opponent for the time being.

"Ladies and gentlemen, welcome to your first fight on tonight's Main Card! This is a middleweight bout at 185 pounds. Fighting out of the red corner, we have Kevin Holladay, a UFC veteran and Brazilian jiu-jitsu black belt..."

I zone out during the introductions, completely consumed by my nerves and wanting it to just get started. Everyone knows the nerves go away once the bell rings, and right now that's the only thing I'm waiting for.

After what feels like an eternity, the ref calls the two fighters to the center of the octagon to go over final rules and offer them the option to touch gloves. They do, and then separate to their individual corners.

"Are you ready?" the ref calls, and I swear I've stopped breathing.

"*FIGHT!*"

The air whooshes from my lungs at the sound of the bell.

Tristan bounds forward, intent on throwing the first punch, just like in every fight. An old Philly boxing coach once told us that the first person to step forward and throw will likely hold the momentum of the fight, and both of us have lived by that ever since.

Sure enough, Tristan holds the center of the cage, setting himself as the aggressor from the very start. He's always had a dominant fighting style but it's especially important in this fight—Holladay is a long-time veteran that's known for his endless gas tank and ability to scrap. If he's allowed to play his game, Tristan will be playing catch-up the whole fight.

So instead, we need to beat him to it and best him at his own game. Stay on him and always be the first and last to throw in an exchange.

Tristan immediately begins to initiate the game plan. He's on top of Holladay from the very first exchange, throwing combos every chance he gets and never waiting for Holladay to get off his heels. There are plenty of shots thrown—it's not like Holladay is just sitting back and taking it—but it's still clear that Tristan has the edge on most of them. Even though they go back and forth with their strikes, the simple fact of the matter is that Tristan is both the first and the last one to land in most of the exchanges.

Tristan's default is boxing, though he manages to throw a few body kicks when Holladay tries to get away from his punches. The exchanges are constant—this fight is already much higher paced than most middleweight fights are. And it's all because Tristan isn't letting his opponent catch his breath long enough to become the aggressor.

Pride flares in my chest at the sight. It's no secret that Tristan is an underdog in this fight. He's a relatively unknown fighter in the very large world of MMA, and he's going against a guy that has triple the amount of fights that he has. Everyone else is expecting a green fighter that only took this fight because it was an easy way into the UFC. Which it is, because as long as Tristan puts on a good fight and doesn't get completely demolished, this likely won't be his only fight for the promotion.

But that's not how Tristan is fighting. If I knew nothing about their fighter stats, I'd say I'm watching two experienced, calm veterans go toe-to-toe in a technical battle. It's a great fight. Even without the sounds of the fans cheering throughout the arena, you can tell it's a highly entertaining bout. Everyone sitting around the cage is riveted by these two fighters.

Tristan holds the center of the cage and continually throws—and lands—more strikes than his opponent does. But with a minute left in the round, he finds an opening to fire a stiff combination straight to Holladay's jaw.

The punches stun Holladay into stumbling back a few steps. It's exactly the opening that Tristan needed, and he wastes no time capitalizing on it. He immediately launches his own attack of strikes.

Unfortunately, he gets a little too excited in doing so. He wants so badly to win by finish that he rushes forward with a sloppy attack. When Holladay steps back and into the perfect range for a kick, Tristan rips a midline kick to the body.

Which Holladay immediately catches. He's too experienced, too much of a veteran, not to see the opening for what it is: a way to shift the tides in his favor in a round that he hasn't been winning.

With the kick caught and Tristan standing on only one leg, he easily takes him down to the mat. I hear Coach let out a curse next to me, even as Tristan tries to immediately right his mistake by wrapping Holladay up in his guard.

The end of the round sees Holladay trying to do damage from his position on top, while Tristan tries to both minimize the impact and look for a way to his feet. The bell signals the end of the round.

Tristan's expression stays blank as he gets to his feet. It's so easy to curse yourself in a moment like this, but what people don't understand is that the judges see and weigh every single action of the fighters. If you act like you've lost, you'll be seen as a loser—act like you've won, and they'll see a winner. So instead of cursing, Tristan keeps his poker face and strides back to the corner for further instruction.

"Forget the end of that round," Coach immediately barks. He slaps Tristan across the face once to make sure he has his undivided attention, then launches into his instructions. "You're doing great with the pressure so I want you to stay on him just like you were doing. He's got nothing for you as long as we keep him on his heels. But you need to lay off the body kicks because he's going to get desperate soon and start looking for the takedown. So keep the pressure, keep the combos, but stay long and don't let him take you down. This is *your fight. Your* victory. *Take it* from him."

I watch as Coach's words hit their mark, Tristan's eyes blazing with determination as he gives a firm nod.

He's barely breathing hard by the time Coach finishes his instructions. The fact that he took this fight on two weeks' notice is amazing in itself, but it's even more impressive that he's not even winded right now. It's truly a testament to his work ethic and no-days-off training regimen that he's doing so well physically right now.

"You got this, brother," I choke out, pride almost causing the words to get stuck in my throat.

He doesn't turn back to look at me but I know he hears my words of encouragement when he nods and jumps up to bounce around on the balls of his feet. The clap sounds that signals the corners need to get out of the cage.

He doesn't waste any time putting Coach's instructions into action. The second the bell rings, he's gone like a rocket out of a cannon, practically running across the cage so he can lay fists on Holladay's face.

Fuck waiting for the last round; he's ready to end this fight *now.*

Holladay tries to shoot for a takedown once or twice between running away from the onslaught, but Tristan's managed to remind himself not to get sloppy. His takedown defense is solid, even as his strikes begin to intensify.

In a last-ditch effort to get Tristan to the mat, Holladay shoots for a very telegraphed takedown. And as his body lowers down to waist level so he can go for the tackle, Tristan immediately spots the opportunity.

The uppercut lands flush on Holladay's chin.

He's out before he even hits the ground.

Tristan doesn't even react, he just raises his arms in victory. Looking every bit like the fighter that knew he was going to win--like it was an inevitable fact.

In contrast, I'm screaming my goddamn head off. Even Coach is clapping loudly, and that guy is one of the most expressionless people I know. We pile into the cage, stepping around the ref and doctor huddled over Holladay and rushing Tristan with enthusiastic hugs and back slaps.

But there are so many chaotic feelings inside me that inevitably my hug ends with me lifting him high in the air, needing to express my excitement because it feels like I'm bursting at the seams with joy. "That was amazing!" I scream when I drop him. Like my face is about to split in half from my smile. "You just won your UFC debut by knockout. *Fuck yeah!*" I punch his shoulder in pure glee before wrapping him in another bear hug.

He's grinning from ear-to-ear, and I swear to God, the sight of my brother happy is one of the greatest feelings in the world. I can't help it, I punch him again.

"Dude, I'm about to be more injured from you than from Holladay," he says with a laugh. "Figure out another way to be happy for me, would you?"

I grin and wrap an arm around his shoulders. "Without a doubt, that was Fight of the Night. You're definitely getting that $50,000 bonus. Guess we're going to have to take the girls out for a nice dinner tonight, huh?"

If at all possible, the mention of his girlfriend makes his eyes glow even brighter. He's probably eager as fuck to get the post-fight formalities over with so he can get to her as quickly as possible.

My smile warms at the sight. He deserves all the good karma in the world.

The winner announcement and post-fight interview pass in a blur. By the time we step out of the cage, my head is spinning with all the flurry of activity. It isn't until Tristan rushes forward to the crowd that I'm snapped back to the moment.

Remy and Hailey are standing on the other side of the divider. Tristan got them tickets to the section reserved specifically for guests of the fighters, but they must've pushed down to the guard rail that separates the crowd from the fighters' path back into the tunnel. Both girls are practically vibrating with the excitement of his win.

Tristan rushes up to his girlfriend and, ignoring the railing between them, lifts her around the waist so he can press an eager kiss to her mouth.

She welcomes his attention, cupping his face in her hands and returning the kiss with just as much fervor. I can distantly hear her whispering how proud she is.

I roll my eyes—even though the smile stays on my face—and turn away from the sickening lovebirds. Instantly, my attention is captured by the tiny blonde at Remy's side.

"Hey, baby girl," I murmur, wrapping an arm around her shoulders and pressing a kiss to her hair. "You good?"

She shines a thousand-watt smile up at me and for the second time tonight, I'm blown away by the happiness I feel for another person's happiness.

"Yeah," she breathes. "I'm good. That was incredible. Does he always fight like that?"

"On good nights, he does. Tonight was a good night. It was a hell of an initiation into the UFC." She nods in understanding. "You up for the after party? Tristan has to get checked out by the doctor, but after that we were planning on taking a shower and going out for a little bit. You down?"

She nods again, eagerly this time.

I chuckle and squeeze her tighter against me. "Good girl."

It's another two hours before we can meet up with the girls again. It's one of the most annoying parts about fighting, that even when you win, you're likely to go to the hospital or at least need to be patched up by the doctor in one way or another. It took forever to get out of there and up to the hotel room to shower and get changed.

By the time we make it to the hotel bar, it's obvious Remy and Hailey have had a few drinks while waiting for us. Remy's only tell that she's drunk is her loose posture and easy smile, but Hailey is clearly much happier and much louder than earlier tonight.

"Hi!" she squeaks when she spots us walking toward the

bar. "You made it! Why did that take so long?"

I let out a heavy sigh. "Doctor stuff. Even when you win, it takes forever to get checked out." I quirk an eyebrow at her almost-empty glass. "I see you two had no problem starting without us."

She giggles, trying to hide the sound behind her hand. *Fuck me, it's the cutest sound I've ever heard.*

She places her glass on the bar. "Sorry, I keep forgetting my tolerance isn't what it used to be. I switched to water already, don't worry. You won't have to babysit tonight."

I tug a lock of her hair affectionately. "Celebrate all you want, baby girl, I'll take care of you. You deserve a little fun too."

She smiles up at me, the blue in her eyes seeming extra bright tonight, either from the alcohol or her general good mood. Her gaze drops down to my white button-up shirt.

Her breath rushes out of her in a whoosh. "God, I always forget how hot you are when you're all dressed up."

I grin. And after her lips part in surprise when she realizes what the alcohol just let slip, it grows even bigger.

"You think I'm hot, Hailes?" I tease.

She swallows nervously but doesn't backtrack. She just rolls her eyes and looks away, saying, "Like you need me to tell you you're hot. You probably have plenty of women telling you that every time you wear a suit in public."

I gently check her hip with mine in an attempt to get her to focus on me again. "I like it better coming from you."

The corner of her lip twitches when she fights a smile. My grin grows even bigger, partly because I got her to smile again, but also because she thinks I'm hot. I lean back to check out what she's wearing so I can return the compliment.

My breath catches when I take in her appearance.

I was too amped up from Tristan's win earlier to really look at her.

Now, I can't *stop* looking at her.

She doesn't look like the usual female UFC fans around the arena. She doesn't look fake, or overly done-up, or like she's only here to appeal to the male specimen and convince one of them to wife her up.

She looks... like herself. Like she threw on something that just so happens to accentuate her natural beauty. Like she doesn't give a shit about what other people think of how she looks, as long as *she* likes how she looks. She's wearing a simple black dress that hugs her from tits to thighs, with thin straps running along her shoulders and the back completely open to anyone's gaze. She's barely wearing any makeup, and her golden hair is unstyled and brushed over her shoulder. Nothing about her outfit screams *look at me!*

She's just... beautiful. As is.

Perfect.

I shake out of my reverie when I realize Hailey's staring at me expectantly.

"Sorry, what?" I blurt, completely clueless about how long I've been admiring her. Hoping she didn't notice.

I've been doing an awful lot of staring at her lately.

"I asked if that's the watch I got you," she repeats with a knowing grin.

She doesn't wait for me to answer, she just reaches out

to grip my hand. "It *is* the one I bought you," she murmurs, brushing her fingers over the face of it.

I nod. "It is. I never go to work without it. I think you gave it to me when I got my first big internship in college."

She confirms the memory with a thoughtful nod. "I knew you wanted to look professional when you started. I saved for weeks for this. It was the most I ever worked in high school."

I swallow roughly at the admission. I know the story, of course. I almost didn't accept the gift when she gave it to me, since I knew how much a watch like this could cost—way more than a high school waitress could make in a small town. It wasn't until Remy told me how much it meant to Hailey to give me the gift that I made my peace with accepting it.

She's not looking at me—she's still lost in the memory of the watch. And I know if I give into the seriousness of this moment that I might admit something I'm not even ready to admit myself, so instead I try to lighten the situation with some humor.

"I remember the girl I was dating got pissed that she was shown up by a sixteen-year-old," I joke with a forced grin.

But it's enough to snap both of us out of the pensive moment because Hailey sighs and finally looks up from the watch.

"Yeah, well, Amanda was a bitch. She deserved to be outmatched by a teenager."

I let out a startled bark of laughter. Hailey grins at me, mischief shining in her eyes.

"So where are we going tonight?" she asks with a bounce. "Remy didn't say where the after party is. What's the plan?"

I look over at Remy, who is currently being accosted—

there's no other word for it—by Tristan. I had a feeling he wouldn't be able to keep his hands off her, but this is just ridiculous.

He's got his hands on her waist and his face buried in her neck, no doubt whispering filthy shit in her ear if the blush on her skin is any indication.

"Am I right in assuming it's going to be like this all night?" I ask dryly.

Remy's blush intensifies, but Tristan only pulls away from her skin with his trademark smirk. "Probably," he drawls. "Tonight might be a short night because I'm less interested in partying and more interested in bending my girlfriend over as soon as possible."

"Oh my God, *Tristan!*" Hailey shouts with a wince.

Tristan just grins before turning to look thoughtfully at Remy. "Huh, that's exactly what she likes to say. Less angry and more breathless, but the sentiment is the same."

At that, Remy finally steps into the conversation. Not with words, exactly, but with a punch to the shoulder.

"That's my sister, you *ass!*" she hisses.

Tristan just rubs his shoulder in mock pain. "What is it with you two punching me?" he grumbles. "I swear I'm in more pain after the fight than during."

Remy just shakes her head with a heavy sigh. "Let's keep it in our pants while others are around, shall we? You act like I've been depriving you for weeks."

The teasing smirk immediately returns to his face. "That may have been the plan, but we both know you couldn't say no to me if you tried."

I finally let out a loud groan. "Dear God, this is going to be the most painful night ever." I aim a glare at them. "Remind me to never hang out with the two of you again."

Remy and Tristan both just grin and step away from the bar. "Come on, let's go dance," Remy chirps. She grabs Hailey's hand and pulls her toward the exit.

"So, how does it feel?" I ask Tristan, settling back into the VIP lounge and taking a swig of my beer. The smile hasn't left my face all night, and right now, sitting in the club with my victorious teammate, I can tell that's not going to change anytime soon.

I watch him stretch out on the lounge across from me, looking every bit the comfortable and arrogant alpha. Sure enough, he aims a cocky smirk my way before he answers.

"Feels like I always knew it would," he replies honestly, taking a sip of the tequila in his hands. "It's going to get harder with each fight," he admits thoughtfully. "This was just the first one. And yeah, I know I wasn't supposed to win, but now that I have they're going to give me someone tougher next time. Tonight's the only night I'll have to relax and enjoy this feeling. Until the next win."

I nod, not wanting to sugarcoat the truth for him. "That's true. But each victory is going to be sweeter than the last, because each fight will be a bigger mountain than the last. Until you get that belt. Which, we all know you will, let's be honest."

He smiles his appreciation at me. And then he seems to actually look at me for the first time since he got the call for the fight. "What about you? Are you going to fight again?"

I wince, knowing Tristan well enough to know he's asking for a reason, and not just to make conversation. I also know that this is the opening I've been looking for to tell him how I've been feeling about everything.

I think about what Hailey said last week, then take a deep breath to answer the question.

"I think I'm done, man," I say quietly. "My head's not in it anymore. Especially seeing the world that you just stepped into... I don't think I can do it anymore. I don't think I *want* to."

And Tristan, despite all my worries, all my nervous reasons for not telling him about what was going on in my head... just nods.

"Okay."

I quirk an eyebrow. "Okay? That's it?"

He nods again. "What else is there? This isn't the kind of sport you can half-ass or push through if your head's not in it. If you're done, you're done."

I lean forward to brace my forearms on my knees, looking down at the drink in my hands instead of the meeting Tristan's eyes. "I feel like I'm giving up," I mumble.

He snorts. "The people that retire are the smart ones in this sport. We should all give up. This sport is fucking insane."

But then he sobers and locks my gaze onto his. "This isn't something you should be ashamed of," he says, knowing my thoughts in a way that only Tristan can. "Any reason is a good enough reason to quit this sport, even at the pro level. It's too hard, too dangerous, to do when you don't want to do it. No one but you would look at it like you're giving up."

I sigh and sit back in my seat, feeling like a weight is slowly starting to lift off my chest. Leave it to Tristan to lecture me in a matter-of-fact way that actually eases my nerves. "That's what Hailey said, too."

Tristan's stare doesn't waver. For a moment, he just studies me. Then, "She's a smart girl."

I nod, looking down at my drink, swirling in my glass. "She is," I murmur.

Tristan is quiet for another minute. When he speaks, his voice has almost gentled. "You seem like you still enjoy training and coaching, but lately it's felt like your priorities have changed. Like you're more interested in moving on from the young man's sport and settling down a little bit more. You like work, you like taking time off, you like being with your friends and family. That's enough for you now, isn't it? That's what you want to settle into?"

Finally, I look up to meet his eyes. He's nailed it, of course. I *do* want to settle down. Not with a house and kids kind of way, but in a life kind of way. I like the *idea* of settling, of being in a comfortable point in my life. Even at twenty-six, I feel like I've hit a point where I know what I want.

My only answer for Tristan is a nod.

And in the way that only men can communicate, he nods back.

"Then do that," he says simply.

I chuckle at the simplicity of his conclusion, even though

he's right. And suddenly—or maybe not so suddenly—I've made my decision to retire from MMA.

A peace settles over me. Between Hailey and Tristan, I feel like I've finally decided on something that I didn't realize was causing me a lot of stress the past few weeks.

I glance up to thank him but get distracted when I notice the glass in his hand for the first time. I frown in confusion. "Since when do you drink tequila? I thought you were a whiskey drinker."

A small smile tips the edges of his lips as he looks down onto the dancefloor. "It's a new thing," he murmurs, mostly to himself.

I follow his gaze, and of course, he's looking at Remy. She and Hailey are at the center of the dancefloor, shaking their hips and clearly having fun.

My attention inevitably drifts to Hailey. She's laughing at something Remy said, her skin glistening with sweat and her cheeks flushed pink from the alcohol and the heat. She has the body of a dancer and the moves to back it up—watching her dance is mesmerizing. I can't help staring as she raises her hands above her head, can't help following the line of her body as she sways…

As I'm watching, I see a guy sidle up to them with a smile.

The air becomes suddenly stifling as both Tristan and I immediately stiffen.

But he doesn't touch them or even get too close, and both girls continue to smile. I hear Remy let out a loud laugh. The guy seems pleased with her reaction, but it's Hailey that he leans down to whisper to. With a small smile, she just looks at him and nods. He grins and steps up behind her, putting his hands on her waist and pulling her against his body. They easily start to sway to the beat.

If I thought I was stiff before, it's nothing compared to how I'm feeling right now. My inner Neanderthal wants nothing more than to jump the VIP barrier and rip the guy's arms from his body for daring to even *ask* to touch her.

But, I'm not a Neanderthal. And I have no claim to Hailey. So I have no right to be upset about the fact that she accepted a dance from a good-looking guy. She's a beautiful girl, of course someone was going to ask her to dance. I should be grateful the guy actually asked and didn't just dance up on her like a lot of drunk assholes like to do.

Still, my rage continues to simmer below the surface. I've spent over a decade looking out for Hailey and I've seen way too many douchebags try to come onto her over the years. It's a natural reaction to want to protect her. Of course I want to rip him away from her.

I somehow manage to keep myself from jumping up and doing just that. I watch as the three of them dance together for a few minutes, Hailey's body moving easily against his, and Remy dancing by herself right in front of her. I should know Remy would never leave her sister unprotected—sometimes I wonder if she's more protective than even I am.

I tell myself that when, after the song ends, Remy leaves Hailey on the dancefloor and makes her way over to where we are. She's dramatically fanning herself when she plops down on the lounge next to Tristan. And I swear I hear him *growl* as he buries his face in her sweaty neck.

I can't actually see what they're doing because I haven't taken my eyes off of Hailey.

"Jax, she's fine," Remy says, and I can practically hear her rolling her eyes. "I wouldn't have left her if she wasn't. He was really nice and just wanted to dance with her."

"Yeah, I'm sure that's all he wants," I growl. When I turn to look at her, she really is rolling her eyes.

"She needs to reacquaint herself with acceptable and unacceptable male behavior. Steve has her so fucked up that she doesn't even know what's right anymore." She nods in the direction of where they're dancing. "He went about it the right way. He complimented her, asked without touching, and waited until she said yes before he did anything. Acceptable."

I sigh in defeat, knowing she's right. Hailey even said something to that effect before.

It's just harder than I anticipated letting *any* man around her again.

"She's not going home with a stranger in Vegas," I grunt, refusing to admit total defeat. It's not that I'm against women having one-night stands, I just don't like *her* doing it in a city where she doesn't know anyone or anything.

Remy rolls her eyes again and I wonder--not for the hundredth time--how they don't get stuck up there with how often she does it.

"Dude, it's *Hailey*. She doesn't do one-night-stands to begin with. Relax." She turns to look at her sister again, just in time to see her throw her head back and laugh at something the guy must've whispered in her ear.

My hackles literally rise.

"I think she just wanted to dance," Remy murmurs thoughtfully. "I think she misses dancing, even if she doesn't realize it." Her gaze hardens. "It's yet another thing that piece of shit talked her into quitting."

That's the thought that finally tames my rage. I know Hailey likes dancing, and I also know Remy's right: she misses it even if she doesn't realize it. And the last thing I want to be is another asshole that tells her what she can or can't do.

I sigh and turn back to Tristan and Remy. She's fully perched in his lap now, and his hands are wandering way too close to her hemline for my comfort.

"You two seriously need to get a room," I wince. "If I knew you'd be this disgusting with the PDA, I never would've approved this shit."

Even as Remy actually blushes, Tristan just sends me a wolfish grin. And now I'm the one rolling my eyes.

But Hailey picks that moment to break away from the guy on the dancefloor and make her way over to where we're sitting. She plops down on the cushion next to me with a contented sigh.

I resist the urge to pull her against me to stake my nonexistent claim on her for any other man to see. "Have fun dancing?" I force myself to ask instead.

She shines her typical megawatt smile at me and nods. "I forgot how much I enjoy it. We danced almost the entire night last week when we were out with Lucy."

Remy smiles at her little sister, even as she curls closer to Tristan. But in typical blunt Tristan fashion, he decides to push the topic a little further.

"Why don't you start dancing again?" he asks, his fingers still tracing patterns on his girlfriend's thigh. "Remy said you used to love it. Why'd you stop?"

When Hailey blushes and looks down at her lap, I aim a glare at his head. He just gives me a blank look like, *what?*

"I didn't have much time because of school," she finally admits. And while that's a partial truth, Remy and I know it's also a lie. Making her quit dancing was yet another tactic by Steve to alienate her from people and places she loved.

But then she looks out at the dancefloor. "I probably have more time now, though," she says thoughtfully. "Maybe I should pick it up again."

At this point I can't resist finally wrapping an arm around her. I pull her against my side, the tension in my body easing when she melts into me.

"You should do whatever makes you happy," I tell her simply. "Dancing, school, a new hobby, whatever it is, do it."

She looks around at our surroundings, from Remy sitting across from her down to the dancefloor where she was just enjoying herself.

Then she turns her attention back to me. "I'm happy now," she says softly, smiling up at me.

And *fuck* if that doesn't hit me in the gut.

Only an hour later, the four of us are walking through the hotel, already over the party scene.

Remy is ahead of me, Tristan's arm wrapped around her

like he can't bear to have even an inch of space between them. "Hailey, are you good staying with Jax tonight? I figured Tristan and I would take our room and you could stay with Jax." She has the decency to look sheepish. "Or I can just send Tristan back to his room and you and I can do a sleepover like old times. I don't really mind—"

Hailey just flaps her hand at Remy as if it's the most ridiculous non-issue she's ever heard. "I'm not staying with you when you're this hard up. You and Tristan can take the room and do whatever God-awful things you've been whispering about all night." She actually shivers at the thought. "I would really prefer if we split up right now and I didn't have to spend another second thinking any more about this conversation."

I chuckle and throw an arm around her shoulders. "I second that idea. Let's get the fuck away from them before they start making out again. We're on the other end of the floor and hopefully far enough away that we don't hear anything."

Tristan needs no further urging because the second the words are out of my mouth, he simply bends down to throw Remy over his shoulder and begins stalking down the hallway.

"Night, all," he shouts cheerfully over the sounds of Remy's protests.

I laugh again and steer Hailey in the opposite direction. When we get to the hotel room that Tristan and I shared this week, I gently nudge her into the recently cleaned room with a hand on her lower back.

"There's only one bed," she says with surprise.

I grunt an acknowledgement as I toss my phone and wallet on the nightstand. "Yeah, don't get Tristan started on it. They screwed up our rooms and everything was too booked to change anything." I aim a teasing grin at where she's standing by the foot of the bed. "It's a good thing I'm secure enough in our friendship to share a king-sized bed with him. Otherwise, things could've gotten a little weird."

She shakes her head, a small smile tugging at the corners of her lips.

I frown and look at the bed with a new perspective. I didn't think about the fact that having Hailey sleep here would mean she has to sleep *with* me, but now that she mentions it, I definitely should have. God knows I've shared a bed with Remy a thousand times in the past decade, but never with Hailey.

"Should I... take the couch?" I find myself asking. "I'm so used to sleeping with Tristan or Remy that I forgot it might be uncomfortable for you to share a bed. I'm sorry, I should've thought of that before we split rooms for the night." By the end of that thought, I come to a decision. I grab a pillow from the bed. "I'm going to sleep on the couch."

Hailey stops me before I can round the bed and settle on the—admittedly way too small—piece of furniture in the corner of the suite. "Don't be ridiculous, a single limb of yours wouldn't even fit on that thing, let alone your entire body. We'll share the bed, I'm totally fine. It just... caught me off guard." She smiles at me to dispel any remaining worries. "I am ready for bed, though. Are you tired? You've had a hell of a day, too."

I groan and drop onto the bed. "You can say that again. Do you want to shower first?"

She nods and immediately disappears into the bathroom. I strip off my shoes and button-up and chug a bunch of water while I wait for my turn in the shower. I'm messing around on my phone when I hear the bathroom door creak open.

"Jax?" her soft voice calls.

I look up to see her standing outside of the bathroom in only a towel.

And she's still wet.

Which means I'm looking at a rosy-cheeked Hailey, with her golden hair plastered to her shoulders, and droplets of water running down her skin until they're absorbed by the fluffy white towel wrapped around her.

My mouth goes dry, and I'm pretty sure there's no air in the room.

She either doesn't notice or ignores my shock. "Do you have a shirt I could wear? I just realized I don't have anything to change into."

"Uhh... yeah. Yeah, I can get you some clothes. Um—I" I snap to attention and start digging through my suitcase. I easily find a shirt to toss her but I lose focus when I see her shapely legs step up next to me.

"Um, I don't have any shorts to give you that aren't grappling shorts," I murmur. "I could give you boxers, but I don't know if that's what you're looking for... I could—"

"Just a shirt is fine, I don't sleep in pants anyway. Thanks, Jax." She spins around and walks back into the bathroom, leaving me standing there with a racing heart and slack jaw.

"Fuck," I breathe out.

Hailey will be sleeping a foot away from me in nothing but a T-shirt. My T-shirt.

Fuck.

I drag a hand down my face in frustration. This is not the same image of Hailey I've had for the past decade. That Hailey was innocent. Childlike.

Not this blonde bombshell who is entirely woman yet has no idea how appealing she is.

Fuck.

I shake my head in an effort to clear it of the inappropriate thoughts. I'm not sure if it works because I'm immediately thrown back to square one when Hailey walks out of the bathroom for the second time, this time wearing only my shirt.

My shirt.

It's so big on her that it almost reaches her knees, but she may as well be naked for how sexy she looks. She looks like every guy's wet dream.

I clench my jaw in an effort to keep it from dropping. I look down at my suitcase, trying to look anywhere but where I actually want to.

"Uh, I'm going to jump into the shower real quick. Make yourself comfortable." I practically bolt from the room.

"Fuck," I can't help but mutter as I step into the shower and let the water run over my exhausted body. *That seems to be the word of the evening.*

I groan and drag my hands down my face. What the fuck is wrong with me? It's not a surprise that she's beautiful. Why is she suddenly affecting me like this?

How does this keep happening?

And to make matters worse, my dick is hard as a rock. My brain is screaming at me to wrap my fist around it, to rub my hand over my length as I imagine that it's not my hand that's gripping it. Instead, it's actually a pair of rosy pink lips wrapped around it. And as they slide up and down my length, I brush away a few golden strands that have fallen to the front, until finally I just collect it all in my hand so I can hold firm and start fucking forward—

With an angry growl, I turn the hot water all the way off. I am *not* jerking off to the thought of my best friend's little sister, who is currently sleeping in my bed on the other side of the wall. Almost immediately, the shower transforms into an icy rainfall—one that, if not immediately, but eventually takes me from a panting bundle of live wires to an annoyed and frozen raisin. Irritating as fuck, but it worked.

I don't bother drying myself off, I just wrap a towel around my waist and yank the bathroom door open. Without chancing even a single look at Hailey—the last thing I need right now is a hard-on that I have zero shot of hiding under a towel—I walk over to my suitcase and pick out a pair of boxers to sleep in. I debate grabbing a shirt too, but then I think, *fuck it, she hates sleeping in pants, and I hate sleeping in shirts.*

It isn't until I've straightened up from my suitcase that I accidentally catch a glimpse of Hailey, where she's curled up against the headboard. It doesn't seem like she's even looked my way, that's how riveted she is by the phone in her hand. And if it wasn't for the pink flush running from the tip of her nose to her ears, I would even believe that she's not affected by me. But between that and the intensity with which she's trying *not* to look at me, I can tell she's just as flustered at the sight of my half-naked body.

Thank God. I guess I'm not the only one suddenly thrown off by this situation.

I brush my teeth and finish getting ready for bed, and then I walk around the room, turning all the lights off. When I finally pull back the covers on the bed, Hailey's already snuggled deep under the comforter.

Neither of us says anything. We don't even look at our phones, we just lie quietly on opposite ends, trying to calm our breathing and ignore the tension that's very clearly lingering in the air.

Hailey's soft voice sounds in the quiet. "Goodnight, Jax."

And *fuck*, my name on her lips.

"Goodnight, Hailey," I manage to choke out.

Despite the long day, I know I'm getting no sleep tonight.

CHAPTER SIXTEEN
Hailey

WHEN I WAKE up it's still dark outside, clearly the middle of the night. I'm confused about what woke me until I feel an arm tighten around my waist.

My brow furrows in confusion at the foreign sensation. While I've never been huge on physical affection, I've always craved the feeling of being held when I sleep, wanting to feel loved and protected in my most vulnerable space.

I haven't felt that way in a very long time.

Right now, I feel warm, and safe, and so comfortable I almost drift back to sleep. But then the grip tightens again, pulling me farther backwards into a hard chest.

And a very obvious erection.

I smother the whimper that automatically tries to sound at the feel of Jax pressed against me. I can't stop myself from circling my hips once, just to feel it.

And choke on my groan when I realize how big it is.

I peek over my shoulder to see Jax's face buried in my neck. He looks peaceful—nothing like how he looked when we went to bed a few hours ago. Then he looked stressed and uneasy.

He couldn't have been farther from me on the bed when we lay down. If what happened at the gym last week was any indication, he's been trying really hard not to crowd me or make me feel uncomfortable.

What he doesn't seem to understand is that he makes me feel the opposite of uncomfortable. He makes me feel safe. *Wanted.*

I know him. I know his expressions and his mannerisms and his moods. I know when he feels guilty.

I know when he's being protective.

And last night, he was trying to protect me from himself. He *liked* seeing me in a towel, soaking wet and standing before him. Grateful for his T-shirt. He liked *me.*

But in the same way that he's been pushing me away the past few weeks, he also erected those walls between us last night. For some reason, he doesn't want to act on this heat that's building between us. Whether it's because of Remy, or Steve, or the fact that our friendship started when I was a lot younger than him, he's been stopping himself from letting go.

And I'm tired of it.

This attraction between us isn't something we can just ignore. Nor do I want to. Over the past few weeks, it's only grown, starting with our friendship that has always been rock-solid, and then blossoming with the gradual physical attraction between two people who never let themselves look at the other in this way before. I never allowed myself to want him again after my schoolgirl crush.

But now... he wants me too.

I see it in his eyes, in the way he appreciates my newfound

style and growing confidence. In the way his breath catches when we're too close together.

I don't want to fight this pull between us anymore. I want to push him, to make him break and acknowledge this new fire. Even if it's just sex, I want to explore this heat with the man I trust more than anyone else in the world.

So I do.

I back into Jax's embrace, flattening myself against his muscular chest and shamelessly wriggling against his lengthening erection, fighting a moan. All I can think about is how right this feels, how badly I want him inside me...

The arm that's slung over my hips bands across my stomach and pulls me even closer. A hum of contentment sounds in my ear where his face is still buried in my neck. And at the feel of his breath along my skin, a full-body shiver runs through my body.

I couldn't stop myself from pressing my ass against him even if I wanted to. My hips automatically begin to move in a circle, and I start to feel wetness gather between my legs from just the feel of Jax at my back.

A choked whimper escapes my lips.

I can't tell if the sound of it begins to wake Jax from his sleep, but a groan rumbles through his chest just as his other arm snakes under my shoulder. It wraps around my chest just as his other hand slips under the hem of my shirt that's already riding too high.

I freeze at the feel of his hand so close to my breasts. And when I suck in a deep breath, my chest expanding with the movement, I actually moan when his hand brushes my nipple.

His hands are large enough they can envelop my breast fully, and I can't help squirming against him and looking for the contact again.

And like two magnets being drawn to each other, Jax seems to subconsciously look for the physical contact, too. He murmurs something in my hair as one hand cups my breast and the other slides underneath my shirt to gently stroke my stomach.

I think I hear him say my name, but I'm not entirely sure because in that moment, his hips rock forward. I gasp at the feeling of his length pressed against me, and instinctually push back against him.

"Baby girl," he mumbles sleepily, his face nuzzling into my neck at the same time that his hips rock forward again.

I let out a whimper as the lust ratchets to suffocating levels. I know Jax feels it too because he immediately groans and reaches down to grip my hip so he can grind into me again.

"Fuck," he moans into my ear.

I have no idea if he's awake. I have no idea if he knows it's me, or if he even knows what he's doing right now. But I'm breathing so hard, trying desperately to get air in my lungs when it feels like there's none in the room, that the questions don't even register. All I know is this burning need to *take, take, take.*

I can't help it when, in a breathy voice, I gasp, "Jax."

His hips pause in their roll. Then I hear a sleepy, "Hailey?"

I suck in a breath because I know this is the moment this becomes real. He's either going to give in or push me away.

And even though I wished so badly for him to embrace

this fire between us, I'm not really surprised when he scrambles away from me with a curse.

"Fuck, Hailey, I'm sorry. I didn't know—I didn't mean—"

I swallow my sigh and turn over on the bed to face him, the lust cooling as if a bucket of ice water was thrown on us. He's sitting up, eyes ready to pop out of his head, and he's breathing heavily as he visibly begs my forgiveness with his eyes. I have to remind myself to focus on his face and not his body, because the sight of a shirtless Jax is way more distracting than I'm prepared for while in this state of mind.

"Jax, it's okay—" I start.

"No, it's not," he panics, standing from the bed. "It's not okay. Fuck, I never should've let this happen, I should've just given you the room..."

I push myself to a sitting position as he starts to pace the room. He's truly freaking out right now, delirious from being woken up and panicking from the severity of whatever was happening between us.

"Jax, you have to relax," I try to soothe him. "Nothing even happened, there's nothing to freak out about. Just lay down and we'll go to sleep."

He stops in his pacing and stares, open-mouthed. "Lay down? I can't get in that bed with you again! Not when all I want is to—" He cuts himself off, his throat bobbing as he seems to swallow his words. But it's not hard to guess what he was going to say because his eyes darken as they glance over my body, pausing on my hardened nipples that are visible through his shirt.

"Jax, please," I beg. "Just come back to bed, we'll forget

about the whole thing. Please don't shut down on me."

He just stares at me for another moment before breathing a quiet, "I can't." His eyes glaze over, his attention shifting back to my face and showing me the depth of his struggle. "I just can't."

I watch as he grabs a pillow from the bed and settles on the tiny couch without another word.

I try not to let the sting of rejection bother me. I know he's not doing this because he doesn't want me—he just thinks this is the right thing to do. So with a heavy sigh, I lie down and try to fall back asleep.

We're both quiet in the morning. Other than a mumbled *good morning*, Jax doesn't make eye contact with me while we pack up the room. I get a text from Remy that they're coming to the room to help grab all the guys' stuff, so an hour after waking up to an awkward Jax, I'm opening the door to a very happy Remy and an equally happy Tristan standing behind her.

"Morning," my sister chirps as she flounces into the room. "How'd you two sleep?" She freezes when she sees the bed situation. "There's only one bed?"

"Don't even get me fucking started," Tristan growls as he walks in. "If I had more energy when we checked in, I would've raised hell with the front desk for not getting us two beds like I asked. Last thing I wanted was to deal with on the night before a fight was Jax trying to spoon me."

Remy giggles. "He does get a little touchy when he sleeps."

Tristan glares at her, and I'm honestly waiting for an actual growl to sound from him. But Remy just rolls her eyes and slaps his chest. "Relax, ever since I punched him in the face that one time, he won't even come near me, even in his sleep. Mission accomplished. You could easily do the same." Her eyes flash with mischief as a grin slides across her face. "Has he tried to spoon you? Because that could be pretty hot."

This time, a growl *does* rumble through Tristan's chest. "I thought I fucked the attitude out of you last night. Guess I have to try a little harder next time."

"Can we not do this first thing in the morning?" Jax snaps.

Everyone's attention shifts to him in surprise. There's no way to hide the fact that he looks exhausted, and currently incredibly frustrated with what's going on. Jax might tease annoyance sometimes, but it's rare to ever see him legitimately irritated like this over something so trivial.

Remy frowns when she notices the same things I just did. She glances at me and asks, "How'd you two do last night?"

"Fine." I somehow manage not to squeak my answer. I don't know if she senses the lie but she looks back at Jax with the same question.

"I'm fine, I just hate Vegas," he grumbles. "Can we get out of here? Even the smell makes me nauseous." He capitalizes on his comment by throwing the last of his clothes in his suitcase.

He goes to reach for Tristan's clothes too, but Tristan darts forward to snatch them from his hand. "Alright, Jesus. Just calm down. It'll take me ten minutes to pack everything." He glares at his friend. "You know, you're going to have to figure out how to make your peace with Vegas if I'm going to be fighting in the UFC. This is where the fights will be more often than not."

"Hey, I held my shit together," Jax defends himself. "At least until last night." His eyes dart to me and away so quickly that even I almost miss the automatic gesture.

It doesn't take long for us to pack up the rest of the room. We take two taxis to the airport, and I'm immediately thankful for the short trip because Jax stays silent through all of it. Thank God we're not on the same flight because I would probably burst from the awkwardness hanging so heavy between us.

The four of us spend the morning together at the airport, Tristan and Remy doing most of the talking and laughing while we eat lunch. Jax's silence is just as unusual as it was this morning, but mine is normal, so no one really says anything. Remy and I have a flight about an hour before the boys do, so when we finally leave them in the seating area, it's with the expectation that we'll meet them back in Philly.

"Everything good?" Remy asks with a skeptical brow raise as we settle into our seats.

"Fine," I answer simply. "Just tired. I think Jax is right, Vegas isn't great."

She chuckles. "No it's not," she agrees, closing her eyes as she drops her head back. Within minutes, she's sleeping, and I'm left alone with the chaos in my head.

I'm stuck in my thoughts for the entire trip home—through the layover, the connecting flight, the Uber ride back to Remy's apartment, all of it. I'm lost in thoughts of not only last night, but also of the past few weeks.

I don't even mean the breakup—that feels like it happened

months ago. I haven't felt any of the sadness that I would've assumed I'd feel, haven't felt lost or like I've made the wrong decision. I've actually felt the opposite. In only two weeks, I've felt my confidence coming back, and I've started to do things that make me happy... I've basically started to settle back into my true self.

And it's all because of Jax.

We may have been able to deny it in the beginning, may have been able to call it natural tension when we were first adjusting to both of us being single in the city for the first time, but this feeling between us is only getting deeper. It feels like lust, but also like something heavier. And I know he's fighting it—because of Remy and our friendship and maybe even my recent breakup—but all of those reasons are sounding but more and more flimsy.

Even before last night, this tension has started to feel suffocating. I've always thought Jax was the hottest alpha male I'd ever met, but it's more than that. He's kind, and funny, and he wears his heart on his sleeve for the world to see. He's also the best man I know. How could I *not* care for him? In a simpler way, it was the whole reason I had a crush on him when I was a kid: because even as a teenager, he had the best heart of anyone I knew. So if, years later, he's finally starting to take notice of me as a woman, how could I not want to pursue him?

I can't regret coming onto him last night, even if the situation started accidentally. I *wanted* him to make a move, to touch me. I wished, for the first time since I was too young to understand my own desire, that he wanted me back. Not because I want to start a serious relationship or because I think he's my soulmate, but because he's one of my best friends and I want to explore this new connection.

I'm not sure how hard I want to push him on it, though. Last night is just further proof that he feels too many reasons not to give into it, and as much as I want to be an independent woman and take what I want, I also don't want to make him do something he'll regret.

When we get back to Remy's apartment it's late enough that Sunday is over, but not quite late enough to go to bed. I unpack my clothes and try to do a little bit of homework, but I don't get very far because my brain is lost in thoughts of last night—of Jax shirtless, of the feel of his skin against mine, of the feel of his length pushed against me...

I slam my computer closed. Just as I'm standing at the tipping point of my decision, I hear keys in the front door, and the appearance of Tristan standing in the doorway when it swings open is enough to decide for me. Without giving myself a chance to second guess myself, I grab my keys and call out, "Remy, I'm going out. Don't wait up."

Tristan looks like he wants to say something, but he must see something in my eyes because instead, he stands aside as I blow past.

One way or another, Jax and I are getting rid of this goddamn tension.

CHAPTER SEVENTEEN
Jax

I CAN'T STOP myself from slamming the front door behind me when I finally get back to the house. I drag my hands down my face with a muttered, "Fuck."

Then, a little stronger... "*Fuck.*"

How the fuck did this new Hailey fascination get so out of control? I've known her for ten years, and now all of a sudden, I can't stop fantasizing about having her under me. And what's worse, I keep somehow saying and doing things that are making these new feelings obvious. I know Hailey notices, because I see her body reacting. I know she's turned on, and as much as it's flattering that she finds me attractive, it just makes me feel guiltier that I'm putting her in these situations.

And whether or not she would want to act on it is irrelevant, because I shouldn't even be giving her the choice. I'm her friend, for God's sake—I should be acting like a friend, not salivating over her like a horny teenager. I'm sick of taking ice cold showers to get rid of the hard-ons that I shouldn't be feeling for my best friend's little sister.

I drag my hands down my face again with a frustrated

growl. I need a fucking drink.

I stalk over to the kitchen and rip open the fridge for a beer. For once, I grab one of Tristan's disgusting IPA's, needing the added alcohol content. I chug half of it, trying not to breathe through my nose so I can ignore the weird sour taste. I'm panting when I finally slam it down on the kitchen island.

Okay, chill the fuck out. Some shit happened last night, but it's not the end of the world. You didn't do it on purpose, for fuck's sake, you were sleeping. You've got bigger problems right now anyway. For example, how to get the girl out of your sex-addled brain.

"Fuck," I mutter to myself again. That's all I have to describe the culmination of the day's insanity. Just... *fuck.*

Suddenly, a knock sounds on the front door, making me frown in confusion. *Who shows up without calling that they're coming over?*

I walk through the living room to the front door, pausing to check the peephole before I open it. My frown only deepens when I see who's outside.

"Hailey?" I ask in confusion when I open the door. At some point, it started raining, because she's standing, drenched, on my doorstep. Her blonde hair is plastered to her cheeks and neck, and her blue eyes look unusually bright. She's also breathing heavily. In a way, she looks as crazy as I feel right now.

"Jesus Christ," I gasp in shock. "Come inside, you're soaked. What're you doing here?" I usher her through the doorway and reach to peel her drenched jacket off her shoulders.

Which immediately turns out to be a mistake because she's only wearing a tank top underneath, and now I'm distracted by her nipples that have pebbled in the cold.

She ignores the fact that my attention has wandered and pushes past me into the house.

"You feel it too," she states simply. "I know you feel it. It's not just me."

I force myself to look away from her. I close the door and ask distractedly, "What're you talking about?"

She closes the distance between us in two determined strides. I turn toward her and suck in a startled breath at the look on her face. She still looks wild, but also determined, and so fucking beautiful.

"Hailey…" I breathe. My heart is pounding out of my chest. I have no idea what's happening right now.

Her gaze on me sharpens, and she takes another step closer. By now, both my breathing and my heartrate are out of control.

I watch as her demeanor visibly calms before me, as if whatever she sees on my face is enough to tame the wildness she was feeling. "I know you feel it too," she repeats quietly. "Tell me how you felt when I almost kissed you at the bar."

Shit.

I can't tell her the truth. This can't happen, we can't let this happen.

"I—I don't know what you're talking about," I force out. I'm practically panting now, pleading with my eyes, begging her not to push me. I already feel guilty, and nothing's even happened. I'm way too close to losing my mind right now, my panic spiraling further.

Her blue eyes remain calm, serene. She knows exactly what she's doing to me right now, and she's not going to stop without an answer.

"I wanted to kiss you so bad," she whispers, making me suck in a breath at her admission. "I want to kiss you right now too." Her eyes trail over my face before locking our gazes again. In her eyes, in this moment, I see pure fire. I see a passion I've never seen in Hailey before, and it's enough to set me trembling with want—even as I try to harden my resolve to not give in. "And then I want to do other things—things I never thought about doing with you. Until now. Now, I can't seem to think about anything else."

I squeeze my eyes shut, like if I can't see her, then she won't be as much of a temptation.

But it doesn't help. Now, all I can focus on is her sweet feminine scent and the heat of her skin next to mine.

I had a feeling she was experiencing the same emotions I was, but I never thought she would be the one to make the first move. And hearing her say it out loud means I actually have a choice to make.

I sense, more than feel, her take another step closer to me. When I still don't respond, she places her hands on my chest and whispers, "Why are you fighting this?"

I open my eyes so I can level an accusatory look at her. "Because you're Remy's—"

"I love my sister, but she doesn't get to say who I can and can't be with," she interrupts, and I hear the conviction in her words. "I've had enough of people trying to dictate my life."

Now my gaze turns pleading. "Hailey, you're like a little sister—"

"Don't," she cuts me off again. Only now she's angry. "You

don't get to do that. You don't get to use that as a cop-out, because you know that's not true. *Remy* may feel like a sister to you, but I've always been something different. You know that. So don't you dare try to lie to yourself about that."

A muffled sound of pain whooshes out of my chest. I'm hanging on by a thread here, and I am one reason away from surrendering completely and giving her everything she wants because fuck knows I want it too.

I feel an intense urge to cup her face and pull her to me but that would draw me further in, so instead I place my hands on her shoulders and gently run them up and down her arms. When I brush her wet hair over her shoulder, a shiver runs through her.

"Hailey, I care about you," I mumble. "If this hurts our friendship, or if, God forbid, I accidentally hurt you, I would never forgive myself. I don't—"

She slides her hands from my chest to the sides of my face, gently cupping my face the same way I crave to do with hers.

"You could never hurt me," she whispers, tenderly brushing my cheeks with her thumbs. "I know you. And it's *because* I know you that I want this. I trust you, I care about you, and I know you feel this spark between us. And I want it. Whatever it is. I want *you*."

She stares at me with such trust, such longing, that I feel the last shred of my resolve crumble. In this moment, I decide I'll give this girl whatever the fuck she wants: my body, my heart, the moon, the stars, anything. It's hers.

There's not enough air in my lungs to breathe. She wants an answer, but I can't even formulate a thought, let alone words.

I'm too far gone in this girl's eyes to do anything but stare at her in wonder.

After a few moments where I still haven't said anything, Hailey stiffens and looks away, annoyance and hurt flashing across her face. The sight of it is enough to shake me out of my stupor, but before I can say anything, she straightens her spine and lifts her gaze to mine again. "But I'm not interested in convincing anyone to want me back, so if I have to push for this, then let's just forget it." She starts to turn away.

I grab her arm before she can walk away from me.

"Don't," I growl.

I hear her sharp intake of breath as she turns back to me. Her eyes widen, the pain in them disintegrating to reveal her tentative hope.

I step forward to do what I've been dying to do since that night at the bar. I cup her face, my fingers tangling in her wet hair, and I fucking *revel* in the feeling of finally touching her like this. My breath catches in my lungs at the look on her face, at the hunger. For *me*.

I don't rush into kissing her. I just hold her, trying with everything in me to memorize this moment, memorize how she looks. My gaze drops down to her pink, plush lips, and then I'm lost.

The second her lips touch mine, I feel an electric charge run between us, restarting my heart and making it beat just for her. I devour her, claim her as mine. My lips part on a groan.

When our tongues touch, I feel Hailey whimper and fist her hands in my shirt. *Fuck*, she's so much smaller than me, so fragile. I want to tuck her against my chest and protect her so no one can ever hurt her again.

But Hailey doesn't kiss like she's fragile. She meets my aggression with her own brand of fire, tightly pressing her body against mine and tugging down on my shirt so she can better reach my mouth. Her tongue spars with mine, her moans getting louder. Hearing them come from *Hailey* is enough to set my heart racing. And when she takes my bottom lip between her teeth and bites down, the act pulls a tortured groan from my throat.

That bite is the reason I force myself to pause for a moment. Before I take this too far too quickly.

I pull back, leaving my hands in her hair and my forehead resting against hers. We're both breathing heavily, both vibrating with the urgency to keep going.

I try to sort through my jumbled mess of thoughts that Hailey's kiss just completely obliterated. I have no resolve left to fight against this, nor do I want to, but something is nagging at the back of my mind to make sure Hailey knows this isn't just sex. It can't be. It's *Hailey.*

I take a shaky breath and force myself to say, "If we do this, I'm not just going to fuck you, Hailey. You can't just be a girl in my bed. I'm not saying you have to call me your boyfriend, but this has to be exclusive. I care about you too much not to value our friendship and treat you with respect."

She nods quickly, eager for more.

But then she glances away. She opens her mouth to say something, but it takes another try before any sound comes out.

"Okay," she whispers hesitantly. "I want that too. But— umm, I also want..."

I know exactly what she wants. It's the same fantasy I haven't been able to get out of my head since that day at the gym I offered to put her on her knees.

I straighten and pull my fingers out of her hair, gently brushing the wet strands over her shoulder to lie along her back. I straighten her shirt too, smoothing it down her waist. I give her an opportunity to take her fantasy by the reins and own it. To say it out loud.

But she doesn't seem to be ready for that yet. She stays quiet, too shy about her request to actually vocalize it.

I give her one more chance to admit her desires. When my adjustments are complete, I lightly grip her chin between my fingers and lean down to place a sweet kiss against her lips. "Hailey, I'll give you whatever you want. Just ask. You don't ever have to hide from me."

Her breath catches, and her eyes go wide. "I want you to show me, like you said you would…"

Her answer causes a pleased sound to rumble through my chest, and a shiver to run through Hailey. "Upstairs," I growl hungrily.

If possible, her eyes go even wider. But then she turns and hurries up the stairs without any hesitation.

A part of me feels like I should feel guilty for what I'm about to do, but the large majority of me is too enamored, too hungry for her, and too weak not to give in to this heat between us. The past few weeks have shown me a Hailey I've never known before, and I don't think I could stop myself from pursuing her even if I wanted to.

I'll deal with the possible fallout later.

I bolt after her up the stairs and reach my room at the same time she does, so I slam the door behind us and push her up against it. I swallow her gasp with a kiss.

We fall onto each other like we're starved. Starved for each other's touch, our tastes, the feel of our hands grabbing at each other as we try to decide what piece of clothing we'll rip off the other first. She somehow manages to rid me of my shirt, but the time it takes is too much time spent apart because as soon as my T-shirt is pulled over my head, Hailey's right back to being plastered against me, panting against my mouth and nipping at my lips.

The feeling is mutual. No matter how close I pull her, how long I kiss her, I still can't get enough. It's like our years of friendship have been building this fever between us and we didn't even realize it. And now that we've given into it, everything's about to explode.

I finally force myself to pull back from her, but only so far as to lean my forehead against hers. We're both panting, both still gripping each other with desperate hands. She looks up at me, the same hunger, same *trust* shining in her eyes as was downstairs.

Chest heaving, I brush the back of my knuckles against her soft, ivory cheek. "Sure you want to do this?" I murmur.

She's nodding before I even finish the question.

"Yes," she breathes. But she must see the last strands of my hesitation because in addition to her words, she also shows me with her actions.

She drops to her knees in front of me.

"Fuck," I gasp before I can stop the word from slipping out.

As much as I've fantasized about Hailey like this the past few weeks, the sight is a thousand times better than I ever thought it would be. Not only is she looking every bit like the obedient partner that I love in the bedroom, but she also looks absolutely breathtaking on her knees. Lust darkens her gaze, and I almost groan when she glances at my pants and licks her lips.

She immediately reaches for my jeans, popping open the button and carefully sliding the zipper down. Just that action is enough to make me start panting. She only pauses for a moment, shooting me a hesitant glance, but then the apprehension is gone, and she's reaching inside my boxer briefs.

This time I can't stop the groan that pours out of me when her hand wraps around my cock. Slowly, and still a bit hesitant, she starts to pump her fist along my length. The pleasure of just that minimal touch has me weakening, and I catch myself with my hands on the door as I fall forward.

Triumph sparkles in her eyes at my reaction, her lip quirking into a smug smile, and then her grip tightens. But when she starts to lean forward to take me in her mouth, and before I can think to stop it, I automatically revert to my dominant side that comes out when a woman is on her knees before me. I grip her hair and pull her head back. She gasps at my forceful action, and for a second, I regret being so aggressive with her. But then I notice she's squirming on her knees and pressing her thighs together.

"Not yet, baby. Use your hands," I say in a rough voice. I loosen my grip on her hair and instead run my fingers through the strands, purposefully offering contrasting sensations.

She lets out a little whimper at my words and slowly starts to pump her hand again. It's only a few seconds before I'm holding back my groan from the pleasure sparking through my body.

I nudge my hips forward, almost far enough to touch her lips. "Suck," I command gruffly.

She keeps her eyes on me as she leans forward and takes the head of my cock in her mouth. I feel her tongue swirl around my shaft right before her cheeks hollow out and she sucks hard.

"Fuck, baby," I groan. My hand drifts to hold the back of her head, and I have to fight to keep my eyes open, so I don't miss a single second of Hailey starting to work more of me into her mouth. She feels like fucking heaven. All I want to do is sink my entire length into her throat.

My dick is big enough that soon she begins to struggle. When I reach the back of her throat, she gags and puts her hands on my thighs, but before I can ease up on her, she grabs the base of my shaft and goes right back to working me with her hands.

I swallow the temptation to let her bob up and down my length until I come from the sheer pleasure of her silk tongue. Instead, I let the part of me out that she's been flirting with ever since that night at the darts board.

I tighten my grip on the back of her head and slowly start to thrust into her mouth. I hit the back of her throat and she gags again, but still, I don't stop.

"Look at me," I growl. Her eyes snap up to meet mine. I push a little deeper into her mouth, and this time, she doesn't gag. *Good girl.* "I want you to take all of me. I want every inch of my cock buried in your throat."

My words must set her off because she moans and immediately reaches forward to claw my thighs and pull me deeper into her. *Fuck.*

I push even deeper. Let myself be a little rougher. Another inch in, and her eyes start watering, though she completely ignores the tears now rolling down her cheeks.

I take the opportunity to look at the rest of her. My gaze travels over her pink cheeks, down to the hair stuck to her neck, and then settles on her breasts, which I can see through her wet, thin tank top. My dick hardens even further at the thought of cupping her perfect breasts and rubbing my thumbs over her pebbled nipples until she's squirming in my hands.

My attention snaps back to Hailey's mouth when she hits a particularly deep stroke. "Good girl," I murmur, holding her head in place and fully fucking her mouth at this point. The tears continue to roll down her cheeks.

Her nose finally reaches my stomach as the last of me sinks into her throat. She goes to pull back, but I stop her with the hand on the back of her head.

"Take it," I growl. "Take every inch." She's squirming, but she stops trying to pull away. I feel her muscles relax as she accepts me completely.

"Fuck, that's so pretty," I murmur. I hold myself there for another second, then ease out from between her lips when I start to seriously worry I'm going to come from the sight. I damn near lose my mind when I see a strand of saliva stretching from the tip of my dick to Hailey's pink, swollen lips.

I growl and reach under her arms to jerk her up to her feet

and press her against the door again with my body. I grip her hips and swallow her gasp, kissing her with a ferocity that I'm physically aching with in her presence.

"You're fucking perfect," I whisper against her lips.

Grabbing under her thighs, I lift her up so she can wrap her legs around my waist. I don't stop kissing her the entire way over to my bed. When I finally tear my lips from hers and lay her down, she's breathless and wriggling against my dick. I groan at the feeling of her being so turned on and responsive.

"I'm going to devour you," I tell her with a growl, unable to stop myself from kissing her again.

I'm wedged between her thighs, holding my weight on my forearms and trying to remind myself that I shouldn't just shred Hailey's clothes from her body and push inside her as quickly as humanly possible. I need to take my time and make this exactly the kind of night that she's been silently begging me for.

I finally rip my lips away from hers and begin trailing them along her chin and down her neck. When I reach the fabric of her tank top, I tease my tongue under the hem and smile when I feel Hailey shiver.

I pull away slightly so I can look down at her. She's breathing heavily and her skin has the most beautiful pink flush. Her eyes are black with lust as she looks up at me with the kind of trusting eyes that only Hailey ever looks at me with—like she's put all of her faith in me.

The only thing that matters is the gorgeous girl lying underneath me, trusting me to give her pleasure she's only ever fantasized about and waiting for me to do it. A growl rumbles through me in male satisfaction that I'm the one she wants.

I lean down to lick and nibble along her neckline. "What makes you come the hardest, baby girl?" I murmur, even as my hands start to inch under her shirt.

"Umm, I'm not sure," she mutters breathlessly. Her eyes close, and she starts panting as my mouth slides farther down to latch onto her nipple through the fabric. "Oral? I only ever really come from oral."

I bite her pebbled nipple through her tank top, grinning when she gasps and arches off the bed. "When was the last time you had more than one orgasm during sex?" When she doesn't answer—just continues to arch for more—I bite the curve of her breast and growl, "Hailey. Answer the question."

She gasps, and her eyes shoot open. "Never. I'm lucky if I come once."

With my suspicions confirmed, and without another word, I grip the bottom of Hailey's shirt and pull it up over her head. And I groan when I see the entirety of her porcelain skin and perfect pink nipples. I can't stop myself from dropping down and devouring the rosy tips. I need to touch them, taste them, bite them.

She arches even harder when I roll one tip between my teeth. I alternate between sucking and biting, worrying the bud until they're pink and swollen from my ministrations. Only then do I switch to the other one.

"Jax," she finally gasps. Her nails dig into my shoulders, and it feels like she can't decide if she wants to push me away or pull me closer. "Jax—yes, I—oh *God*—"

Her words fade into a moan when I pinch one nipple as I

suck the other into my mouth. "I know what you need, baby girl," I say with a kiss to the curve of her breast. "And I'm going to give it to you." I kiss my way down her stomach until my tongue is once again trailing under the fabric of her clothes. I hear her breath hitch at the tease. I quickly undo the buttons of her jeans, then tug on the sides. "Lift up for me."

She lifts her hips, and I swiftly pull her pants and underwear off in one motion. When I go to settle between her thighs again, I realize she's snapped her knees together and now has a hesitant look on her face. Like she's just realized how exposed she is.

It's enough for me to pause the grand plans I have for her body and instead crawl up the length of her and press a gentle kiss against her lips. I take my time kissing her, waiting until she relaxes and opens her mouth to me before I end it.

"You're perfect," I whisper against her lips. "You're so fucking beautiful. Don't ever doubt that your beauty absolutely ruins me. It always has."

A shaky breath sounds between her lips as she nods. I kiss her again, letting her feel the truth in my words.

I continue to kiss her, even as my hand drifts down her skin to her waist, and then across her stomach. I feel her breath hitch when my fingers travel farther.

"Let me make you feel good," I murmur. "Let me show you how it feels when a man would die if he couldn't have you." I punctuate my words by letting my fingers lightly graze her clit.

A shudder runs through her at my touch. And I hear her gasp, "*Yes.*"

I let my fingers slip even farther. I circle her entrance,

teasing her by keeping everything light and not giving her the touch that I know she's aching for.

"Jax," she whimpers. And at the sound, I know I've broken through her final wall of insecurity.

I nudge her legs open so I can settle between them on my stomach. I think I'm trembling, finally seeing her in this way that I haven't even allowed myself to think about. My arms wrap under and around her thighs, my head only inches from her beautifully glistening pussy. When I inhale deeply, my senses are overwhelmed with the intoxicating, *womanly* scent of her.

I look up to see Hailey biting her lip, her eyes blazing with hunger and excitement. I smile and tell her, "I've been dreaming about what you taste like, baby girl."

And then I drop my head and *eat*.

The second my lips touch her clit, the sexiest moan I've ever heard leaves her lips, right as she arches hard against my mouth. The sight and feel of her craving me so intensely is enough to make me groan and dive even deeper.

I can't get enough of her taste, her smell, her feel. My tongue dips from her clit to her entrance, and I thrust inside so I can drink straight from the well. She tastes like fucking nirvana.

My dick is even harder than it was while Hailey was on her knees before me, and my hips automatically want to start grinding on the bed for some relief. But I'll be damned if I come anywhere except on or in Hailey, so I slide my tongue back to her clit and slip two fingers where my tongue just was.

Hailey's moans turn to whimpers at the feeling of my

fingers pushing inside her. She reaches down to grip my hair as her hips start moving even more.

"Fuck yes," I growl against her skin. I can't take my eyes off of her—off of her pure *need* for me. "Ride my face, baby, take what you want."

She moans and starts to do just that. I let her hold my head where she wants me, continuing my finger's thrusts inside her even as she uses my mouth so unashamedly. *Fuck,* I might come from just the sight of her like this.

"Jax," she whimpers, and I see a little bit of awe, mixed with a little bit of fear in her eyes. Her hips stop rolling, and she starts to slightly pull away. "I—I can't, it's t-too much..."

"Fuck that," I growl, increasing the intensity of my fingers. I suck her clit into my mouth and suck hard, determined to *pull* the orgasm from her body if I need to.

I wrap an arm under her thigh so I can drop it across her stomach and hold her in place as I double down on my mission to pull a God-seeing orgasm from this beautiful, deprived creature in front of me. And when I finally curl my fingers inside her, I do just that.

Hailey *screams* at the force of it. I watch, completely enraptured, as her face crumples at the sheer waves of ecstasy rolling through her—as she finally succumbs to the feelings she's been fighting. And just when I think the sight couldn't get any better, I feel a gush of liquid hit my lower lip.

When the sensations finally abate, her exhausted body drops, limp, back onto the bed. Her eyes, which had closed from the force of it, finally blink open slowly. I'm drenched, and grinning wildly, when her gaze finally settles on me. Her brow furrows in confusion.

"If you tell me you never knew you could squirt, I can tell you right now I am never going to want to leave this spot between your legs again," I say as my fingers lightly graze her clit.

She flinches from the oversensitive bundle being touched. But then her eyes go wide as she registers my words. "I—what? I did not!"

I push onto my hands so I can crawl up her body. Once I'm braced over her, I make her watch as I lick my glossy lips. She actually moans from the sight.

And that's even before I do it again, this time licking her taste off my fingers before rubbing them across her lips.

"Taste yourself," I growl. "Taste how eager you are for my tongue, my fingers, my cock. I've never seen or tasted anything so beautiful."

"Oh my God," she whispers.

Then she sucks my fingers into her mouth.

At the feeling of her mouth's suction, I'm reminded of how it felt to be in her mouth. Which immediately makes me desperate to be inside her again.

"I need to fuck you," I tell her. "It feels like I'll die if I don't get inside you right now." I lean over her to reach for the condoms in my nightstand, but I don't get very far because Hailey wraps her arms around my waist and pulls me back.

"No," she breathes. "No condom. I just got tested, and I'm clean, and I'm on the pill. Are you?"

"On the pill? No." She giggles at my stupid joke and tucks her face against my neck. I smile, the charged tension between us pausing for just a moment and reminding me that Hailey isn't just someone I want to fuck. She's also a friend I care about.

The thought is sobering, especially with her question. "I'm clean," I tell her. "I just got tested, and I haven't been with anyone in a few months." I gaze down at her and study her features. "You don't want me to use a condom? Are you sure?"

She nods immediately. "I want to feel you," she whispers.

And that's all it takes. I groan, dropping my own face into her neck. "How am I supposed to say no to that?"

"You're not," she says. "You're supposed to start fucking me because you're not the only one that feels like they'll die if you don't." And then she wraps her legs around my thighs and starts pushing my already loosened jeans off my hips. Between the two of us we manage to quickly pull my pants off so I can settle back between her legs.

I slide my forearm under her shoulder so I can drop my chest to hers. In this position, our lips are only inches apart.

I let my gaze roam over her face for a moment. With my other hand, I brush a gentle hand over her hair.

"Are you sure you want to do this?" I ask. "There's no going back after this."

She doesn't even hesitate; she just wraps her legs around my waist and pulls me in close. I groan when my dick presses against her drenched pussy.

"I just came on your face, Jax," she says matter-of-factly. "There's already no going back."

I choke out a laugh. I think my mouth gapes a little, unused to—but also completely mesmerized by—the idea of a dirty-talking Hailey. "Who are you and what have you done with my sweet Hailey?"

She rises right up and kisses me, her tongue boldly tangling with mine as she whispers against my lips, "I don't want you to fuck me like I'm sweet. I want you to fuck me like I'm yours."

Her words snap any remaining restraint inside me. I'm powerless to give into her wants, her needs—powerless to give into *her*.

I lean down and capture her lips with mine.

The kiss is intense—there's very clearly a desperate surrender from both of us. Because everything is about to change.

When I can't stand another second of not being inside her, I reach down to fist my cock and slowly slide inside her.

She whimpers at my size and starts to squirm, so I pause to give her a second to adjust and lean down to kiss along her neck.

She grabs my face and pulls my mouth back to hers. "No—" she gasps. "I want you inside me. Don't stop."

"I don't want to hurt you," I murmur against her lips.

She shakes her head and reaches down to grab my ass. With one pull she hauls me completely inside her.

"Fuck," I gasp as I bottom out. It feels like the only thing I'm capable of saying around this girl.

She moans against my mouth as her hands start to claw at my back. "Yes. Move. Oh my God, I need you to move."

I groan and start to move slowly. Then as I feel Hailey adjust to my size and relax, I pick up my pace. It's not long before she's rocking her hips and urging me faster.

"*God, you* feel so fucking good," I breathe out. The

sensations are too much, I'm already too close to exploding. I close my eyes and bury my face into the crook of her neck, angling my body low over hers so I can piston my hips into her.

Every plan I had for fucking her seven which ways immediately flies out the window. Now, all I can think about is fucking into her as deep and as hard as I can, until I feel her explode around me. Hailey must feel the same way that I do because her thighs start to tremble around me, and little moans fall from her lips.

Her responsive sounds drive me to madness. I can't bring myself to take the time to pull away from her, but this fever inside me is enough to bring the animal out of me. I slide both hands under her ass and lift up, which puts me at the perfect angle to grind on her clit when I drive forward. I hear her gasp in surprise at the sensation, then let out the sexiest moan I've ever heard in my life.

Her reaction makes me want to pull more of those sounds out of her. With her hips off the bed and my hand already on her ass, I'm in the perfect position to spank her and then knead her cheek in my hand.

"Jax, oh my God," she gasps. "I—I'm going to—"

"*Yes*," I growl as I spank her again, harder this time. I finally straighten up so I can look down at her, continuing to hold her hips in my hands. Her lips have popped open and her skin is flushed the most incredible pink color. "Come for me, baby."

"*Jax*," she says on a final intake of air. And then her orgasm washes over her.

All remaining sanity leaves me the second I feel Hailey's release. Her scream is soundless, her head rolling back as her back arches. I almost lose my mind when her hands scratch down my abs, and pride wells in my chest at the knowledge that she's leaving marks on me. Her muscles squeeze me so hard that it's almost a struggle to keep pulling out and thrusting back in; her orgasm makes me want to stay buried in her and shoot my own release as deep into her as possible.

But I force myself to hold off because I'm determined to make Hailey finish again. Even as she comes down from her orgasm, I'm already picking up my pace and grinding into her clit on every thrust. And when her breath starts to stutter again, I hitch one of her legs over my arm so I can get even deeper.

"Oh my *God*," she chokes out. "You're so deep, I—I can't—"

I drive into her, *hard*, determined to force another orgasm from her body. And because I think she might like my filthy mouth, I lean down to suck my mark into her neck before whispering into her ear, "You can and will, Hailey. You're going to come on my cock like a good girl." I follow my words with another hard spank.

I feel, more than hear, her breath hitch. But then her hands grip my waist and she starts pulling me into her, her hips meeting mine on every thrust. And when I take her neck with my teeth once more, her whole body freezes—before exploding with pleasure once again. Her moans become rabid, and I feel her trembling from the overwhelming sensation of another orgasm being wrung from her body so soon after the last one.

"*Fuck*," I gasp. The second her body starts clenching, I feel my own release barreling down my spine. I thrust one more time, to the hilt, and then groan as I spill inside her. Hailey shudders beneath me as the last of her orgasm abates.

I have no sense of time after that. It could be seconds—it could be hours—before the tremors stop for both of us and we're left breathless, panting messes. I've collapsed onto Hailey, and my face is once again pressed against her neck.

"I had a few more positions in mind when we started that," I murmur into her skin. She giggles, and the sound is so light and elated that I can't help smiling and pulling away so I can see her face.

She's glowing. And that's not even an exaggeration—she's so relaxed and flushed and *happy*.

It's the prettiest sight I've ever seen.

"Hi," she whispers with a smile.

"Hi, baby girl," I whisper back. I can't help leaning down and stealing a soft kiss from her lips.

"I'm kind of in shock that that just happened," she admits. "I fantasized about kissing you when I was younger, but I never thought *this* would happen."

"Did it exceed expectations?" I tease with a grin.

She rolls her eyes in answer.

I just chuckle and slowly pull out of her, frowning when she winces.

"Did I hurt you?" I ask with a worried frown.

Her smile comes right back as she shakes her head. "No, I just kind of hate the feeling of you pulling out." *Fuck,* but my inner caveman beats his chest at that. "And your dick is huge, so I'm a little sore." *And that.*

"I'll make sure to keep my hands off you for a day or two," I reply with a grin.

Her eyes flash at that. "Don't you dare," she whispers,

pulling me closer by my waist.

This fucking smile is never going to leave my face.

I drop a kiss to her nose and stretch out beside her, and she immediately curls up under my arm against my side.

"Do... do you want me to leave? I don't want to make it weird—"

"What?" I look down at her in shock. "Why would you leave?"

When she doesn't say anything, just nuzzles into my chest, I think about the reason behind her question. "Did you think this was just going to be about sex? I already told you I want more than that."

She shrugs without looking up at me, her fingers nervously tracing patterns on my abs. "I didn't know if you'd change your mind once it was over."

I have to swallow the growl that wants to tear out of me at the knowledge that she thinks *anyone* is capable of using her just for sex.

I tighten my arm around her and soften my voice. "Not a chance. I told you it doesn't have to be a full-blown relationship if you don't want it to be, but you're still Hailey and I'm still Jax, and we're friends." I sigh and shake my head, murmuring absentmindedly, "And how you think I could kick you out of my bed after I just saw God, I have no idea."

She giggles at my comment, but I'm pretty sure I hear an air of relief in the sound.

It sobers me even further.

I grip under her chin and tilt her face up to look at mine. "Hailey," I start gently. "I will fuck you however you want—

especially the next time I can get you in more than just missionary without losing my mind—" Another giggle. "—but you could *never* be just sex to me. You're worth so much more than that. You hear me?"

I see tears line her eyes, but she doesn't let them fall.

"Yeah, I hear you," she whispers, a shaky smile appearing on her face.

Satisfied with the fact that we've waved away some of her insecurities, I tilt her chin up a little more and kiss her again.

I only mean for it to be a peck, but Hailey weaves a hand into my hair and deepens the kiss. It only takes her tongue sneaking out and teasing along my lower lip for me to open my mouth with a groan and slide my tongue in to meet hers. I roll her onto her back before I even realize we've escalated.

I force myself to pull away. "Fuck, wait, I wanted to offer you a shower. And if you're sore, I don't want to push you." Before she can tempt me with another intoxicating kiss, I roll off the bed and tug her to a sitting position. "Come on, let's get you in the shower and then we'll order some food and hang out."

Her eyes light at that, and I'm once again knocked off my feet from the vision that is Hailey. I don't even care that she's naked, I just always want her to look as content as she does right now—her cheeks flushed with pleasure, her lips swollen from my kisses, and a relaxed smile on her face.

She's never been more beautiful than she is in this moment.

I CAN'T KEEP the smile off my face as Jax pulls me off of his bed and down the hallway to the bathroom. I'm completely mesmerized by not only his body, but by his absolute lack of bashfulness as he walks through his house butt naked.

I didn't even know it was possible for someone to feel this comfortable in their body. I never quite reached the point where I was walking around the apartment naked, but there were plenty of times where I felt sexy enough to wear lingerie or dress up in a skimpy outfit. It only took a few looks from Steve before I started questioning those decisions and instead began to cover up more.

Now looking at Jax's naked body, I can't remember a single reason why anyone would want to cover themselves. I've always been mesmerized by Jax's physical appearance. It obviously stands out that he has such a massive stature, but it's not just his size: it's also size with a *purpose*. Every muscle on his body was built through hard work and a lot of sweat. Also, a lot of food. It's the functional kind of muscle that he earned through millions of reps, thousands of hours training, and a dozen fights. His body is a masterpiece.

And right now, trailing behind him, all I can think about is how badly I want to lick over every line of every muscle. How badly I want to trace over the tattoo on his back, to use my tongue to follow the ink from his shoulder, across his back, down his spine, then find my own way across his trim waist and perfectly grabbable ass…

A bolt of lust fires through me at the memory of grabbing that ass while he thrusted into me. And then another as I remember exactly how those thrusts felt.

Part of me still can't believe we just had sex. I was sure he was going to turn me away when I showed up tonight.

But I'm so glad he didn't, because that sex was… otherworldly. I had no idea sex could feel like that.

Despite what Steve seemed to believe, I wasn't that experienced when it came to sex. I've always had a feeling that I crave a different kind of sex, but high school boys aren't exactly known for being very good at or adventurous with sex. I've barely even skimmed the surface of what I want.

In only one hour, Jax smashed through that.

I never knew you could experience sex like that. I had a feeling Jax would be in tune with my needs, solely from our past conversations, but what he did to my body was something else entirely. I've never been so turned on—or come so hard. Between the manhandling, the dirty talk, the sweetness contrasting his roughness… Jax just proved that it wasn't my fault that I could only come occasionally from oral sex; there was nothing wrong with me that sex wasn't always enjoyable.

My mind drifts back to what it *should* be like. Jax spanking me, Jax fucking my mouth, Jax going down on me like it's the last meal he'll ever have…

A shudder runs through me at the memory. Which of course Jax notices.

He pulls me into the bathroom so he can shut the door behind me. He must think I'm cold because he immediately turns on the hot water and ushers me into the shower enclosure.

Through the glass, I watch him throw two towels into the towel warmer that Jax is notoriously fond of. The running joke is that it was exactly the kind of drunk midnight purchase Jax would make—only no one is laughing anymore because that thing is priceless.

When Jax finally steps in behind me, I can't stop the giggle that slips from my lips.

One side of his lip tips up. "What?"

"You're huge," I say with a laugh. He raises an eyebrow, the grin on his face growing. "You probably barely fit in here even when I'm not here. How are we supposed to shower together?"

"Easy. We just stay close." To emphasize his point, he presses his chest to my back as he reaches past me to grab the body wash. Squeezing some of it in his palm, he starts to work it into a lather on my skin.

"You don't have to do that, I can wash myself," I say awkwardly, trying to spin to face him.

He holds me in place and continues to work the soap down my back. "I want to," he responds simply. "I like taking care of you. I always have."

That quiets me. I know it's true because he was always the one to look out for me when I was a kid. Anytime I needed a hand, a savior, or even just a friend, he was there. He was always taking care of me.

I blush and stand still, letting him wash me.

When he reaches my lower back, he works the soap over my ass and down my thighs. I'm fairly certain he's avoiding a certain area on purpose. He just drops into a squat behind me and washes down the length of my legs.

"You're so fucking beautiful," I hear him whisper. And when I turn slightly to look at where he's kneeling behind me, my breath catches at the look on his face. He's looking up at me with awe, and love, and lust.

He looks at me in a way he's never done before. In a way *no one* has ever done before.

"Jax," I whisper helplessly. I don't know what comes after that, I just know I'm being shattered by the look in his eyes.

He either ignores my tone or is completely oblivious to it, because he straightens to his full height and asks in a worried voice, "Did I hurt you tonight? Does anything hurt right now?"

He looks over my body for any signs of pain or discomfort and, finding none, he zeroes in on my neck. And when he wraps a big palm around my throat, I'm shocked I don't pass out right there in the shower from the tsunami of arousal that rolls over my body at even the lightest, non-sexual touch.

"I wasn't too rough?" he murmurs, pressing a gentle kiss to my neck. "Your throat is okay?"

The only thing I can manage is a head shake. "I'm fine," I manage to say.

I see him relax the tiniest bit. When his shoulders loosen, I'm reminded that he just spent a few minutes massaging my muscles. No one has ever given a shit about aftercare before, but of course for Jax, it's automatic. He probably didn't even notice what he was doing.

I spin and reach for the body wash, squeezing a big dollop of it into my palm before I turn around and start washing Jax the same way he just did for me. I start on his upper body, pushing up on my toes so I can reach his neck and shoulders. And when I come close to his face in the process, he dips down to kiss me.

I kiss him back for a moment, eventually pulling away with weak knees and a flush on my cheeks. I start washing his arms, his chest, his abs, looking everywhere but in his eyes, which are staring down at me.

"Does that feel weird?" I manage to ask him, taking a curious peek at his content expression.

He rests his hands on my hips. "Not even a little," he admits. "It feels like I should've been doing it this whole time."

I can't help the smile that stretches across my face. "Well, in the beginning it was illegal, and then afterwards, it would've been cheating. So it's probably a good thing we waited until now."

He chuckles at that. "I'll admit I only recently started thinking about kissing you. Obviously I thought of you as a kid when we were in school, and then when you were with Steve you looked happy." He pauses, a frown appearing on his face. "For a while, at least. That's why I never said anything. But you look much happier now."

I smile at that. "I am. A lot of that has to do with you, honestly."

He presses another kiss to my lips. "I only ever want to make you happy, baby girl."

I can only stare at him in disbelief for a moment, then shake my head. "You're too much of a white knight for your own good, Jax. I still have no idea how you don't have women lining the mats trying to seduce you."

He grins down at me. "What makes you think I don't?"

I shake my head, this time with a smile. But then something occurs to me and it slips from my face.

I know we're teasing, but it's also true. He could have anyone he wants. There are plenty of older, hotter women who could give Jax everything he needs, why would he want me?

I continue to wash him without meeting his eyes. "I mean, of course you do. Any of them would be lucky to have you."

Before I even realize he's caught onto my self-conscious train of thought, he's turning and pressing me into the shower wall, his big hands cupping my cheeks as he stares down at me with the most intense look on his face.

"I need you to listen to me, Hailey. I meant what I said. I don't know what this is, but it's important to me. *You* are important to me. Whatever you want us to be, is what we'll be. But you are, and have been, the only woman on my mind. The only woman I want. You hear me?"

I can't do anything other than stare up at him with wide eyes and give a breathless nod. "Okay," I breathe. "I—I hear you. I don't want anyone else either. Just you. Just this."

He looks over my face for a moment, searching for my truth, and when he finds it, he nods and bends down to kiss me.

I press up on my toes again, desperate to get closer to him. His tongue swipes at my mouth, and I open eagerly. I can't get enough of him. His hands still cup my face, so all I can do is claw at his chest and abs.

"Jax," I whimper, my blood rushing hot with desire. Even though he was inside me not long ago, and even though I'm still sore from his size and rough treatment, I already want him again.

He ignores my desperate pleas, lazily stroking his tongue against mine and taking his time kissing me, so I take matters into my own hands.

I let my hand slide down until I'm gripping his hard-again shaft in my hand.

"Hailey," he groans against my lips, his hips bucking forward into my hand. "I thought you said you were sore."

I continue stroking him, tightening my grip and increasing my pace. "I didn't say I didn't want you again. I do. Right now." I press closer and kiss him again. "Please fuck me," I whisper against his lips, my tone pleading.

The sound of my begging seems to break his restraint. He groans and reaches under my thighs to quickly and easily hoist me up against the shower wall. My legs automatically wrap around his waist and my arms around his shoulders.

"I don't know if you know this, but you could beg me to do anything and I would do it. You've always had that power over me." He connects our lips again, the intensity of this kiss already ratcheting up to another level. "All you have to do is say my name with a please at the end of it."

I tighten my legs around his waist. "Jax, please," I whisper against his lips.

"*Fuck*," he growls. And in one slick motion he reaches down to fist his cock and thrusts inside me with one rough push.

I moan at the feeling of him seated so deep inside me.

"Jesus Christ," he chokes out, burying his face in my neck. "You're so fucking wet. You're going to make me come like a teenager again."

I scratch at his shoulders, panting from the overwhelming sensation of being so filled. "Jax, please."

He groans. "There's that fucking word again." But then he starts to move, not bothering to start slow this time. He just grips my ass and starts ruthlessly pounding into me.

Between the cold tile against my back and the heat of Jax's body pressed to my front, the sensations are overwhelming. And when Jax snags one of my nipples in his mouth, the feeling multiplies.

His tongue circles the rosy bud before suctioning his mouth over it entirely and sucking hard. My back arches off the wall in bliss.

"Bite me," I gasp.

He does, but it's not enough.

"Harder," I whimper.

It takes me a minute to get the courage to ask for more, even though I know Jax would never judge me. I've only ever made that request once before, and it turned Steve off so much that he barely managed to finish. He had to turn me and take me from behind, and I suspect it was so that he didn't have to look at me or my nipples.

Jax doesn't even hesitate.

He bites down with a growl. And if the feeling of his cock thickening is any indication, it has the opposite effect from the one I'm used to.

It turns him on to turn *me* on.

That knowledge is enough to bring the wave of my orgasm even closer than it already was. My eyes close and my head drops to the tile, my fingers still curled into Jax's hair and holding his head against my chest. He switches to my other breast and gives me the same attention all over again.

My orgasm rolls closer. I start to pant, squirming against Jax's rock-solid hold and once again wanting to pull away from the insane amount of pleasure that's about to overtake me.

"Jax," I whimper, my eyes popping open in panic.

And once again, he knows exactly what's happening inside my head and body. He pulls away from my nipple with a *pop* and creates just enough room between us for his hand to slide down to my clit.

"Give it to me, baby girl," he growls, rolling his thumb over the small nub. "Drench my cock, I want to feel how good I make this sweet pussy come."

Where his touch is the kindling, his words are the spark.

I shatter from the explosion of pleasure that takes over every inch of my body. My eyes roll to the back of my head, and I scream from the sheer power of this feeling.

I vaguely register Jax cursing and his hips jerking as my body continues to shake. It feels like I'm suspended in midair for seconds, minutes, hours, as the sensations roll through us both.

When they finally abate, I collapse, exhausted, in Jax's

arms.

"Goddamn, baby," he mutters in my ear, one of his hands stroking my back.

I can only mumble something incoherent.

His chuckle sounds against my skin, and the sound warms my heart almost as much as the after-bliss of the orgasm he just wrung from me.

Gently, he slides out of me so he can set me down. He nudges me under the water so he can rinse my skin once more, this time taking the time to wash between my legs. I shudder when he touches my oversensitive sex.

We somehow manage to maneuver and switch places so he can rinse himself, and then the water is shut off and he's wrapping the warmed towel around me.

"Oh my *God*...." I moan. I grip the edges of the towel, pulling it tighter around me. The feeling is so heavenly that I don't even focus on the fact that Jax's caretaking includes drying and bundling me. "I will never again tease you for this; it's the greatest thing I've ever felt."

He grins, wrapping his own towel around his waist. I'm momentarily distracted by the sudden need to lap up the water droplets that are currently running down his abs and disappearing into said towel.

"Better than the orgasm you just had?" he teases, interrupting my daze.

Dear Lord, how do I want him again? *I've never been this hard-up before. This is insane.*

"Even better than that," I tease with a smile. His brow furrows, and he slaps my ass in retaliation.

"Want me to make you eat your words?"

I raise an eyebrow. "I'd rather eat you," I counter smoothly.

Now it's his eyebrows at his hairline. I've hardly ever been a confident, dirty-talking sex fiend, so even I'm surprised at the words that leave my lips.

Looks like I just needed a few orgasms.

"Not before I've fed you," he responds seriously, turning and nudging me out of the bathroom. "I assume you haven't eaten since the airport so we're ordering in and watching something on TV while we wait. No sex-eyes until then."

I breathe an exaggerated sigh but start to walk toward his bedroom. "Yes, sir."

I don't see it, but I *feel* his pause. I look over my shoulder with a smirk.

He's standing frozen in the doorway, even the water droplets freezing on their path down his body. "I... don't know how to feel about that one," he admits. "But you should probably put your clothes on before I decide I like it a little too much."

I chuckle but do as he suggests.

We spend the night watching *Office* reruns on the couch, where I sit curled up under Jax's arm and fighting the urge to fall asleep. I'm feeling too elated, too *light*, to let the night end. Even the sight of a bear-sized Jax opening the front door to the wide-eyed Chinese food delivery driver makes me stupid happy. I laugh at the bewildered look on the man's face, and again when Jax winks at me.

We eat our food, half watching the TV and half talking about nothing in particular. We're both full, sleepy, and sated from the past few hours, cuddled up on the couch with my head in Jax's lap, his fingers running through my hair. When I inevitably start to nod off, Jax leads me to bed and once again settles me under his arm. I fall asleep with a smile on my face.

It's the best night I've had in a very long time.

The next few days pass in a blur. I'm swamped in the café, and it's all I can do to stumble out of there every afternoon and somehow summon the energy to go home and do schoolwork. Thank God I'm only a part-time student right now because with the amount of responsibilities Stacey is pushing on me at the café, I would never have enough time or energy to do more than a three-class course load.

I spend every night with my nose in a textbook. Some nights, when she's not at the gym, Remy sits with me in the living room. Occasionally, she helps with my work, but more often than not, she's just there for moral support.

It's actually kind of nice. We both spread out on opposite ends of the couch, me running numbers for statistics and Remy plotting madly on her computer for whatever new novel idea she has in her head.

Despite the reason for me being in her apartment in the first place, I'm actually glad that I get to spend more time with my sister. Before she quit her job—and before my breakup—we rarely saw each other more than once a week. Now, it feels like we get to settle back into our pre-college relationship.

And other than the fact that I'm lying to her and sleeping with her best friend behind her back, everything is going great.

A nagging pit of dread appears in my stomach at the thought. Jax and I didn't exactly talk about Remy the other night, so I have no idea how we're supposed to handle this turn of events.

Should we tell her? Will she be mad? I have no idea how she'll react, and the thought of her being disappointed in me—or worse, in *Jax*—has me hesitating to say anything.

Maybe I'll just wait a little bit before I tell her, just to see where this thing with Jax goes.

I automatically check my phone for the tenth time since I sat down. Jax and I have texted a little since the morning after I left his house—nothing really out of the ordinary for us, just the usual checking in during work and asking how my day went-type texts. The only difference now is the slight flirtatious undertone of each exchange. Or maybe that's just my imagination because I can't get Jax out of my head. He's been busy with work and the gym during the week, so I haven't really been able to talk to him, let alone see him again.

And I'm not too ashamed to admit that it's driving me a little crazy.

Remy shakes me out of my dick-obsessed reverie when she closes her computer and stretches her arms above her head. "I think I'm going to skip the gym tonight," she groans. "Coach put us through an insane workout this week, and I swear I'm still feeling it days later." She drops her arms and turns her attention to me. "Wanna hang out instead? I feel like the only time I've seen you lately is when we're both working. What have you been up to?"

I have no idea how my face doesn't flame red at her question.

Oh, nothing. I've just been flirting with your best friend, until finally we both gave in, and he fucked more orgasms out of me in one night than I can count on one hand. Nothing special.

"Um, you know, same old," I somehow manage to mumble. "Work and school, nothing new." I scramble to change the subject. "But I'm down to take a break. What do you want to do?"

She doesn't seem to pick up on my nerves because she moves on without question. She just shrugs and says, "Depends if you want to go out or stay in. It's Thursday, so we could get dinner and maybe a drink? Or I know you work tomorrow, so we could just stay in and cook something instead."

My nerves fizzle as a smirk inches onto my face. "You mean, *I* could cook something," I say with amusement.

Remy grins. "You said it, not me." Her smile fades slightly as her focus on me tightens. "Is there anything you *want* to do? Anything you maybe haven't... had the chance to do in a while?"

And in that moment, I love my sister more than I've ever loved her. Because I know what she's asking. I know she's trying to be sensitive about the things I've given up in one way or another over the past year, and trying to give me an opportunity to grab a little more of my freedom.

So I smile and say, "Let's stay in and relive the raves we've been to. We can play the live sets and reminisce. What do you think?"

Her grin is back, tenfold this time. "That sounds like a great fucking idea. Let's do it."

Our excitement is palpable as we start to put away our

computers and straighten up our work area. Remy's so excited that she gets distracted mid-cleanup, already looking through her favorited EDM playlists to find the artist whose show she wants to bring up on the TV. I'm hurrying into the kitchen to make us a mixed drink—although we never did drugs at the shows, we did enjoy the occasional overpriced Lime-a-Ritas from the food stands.

I'm in the process of making us loaded Coronas when the door unlocks and a grinning Jax walks into the apartment.

Remy and I both look up in surprise.

"Jax?" my sister asks with a furrowed brow. "What're you doing here?"

His smile freezes in place when his eyes lock on hers. I don't know what's going on here, but I can tell by his body language that he's not exactly excited—or at least prepared—to run into Remy.

"Uh... I was... I was hoping to catch you before you left for the gym," he fumbles through his explanation.

She looks even more confused at that. *That makes two of us.*

"I'm not going to the gym," she says. "What did you need?"

He darts a glance my way, and that's when I realize... *he came here to see me.* Remy was supposed to be at the gym, where she usually is on Thursday nights.

"Uh... I need... I mean, I just wanted—" Jax is struggling so hard to come up with an excuse that it would be adorable if it wasn't risking our secret coming out before I'm ready. So I decide to jump in to try to salvage this clusterfuck.

"He's been talking about making a shadow box for your jiu-jitsu medals," I cut in. Both Jax and Remy's attention snaps to me, Jax's eyes going wide with equal amounts of shock and panic. If he wasn't such a mess right now, that look would make me giggle and *then* drop to my knees in front of him.

"A shadow box?" Remy repeats, looking at Jax again with questions written all over her face. "Since when are you crafty?"

At the sight of a blush lighting Jax's face, something lances through my chest.

"I'm... not," he stutters. "I just thought—"

"He just thought, since he's paying for someone to make one for Tristan's first UFC win, he'd do one for you, too," I cut in again, the lie slipping easily from my lips that are now curved into an amused smile. "He's so thoughtful, right?"

Remy finally relaxes when understanding sets in. Her eyes light up and a smile stretches across her face as she focuses back on Jax. "That *is* thoughtful," she agrees. She starts to walk out of the living room and toward her bedroom, stopping to affectionately shove Jax as she passes him. "You're so *thoughtful*, you big bastard."

The second she disappears into her bedroom to look for her medals, Jax's panicked gaze swings my way.

I have to bite my lip to keep from laughing out loud.

He strides over to me, his massive stature taking up so much room in the tiny kitchen that I can feel his body heat against me when he comes to stand in front of me. "What the fuck is a shadow box?" he hisses, only loud enough for me to hear.

I can't help it. I finally let out the snort-laugh that's been building in me since I realized why he's freaking out.

His eyes widen at the sound, a look of awe smoothing his

stressed expression. "Did you just laugh at my pain?" he asks. "Actually no, scratch that... did you just *snort* at my pain?"

Another laugh bursts out of me, and I drop my face into my hands, my shoulders shaking with laughter I'm trying to keep quiet.

"You should've seen your face," I choke out, eventually lifting my head to look at him again. He's gone from panicked, to awed, to now a combination of amused and tender as a half-smile tips the corner of his lips.

"You couldn't come up with a better lie?" he asks with a chuckle.

I snort again. "*You* couldn't come up with a better lie." My laughter settles, and I finally look at him with curiosity. "Why *are* you here? Clearly, it's not to gather materials for a shadow box."

He winces. "Real quick, though, what the fuck is that? Let's sync stories before she comes back and catches me lying about how the real reason I came over is to bend her sister over because I can't stop thinking about how sweet her pussy felt the other night."

At that, all laughter fades away. I swallow nervously, my body heating from his words. Images of him doing exactly that immediately wipe all other thoughts from my brain, leaving me distracted and panting.

"Hailey," he says with a chuckle, pulling my attention back to him.

I snap out of my daze. "What?" I ask, the word escaping my lips on an exhale.

"What's a shadow box?" he repeats, amusement coating his

tone.

"It's like a photo frame but for items instead of pictures," I answer automatically. "You know that clear box one of your fighters made for Coach for his big career win? The one that's on the wall at the gym with all the belts and medals?" Understanding dawns in Jax's expression. "That's a shadow box. Which you now have to make for Tristan *and* for Remy."

The panic starts to return. "How am I supposed to make one of those? I have no idea where to even start with that." He groans and drops his head back. "This is what I get for being so infatuated. Now I'm stuck with an art project when all I wanted was to see you."

My heart flips over in my chest. "Really?" I ask quietly.

His gaze focuses on me again. "Of course. I haven't been able to think of anything else since you left my bed on Monday. I've been dying to see you again, baby girl."

My cheeks pinken at his words. "I missed you too," I whisper.

Jax chances a look over his shoulder to make sure Remy is still in her room. Then he takes a step forward and cages me in, his hands bracing next to my hips against the counter.

"Yeah?" he breathes against my lips. When I nod, he lets out a heavy exhale and asks, "When can I see you again? I'm going crazy without you."

"Umm, I think—"

"Found them," Remy calls from her bedroom. In an instant, Jax is stepping back to create some distance between us. By the time my sister walks back into the living room, I've managed to disguise my flustered expression by turning back to the drinks I had already pulled out of the fridge.

Remy drops her gold medals on the kitchen counter. "Does Tristan know you're making these?" she asks Jax.

"Uh, no," he admits. "It was a spur of the moment idea."

I just barely cover my grin with a cough. But when Jax gently kicks my foot where we're hidden behind the counter, I have to erupt into a coughing fit to keep my laughter from slipping out.

Remy gives me a confused look but doesn't comment on it.

"So... what're you two doing tonight?" Jax asks quickly in an attempt to change the subject.

At that, Remy grins and says, "We're going to play old Illenium rave sets and relive the shows we've gone to. Wanna join?"

Jax winces. "I think I'll pass, that's not exactly my kind of music. But you two enjoy."

Remy shrugs. "Suit yourself."

Jax grabs the gold medals, and I grab a tote bag for him to carry them in, swallowing my laugh when I realize I grabbed the one that says *she believed she could, so she did*. When he takes the bag from me and starts to turn toward the door to leave, I see him pause, indecision warring in his eyes. Then, as if making up his mind, he quickly leans forward to kiss my cheek.

Just as quickly, he turns away and leaves with a *Bye, you two have fun*.

And even though Jax has kissed me in front of people dozens of times, I'm still fighting the blush that wants to flame my cheeks as I avoid looking at Remy.

I can still feel her studying me when she says, "Sometimes

I wonder how you ever started dating with Jax around. I have no idea how any guy looks at how he is with you and thinks *that guy's not threatening at all*." She shakes her head and reaches for one of the loaded Coronas in front of me. "I guess it's probably a good thing for now, since I assume you want to take a little time away from guys, right?"

I frown. "Why would I need time? It's not like I'm heartbroken and need to get over Steve. It's actually the opposite—I've been sick of that guy for months. I just didn't know how to get out of the relationship."

Remy nods in understanding. "I know, I know. But you still only got free of him three weeks ago, right? There's a difference between being over a guy and being single. Don't you want to live for yourself for a little while? Isn't that why we're putting house music on and getting drunk right now?"

I can't stop the smile that takes over my face at that. I know what she means, and she's right. I *do* need to get used to being independent again.

What she doesn't realize is that I can do that even with Jax by my side.

But I'm not quite ready to share that part of my life with her, especially after what she just said. So instead, I distract her by grabbing my own drink and taking a big swig.

"I can be drunk with or without a man. Right now, I want to listen to Illenium and forget that I have Karens to deal with in the morning and statistics to worry about at night. So can we just turn the music on? I want to see how long we can go before your neighbors come banging on your door again."

Remy's grin is both delighted and vicious. "Yes, ma'am,"

she says, grabbing her phone.

Twenty-four hours later, I'm in the exact same position: sitting on my computer, lost in the confusing universe of statistics, while Remy sticks her fifth pen in her hair as she tries to muddle through a plot hole in her new novel.

Only, instead of ending the night giggling on the couch watching old videos that we've taken of light shows, our study session ends with Remy announcing her brain is done for the night and that she needs to go punch her boyfriend in the face a little to relax.

I turn toward my sister with an amused grin. "Are you coming back here afterwards?"

Remy looks slightly guilty as she answers. "I was going to stay with Tristan, if you don't mind the empty apartment. You can sleep in my bed if you want." She studies me for a moment before adding, "But I can have Tristan come here instead if you want the company. I don't want to leave you here alone if it bothers you."

I wave her off. "Don't worry about me, I'm fine here. It might even be nice to get some peace and quiet without your big mouth and loud moans for once." When her jaw drops in shocked outrage, I can only chuckle. "The second part was a joke. You're not *that* loud."

She narrows her eyes at me, then grabs a pillow and chucks it at me. "Brat," she mutters under her breath.

I turn back to my homework with another chuckle. It's not

long before I hear her sing her goodbye and leave the apartment.

I manage to immerse myself in my homework enough that I completely zone out of the real world. So when my phone rings, I startle hard enough that I almost fall off the couch.

Jax's caller ID lights up my screen. "Jax?" I answer in surprise.

"Hey, Hailey, what're you doing right now?" his deep voice comes from the other end of the line.

"Um, I'm doing homework. Aren't you at the gym? What's going on?"

"I got the night off. Open the door."

I look to the front door in surprise. "You're here?" I ask incredulously.

"Don't make me ask again, baby girl," he growls through the phone. And I swear he can sense the shiver that runs through my body at his deep timber because I'm fairly certain I can also sense the smirk on his face.

I stand up and open the door to find Jax leaning against the doorframe, looking just as delicious as he always does. He towers over me, and yet again, I find myself wondering if he's ever gotten stuck in doorways—that's how huge he is. He's wearing worn jeans and a slate-colored Henley that looks like it's straining at the threads to cover his broad chest. With one hand holding his phone to his ear and the other in his pocket, he is the epitome of effortless self-confidence.

I don't even realize I lick my lips at the sight of him until Jax's smiling expression morphs into intense focus at the sight of my tongue darting out.

"Is Remy here?" he asks, tucking his phone into his pocket.

I drop my own phone. "She left for the gym not long ago."

He wastes no time. "Good," he growls, pressing me back into the apartment and slamming the door behind us. "Because I need to kiss you more than I need to breathe right now."

In the blink of an eye, I'm spun and my back is against the door. I don't even have time to gasp in surprise because Jax steals the breath right out of me.

The way that Jax kisses me is… epic.

Everything he's ever done for me has been to protect me, to support me. To love me. I don't know why I ever thought his kissing would be any different. His touch is frenzied because of the week spent apart, with his hand sliding into my hair and his lips eager against mine, but even still, the kiss is reverent. Like he's showing me how much he adores me, how much he's been thinking about me.

How much he doesn't want to be anywhere else in this moment.

I've never been kissed like this, and I can't imagine how I ever would be again.

My knees actually weaken and buckle, so Jax reaches down to grip under my thighs, hoisting me up against the wall. He tears his lips away from mine so he can trail them along my jaw and down my neck. "Fuck, Hailey, I almost lost my mind yesterday not being able to kiss you. I've been dying for this all week. For you. I had to beg Aiden to take my classes tonight so I could come see you." The second the words are out of his mouth, he goes right back to devouring my mouth, kissing and nipping at my lips.

I can't find the motivation to separate us again long enough to answer, so instead I tighten my legs around his waist and sink my fingers into his hair so I can kiss him better.

Jax groans at my renewed vigor. Before long, his hips start pumping against me—or maybe it's my hips that are moving—and we're both panting from breathlessness.

He somehow manages to rip himself away and create a little bit of distance between our mouths. "Wait, wait, this isn't what I came here for," he pants. When I raise an eyebrow in disbelief, he amends his statement. "I mean, *obviously* I've been thinking about this all week. But I have a whole night planned out for us. I didn't come over just to bend you over and make you scream."

My insides liquefy at his words. I tug his head back to me and whisper against his lips, "Make me scream first, then we can go do whatever you have planned."

A desperate groan is all I get before he's attacking my mouth again. His hands tighten on my ass and he starts rolling his hips into mine, all while kissing me like a man starved.

"Say please," he growls.

I purposefully wait a moment before I beg, "Jax, please."

A purely animalistic, male growl rumbles through his chest as he pulls me away from the wall. Taking a quick glance around the apartment, he immediately strides over to the wall of floor-to-ceiling windows and presses me against it. I gasp at the shock of the cold glass against my back, and Jax takes the opportunity to slide his tongue in my mouth again.

"I'm going to fuck you against this window." He whispers the promise into my skin. "The whole city is going to watch you come apart on my cock."

I can only whimper in excitement. He's barely even touched me, and I can already sense the orgasm simmering inside me. It's not going to take much for it to explode. In fact, just hearing him describe what he's going to do to me would probably be enough to set me off.

He unwraps my legs from his waist and sets me down on the ground. And without another word, he rips his own shirt off and then leans down to yank the leggings and underwear off my body.

I yelp and reach for his shoulder to steady myself. But it doesn't make a difference, because just as quickly he spins me around and has me face the window. I can barely focus enough to brace with my hands.

"Spread your legs for me," he orders as he steps away. I don't even hesitate before I do it. "Good girl. Now arch your back. Show me how badly that pretty pussy has been begging for me all week."

"Oh my God," I whimper, my forehead falling to the glass as my body threatens to combust from the erotic words. I'm definitely only a touch away from exploding. *How does Jax have such a filthy mouth?*

I follow his directions, and I'm rewarded with a groan, the only proof that he's just as affected by this as I am. I peek over my shoulder to see him standing there with his fist in his mouth and a pained look on his face.

And in this moment a little piece of me—one of the pieces that Steve destroyed with his dirty looks and passive aggressive comments—heals, as if it was never even damaged in the first place.

It makes me more desperate for Jax than I already am. I squirm in my stance and whine, "Jax, please."

He groans and drags his hand down his face. "That *fucking* word," he growls. But immediately he reaches down and unbuckles his belt, opening his jeans just enough to pull his cock out.

I start panting as I watch him stroke his length. I thought begging would get him to hurry up, but Jax won't rush this moment. Because he's *reveling* in it.

He continues stroking himself as a finger trails down my spine. When he reaches my ass cheeks, he cups one almost lovingly.

"Such a perfect little whore, ready for my cock," he whispers.

I suck in a breath at the words. I've been fantasizing about hearing something like that for as long as I've been having sex, but I never thought about how it would feel to actually hear them. I never expected the way my muscles would tighten in anticipation and excitement. I never expected to feel the rush of arousal in my core at the filthy sentiment.

I never expected that hearing them from *Jax* would set me on fire.

I can't see him, but I can sense him closely watching my reactions. He's stroking my skin with a tender touch, waiting to see if I want to play or if he needs to slow down. And when I let out a shuddering moan, he gets his answer.

"Good girl," he praises as he drops a slap onto one cheek. At the sound of another moan, he repeats the motion on the other one.

"You're fucking perfect," he growls as he finally steps closer to me. When he grips my hip and touches his tip to my soaking-wet entrance, I know I'm only seconds away from losing it.

And when he pushes inside me with only a single hard thrust... I do.

The second he's filled me entirely, it's like someone lit the fuse and set off the explosion. I'm barely able to brace myself on the window as my orgasm tears through my body, and I'm completely oblivious to the fact that Jax hasn't even moved, he's just holding my hips and keeping me upright as my body shudders underneath him.

When the sparks finally fizzle, I hear Jax ask in an awe-filled voice, "Jesus Christ, Hailey, what was that?"

I can only shiver again in response.

He slides out of me so he can pull me upright and plaster my back to his chest. "Are you okay?" he whispers in my ear, brushing his fingers lightly over my neck. "Do you want to stop?"

I immediately shake my head. "Don't stop, that felt amazing. I think it was just because I didn't see you all week."

He hums thoughtfully in my ear. "Were you horny for me, baby girl?" When I whimper and nod my head, he nips at my earlobe. "You didn't touch yourself?"

That orgasm must've destroyed all of my self-consciousness because when before I would've blushed and hid from the question, now I just shake my head.

Not that I need to tell Jax this when his dick is still covered in my release, but Steve always frowned on masturbation. I think he thought of it as cheating, or as a sign that he couldn't satisfy me. He caught me doing it one time and didn't talk to me for two days.

Jax runs his nose along my cheek. "Hmm. Let's remedy that."

He takes my hand and guides it down the front of my body. With his fingers covering mine, he presses against my clit and slowly starts to move in circles. And even though I just came, the combination of Jax's touch and him telling me to play with myself is already making my body heat again.

"Don't stop," he says in my ear. He pulls his hand away from mine and goes back to holding me by the hips, a pleased sound rumbling through his chest when I do as he says.

"Look at how pretty you are," he murmurs in appreciation. His words cause me to look down at where my fingers are moving between my thighs, but almost immediately he tips my chin up and says, "Not there. Look at yourself in the window. Look at how magnificent you are touching yourself like this."

I jerk my head up in surprise. Sure enough, there's a slight reflection in the massive window, enough that I can see my almost-naked body and Jax's hungry expression over my shoulder. Our eyes meet, his lip curling in a smile when my face flushes.

"There you are," he practically purrs. "So fucking pretty." I see and feel his lips dropping to my neck, laying kisses on my skin and along my shoulder.

I moan at the contact and drop my head back against his chest. My fingers automatically start to move faster, the erotic sights and sounds and sensations already spiking the pleasure inside me higher than it's ever been before.

"Put two fingers in, baby," he instructs. I do it eagerly, craving exactly this kind of dominance. I feel his growl against my back when my fingers sink inside me easily. His grip tightens on my hips. "Do you know how many times I thought about you this week? How many times I touched myself to the thought of you like this?"

At the feel of his cock grinding into my ass, Jax's words finally register. My eyes shoot to his in the window's reflection.

"How many—" I swallow roughly and try again. "How many times did you touch yourself?"

A grin stretches across his face. His lips trace over the shell of my ear, teasing me because he knows I wouldn't have made myself ask that question if I wasn't dying to know the answer.

"Every morning when I woke up without your ass pressed against my cock," he says, his lips continuing their lazy path. "And every night when I had to go to sleep without first burying my face in your sweet pussy and making you scream my name."

"Jax," I gasp. I add another finger inside, the sounds of my arousal loud in the empty apartment. Normally, I would be mortified by the fact that I'm this wet and making this much noise, but between the orgasm that's threatening to take me under and Jax controlling the scene, there's not an ounce of me that cares right now.

But just when my breaths start to quicken and the pleasure starts to crest, Jax grabs my hand and pauses my movements. My eyes meet his in surprise.

"That orgasm belongs to me," he growls. "Put your hands back on the window for me, baby." I do as he says, so desperate for release that I can feel my legs shaking. I automatically arch my back for him.

"Good girl," he murmurs. His hand caresses my ass and thighs in appreciation. I'm too close to the window and too far gone in my lust to see what he's doing, but then I hear his groan. "Fuck, you're so wet. That was the sexiest fucking thing I've ever seen." Then without another word, he slides inside me.

My head drops between my shoulder blades as the pleasure roars to a bonfire in the span of only a second. Jax's thrusts aren't fast, but they're hard and they feel like they touch every nerve ending.

"Lift your head up," he says darkly. "Look out at the city while I fuck you."

I gasp and raise my head, looking out at the quaint neighborhood of South Philadelphia. It's 6:00pm, just light enough that the city lamps aren't on yet and light enough that people would definitely be able to see us if they looked up.

"Do you think anyone can see you right now? Is anyone watching you get fucked?" I feel Jax reach around and tug down the cups of my camisole, exposing my breasts to the city. For some reason, that's the thing that suddenly makes me feel truly naked.

Another orgasm threatens to roll me under.

With both hands, Jax reaches around to tease me. He alternates between rolling the hard tips between his fingers and making me gasp with a hard pinch.

"I bet if anyone looked up here right now, they'd be torn between wanting to suck these rosy nipples and wanting to take my place behind you. I bet they'd love to be the one pounding into your sweet cunt right now."

His words are enough to ignite a second orgasm. I cry out in surprise as it overtakes me, Jax muttering a quiet *fuck yes* as he speeds up his thrusts.

When I once again deflate in the aftermath of Jax-induced chaos, he pulls out of me and spins me around. He lifts me up and puts us right back in the position we were in when he first showed up—only this time there are a lot less clothes and a lot more sweat.

I gasp when he slides inside me again, tightening my arms around his neck. He goes straight for my exposed nipples, dropping his head to my chest even as his thrusts start to pick up again.

"You taste like the sweetest candy," he moans as he rolls a hardened bud between his teeth. I whimper at the pinch of pain and arch harder against his mouth. He nips once more before switching to my other breast.

When I can't take the torture anymore, I tug on Jax's hair and squirm in his arms. The only thing I manage to gasp is his name.

By now, Jax seems to know my body better than even I do. Somehow he can sense the pressure building inside me, the frustration peaking as I get closer and closer to another orgasm. Not only that, but he knows what is going to set me off, too.

His thrusts never slow, even as his lips trail along my collarbone and up my neck. I feel him nip my skin, just hard enough to draw a whimper from my throat. And just as I start to lose my grip on reality from the overwhelming pleasure building in my body, he presses his lips against my ear.

"You're going to come for me and then I'm going to put you on your knees and paint you with my cum for the whole city to see."

I'm helpless to do anything but open my mouth on a silent scream as I shudder in Jax's arms, bound by the effect he has on my body.

He has a look of wonder on his face as he watches me fall to pieces. "You're so fucking beautiful when you come," he whispers. By the time my orgasm dies down, I'm too tired and too bashful to respond to that, so I just drop my head against his shoulder.

"I have a feeling you'll look just as good with my cum on your lips, though," he purrs in my ear.

And just like that, my lust fires up again. Only this time it's not because I want to come, it's because I want to please *him*. I want to show him the same kind of pleasure he's shown me, and I want to watch his face as he experiences it.

I scramble out of his arms and drop to my knees, placing my palms on my thighs and gazing up at him with reverence.

"Fuck, baby, you're so pretty on your knees," he whispers as he runs a thumb along my bottom lip, looking down at me with adoration. I open my mouth and suck his finger into my mouth, silently begging him.

A growl rumbles through his chest as he reaches for his cock. His fist rolls easily over his length, made slippery by the mind-numbing orgasms he just wrung from me.

"Open your mouth for me," he says through gritted teeth. I comply immediately. "Do you like that your neighbors are seeing you like this? So eager for my cum?"

I can only whimper with my mouth open, squirming where I sit on my knees. And when I stick my tongue out in a silent invitation, it's the action that finally sets him off.

With a groan, his release shoots across my lips, my chin, my breasts. My eyes close automatically, but I moan at the feeling of Jax's pleasure painting my skin—at the knowledge that *I* brought that on. That I drove him crazy.

After a moment, I open my eyes, staring up at this amazing, sexy-as-sin man in front of me. Holding his gaze, I lick my lips, savoring the taste of him. Jax watches, riveted, as I drag a finger across my chest and suck my finger into my mouth.

He falls forward to catch himself on the window with one arm, groaning "Fuck, Hailey, you're like a dream."

I just smile at him and scrape another finger over my chest.

Jax seems to finally snap out of his lust-drunk fog and rushes to the kitchen to grab some paper towels. When he walks back to me, he doesn't just hand me the towels like I expected, he drops to his knees and carefully cleans me himself.

"I can do it," I mumble awkwardly, trying to take the towel from him. But in typical Jax fashion, he brushes my hands away and continues to take care of me. When he's finished, he leans forward with a smile and presses a kiss to my lips.

I jerk back in surprise. "Jax! I still have your—umm… doesn't it bother you that I'm covered in…"

"Fuck that," he growls, and then he grabs me by the base of the neck and pulls me in for a toe-curling kiss. He kisses me until I'm breathless and can't remember what I was worried about.

He grins at my dazed look. In one quick motion, he stands

and offers me a hand. "Come on, baby girl, I have big plans for us tonight. Get dressed."

I let him pull me to my feet, but the suspicious look on my face lingers. "What are we doing?"

His grin only grows bigger. "We're making a dent in your *Fuck Steve List*."

CHAPTER NINETEEN
Jax

An hour later, I'm pulling Hailey into our favorite burger bar in Center City. I don't even have to ask her what she wants, I just order her favor burger and fries with an Oreo cookie milkshake combo.

Plus, two double burgers for myself.

She looks around the food joint with a skeptical look on her face before finally settling her gaze back on me. "Umm, I don't remember having Burgerfi on my *Fuck Steve List*," she comments, an eyebrow raised in question.

I chuckle at the name we keep using for her bucket list. "This is just a pit stop, baby girl. The real destination is after this, but I can't have you going in there on an empty stomach. So... burgers first."

Now, I've piqued her interest. "What's the real destination?"

A sly grin curls my lips. "Tattoo shop."

Her eyebrows shoot to her hairline. "What?! Jax, I can't get a tattoo!"

I settle back into my seat, my arms crossed over my chest. I cock an eyebrow. "Why not?" I ask simply.

Her jaw drops open in shock. "Because! Because... that's crazy. People don't just get tattoos on a whim."

My questioning stare doesn't falter. "I'm pretty sure that happens more often than not. Plus, this isn't on a whim. You've known what you wanted to get since you were eighteen."

For a moment, she's speechless. And if I didn't know her as well as I do, I would think she's angry. But she's not, she's just calculating the information. The wheels in her brain are spinning, weighing the truth of my words and her own feelings, trying to figure out what to do next.

"Jax, this is crazy. It's a big decision, you can't just spring this on me."

I give her a nod in acknowledgement. "You're right, this isn't a decision to be taken lightly. And if you're not comfortable, we'll go do something else. Anything you want. But you and I both know that this is not a whim, and you've just been putting this off since you were old enough to get it done. And now that Steve's gone, you don't have a good excuse anymore."

Her sputtering outrage morphs into a glare of frustration. She knows I'm right. And after a few moments, she finally concedes.

"Fine," she mutters. But then something occurs to her, and she looks up at me in surprise. "Are you getting something too?"

I shake my head. "No. Tonight is all about you, baby girl."

Whether it's from the nickname that I know she loves or the sentiment itself, she practically melts at my words. A happy smile stretches across her lips right before she leans over the table between us and presses a kiss to my mouth.

But the second she pulls away, she freezes when she realizes what she's done. The smile drops from her face, and she looks at me, stunned and nervous, waiting for my reaction.

"Sorry, should I not have—"

I don't even let her finish her sentence. I lean closer to meet her halfway and slide my hand around the nape of her neck, bringing her lips back to mine. I take a few lazy seconds to tease her, sliding my tongue along her bottom lip and nipping gently. And then eagerly swallowing her gasp with another hungry kiss.

"You don't ever have to question if you can kiss me," I tell her when I finally pull away. I'm pleased to see her cheeks are now a rosy pink.

She flushes even more, seemingly embarrassed. "I just wasn't sure if we wanted to keep us private. What if someone sees us?"

I shrug. "Then they see us. I meant what I said about this being more than sex. The last thing I want to do is hide you away."

She still looks unconvinced. "What if it's someone from the gym and they tell Remy or Tristan?"

For the first time, I see uncertainty in her features. And the knowledge that she might be worried or regretful about what's going on between us hits me like a bolt of lightning. Not wanting to make her feel uncomfortable, I lean back in my seat, and she does too, but I reach for her hand before she can drop it into her lap. "We can handle this however you want, Hailes. I'd like to be honest with Remy, but if you want to keep this between us, then I'm okay with that, too."

She frowns at that and automatically squeezes my hand. "I would never want to hide you. Any girl would be screaming from the rooftops that she's on Jax Turner's arm." The uncertainty returns for a moment. "But I think... I'd rather keep this private until I tell Remy. I wouldn't want her to find out about it in a way that's not me telling her directly."

She studies my face for a moment before reaching up and cupping my cheek with her palm. She looks nervous as her thumb strokes my cheek. "Is that okay?" she whispers.

I smile and press a kiss to her palm. "Of course," I tell her honestly. "Whatever you want to do."

She must sense the truth in my words because a warm smile appears on her face again. With the hand still cupping my cheek, she pulls me closer so she can kiss me again.

"I thought we just said we're keeping this private," I say with an amused chuckle.

She smiles. "We are. But you were too irresistible and I wanted one more. So I took it."

I grin and lean forward to take her lips one more time. "You can take me anytime you want, baby girl. I'm yours to command."

Her eyes sparkle with mischief as she says, "Don't worry, I'll take plenty of what I want later."

Three burgers and twenty minutes later, I'm finally able to focus on something other than my insane need to call off this whole plan and take Hailey home to see exactly what she *wants*. It takes seeing her squirming nervously on the tattoo bench to switch from animal-Jax back to caring-Jax.

I take a seat next to where Hailey is perched on the edge of the chair and wrap an arm around her waist. I pull her against my side and press my lips against her hair.

"Relax," I murmur. "It doesn't hurt as much as you think it does, and it'll be over before you know it. Just take a deep breath and remember why you're doing this."

I can feel her relax in my arms. She takes a deep breath, then another, and then smiles gratefully at me.

My heart feels like it wants to fucking explode at the sight.

"Hey, guys, how we doing tonight? Jax! Hey, man!"

I turn to look at Tyler, my usual tattoo artist. Not that I have a bunch of ink, but when I do commit to something, he's my guy.

"Tyler, what's up, man? How's it going?" I extend my hand for a fist bump, which he meets with a big grin. All of the fighters at the gym get their tattoos done here, so the running joke is that we keep the shop in business; all of the artists are always happy to see one of us walk through the front door.

"Ah, you know, can't complain. Remy actually just called me and set up an appointment for some crazy back ink next month. What're we doing today? Are we finishing the color on your back?"

I shake my head with a chuckle. "Stop trying to put color on my designs, man, you know I only do black and white."

Tyler raises his hands in mock-surrender, though a guilty smile appears on his face. "I had to try. That thing would look dope with some color."

I laugh again but turn toward Hailey. "I'm actually not your customer today. Hailey wanted to get some ink."

Tyler turns his attention to Hailey and notices for the first time that my arm is around her. "This your girl?" he asks with a kind smile.

I squeeze Hailey tighter to my side, just as that word squeezes something around my heart. I know I look like a grinning idiot right now, but I couldn't give a flying rat's ass. All I manage to get out is, "Yeah, she is."

Hailey's eyes are wide as she looks at me, but she doesn't say anything to correct me. I know we haven't put a label on what's going on between us, but I don't think either of us could deny that 'my girl' sounds more right than anything else we could've called it.

"It's nice to meet you, Hailey," Tyler says, interrupting my silent conversation with Hailey. "I'm Tyler. What were you thinking of getting today?"

Her nerves immediately return, so I give her a reassuring squeeze to remind her I'm here. "Umm, I've always wanted to get a compass tattooed on my ankle. Something medium-sized, not anything too big, but I do have a few details in mind. I have a design I can show you, I just need to find it on my phone—"

"I've got it," I interrupt. I pull my phone out of my pocket and swipe to the picture, then hand it to Tyler.

"You remembered which design I wanted?" Hailey asks, surprised. "We talked about it years ago."

I shrug as if it's no big deal. "I looked it up when I made this appointment. I knew you wanted a very specific design." I don't mention the part where I spent almost two hours searching through compass tattoos, just so I could find this particular one.

"This is great, we can definitely do this," Tyler chimes in

after looking at the design. "How big are you thinking? Can you show me on your ankle?"

Hailey stares at me in shock for another moment before tearing her gaze away to look at Tyler. She pulls her right ankle up across her opposite knee and tugs her socks down so she can estimate a circle with her fingers. "Umm, I'd like something about this big if you can still keep the detail. I don't know how small or big it has to be."

"That size is fine, I can still get the details in. Why don't you take your shoe off and lie back on the chair while I go print the stencil for this? I can have you out of here in about an hour."

Hailey does as he says, and by the time Tyler comes back a few minutes later, her nerves have gotten increasingly worse. He goes through the process of setting up the ink, cleaning her skin, placing down the stencil, by which point she's breathing heavily and squeezing her hands into fists.

I pull a chair up on her opposite side and reach for her hand. I gently pry open her fists so I can take her hand in mine and give her a reassuring squeeze.

"Breathe, baby," I murmur. "I promise it's not that bad."

"Ready?" Tyler asks gently.

Still wide-eyed and looking more nervous than I've ever seen her, Hailey just nods.

I watch her as I hear the buzzing start up, rubbing gentle circles on her wrist in an effort to move her focus from the needle to my face. It doesn't work, but her mouth pops open in surprise.

"How did that feel?" I hear Tyler ask.

Hailey swallows thickly. "It's... not as bad as I thought it was going to be. It kinda feels like a cat scratch."

I grin. "I told you." She shoots a glare at me and motions for Tyler to continue.

"So why a compass?" he asks as the gun starts up again.

Hailey doesn't take her curious gaze off her ankle as she answers. "My family always traveled a lot when I was growing up. My parents taught my sister and I that it was important to see other cultures to better understand the world, so it just became this inherent thing to travel. By the time we were old enough, my sister and I were obsessed with seeing as many new places as we could."

She pauses when Tyler hits a sensitive area, squeezing her eyes shut and forcing herself to take deep breaths. When it passes, she continues talking. "I've always wanted a compass tattoo as a reminder not just to keep traveling and learning about the world, but also to keep doing the things that make me happy. Some of the best memories of my life were on trips with my sister." She sighs and drops her head back against the chair. "It's probably the ideal timing to get it inked right now. I haven't been anywhere in almost two years. So much for prioritizing the things that make me happy..."

She trails off at the end and she looks so unhappy that I squeeze her hand—that I have yet to let go of—in order to get her attention.

"That's an easy fix, Hailes. You can hop on a plane whenever. I'll take you to Spain tomorrow, if you want."

She's still distracted by the pain when she says, "So we can get arrested together? Not sure that's my idea of fun, even if I *am* impressed that you could sweet-talk your way out of the station."

My mouth opens in shock. My college roommate is the only one that knows about my drunken argument with a group of locals that ended with me outraged and committed to proving to them that circumcised dicks do *not* look like naked mole rats. If I had seen the cops standing across the street, I may have paused long enough to at least question the decision, instead of dropping trough without a second thought. Thank God the cops were amused by the argument and too tired to actually arrest me.

"How did you…?" I trail off in amazement.

She grins, and for the first time, she doesn't seem completely wrapped up in the pain. "I know you just as well as you know me, *baby boy*."

The nickname shocks my eyes even wider—and then they narrow suspiciously. "That doesn't answer my question, *baby girl*," I growl. "How did you know about that? Even Remy doesn't know. And I know she doesn't know because if she did, she would never let me live it down." I actually shudder at the thought of the teasing I would receive.

She chuckles, finally oblivious to the hum of the tattoo gun. "It was the one country of your European spring break trip that you never talked about. You'd always blush and change the subject. And you always get really nervous anytime someone talks about getting arrested when they're drunk, so I just made the connection." She shoots me another grin. "The sweet-talking your way out of it was just a guess."

For a moment, all I can do is blink at her. *She picked up on all that? When she was a* teenager? *Even my best friends didn't know me well enough to deduce all that.*

Tyler's chuckle breaks me out of my shell-shocked stupor.

"Sounds like she's got ya there, man." He grins, sharing an amused look with a smug Hailey.

"So what was the actual arrest for?" Hailey teases.

I swear to God, I *feel* the blush flame my face. And I know it's visible because Tyler and Hailey immediately crack up.

"It's not funny," I grumble, even though my heart is soaring at the sound of Hailey's laughter. "I can never drink anything with Vermouth in it again because of that night. I didn't drink at *all* for the rest of the trip."

Hailey's giggles finally subside. "One day, you'll have to tell me what happened because I'm fairly positive the ideas I have are way worse than whatever it is you actually did."

"I wouldn't bet on that," I mumble under my breath.

She smiles at me, and I immediately forget my embarrassment, my annoyance, my reluctant amusement, all of it. Because she's giving me *that smile.*

The smile that she only ever gives when she's truly happy. The one that makes her eyes shine and that lights up her face. That stretches her lips in a way that makes me incapable of focusing on anything other than how badly I want to kiss her. That makes me singularly obsessed with finding all the things that could possibly cause this smile to appear.

The one that I haven't seen in over a year.

"Okay, so maybe no Spain," she teases.

"Whatever you want," I agree in a breathless trance. "No Spain." I shake myself out of my daze and focus back on the original topic. "We'll go anywhere else. What do you want, baby girl? Italy? Finland? Japan?"

She considers my question. "I always think about going back to Italy. I feel like Remy and I have spent so much time in the smaller cities but never enough in Rome. I think I'd like to go there."

"Done. When are we going?"

"Jax," she admonishes with a small smile.

"I'm serious. I'll take you wherever you want. Just say the word."

She studies my face for a moment. "You probably would, wouldn't you? You'd really drop work to take me somewhere."

"One hundred percent."

Her expression becomes sad as she looks away. "I can't, Jax. I have school. And work. It's just not a good time right now."

I soften my tone, wanting to push her because I know she's making excuses but not wanting to push her too far. "What about the whole point of the tattoo, Hailes? When will be a good time? You'll always have school or work. You should make yourself, and your happiness, a priority."

I can see the moment she shuts down because she stiffens, a fake smile on her face this time. *Too far too soon.* "What cities are on your travel bucket list, Tyler?" she asks, deflecting my question. "Where do you want to go?"

"I can't say I've really been anywhere outside of the States, to be honest, other than Mexico for spring break, so I'd love to go anywhere. Italy sounds good. Or maybe Spain?"

"Spain is beautiful," she sighs wistfully. "Especially the small beach towns around the coast. I would go back to Barcelona in a heartbeat."

"Ever been to Asia?" Tyler asks without taking his eyes off his work.

Hailey shakes her head. "No. European history has always interested me more because of my family living over there, so that's where we usually end up going. Not that there aren't plenty of places in Asia I would love to visit, I just haven't made it there yet. My sister seemed to really enjoy Thailand, though, so that's probably where I would go."

"Where else have you been?" Tyler asks, having discovered the topic that will keep Hailey distracted and talking.

And for the next twenty minutes, she does. She settles into her favorite travel memories, becoming more relaxed with each story. Her smile never drops, and even when Tyler has to retrace a few lines, she barely winces.

Despite the fact that she's handling it well, I never let go of her hand and never stop rubbing circles on her wrist. I think a part of me likes being in contact with her heartbeat that way.

"Alright, Hailey, you're all done. You did really well, especially for your first one. Do you want to take a picture of it before I wrap it up?"

A huge smile lights up Hailey's face as she nods eagerly. I finally let go of her hand so she can lean forward and take a closer look at her new ink.

"It's beautiful," she breathes in wonder. She just stares at it for a few seconds, looking like she wants to touch her fingers to it, before she grabs her phone to take a picture.

Tyler wraps it up and goes over the instructions on how to take care of it for the next few weeks, then we're walking up to the front desk to check out. The whole time, the smile never leaves her face.

When Tyler tells us the total cost, I stop Hailey from reaching into her purse and slide my card across the counter instead.

"Hey!" she exclaims in surprise. "Jax, you're not paying for me. I'm the one that got the tattoo."

I just shrug, not even bothering to hide my smile. "Doesn't matter. It was my idea and my date, so I'm paying. Deal with it."

She splutters a few choice words and tries to pay with her card, but Tyler just grins and swipes mine instead.

"You're incorrigible," she mutters, admitting defeat.

I grin and slide an arm around her waist. "I am no such thing."

She looks up at me as if she's realizing something for the first time. "You're right, you're not. You're compassionate. You have the biggest heart of anyone I know and you take care of the people you love, in every way. It's just who you are."

I shuffle awkwardly at her praise, unsure of how to respond. I open my mouth to make a joke before I can let myself think too hard about why I like the sound of the word *love* on her lips so much.

But she doesn't seem to be as thrown off by it as I am because she continues to stare at me with a warmth in her eyes that makes my heartrate speed up. And when she slides her hand behind my neck and tugs my face down to hers, I *really* lose the ability to talk.

This kiss feels different than any of our other kisses. *This* kiss is not only led by Hailey, it's also intense in a way that I know in this moment I can only ever experience this feeling with her.

"Thank you," she whispers against my lips. "For this. And for being a good man. The best man."

If I thought I was speechless before, it's nothing compared to how I feel now. I just stare at her, wide-eyed and dazed. Eventually, I force myself to swallow and nod. "Of course."

CHAPTER TWENTY
Jax

Two WEEKS AND a few secretive dates later—spent cooking together, watching movies, and exploring this new connection between us—we're ready to check another item off her list.

"So what are we doing tonight?" Hailey asks, prancing into my house.

I'm mesmerized by her once again as I take her in her appearance, not just because she's wearing a skirt that shows off her trim waist and gorgeous legs, but because she's *glowing* with happiness.

"So… where are we going?" she asks, shaking me from my thoughts. Her grin is enormous, and she's practically vibrating with excitement. "What's on the *Fuck Steve List* tonight?"

"Uh, hookah bar," I stammer, still lost in the spell of Hailey. "There's a Moroccan restaurant in Old City that has a hookah bar inside, so I thought we could go out for some drinks and to hang out a little bit."

If it's possible, her face lights up even more. "I haven't been to a hookah bar since high school." Her expression fades a bit when a memory takes over. "I could never get Steve to understand that shisha wasn't a drug. I think he thought of it as kind of a weed-type thing, since it makes you chill out and a little dizzy. Plus, any substance was always a huge no-no." She rolls her eyes at the last part, all joy vanishing completely in the face of her anger at the idiot ex.

And I'm once again reminded that I'd love to beat the guy's face in. For more reasons than I can count.

I step up to her and wrap an arm around her waist, lifting her slightly. I play with a strand of hair, once again sucked into her vortex, this time because of her delicious, womanly smell. Part of it is the hint of coconut that follows her everywhere, but the other part is just her personal, feminine essence—that's tinged with the heat of her arousal now that she's pressed against my body. As soon as she's in my arms, her skin flushes and her breathing becomes erratic. My cock hardens instantly at the sight, and it takes all of my willpower to voice my thought instead of taking her to the floor right now.

"We should stop calling it the *Fuck Steve List*," I tell her, still absently running her hair through my fingers. Anything to take my focus off my anger for that shithead and my desperate need for Hailey. "You don't need any more reminders. And even though the list was made because of him, we should move on from associating it with him. Why don't we call it the *Carpe Noctem List* instead?"

Her brow furrows. "Seize the… night?"

I nod my confirmation.

She thinks about it for a second. When she finally answers, she looks like she's come to a monumental decision. She gives me a stiff nod. "You're right. I need to stop wasting energy on being mad at him; it's just going to drain me. *Carpe Noctem List*, it is." Her look of determination fades into a pleased grin. And when she pulls me down for a kiss, my heart practically melts at her taking back her life, one step at a time.

I swoop down to steal another kiss from her lips, smacking her ass once for good measure. "Good. Then let's get out of here and go seize the night, baby girl."

She doesn't immediately turn to leave. She has a teasing glint in her eyes, and I swear I'm hard from just that look. I try to remember why I shouldn't drag her upstairs with me right this second.

"Can I add something to the list for later?" she asks coyly. "I have something I'd like to seize too."

And when her hand skates down my abs to grab my belt buckle, I *really* start to have trouble remembering why that's a bad idea.

I lean down to nip her neck. "Naughty," I murmur in her ear. "I am *this close* to canceling this entire plan and instead spending the night between your legs." I hear her moan and feel her hand slide even farther to cup me through my jeans.

The contact is enough to shake me out of my stupor. I pull away so I can look down at her and say, "But I really do want to take you out tonight."

She looks lust-drunk, barely even registering my words. "Okay. Whatever you want to do."

I frown. *I don't like the sound of that.*

I pull her hand off of me and lift it up so I can kiss her knuckles. "Hailes," I say gently, bringing her attention back to me. She looks up to meet my eyes. "I don't want to do anything you don't want to do. You'd tell me if you didn't want to do something, right?"

"Of course," she answers quickly. Maybe *too* quickly.

My eyes narrow slightly as I study her expression, trying to figure out if she's lying. I'm not blind to the fact that Steve's influence made her into the ultimate people-pleaser, and the last thing I want to do is watch her continue that with me.

She squirms under my attention. "I really do want to go tonight, I promise."

I watch her for a moment longer before nodding and reaching for my coat. I grab my wallet and keys in one hand and Hailey's hand in the other, and then we're out the door.

Fifteen minutes later, we're being seated inside the Moroccan restaurant. Although *restaurant* might be the wrong word for it—despite there being a menu for a seven-course traditional dinner—because it's set up to feel like a Moroccan tent on the inside, with people being seated in lounge areas instead of actual tables. Colorful tapestries hang from the ceiling and on the walls, making it feel like we're actually sitting inside a tent. Coupled with the couches and small round tables placed all over the tiny restaurant, and it really does give off a Moroccan vibe.

"This place is amazing," Hailey breathes, looking awestruck. "I can't believe I never knew this was here." Before I even realize what she's doing, she bounces into my lap to wrap her arms around my neck, then plants a big kiss on my lips. "Thank you for bringing me here," she whispers. "I love it."

I'm too surprised to do anything more than smile at her. It feels effortless to squeeze her to me and drop a playful kiss on her nose, at which she giggles and squirms out of my lap. I don't let her go far, wrapping an arm around her shoulders and tucking her into my body.

I hadn't thought this would be a big deal, though Hailey's reactions lately to some of the things we've done are probably proof that she hasn't been taken care of in a while. She's not a high-maintenance type of girl—it's easy enough to pay attention to what she likes and put some effort in to make those things happen. It wasn't exactly rocket science to google 'hookah bars in Philly' and then make a reservation. Two hours of my time and $100 for a hookah and some drinks, and my girl will be brimming with happiness.

"What flavor hookah do you want to get?" I ask when she's settled beside me again. Despite there being plenty of space on the couch, she's nestled against my side with her hand resting on my thigh, as if she can't stand the thought of there being any space between us.

"Something fruity," she chirps. "I never liked the harsh flavors. Orange? Or maybe a berry flavor?"

"Order whatever you want, baby girl."

After I place our order with the waiter, I see her eyes widening as she spots something behind me. I hear the music change and notice the lights dimming, so I don't even have to turn around to know what caught her eye. A slow grin slides across my face.

Sure enough, the upbeat music picks up and the conversations around the restaurant dull to a quiet murmur. Everyone's attention is fixed on the tent flap opening at the back of the restaurant.

Everyone's except mine, because I can't stop staring at Hailey's expression.

She's awestruck, but also surprised, and a little bit flushed. That flush spreads when the target of everyone's attention begins moving through the restaurant, closer and closer to where we're sitting. When she reaches our table, I finally tear my gaze from Hailey and turn to the stunning belly dancer gyrating her hips beside us.

She's Moroccan and absolutely stunning—the tan color of her skin, the bright green of her eyes, the shiny, dark hair that falls to her waist. She'd be captivating even if she wasn't dancing in a way that could only be described as hypnotic. But combine her looks and her movement, and everyone in this restaurant is entranced by her.

And the dancer, it seems, is entranced by Hailey.

Where she passed by everyone else's table, she seems to linger beside ours. Her hips continue to move in a way that only a belly dancer's can, in a way that captivates anyone watching. Hailey herself seems like she's under a spell. But so is the dancer, because she can't take her eyes off the girl currently tucked under my arm.

I squeeze Hailey closer and press my lips against her ear. "I think she likes you."

She blushes, but she still doesn't take her eyes off the Moroccan woman.

"She's pretty, isn't she," I murmur. Hailey glances at me, startled, but I just grin and assure her, "Don't worry, you're the only one I have eyes for, baby girl."

She turns back to the dancer, pulled under her spell once

again by twirling hands and the circular motion of her hips. "Do you like her?" I continue whispering in her ear. "Do you like watching her move? Because I think she's dancing for you."

Hailey doesn't answer, she just swallows nervously and continues staring. I can't stop grinning at the sight of a flustered Hailey—and by a woman, no less.

It reminds me of something, and I let my hand start to drift along Hailey's skin in a pattern that makes her shiver. "Wasn't kissing a girl one of the things on your list?" I ask with a smile.

Her head snaps to me in surprise. "What?"

My grin only grows. "You heard me." It distantly registers that the dancer has moved on to another table.

Her expression morphs from shocked to thoughtful. "You would let me do that?"

My smile falters at the reasoning behind her question. But I answer honestly and tell her, "It's not up to me to *let* you do anything, Hailes. You heard what Tristan said about Remy; same goes for me, and for any other self-respecting man. Your decisions are your own. It's not my place to tell you how to live your life."

For a moment, she just stares at me. I can't tell what she's thinking right now, so I let her process that however she needs to, my touch on her arm and neck never stopping.

"What about sharing me?" she finally asks. "You'd let me kiss a girl even though we're… together?"

I force myself not to focus on her hesitation with that word. Instead, I run my nose along Hailey's neck and answer honestly, "Baby girl, I'd let you bring another man into the bedroom if I thought that was what you wanted."

"Are you serious?" she squeaks. "You would do that for me?"

My brow furrows as I pull away to look down at her. "Of course. Your happiness matters to me. And it's definitely more important than whatever jealousy issues I may or may not have."

She stares at me for another moment before shaking her head with a quiet, "You can't be real." But then she quirks her head and asks, "Is that something you'd want? Someone to join us in the bedroom? A girl, I assume?"

I shrug. "You're more than enough for me. I'd do it for you, but I don't have any interest in bringing anyone else into the bedroom with us."

Hailey nods and settles back against my side, her gaze moving around the restaurant and eventually settling back on the dancer. I can't tell if she's thinking about the girl or about my words, but her posture is relaxed, so I don't push any further.

It isn't until the dancer starts making her way back to our table that I break the silence. "She liked you," I observe, taking another puff of the hookah.

"She was just doing her job," she mumbles with a blush as she looks away.

In moments like this, I feel an urge burning deep inside me to figure out how to convince her that she's the most beautiful woman I've ever seen, both inside and out. Which isn't even an exaggeration stemming from my feelings for her, it's just the plain truth. How can she not see that her sweet smile and kind heart attract people to her like a magnet? How does she not realize how incredible she is?

So I weave my hand into her hair at the nape of her neck and run my nose along the long line of her neck. She shivers beneath my ministrations but automatically leans into my touch. "She wasn't just doing her job, Hailey, she was mesmerized by you," I whisper against her skin. "She wanted you, just like everyone in this restaurant wanted you when we walked in. You're breathtaking, baby girl. It's about time you believe it."

She blushes even harder but forces herself to look into my eyes instead of hiding against my chest the way she obviously wants to. *Good girl.*

We don't speak for the next few minutes, just share the hookah and watch the belly dancer as she makes her way through the restaurant. But I'm only half-watching her, because even more of my attention is focused on the girl tucked under my arm who has no idea how powerful her beauty really is. Who has been locked away for so long that her wings are cramped and believed to be broken.

So when the dancer comes back around, looking just as eager to be in Hailey's orbit as she was on her first pass, I jump on an idea as soon as it pops into my head.

"Can you show her how to dance?" I ask the girl when her sultry gaze lands on Hailey again.

She nods eagerly, even as Hailey's mouth drops open in shock.

"*What?* Jax, no, I can't!"

I wink and nudge her toward the dancer, who's already reaching for her. "Sure you can. You're already a dancer, just think of it as learning a new style."

She bites her lip and glances at the girl, looking nervous but also like she wants to try it. I tug on her hand to bring her attention back to me. "You never have to do anything you don't want to, Hailes. Especially not because of me. But if you want to try it, you should take a chance. Carpe noctem, remember?"

That seems to do the trick because she takes the dancer's hand and stands to her feet. She's led around our table to the aisle running through the restaurant, where the dancer immediately puts her hands on Hailey's hips and begins murmuring instructions on how to move her body.

Hailey shoots me a nervous glance, but I just smile and nod my encouragement. She turns back to the girl, a determined glint in her eyes, and begins rocking her hips the way she's being instructed to do. I settle back in my seat to stretch my arms over the top of the lounge and get comfortable.

It doesn't take long for her to get the hang of it. The dancer glances up at Hailey with surprised glee as soon as she starts to move without guidance. She watches her for a minute before taking her hands off Hailey's hips so she can untie the sash from around her own waist. The gold coins on the sash clink beautifully once they're around Hailey's waist.

Hailey glances at me with surprised wonder when she starts to move her hips again.

I feel an ache hit my heart while I watch her. I watch the joy on her face grow just from dancing, from being made to feel talented and sexy. Exactly what she is.

So I lean forward to rest my arms on my thighs and show her just how much of my attention she has. I return her look with one that I hope she can read as, *You're incredible, baby girl.*

Show me how sexy you are.

I think she understands because her entire body relaxes and she shoots me a smile that is equal amounts grateful and pleased.

I know you want to embrace it. Show me, baby girl. I want you to see how enamored I am with you.

Lust flares in her gaze. She turns back to the belly dancer, who takes her hands and lifts them up so they can stay connected while Hailey mimics her moves. Together, they dance in the aisle, sometimes twirling in place, sometimes shifting in a circle, always moving together in a way that has the entire restaurant spellbound.

And when the belly dancer drops Hailey's hands so she can grip the edges of Hailey's top and give her a look silently asking for her consent, the charge in the air multiplies tenfold. After a moment's hesitation, Hailey nods her answer and lets her top be tugged up just high enough so her stomach is on display.

My own breath catches in my fucking lungs. I was enraptured even just watching her dance, but now, with her taut stomach and porcelain skin on display, I'm more focused on the sight in front of me than I've ever been on anything in my life.

I'm hypnotized by the sight of Hailey taking back her power.

She knows everyone in the room is looking at her. Appreciating her. I can see it in the confident, pleased expression on her face as she continues to move her hips to the music. She knows she's the center of attention, and she's embracing it.

Reveling in it.

She's not looking to me for permission, she's just harnessing the power that comes from her femininity and telling the world, *You're welcome for this*.

I just watch, awestruck, as the girl who was made to feel worthless finally understands the lie and takes back her power with the truth.

I think I'm still staring, open-mouthed, when the song finally ends and cheers erupt around the restaurant. Hailey's smile is slightly shy when she hears the applause and when she reaches for the sash around her waist. She hands it back to the dancer, who immediately pulls her in for a hug. I see her whisper something into Hailey's ear—and whatever she says makes a blush flame across her cheeks, though there's also a pleased smile.

She pulls away from Hailey and takes one of her hands so she can show her off to the restaurant, turning them in every direction and fully absorbing the applause. I watch in awe as Hailey keeps her chin tipped up in pride. And when she's finally led back to our table, she stays tall when she takes her seat next to me, instead of curling into my side for security or assurance.

But that doesn't mean I can resist pulling her into my side the second her ass hits the cushion. I wrap my arm around her shoulders and bury my face in her hair, trying to inhale her very essence into my soul.

"Fuck, baby, that was incredible," I murmur into her neck. "You're the sexiest thing I've ever seen. Holy fuck."

"Really?" she asks breathlessly. "It didn't bother you that

others were watching?"

I finally pull away so I can look at her. "Fuck, no. I love showing you off. And you should enjoy showing off." I tuck a strand of hair behind her ear. "Did you enjoy yourself?"

She just stares at me, breathless and wide-eyed, before she finally nods. "Yes," she breathes. "I liked when they looked at me. But I liked when *you* looked at me even more."

A possessive sound rumbles through my chest. I feel an urge to kiss her and I don't even try to fight it, I just lean forward and capture her lips with mine.

"I can't wait to get you home," I growl into her skin. "I'll show you off every minute of every day and I don't care who watches you, as long as it's my bed you end up in."

She shivers in my arms and presses closer. "Take me home," she says quietly. "I need you." But before I can respond, she glances at the barely half-smoked hookah and starts to backtrack. "I mean, I know we've only been here for half an hour, so we can finish the hookah first if you want—"

"Screw the hookah," I growl. "If you want to go home, we'll go home. It's your night, Hailes. What would you rather do?"

She takes another look at the table, with our barely touched drinks and still-burning shisha, then says, "We should probably stay a little longer." She cuts off my protest when she repeats, "Let's stay a little longer."

I study her expression but eventually nod my agreement.

It takes us twenty minutes to smoke the rest of it. We chat a little, but for the most part we just enjoy each other's silent company as we take turns smoking.

It's an odd combination, the feeling of the shisha mellowing us out while the sparks of our sexual tension charge the air between us at the same time. I never take my hands off her. I alternate between teasing touches along her neck, her side, her thigh, and gentle brushes of my lips against her skin. With every touch, every heated glance, the flame of our lust ratchets higher. So I'm not surprised when she finally grabs my hand and breathes, "Let's go."

As soon as we get home, I'm pushing her against my bedroom wall and ducking down to drag my tongue up her neck. When I reach her ear, I gently nip her earlobe before asking in a rough voice, "Would you like to be a queen or a whore tonight, baby girl?"

Her eyes darken with her desire. But she doesn't even hesitate before she whispers, "Both."

I nod. "As you wish." Then I reach for my belt buckle and order, "On your knees, then."

She drops to the floor, and I almost blow my load at just the sight of her. She looks up at me with eyes so trusting, that for a moment I freeze and just stare at her, awed by the sight of Hailey feeling so comfortable with me.

But when her eyes flick to my pants and her tongue darts out to lick her lips, I snap back to reality.

I hurriedly pull the belt from my pants, then I lean down to loop it around Hailey's neck. Her eyes widen when she realizes what I'm doing.

"Do you trust me?" I murmur, stroking her cheek with a gentle touch. She leans into it for a moment, her eyes closing, but then she focuses back on me and nods.

345

"Yes," she whispers on a breathless exhale.

I let my fingers trail for another moment. "Good girl."

Then I grab the end of the belt with one hand and unzip my pants with the other.

"I'll start slow, and I won't do anything that will hurt you," I promise her. I gesture toward her hands. "Put your hands on my thighs. If at any point you want to stop, I want you to slap my leg. Do you understand?" She gives me an eager nod and places her hands where I need them.

"I want to hear you say it out loud, baby," I say firmly.

She swallows and answers, "I understand. I'll slap your leg if I want you to stop."

"Good girl," I murmur. I pause one more time to make sure this is something that she wants, but when I see the readiness blazing in her eyes, I have my answer. When I free my leaking, swollen cock from my jeans, those eyes glaze over with lust.

"Suck me," I murmur, pairing my order with a light tug on the belt.

She immediately takes me in her mouth, her tongue wrapping around my head and sucking enthusiastically. I groan in ecstasy.

"Such a sweet mouth," I praise. "Look at me."

Her eyes shoot open and look up to lock with mine. And when she holds my gaze and takes most of my dick in her mouth, I groan and brace my hand on the wall.

"Fuck, baby. That's so good. Take me deeper."

Her gaze never leaves mine as she does just that.

My eyes close with a groan. For a few moments, I don't do anything but enjoy the feel of her wet, warm mouth sliding along my length. But when she goes deep enough that I hit the back of her throat and then more, my blood suddenly feels like it's on fire.

With a growl, I get a better grip on the end of my belt. I make sure it's tight on her neck but not tight enough to block off her air—yet.

I tug on it to pop Hailey's mouth off of me. "I'm going to fuck your mouth now. Okay?"

She nods, her lips pink and swollen. I want so badly to slide between them again, to make them swell even more and to watch spit dribble from the corners.

I revel in the anticipation for a moment, lazily stroking myself as I watch Hailey start to squirm with need and impatience. When a whimper slips from her lips, I take pity on her and slide my cock back into her mouth.

Holding her head in place with my grip on the belt, I start to push into her mouth with slow, even thrusts. I don't push her yet. I just appreciate the sight of Hailey on her knees, eagerly taking my cock.

After a minute, I push a little deeper. The first time I hit her throat, I expect her to gag, but she doesn't—she just stares up at me, her blue gaze unwavering.

I growl and tighten my grip on the belt, applying a little bit of pressure on her neck. Just from that, I see her start to squirm. I increase my thrusts and go deeper, pausing when I reach her throat.

"Swallow," I say through clenched teeth. She does, and I can't stop the groan that rumbles through my chest at the feeling of her throat contracting around my cock.

"Fuck, baby, that's so good," I murmur. I pull a little harder on the belt—it's tight enough now that I can feel her breaths are starting to come quicker. My voice is rough as I ask, "Are you going to let me finish in your perfect little mouth?"

Her moan travels the length of my dick, making my abs clench and my orgasm move that much closer. *Fuck,* I've never been this hard in my life.

She answers my question with an eager nod, her gaze never looking away from mine. "Keep your mouth open and don't swallow again until I tell you to," I order through gritted teeth. Then I start to fuck her mouth.

It doesn't take long for her tears to run and the saliva to drip from her mouth. Yet she never once drops my gaze or lifts her hands to push me away. She just takes what I want to give her.

"I'm going to come," I choke out.

I finally pull the belt tight and push as deep as I can go. And when I stay there, buried in her throat, I can only watch in rapture as the tears fall like diamonds from her eyes.

I put slack on the belt and pull out far enough that I'm not shooting down her throat. I drop my hand to my dick and start to tug in rough strokes, trembling from the orgasm that's barreling down my spine. I watch in awe as Hailey follows my instructions to the letter: she's pulling hasty breaths into her lungs, but she's kept her mouth open, spit still dribbling from the corners as she waits to swallow.

After only a few pulls on my dick, I groan, my mind splintering with my release. I force myself to keep my eyes open and watch as my cum lands on Hailey's tongue. The sight of her kneeling at my feet, waiting for my instructions while she's covered in and full of me, is the most erotic thing I've ever fucking seen.

I'm panting by the time the pleasure fades. I still have a grip on the loosened belt in one hand, but with the other I cup her chin and tell her honestly, "You've never looked sexier than you do right now. Swallow for me, baby."

Her mouth closes, and I watch as her throat works in a swallow.

Immediately, I drop the belt with a clatter and fall to my knees.

"Baby girl," I murmur, cradling her face and wiping the tears from her cheeks. I press an adoring kiss to her lips, uncaring about the cum on her mouth and the saliva still dripping down her chin. I pull back to look at her, wanting to make sure she's okay. But she just gazes at me with a content smile, her love and trust shining bright in her eyes.

"You treat my cock so good, baby. Such a perfect little whore," I whisper, brushing the hair away from her face. "Are you ready to be a queen now?"

Her gaze goes from lazy to heated in an instant. She only nods her head in response.

I stand so I can lift her to her feet. With her back against the wall, I cup her face again so I can kiss her sweet and slow. She hums appreciatively, her hands gripping my wrists as she revels in our closeness. And when I deepen the kiss and slide my tongue in her mouth, her sounds morph into moans and her hips push forward against mine.

I press my hand to her stomach and flatten her against the

wall again. She makes a small sound of annoyance, protesting the distance between us, but I just chuckle and end our kiss.

"Patience, baby girl," I scold gently. "You'll get what you need." And then I quickly pull my shirt over my head and drop to my knees before her, wrapping my big hands around her slim thighs.

"I've been thinking about putting my mouth on you for days," I murmur. My gaze travels over her skirt, as my hands slide up her thighs.

Her breath hitches when they move under the soft material and reach the sides of her thong.

"Do you like seeing me before you like this?" I ask her, holding her gaze as I slowly pull them down. "Do you like seeing me kneeling? Mesmerized by the sight, the feel, the smell of you and going crazy with the thought of tasting you?"

As she steps out of her underwear I watch her chest heave with shallow breaths as she waits for me to move her skirt aside. But I don't move to touch her again, I just wait for her to answer.

"Do you?" I nudge gently.

She swallows nervously and nods. "Yes," she gasps. "Yes, I like seeing you on your knees."

My hands return to her thighs and begin to gently caress her soft skin, slowly moving higher and higher on her leg.

"Does it make you feel like a queen? To see me kneeling before you like this? To hear me begging to worship you?"

Her eyes are black with lust and she's panting, trying to get air in her lungs. Internally I thump my chest at the knowledge that I can affect her like this without even really touching her.

That I can make her wet with just my words.

"Yes," she breathes. "I love it. You make me feel like—like I've never felt before." Her gasps start to come quicker. "Fuck, Jax, I—I—"

Her words cut off with a moan when my touch nears her core. Then when I change the glide of my hands from teasing to soothing, she starts to pant again. "Breathe, baby," I whisper. Let me take care of you."

She swallows nervously and nods, her head dropping back against the wall with a heavy exhale. I press a calming kiss to her outer thigh.

I decide not to pull her skirt off, I just push it up to her waist. I like the thought of her being almost fully dressed while I eat her out.

I hum in contentment when her glistening pussy is bared to my sight. I lean forward to press my cheek against her thigh and take a deep breath, needing to inhale some of her essence. I almost groan at the beauty of it.

"You're so fucking perfect," I murmur. "I don't think I'll ever get enough of you." Then I lean forward and lick the length of her slit.

She immediately moans at the contact and sinks her fingers into my hair. I dive in and start to caress her with my tongue, my hands digging into her thighs hard enough that I know she'll have bruises in the shape of my fingerprints tomorrow.

I groan when my tongue spearing inside her rewards me with another rush of arousal. "Fuck, baby, you get so hot," I groan. "Are you going to come on my face for me?" I press one finger inside her while I'm talking, slowly pushing in and out of her, stoking the fire that's about to explode any moment.

"Yes," she gasps, her grip tightening in my hair. "*God*, yes, I'm going to come."

"Not yet." I nip the inside of her thigh, and I hear her squeak in surprise. "Not until I say so."

Her whimper is proof enough that she's already struggling.

Just then, I hear a door slam shut downstairs.

"Jax?"

I feel Hailey freeze at the sound of Tristan's voice. I stop too, and I know we're thinking the same thing: *is Remy with him?*

But after a minute, we only hear one set of footsteps come up the stairs. "Jax, you up here?" he calls again.

"Yeah," I respond with a shout. Hailey's eyes snap to me in horror, but I just grin. My finger never stops moving inside her.

"I'm going over to Remy's, do you want to grab dinner with us tonight? We want to check out that new burger spot near her apartment."

I lick a quick line along Hailey's pussy before answering, "Nah, I already have plans for dinner."

Hailey's mouth drops open at the brazen move. And when I slide another finger inside her, I feel her thighs start to quiver with the force of holding back an orgasm.

Don't come, I mouth.

She claps a hand over her mouth to smother her whimper.

"Alright, well I'm heading out, then," Tristan continues from the hallway. "I don't have my private lesson with Jacob until later in the morning, so I'm going to stay at Remy's tonight, but I guess I'll see you tomorrow night at the gym.

Let me know if you want to get some rolls in during your lunch break, I could always use—"

"Goddamnit, man, I'm a little busy right now. Can you just get the fuck out?" I finally snap. Tristan rarely goes on tangents, but when he does, it's always at the most inopportune times.

"Oh, Jesus Christ," I hear him mutter. "Yeah, I'm out. Fuck. Sorry."

Almost immediately his steps can be heard going down the stairs. And by the time I seal my lips to Hailey's clit, I hear the front door slam shut.

"Such a good girl," I murmur against her skin. I glance up to where she's still smothering her sounds, still trying to follow my instructions. So I take pity on her and say, "Come for me, baby girl."

I've never seen a woman finish on command, but right now, in this moment, my words are what finally break the dam. At the sound of my command, Hailey lets herself go with a cry.

I hold her steady with one hand and eagerly lap up her honey while my fingers continue thrusting into her. I can *feel* the orgasm rush through her, the force of it making her entire body tremble and causing her knees to weaken. It's enough to make me hard all over again, despite the fact that she just sucked the life out of me a few minutes ago. I greedily continue licking her until her legs finally buckle and I sweep her into my arms.

"So fucking pretty," I murmur as I nuzzle her neck. "I don't think I'll ever get enough of the sight of you coming with my tongue in your cunt and my name on your lips."

She's still shaking when I lay her down on my bed. I quickly strip her clothes off before settling on top of her, my face buried in her neck and laying teasing kisses on her skin. I can barely take a second to kick my pants off before I'm sliding inside her on a groan, my kisses turning to bites as our lust ratchets higher.

"Oh my God," Hailey gasps, spreading her legs wider as she tries to get me deeper. "Jax, you feel—I—oh my *God*…"

I growl my satisfaction when I see the overwhelming pleasure on her face, in her body. "Fuck yes. Take me. Take all of me."

I hike one of her legs over my arm and drive even deeper, the animalistic side of me finally making its appearance. Suddenly, all I want to do is fuck her as hard as I can, to drive so deep into her that afterwards she feels empty without me. I want to hear her scream my name until she's too hoarse and limp to do anything but moan as she begs for more.

"Tell me how much you love my cock," I growl. "Tell me how much you love me fucking you."

"I love—your cock." She gasps out each word, too mindless in her pleasure to even feel embarrassed about my demanding crude language from her. In our state of frenzy she can let go, can let her inhibitions disappear and finally dive into the kind of sex she's always wanted.

"Say it again," I say through gritted teeth, leaning down to suck her nipple into my mouth. When I bite her, she gasps in surprise. "Say it."

"*God*, I love your cock," she says on a breathless moan. Her body, slick with sweat and flushed with her desire, arches beneath me. "I love how you fuck me. I love how deep you get. Please, please, *please,* I want it harder, Jax I want—"

I pull out of her and quickly flip her onto her hands and knees. I grip her hip with one hand and fist a handful of her hair with the other, and before she can even react, I've slammed back inside her, reveling in the sound of her choking on a gasp.

"Is this what you want?" I growl as my hips brutally drive into her from behind. "My cock so deep inside you? Fucking you so hard that you'll wear my bruises for days?"

She can barely manage a moan, she's so delirious with pleasure. When I feel her muscles start to tense I drive deep and tighten my grip on her hair. "Don't come yet," I growl. "Not until I say so."

I feel her breaths start to quicken as she tries to obey. Her body clearly wants to come, but even still, she does as I say and holds herself back.

"Good girl," I praise. I reward her by pushing forward and flattening her body against the bed, keeping my grip on her hips so I can continue driving into her. I nip at her earlobe before trailing sucking kisses along her neck. "Such a good little whore for me," I whisper against her skin.

A desperate whimper escapes her lips at my words, and her body starts to tremble at the force of stopping the orgasm that I know is about to consume her. And at the knowledge that I could easily tip her into ecstasy right now, I can't resist teasing her a little more.

My hand drifts from her hair down to slip under her body. I play with her clit, my touch lazy even as I continue to fuck her hard.

"Sweet Hailey, so hungry for my cock," I taunt. "You'd give me anything right now, wouldn't you? Anything I asked for?"

"Yes," she gasps. "Anything you want. *Jax*—"

My fingers press a little harder on her clit, drawing a heady whimper from her. "Earlier I wanted to wipe my spit-soaked cock all over your face. I wanted to cover you in my spit and my cum. Would you have let me?"

A breathless *yes* sounds from her lips.

I drive harder into her with my hips. "What if I wanted to take your tight little ass, would you let me do that?"

Her hands fist in the sheets as she starts to beg. "Yes, yes, anything, I want it all… Jax *please*—please, just let me come, please—"

I pull away from her clit for only a moment, just long enough to push one of her legs up to bend at her side and open her up completely. I don't give her a chance to breathe, I just capitalize on the better, *deeper* position by driving into her as hard and as deep as I can go.

She *screams* at the force of it. Part of me is shocked that she doesn't come from that alone, and that she somehow waits for my command.

"I know you'll give me anything I want," I speak into her ear. Then my hand slips underneath her again so I can go back to stroking her clit, this time without taunting—this time, I let the desperation between us fuel my hard, fast circles. "And right now, I want to feel you coming around my cock."

My thrusts are animalistic and out of control. I feel my release barreling down my spine but I'm so hyper-focused on Hailey's pleasure that I push my orgasm off by sheer force of will. I just bear down on Hailey—with my weight, my hand, my hips.

"Give me what's mine," I growl.

"Oh my God," she breathes, seconds before I feel her pussy tightening around me, so much so that it's a struggle to pull out so I can push in again. But then her muscles start to flutter and clench around me, and her orgasm rolls through her so hard, it's all I can do to hang onto her.

It immediately triggers my own release. I drop forward to latch onto Hailey's shoulder with my teeth, pinning her to the bed in every way I can. I groan as I empty inside her.

I fuck her through every wave, every ripple, until finally she slumps against the bed with a tired whimper.

I collapse on top of her, just barely holding my weight up on my forearms. We're both breathing heavily from the force of our orgasms. I don't even have enough energy to kiss her, so I just press my lips against her shoulder and mumble, "When Tristan demolishes me in the gym tomorrow, I'm going to blame you for draining all my energy."

She lets out a weak giggle and buries her face in the comforter.

I don't want to crush her so I roll off to the side with a groan. When she whimpers from the loss of me, I turn and pull her against my chest.

"Are you okay?" I manage to croak. "Did I hurt you at all?"

She shakes her head, her face still buried in my chest. "I loved it," she whispers. Then, finally, she looks up at me and meets my eyes for the first time since I had her on her back. "I loved all of it. I—I've never come that hard."

I can't stop the very smug smile from appearing on my face. I don't even try to hide it.

I weave my fingers through her hair and start to play with the strands. "Me neither, baby girl. I think I blacked out for a minute."

Her eyes widen in surprise. "Really?"

I nod, my smile gentling as I follow her train of thought. "Really. You and your pretty cunt will be the death of me." I reach down to slip my fingers inside of her, groaning when I can feel how filled she is with me.

"Fuck, that's sexy," I murmur, looking down the length of her body. I love the sight of my cum dripping down her thighs. But before I can dive too deep into that particular thought, I push off the bed to grab a towel.

I gently push her legs open, kissing the inside of her knee before I start running the cloth over her skin. I keep my eyes trained on her body, mesmerized with the sight before me, but I can feel her gaze on me. She's studying me. Studying me taking care of her in this way.

I let her watch. Even after I toss the towel and drop between her legs again so I can kiss my way up her body and eventually pull her against my chest, I let her watch. I let her see how much I enjoy worshipping her.

I let her see how enamored I am with her.

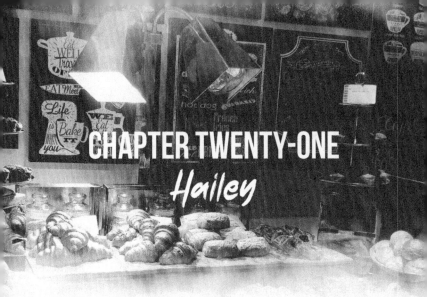

CHAPTER TWENTY-ONE
Hailey

I WAKE UP with a smile on my face, the same way I have for the past three weeks. It's Saturday morning, and my busiest workday of the week, but this week has been so amazing that I don't even care about how tired I know I'm going to be by the end of the day. I'm just excited to get more time with Jax this weekend.

I stretch my body before reaching for my phone, automatically starting my day with notifications and social media.

And frown when I see I got a series of texts last night.

9:38PM STEVE

I miss you.

10:02PM STEVE

Can we talk?

11:13PM STEVE

I'm dying without you, Hailey. I don't want to be without you anymore. I can't.

7:56AM STEVE

Please just meet me for an hour. 30 minutes. Whatever you can give me, I'll take. I just want to work this out.

8:18AM STEVE

Please, Hailey...

I sit up against the couch cushions on my makeshift bed and frown at the phone in my hand. I haven't heard from Steve since he blew up my phone a few weeks ago when I never responded. I figured he'd get the hint, since there was nothing he hated more than being ignored. Which is ironic because his favorite way to punish me was always the silent treatment. But when I didn't hear anything afterwards, it was a relief, and I thought he would give up.

That doesn't seem to be the case. And if his current texts are any indication, he's likely not going to stop until he actually talks to me.

I wince as I think about how that would go. I have zero desire to talk to him, partly because it would be pointless since I definitely don't want to get back together with him, but also because I'm worried he might still have enough of his claws in me that he'll manipulate me somehow. Not necessarily into taking him back, but into confusing me about something. The last thing I need is to take even a single step back in all the progress I've made on myself.

Except... do I need closure on anything?

The actual breakup was a long time coming, so it's not like I'm worried I made the wrong decision or need to revisit the actual night it happened. But I was so eager to get out of the relationship that I just focused on the one reason he gave me and didn't spend any time on the hundred other reasons I had accumulated.

Would it benefit me to get all the things I hate about him off my chest?

I sigh and start to massage my temples. This is not what I wanted to start my day with.

But after a while, I decide that I'm not exactly dying for any kind of closure, and I'm not eager to open up any can of worms, so it's probably best to shut this down immediately. I send a response back to Steve.

8:25AM HAILEY

> There's nothing for us to talk about. We both said what we needed to, and my decision still stands. We're not getting back together. Please stop calling me. Just leave me alone.

Then I mute his messages and jump out of bed to start getting ready. I need to shut Steve out of my brain in order to have any kind of productive day, so I vow to myself that I'm done with any further back-and-forth. He can text all he wants but I'm not going to check them and I'm definitely not going to reply to any more. My message just now was crystal clear, and he'll figure it out sooner or later that I'm serious and then give up on trying to talk to me. He never apologized or begged for anything during our two years together so he's bound to give up pretty quickly.

I get ready for work with my usual routine, then greet

Remy when she finally stumbles out of her bedroom an hour later—probably having woken up to the smell of bacon that I purposely burnt for her. She just grunts her agreement when I ask if she wants to hang out at home once I'm done with work.

I get through the entire brunch rush without once thinking of Steve. It isn't until I go to text Jax that I realize my phone is lit up with text messages.

8:29AM STEVE

Baby, please. We spent 2 years together, don't you think that's worth at least one conversation?

8:42AM STEVE

I love you. I don't want you to throw us away because of one fight, I want to fight for us. For you.

1:58PM STEVE

If you don't want to give us a chance, at least give us 10 minutes for a goodbye. We can't leave it like this, Hailey.

I scowl at the messages, annoyed that Steve is showing persistence for the first time since I've known him. My mood instantly sours—not that it's been particularly great since I also started my day with these kinds of messages—and I'm annoyed with myself for checking messages that I knew would further ruin my day. I should know better. I know I should probably block him entirely, but part of me is worried about missing his communications for fear of being ambushed or caught off guard—God knows he's shown up unannounced to plenty of places when I didn't answer his texts fast enough. And not only that, but there's a part of me, deep, *deep* down, that isn't ready to block him yet, for reasons I can't bring myself to dissect. Whether it's from guilt or just fear, I can't do it yet.

No, I'd rather see the texts but ignore him otherwise. That's a much better plan, even with the annoyance that it comes with.

I'm just about to slide my phone back in my pocket when I realize I have another text message. I'm still frowning when I click on the message.

1:58PM JAX

> Baby girl... I know you're working right now, but I needed you to know you've taken over my every thought. I can't think of anything else. I can't wait to see you later.

2:00PM JAX

> Also... I'm seeing you later, right? I want to see that pretty tattooed ankle of yours thrown over my shoulder while I pound into you because I'm officially addicted to you.

2:01PM JAX

> Text me when you're home? Have a good day at work.

The biggest, goofiest smile spreads across my face, instantly causing my foul mood to evaporate. With those three texts, my day has been completely flipped right-side up again. Now when I slide my phone in my pocket, it's with a flush on my skin and a happy smile on my face.

The rest of the afternoon flies by. By the time 4:00 rolls around, I'm dead on my feet and so ready to go home. But even throughout the insane pace of brunch and the inevitable employee and customer incidents, the happy feeling never leaves my chest. Jax's warmth has infected my entire day.

I wonder what he has planned tonight—if it's another thing off the *Carpe Noctem List*.

And if it is, I can't wait to find out which one he's picked.

I finish closing up the café, and then twenty minutes later, I'm making the somewhat long—but very pleasant on this fall day—walk back to Remy's apartment. I sigh happily as I begin the trek, eagerly breathing in the crisp fall air and tugging my sweater closer around me. *I love this city.*

I quickly shoot a message to Jax, telling him that I'll be home soon. And again, the second I go to put my phone away, it lights up with a message from Steve.

4:48PM STEVE

Hailey, come on. Just meet me for 10 minutes. Anywhere you want, I'll come to you. I can even come to Remy's, so you don't have to leave. I'm sure you're done work by now.

I scowl at the message, more of my happiness seeping away.

I debate texting him back but once again decide it would just encourage him. It's not likely that he'll show up at Remy's—he's too much of a pussy for confrontation, especially if there's a risk that my big bad sister will be around who's always wanted an excuse to punch him.

When I finally make it home to the apartment, I realize Remy and Tristan are both here. It's Saturday night, and they usually make plans to go out or watch fights somewhere, so I'm surprised to see my sister sitting at the kitchen island.

She looks up when I open the door. She's on her computer, clearly writing something because just from the doorway I can see she's got at least four pens tucked into her hair. Any more than four and we all know she's frazzled to the point of overwhelmed and in dire need of a few shots. So she's getting close.

"Hey," she says. "How was work?"

I shrug. "The usual. Just glad to be home and off my feet." I pop up on a barstool next to her and peek over her shoulder. "What're you working on? That murder mystery idea?"

She nods and turns back to the screen. "Yeah, I'm just trying to figure out the plot holes. There's one that's driving me up the fucking wall. I don't know how to fix it."

"I can help you with those holes," a teasing voice says from behind us. I roll my eyes without turning to give Tristan's comment any credit.

"You're an idiot," Remy mutters under her breath. "Or a child. Sometimes I can't decide which."

He ignores her jabs and instead comes up behind her to slide his arms around her waist. He perches his chin on her shoulder as he looks at her screen.

"I still think you should make the butler do it. No one would ever believe it was him. It's perfect."

This time Remy's the one to roll her eyes, even though I can see a small smile tugging at the corner of her lips.

"You two are disgustingly smitten," I sigh. I twist off the barstool so I can walk over to the couch and throw myself on the cushions. "Yet you can't even be in the same room without snapping at each other. And it's funny until Tristan inevitably uses an obnoxious innuendo and makes it awkward for everyone."

With zero shame, Tristan gives me an obnoxious wink before peeling himself away from his girlfriend.

"I'm going to take my innuendos back into the bedroom," he quips. "I know when I'm not wanted."

Remy and I share a look of amusement. Sulking Tristan is rare, even if he's sarcastic, but it's always entertaining to see him be anything other than arrogant as hell.

As Remy turns back to her computer, I turn my focus to my phone. I'm lazily browsing social media when the knocking starts.

"Hailey, *open the door!*"

I wince at the same time that I see Remy frown from her place at the kitchen island. To make matters worse, Tristan walks out of the bedroom with a frown.

"Who's that?" he asks in that no-bullshit voice of his.

I sigh and decide to rip the Band-Aid off in one go. "It's Steve. He's been texting me that he wants to talk. I keep telling him I have nothing to say to him, but he doesn't really seem to be taking *no* for an answer."

To emphasize my point, Steve pounds on the door again. "Hailey, I know you're in there. I just want to talk, let me in!"

I jump up from the couch, ready to rush to the door before my two bodyguards can get to it, but Tristan is too quick.

Remy might have beaten him to it if she hadn't stopped to grab a bat out of the coat closet.

Tristan rips the door open to reveal a red-faced, panting Steve. The fact that he can glare at the mountain of muscle in front of him instead of shrinking in fear speaks to how furious he must be.

I look at Steve, waiting for all the guilt, and the fear, and the internalized need to please him to come rushing back. I wait for the moment when I'll freeze and apologize and tell him I never meant to hurt him, that I know he didn't mean the things he said and that I'm sure he'll never do it again. I wait for the feelings that will demolish the progress I've made toward my own happiness, that will knock me right back into a world where I'm miserable and a shell of the person I'm meant to be.

They don't come.

They don't fucking come.

I feel *nothing* when I look at him.

Nothing but sadness and pity for him. Nothing but love and compassion for the girl that was too young and too eager for his love to realize what a broken little boy he really was.

I'll never be able to help him; I never even had a chance. Not only does he not realize that there's a problem to begin with, but it's also not possible to help someone if they don't want to be helped. And when his issue becomes detrimental to my happiness and my well-being... it's time to let him go.

I turn my attention back to the people in the doorway, finally having made my decision. And my heart feeling so much lighter for it.

"You need to leave. Now." There is zero room for discussion in Tristan's cold order.

Steve tries anyway. "I just want to talk to her."

"Like hell you will," Remy snarls, shoving in front of her boyfriend. "You can get the fuck out of my apartment and forget about ever contacting my sister again."

Gently, without moving too quickly, Tristan peels the baseball bat away from her. He sets it behind the door, and I can faintly hear him mumble, "Jesus, babe. Let's set Bennie down. I don't feel like going to jail tonight."

I huff a laugh, even though Remy is no less terrifying without the bat than she is with it.

I step forward to touch her elbow. "Guys, it's okay. I just want to get it over with. Let him in."

Remy spins to face me, a mixture of panic and pain on her face. I know she wants nothing more than to take over for me and kick Steve out on his ass, but she's visibly fighting the part of her that wants to do that. She wants so badly to let me do this on my own.

Finally, she swallows roughly and asks me, "Are you sure?"

I nod. "I'll be fine, I promise. I want to do this on my own."

My sister exchanges a glance with Tristan, who looks just as unhappy about opening the door as she does. But after a tense moment, the human shield in front of me parts. Steve glares at Tristan in mistrust, then takes a tentative step forward. I walk back into the living room area, signaling him to follow me.

When I reach the open space, I turn back to my ex-boyfriend with crossed arms and a deep frown on my face.

"What do you want to talk about?" I start, my tone one of

boredom.

Steve opens his mouth to say something but immediately shuts it when Remy and Tristan glue themselves to the wall behind him. They, too, have crossed arms and a heavy scowl.

"Can we get some privacy?" he snaps at them.

"No," Tristan says simply.

Steve looks to me for help. I have to tamp down on the small smile that wants to appear at the vision of Steve being in anything other than a dominant position. But I smother the urge before he can see it. I'm not quite ready to start antagonizing him.

Before I can tell him to either talk or leave, I hear the front door bang open again.

"Honey, I'm *home!*"

Jax's happy grin slides off his face the second he sees us all gathered.

I watch as his face transforms from the happy Jax that I know and love, to the vicious fighter that I know he's capable of being. He doesn't even look at me, he's so focused on shredding Steve with his eyes. "What the fuck is he doing here," he finally snarls.

I don't even bother trying to calm him down with words. I step up to him and place a soothing hand on his arm. "It's okay, I told them to let him in," I tell him softly. "I just want to end this once and for all."

His gaze finally settles on me. He calms, slightly, right in front of my eyes. I can tell he's searching for something, probably trying to figure out first and foremost if I'm okay, and then to see if I'm thinking about taking Steve back.

I let him see the truth in my gaze—I don't want Steve. I never will again.

He softens even more. Sliding an arm over my shoulders, and with a final glance toward Steve, he lets out a heavy exhale and nods.

"Okay. Talk."

I know Steve not only watched but understood the exchange. I can see it in *his* eyes. He's right back to being furious, this time at the knowledge that I've likely moved on and that this is a fruitless mission.

Still, he doesn't give up. I should've known, I could always tell how much he hated being bested.

"Can we get some privacy, please?" he snaps.

"*No*," three people say at once.

I sigh and look at my overprotective bodyguards, taking a moment to be thankful for the fact that I have three people who want to protect me at all costs.

"Guys, it's okay," I tell them gently. "We just need a few minutes. Can you give us the room? Please?"

I think it's the *please* that does them in. I can hear Tristan and Remy grumbling under their breaths, but they disappear into the bedroom. Jax stays right where he is.

I touch his arm again. "Jax, please? I want to do this by myself."

At that, he sighs and drops his arm from my shoulders. He plants a gentle kiss at my temple before turning his murderous glare back on Steve.

"You hurt her and I will rip you apart."

The threat manages to surprise Steve, but Jax is already

walking into Remy's bedroom to give us some space. I cross my arms and wait patiently for him to start talking.

But Steve is still looking at the room where Jax disappeared to. His own expression becomes more and more angry, until the question practically explodes out of him.

"Did you fuck him?" he seethes.

I just raise an eyebrow in response.

"I never knew you were into the meathead type," he spits. "I guess it makes sense why we didn't work out, then. Does a guy's IQ have to be in the gutter for you to—"

"You say one more word against him and this conversation is over," I interrupt coldly. I don't let Steve's words strike where he wants them to because I know he's just trying to get a rise out of me.

Fury still glitters in Steve's eyes, so I turn toward the front door, ready to escort him out.

"Wait," he blurts. "I want to talk. Just hear me out."

I turn back around. "So talk. But if I hear you insult my family or my friends again, I'll get Jax to throw you out. And I won't care if he breaks a few bones in the process."

Steve must sense that I'm not bluffing because he swallows and schools his expression to look apologetic.

Even though I know he's not actually capable of the emotion.

"I—" He swallows and tries again. "I want you back, Hailey. I fucked up, and I'm so sorry. I got complacent when we moved in together and stopped treating you how you deserve. I have no excuse, and I'm sorry that I ever hurt you or made you feel bad. You deserve only the best, always. Just how it was in the beginning."

I don't buy a single word coming out of his mouth. He might believe it, but I doubt even that. I think he's just saying what he thinks I want to hear. He wants so badly to "win" that he's saying whatever is necessary to get me back. He doesn't want me; he wants his power over me.

I don't interrupt. I let him talk, because I want to hear everything he has to say before giving my answer. I just watch him with crossed arms and a blank stare, feeling absolutely nothing as he talks.

He either finds his courage, or he interprets my silence as a good thing, because he takes a tentative step forward. When I don't push him away, he takes another, until he's standing in front of me. He reaches forward to cup my elbows. When I still don't move, he begins to gently rub my arms in a pattern that's meant to be soothing. I don't want his touch, of course, I'm just curious to see how he plays this and how far he tries to push it. It's also further proof that he doesn't know me or care what I need, because if he did, he'd feel my tense posture or see my lips twitching with disgust.

"Give me another chance," he whispers pleadingly. "Please, Hailey. We're so good together, you know we are. Just give me another chance. Please..."

With another tentative glance over my face, he slowly leans in to kiss me. I can't even fault him for it, because it's worked in the past more times than I care to admit.

I stop him with a hand on his chest.

"You're a narcissist," I say bluntly.

He jerks back in surprise. "What?"

I give him a firm push to move him back a few inches. "You're a narcissist," I repeat. "You're entitled, you can't accept anything less than total admiration, and you completely disregard other people's feelings."

His eyes widen as he falls back another step.

"You manipulated me during the entire relationship," I continue, deciding to tell him exactly what he's done. If he's not pulling punches then I won't, either. "You used to treat me like dirt one day and then like a princess the next, just to reel me back in and make me fall in love with you again. You'd be nice for just long enough that when you'd mistreat me again, I wouldn't be ready to leave you. You probably didn't even realize you were doing it—though that doesn't make it any less wrong. You can tell me you're sorry you stopped treating me the way I deserve and that you'll never do it again, but you don't really mean it, do you? It might take a week, or a month, or six months, but you'll go back to shitting on me. You'll make little comments about my appearance, or my job, or my past, all so you can cut down my self-esteem and make me dependent on you for even a sliver of a compliment. Because you like having that power over another person. That power makes you feel like a man."

I shake my head, sadness lacing my expression. "I quit jobs for you, and hobbies. I alienated all of my friends and family because of you." I let out a bitter laugh and plant my hands on my hips. "*God*, I even stopped listening to the music I like. That's how much control you had over me. And you've been getting off on that, haven't you? That you did it to someone strong? Someone like me?"

Steve's expression flits back and forth between shock and anger. I can't tell if he's pissed that I'm calling him out on his issues, or if he really doesn't realize he has a problem, but he's definitely too conflicted to even respond to my accusations.

I sigh and let my hands drop to my sides, exhaustion settling into my bones. I've been wanting to get that off my chest for months, and now that I've said it, I'm tired. I just want to curl up in bed and let Jax whisper praises in my ear, erasing every horrible thing Steve has ever made me think about myself.

I walk to the front door and open it, then turn to face him again to deliver my last message. "We are never getting back together, Steve. You and I are never going to talk or see each other again. So get out and erase my number from your phone, because this is the end for us. Nothing you can say or do is going to change that."

Steve's expression finally settles on anger. He opens his mouth to most likely snap at me, but a quick glance to the side has him shutting his mouth. His nostrils flare and his fists clench in an effort to restrain himself.

He stalks over to the door but pauses before he actually steps over the threshold. He turns to face me, and in this close proximity I can clearly see the fury flashing in his eyes, can see his true colors finally coming out to play. Right now, he really does hate me. And I can tell before he even opens his mouth that he can't leave without trying to win the final word, without cutting me deep with something truly vicious.

"I always knew you were a dirty whore," he snarls. "I don't know why I even bothered with you. Good luck ever finding someone better than me. You and your shitty sister can have fun fucking the brainless assholes. Maybe you can enjoy a nice orgy like you've always wanted—"

He doesn't get another word out. I am so goddamn *tired* of being shit on by this man. I never want to hear another insult from him again.

So I cock my fist back and fire it straight at his chin.

The force of my punch knocks him back. He doesn't fall down, but he stumbles through the doorway and barely manages to catch himself on the other side. As he reaches a hand up to touch his chin, I can see the dazed look in his eyes and mentally pat myself on the back for a shot well-placed. I could've broken his nose, but Steve values brain over appearances so I went for the knockout button on the chin, instead.

"You know what I've always wanted to tell you, Steve?" I say thoughtfully. He blinks a few times as he tries to focus on me. "I want you to leave here knowing that I never regretted that threesome in high school. I actually enjoyed it ten times more than I ever did when you would stick your little dick inside me."

He just stares at me, wide-eyed and slack-jawed.

"I just wanted you to know that," I shrug. "Goodbye, Steve."

He's still staring at me in shock when I slam the door in his face.

I look up to see Jax, who is nervously waiting for my reaction.

"Baby," he whispers, placing his hands on my hips and glancing between my eyes as he takes stock of my well-being.

I let out a shaky exhale in an effort to let go of any residual negative feelings. And again, I just feel tired—proud, but tired.

I stand up on my toes so I can wind my arms around Jax's neck and bury my face in his warm skin. He already knows what I need so he grips under my thighs and winds my legs around his waist. He squeezes me tight to his body.

"Come home with me?" he murmurs in my ear. "I need to make sure you're okay. And then I want to worship at your feet all night long." I nod quickly. I feel him walking but I refuse to pull my face away from his neck and his comforting scent, so I can't really tell where we're going. When he tries to set me on the island, I protest and tighten my grip on him.

"What… is happening right now?" My sister's voice cuts through the fog in my brain.

I look up to see her standing in the hallway, staring at Jax and I in shock.

"Not now, Remy," Jax says stiffly.

His order seems to snap her out of the daze she's in. She turns her trademark glare on Jax. "You didn't think to tell me first? How long has this been going on?" She drags a hand down her face in frustration. "Goddamnit, Jax! She's my *sister!*"

I watch Jax's face crumble with guilt. Being treated like a little girl is enough to set me off, but hearing her blame *Jax* when he's been nothing but a goddamn saint makes me see red.

Just as I'm about to snap at her with words that I already know are going to be too cutting, Tristan grips his girlfriend's chin and turns her to face him.

"Remy," he admonishes quietly. "You don't get to make decisions for Hailey. She's a grown woman, and Jax is your *best friend*. If you're going to trust anyone, trust them. They can make their own choices." He shifts his grip to the side of her neck so he can stroke her cheek with his thumb. "Plus, Jax accepted us without a single complaint. You're being a little hypocritical right now."

At that, Remy's cheeks flush and she looks down at her feet, looking properly chastised. She sneaks a guilty peek at Jax and I.

"I'm sorry," she whispers. "I'm just surprised. And you're my *sister*." She looks down at her feet again as she mumbles, "We already know I'm a little overprotective. My mama bear instincts are shot today."

That makes me laugh, even though it sounds wet. I don't know when I started crying but when I touch my face it's definitely wet with tears.

The sight softens Remy. "I'm sorry," she repeats. "It's just a knee-jerk reaction when I see you with a guy." Her gaze hardens when she turns back to Jax. "But I'll tell you the same thing you told Tristan. Even though I love you like my own brother, I love Hailey more. So don't you dare hurt her. Because I'd hate to have to kill you after everything we've been through."

I let out another laugh as I bury my face in Jax's shoulder, relieved to feel the tension in the room immediately easing.

"I would never hurt her," Jax says gruffly. "You know that."

When I turn to peek at Remy, she's studying Jax with a stare that looks like she's trying to cut through his very soul to his deepest secrets. I feel Jax shuffle under her piercing gaze.

After what feels like an eternity, Remy just nods and says, "I know that."

The relief in Jax is obvious; the tension goes from his

shoulders and he lets out an audible breath. He wraps a protective arm around my waist and says, "I'm taking her home with me tonight."

Again, Remy just nods. "Okay." And in a very uncharacteristic move, she walks over to me and wraps me in a tight hug, expressing more love and affection in this one moment than she ever has before. A warmth spreads through me at the knowledge that all three people in this room went to bat for me tonight without my ever having to ask.

When Remy motions for Tristan to follow her into the bedroom in order to give us some space, Jax gently brings my attention back to him. "Are you staying with me this weekend? Do you want me to pack up some clothes for you?"

I smile up at this man that will do anything to make sure I'm taken care of. "I'll do it, I just need to grab a few things." I straighten so I can kiss him lightly before saying, "I don't want to move from your side until we both go back to work on Monday morning."

He returns my kiss with one of his own. "That need is mutual, baby girl. Go grab your things so I can take you home."

I start to look around the room. "In a minute," I say distractedly. When my eyes land on what I'm looking for, I point at my phone on the couch and ask, "Can you hand me my phone, please?"

Jax grabs my phone and hands it over, his eyebrow quirking in question as he waits for me to do whatever it is I need my phone for.

With a sense of finality, I scroll to Steve's contact in my list. And when I click the *Block Caller* button, I feel a weight lift off my shoulders. For the first time in months, I feel like I can finally take a deep breath.

I power my phone off and look back at Jax. "Okay?" he asks gently, brushing his knuckles against my cheek.

I smile, tears of relief shining in my eyes.

"Okay," I whisper.

I DON'T LET go of her hand from the moment I take the bag from her and lead her out of Remy's apartment—not through the car ride, not as I usher her into the house, and not when I lead her to my bedroom.

I take a seat on my bed and gently pull her to stand between my legs. I take a moment to stare up at her, amazed by her beauty and her strength.

I press a kiss to her stomach, to the sliver of skin exposed between her pants and her shirt. "What do you need, baby girl?" I murmur as I grip her hips and press my forehead to her stomach. "What can I give you?"

She combs one hand through my hair, forever soothing even when she's the one that should be soothed. "I'm not fragile, Jax, you don't need to treat me like I'm going to break."

I pull back so I can look up at her, so she can see the truth in my expression when I say, "You were never in any danger of breaking. You're too strong for that. But that doesn't change the fact that I want to treat you the way you deserve to be treated." I take a deep breath, suddenly overwhelmed by tonight, by our connection—by *her*. "Tell me what you want. I'll give you anything."

She tilts her head, studying me for a moment. I wonder if she can see the truth, the desperation in my eyes—the need to take care of her. Because at some point tonight something changed, and we became more than just two people who care about each other.

We became... *more*.

And by the way she looks at me, I realize she can feel it too.

Up until tonight, we've still only been two friends having sex. It's still only been our original bond, except set on fire from our chemistry.

Now, it's so much more than that.

Now, it's like we've gone from two friends having sex to two souls connected.

I swear I can feel the moment the connection slots into place. The moment I realize that what I feel for Hailey is unlike anything I've ever experienced in my life, and something I'll never feel for another human being. It's like she's become a part of me, an extension of me—a piece of my heart beating outside of my body.

My breath catches as I hold her stare, her expression not giving anything away except for the trust I know she feels for me. I can't tell if she's feeling what I am. It might be too early for her after everything she's been through. So even though it feels like I'm drowning in these emotions, I take a shaky breath and remind myself that I still need to take it slow. That she still needs time and space to see if she could feel about me the way I'm realizing I feel about her.

"What do you want, Hailey," I whisper on a broken breath, consumed by my emotions and physically trembling from the force of it all.

She sucks in a startled breath at the raw power in my stare. And then without a word, she reaches down to grab the hem of her shirt and pull it over her head.

It's all I can do right now not to drop to my knees before her, made helpless by my awe of her. Even before tonight, she's shown a strength these past few weeks that many people never find in themselves. They never learn how to get away from the bad in their lives, or how to turn it into good. They never learn how to fight.

Hailey did.

"You're perfect," I whisper, my thumbs gently caressing her hipbones as I stare up at her. "And if I could stare at you like this until my heart stopped beating, then I'd die the happiest man that ever lived."

A muffled sound rushes through her chest only a second before she leans down to press her lips against mine. That contact is enough to snap the last of my restraint.

I groan when I finally give in to her. I tug her down to straddle my lap and weave a hand into her hair so I can grip the nape of her neck, holding her lips against mine and devouring her with my mouth, my teeth, my tongue. With one kiss, I try desperately to show her what I can't bring myself to say.

"Jax," she gasps, and with just my name I understand her urgency, her sudden need for my touch, because I feel it too. Like our closeness is the only thing that can quell this fire between us.

"I know," I murmur, slowing my kiss just long enough to say, "I'll take care of you, baby. But I'm not going to be rough tonight. I want to take my time with you. Okay?"

She pulls away so she can cup my face and looks into my eyes, and I wonder if she can see everything I'm not saying in the way I look at her.

And I think she can, because she just whispers, "Okay."

I grip her thighs so I can roll to the side and lay her down on the bed. I can't stop myself from kissing her again so I don't even try; I just seal our lips together and caress her tongue the way I want to caress her body. She sighs when my weight presses down on her.

It's harder than I thought it would be to tear my mouth from hers and begin trailing across her cheek, her neck, her collarbone. I keep my touches gentle and fleeting, wanting to show her my adoration in every sensation.

When I reach her breasts, I circle her nipple with my tongue before sucking it into my mouth, my other hand trailing down to grip her hip in an effort to center myself. I give her other nipple the same treatment.

By the time I've finished teasing her breasts, Hailey's arching off the bed and panting heavily. I start to kiss along her sternum, down to circle her belly button, before finally reaching her leggings and dipping my tongue under the hem.

"Jax," she finally gasps. "I need you."

I look up the length of her body to see her chest heaving and her eyes locked right on mine, and I know what she needs because I need it too. I push up to a sitting position and murmur, "I know, baby. Lift your hips."

I tug off her leggings and thong when she does as I ask, then I settle between her legs again. I stroke her lightly for a moment before dropping my mouth to where she's drenched and quivering.

I caress every inch of her with my tongue, my lips, my fingers. I revel in the fact that I get to kiss her like this, that I'm the one making her breath speed up and her fingers clutch my hair.

"Jax," she gasps. "Jax… I'm going to—"

I slip two fingers inside her and lift my tongue long enough to say, "Come for me. Break for me, for only me."

It only takes a few swipes of my tongue before she explodes. I ride out the wave with her, my fingers and mouth slowing as her body drops to the bed and twitches with the aftershocks.

I straighten up so I can look down at her and bask in the sight before me—Hailey naked and blissed out with color in her cheeks and a smile on her face is the most intoxicating vision I've ever seen.

"You're so goddamn beautiful," I breathe.

And instead of blushing or waving me off, she just smiles.

Fuck, I love watching her own her beauty. Love seeing her come into her own again. It wrecks me.

When she reaches for me, I quickly pull my clothes off before settling my weight over her body again. Her arms wrap around my neck, her legs around my waist, and then we're kissing. Kissing like we'll never get enough of each other and like we both know something's changed.

"I need you," she whispers against my lips. I don't even stop kissing her, I just reach down and slide inside.

I swallow her moan, obsessed with every sound she makes, every expression. My hips pick up an easy rhythm as I start to fuck her. I grip her hip with one hand, holding her in place so I can grind down on her with every thrust. My other hand tangles in her hair and angles her head so I can deepen our kiss, needing to be as close to her as possible.

Soon her moans get louder and she starts to squirm underneath me. "Fuck, baby," I groan, latching onto her neck to nip at her skin before soothing it with my tongue. I pick up the pace of my thrusts when I feel her start to tighten around me.

"God, yes," I groan. "I want to feel you come again."

She grips my head in her hands so she can pull me up to look at her again. Her cheeks are flushed and her eyes look frenzied, and I know she's close.

"I want you to come with me," she pants. "I want to go at the same time."

Her words do something to me. That same feeling from earlier that made this feel like more than friends, more than just sex… it hits me tenfold right now.

My gaze darts across her face, trying to see if she feels it too. Trying to see if she wants this because it feels like there's this insane force between us trying to fuse more of us together.

But I can't read past her pleasure and desperation right now—and I vaguely remember my vow earlier to take it slow with her—so I don't voice any of that out loud. I just nod and kiss her again.

It doesn't take long for her to start moaning into my mouth and pushing down against my thrusts.

"Jax," she gasps, her hands grabbing at my arms, anchoring herself as her orgasm bears down on her. "Wait, no, I—I want to—"

"I know, baby, I'm there," I manage to choke out, my hips starting to stutter. "I'm right there with you." And when she clamps down on my cock, my brain fragments into pieces as my own orgasm tears through me. "Hailey, *fuck*—"

She shatters with a silent scream. And even as I'm pulled under by my own pleasure, I can't help but be mesmerized by the sight of Hailey lost to feelings of bliss that *I* brought on.

I empty inside her on a groan, burying my face in her neck as she shudders beneath me. When the sensations finally abate, I slump forward, trying to hold most of my weight on my forearms beside her head.

She snakes her arms around my waist and nuzzles into my chest with a happy sigh. I cup her head and hold her against me, reveling in the closeness as I'm still inside her.

She must feel the same way because when I try to pull out of her, she tightens her grips on me and whispers, "No, stay. I like you inside me."

I settle back on top of her, pressing my lips against her temple and stroking her hair.

And I realize, *I could stay here with her like this forever.*

"I want to stay like this all weekend," she says against my skin.

Not quite forever, but I'll take it.

I pull back so I can smile down at her. "Then we'll stay like this all weekend, baby girl."

It takes way more willpower than I would've thought to let Hailey leave my bed on Monday morning. I have to go to work, too, yet for the first time since I graduated college I'm debating calling in sick just so I can stay with her.

Even if that means sitting at the café all day while she works. That's how obsessed I feel right now.

I'm so wrapped up in the memories of this weekend—watching Seinfeld reruns, cooking every meal together, and even that weird hour when Hailey tried to introduce me to some weird electronic music subgenre called trap—that I don't notice Tristan and Aiden laid out on the mat until I'm already halfway through the room. The stupid smile immediately drops from my face.

Tristan has his usual no-bullshit stare on his face, but Aiden is grinning like an idiot. It doesn't take a genius to know he found out about Saturday night.

"You told Aiden?" I say with a resigned sigh. "Do we really have to act like high school girls and spread *all* the gossip?"

"I didn't tell him," Tristan says. "But it's kind of hard not to put two and two together when Remy bulldozed through here growling about friendship, best friends, and little sisters."

My shoulders tense. "She's here?"

Tristan just nods. "In the bag room, probably destroying a heavy bag right now."

"Fuck," I mutter. I drop my gym bag on the benches and then turn back to my friends, trying to figure out how I'm supposed to deal with this. *Does Remy hate me? Will she forgive me? Is Tristan mad?*

I look nervously at my best friend, searching for any disappointment or anger. But I see nothing.

"Did she say anything this weekend?" I ask him quietly.

He just shakes his head at me. "You have to talk to her, dude, don't put me in the middle. You two can figure it out." He takes a moment to study me, though. Then he asks, "I know you well enough to know you wouldn't start with Hailey just for sex, so out of curiosity, is it serious?"

I drag a hand down my face in frustration. "I'm not sure. It's *Hailey*, so everything is kind of automatically serious. But I don't know what she wants." I wince. "Does that make my betrayal better or worse?"

Aiden finally joins the conversation with a snort. "Dude, you're acting like you just stabbed someone in the back. Remy might be pissed, but it's just because she's protective of Hailey. It doesn't mean she's going to hate you forever. The second she calms down and remembers you're actually the most protective bastard we know, she'll see that this is a good thing. She just needs to get over herself."

Tristan aims a scathing glare at our friend. "You're lucky I agree with you, or I'd be choking you unconscious right now. But you better make sure she never hears you say that."

Aiden just grins, looking like he doesn't have a single care in the world. "Why not? I like when she gets feisty. She's fun to roll around with when she's angry."

With a growl, Tristan launches himself at Aiden and within seconds, the two are rolling around on the mat, angling for better positioning so they can finish the other with a submission. I just roll my eyes and start walking toward the bag room at the back of the gym.

"For the record, I saw you and Hailey coming from a mile away," Aiden says in a tight voice. But he doesn't say anything more because by the time I glance at him over my shoulder, Tristan is on his back and choking him with a forearm on his throat.

"Tap out, motherfucker, and admit my girlfriend could hand you your ass," Tristan hisses.

I just shake my head and leave them behind. With every step closer to Remy, my nerves grow and tangle in my stomach. I swallow nervously.

When I finally open the door to the bag room and step inside, I experience the full force of Remy's frustration—the sounds of her hitting the heavy bag are nonstop and so loud that by opening the door, I've filled the whole gym with them. I can't even hear the guys taunting each other over Remy's punches.

It doesn't take her long to notice me. When she does, she throws a few more shots before finishing her workout. She just stares at me, breathing heavily and waiting for me to say something.

"Hey," is the only thing I manage to choke out.

A heavy breath rushes from her lungs. "Hey," she says quietly.

I swallow nervously. "Can we talk for a minute?"

She just nods and pulls her gloves off. She grabs a bottle of water and takes a few swigs before joining me on the steps that lead me down to her.

We sit like that for a little bit, neither of us knowing what to say or how to start it. And even though I know I'm the one that needs to open with an apology, it still takes me a few moments to initiate the conversation.

"I'm sorry," I blurt out. "I know I should've talked to you first. There's no excuse for my behavior, and honestly, I'm not sure why I didn't. The only thing I can think of is I got a little Hailey-crazy." I could tell her that Hailey wanted to wait to tell her the news herself, but that feels like I'm throwing her under the bus. And if anyone is going to eat Remy's wrath, I'd rather it be me.

At that, Remy breathes a heavy sigh—and if I didn't know better, I'd say it almost sounds relieved. "Just tell me, is this casual for you?"

I startle and turn toward her. "Are you serious, Remy? Fuck no."

She winces at that. "Yeah, I figured," she mutters. Then she sighs. "I don't know if that makes it better or worse."

I'm still staring at her in shock. It takes me a moment to compose my thoughts because there are so many confused ones bouncing around my brain right now. "Just to be clear, what... what exactly are you upset about? Is it because I didn't ask you beforehand? Or because I slept with her?" That makes her wince again, but she still doesn't say anything. And when another, more painful thought occurs to me, my heart drops. "Do you not think I'm good enough for her?"

That seems to startle her. She turns to me in surprise, her wide eyes taking in the hurt in my expression and immediately causing her to soften. "Of course not," she says quietly. "You're my best friend, Jax, and the best man I know. How could I think you're not good enough? Even for Hailey?"

Her confession eases the tightness in my chest, but only a little bit. "So then what is it?"

She sighs and looks down at the water bottle between her feet. After a moment, she admits, "I just... I don't think she's in a good place after Steve. I won't pretend to know what she went through or what she needs now, but the last thing I want to see is her accidentally making you a rebound."

The idea shocks me enough that I freeze. "Just because I'm her first guy after a long-term relationship doesn't mean I'm a rebound."

"It's not just because you're the first guy, it's also because it's *so soon*. She's still so fragile. And if I know you at all I know you're helping her with all the shit in her head but... I just don't want to see you become a crutch for her. She needs to fix herself on her own." Remy shakes her head. "Just... do me a favor. I know you both better than you know yourselves, and after what I saw on Saturday, I know this thing is important enough to both of you that you won't give it up, but... just don't get too serious too fast, okay? Give her enough space to heal first."

I'm still in shock so all I can do is nod. The idea that my help might be a hindrance hadn't really occurred to me.

"Yeah, okay," I mumble.

Remy smiles at me but I can't help thinking it looks a little sad. And that hurts, so instead I choose to focus on the fact that Remy and I just made peace after our first fight in several years.

"So, are we good?" I mumble awkwardly.

This time, her smile is warm. "Yeah, Jax, we're good. We'll always be good. You're my brother."

I smile at that. Remy's only ever called me her brother a handful of times when she's gotten emotional, but it hits just as hard every time. I throw an arm around her shoulders and hug her against my side, knowing she's two seconds away from making some kind of sarcastic comment to lighten the mood. I kiss her temple. "Love you too, Remy baby."

Sure enough, the affection and teasing nickname that she hates are enough to snap her back to her alpha bitch persona. She rolls her eyes and shoves me away from her, but she can't quite hide the small smile on her lips.

"So. I'm the best man you know, huh?" I tease with a grin. "What about your boy toy?"

She rolls her eyes but that smile is still there, trying to get even bigger. "My statement still stands. He's too much of an asshole to be the best." Finally, the grin takes over her face. "But don't tell him that. He might be an asshole but he's also a baby, and it would hurt his feelings. Which means I wouldn't get any dick."

I wince and remove my arm from Remy's shoulders. "If we could not talk about you getting dicked down by my best friend, that would be great."

Her grin turns evil as she stands up and holds a hand out to me to pull me up. "That's payback for sleeping with my sister."

I grab her hand with a sigh and let her tug me to my feet. "Okay, that's fair. But can we please go back to never talking about our sex lives now?"

At that, it's Remy's turn to wince. "Yes, please. I need to hear about my little sister even less than you need to hear about Tristan's dick."

I only chuckle in agreement. We climb the stairs to go back out to the mat room, where—surprise, surprise—Tristan and Aiden are still trying to take each other's heads off.

At the sight of us, Tristan quickly capitalizes on his position on top and swings his legs around to trap Aiden's arm and force him into tapping from the armlock submission. Aiden pulls away with a grumble.

"You two make peace?" Tristan asks as he stands to his feet. When Remy nods, the tension visibly drops from Tristan's shoulders. He walks over to Remy and wraps his arm around her, pressing a kiss to her hair.

Aiden finally pops to his feet and glares at us all with his hands on his hips. "Alright, now that the family has made up, can we get back to training? I have a theory that all of you have gotten soft in your lovebird days."

Before Tristan can do more than growl in warning, Remy puts a hand on his chest and pushes him back so she can walk past him to Aiden.

"Come here, pretty boy, I'll show you how soft I've gotten…"

It's Friday night when Remy and I walk into the bar, and the first thing we hear is Jax's raucous laugh. At the sound of it, I can't help the ridiculous smile that appears on my face. It's as natural as the warmth that stirs in me whenever I'm near him.

I notice Remy studying me, but I can't bring myself to turn toward her. Things have been normal between us this week, but I haven't worked up the courage yet to actually have a conversation with her about things. Not because I'm worried that she's mad we hid it from her, but because I'm scared she'll have an issue with our relationship. I didn't exactly expect her to gush over my "new boyfriend," but I'm sensing more wariness than excitement from her about it.

And hearing her voice that out loud will hurt. So I'm not ready to hear it yet.

"Remy, Hailey, over here!"

I'm snapped out of my thoughts by the sound Lucy calling us over. I smile and follow Remy to the pool table in the back of the bar.

There is a core group of about six fighters that makes up

their friendship group, almost all of which are here right now. The only one missing is Tristan, who Remy said is traveling tonight for an MMA seminar that he's teaching in the morning. But beside Lucy are Max, Aiden, and Jax.

My heart stalls at the sight of him.

He's always been the kind of man that catches your eye. His smile and laugh are absolutely infectious, and every time he turns his attention to someone, it's impossible not to feel like you're the most important thing in his world in that moment. It's his personality that makes him breathtaking.

But even that is eclipsed by how he looks right now. His dark jeans are tight on his muscular thighs, and his slate-blue Henley stretches across his broad chest. The shirt's color is stunning against his lightly tanned skin and blonde hair. Not to mention, it brings out the blue in his eyes.

He really does look like a Viking god.

And right now, he's staring at me like *I'm* his goddess.

His smile grows larger and his eyes sparkle the second they spot me. It doesn't seem like he even notices Remy beside me, because he beelines straight to me with brisk, determined steps. Before I can even mumble a greeting—I might not have even gotten one out—he sweeps me off the ground and kisses me.

It's a chaste kiss, but I'm so overwhelmed by his presence that I still end up panting by the end of it. He just smiles up at me, looking happier than I've ever seen him.

"Hi," I whisper with a small smile.

His smile grows even wider. He nuzzles into my neck, trailing his lips along my skin and pressing light kisses everywhere. "Hi back," he murmurs.

I let out a nervous laugh, and I'm sure I'm blushing by now. "I didn't realize you were into PDA. Especially in front of your teammates."

He places me back on my feet. "Sorry. I should've asked you before how you feel about it. I... can't really help myself around you." He glances away, and I swear I can see a flush on his cheeks. "I just wanted to let everyone know—"

"That I'm yours?" I chuckle knowingly. I'm well-aware of how possessive men can get.

His gaze darts back to mine, looking startled. "No. That I'm *yours.*"

My lips part in surprise, Jax's words echoing in my head as I try to make sense of them. That's not a claiming, that's...

An *offering.*

"You're... what?" I ask in disbelief.

He weaves his hand into the hair at the nape of my neck, holding me in a tight grip so I can't look away. "I'm yours, baby girl," he murmurs. "I know it, you know it, now everyone knows it."

It's all I can do to stare at him. No one has ever cared about my feelings so much, or understood me so wholly, as to say something like that. I *know* Jax is the type to wear the pants in his relationships—I know he'd prefer to mark me as his. But he doesn't. Instead of doing what *he* wants, he gives me what *I* need.

He gives me a choice.

I fist my hands in his shirt and press my lips to his, overcome with emotion—overcome with love for this selfless man who cares so deeply about me. Who's always cared for me, even when I was just a little girl who followed the teenagers around. And now that we're together, he cares for me the way a man should care for a woman.

"You're mine," I whisper against his lips. "And I'm yours."

A pleased sound rumbles through his chest. It's accompanied by a rough kiss when he pulls me in by his grip on my neck. He devours my lips, pressing me tight against his body and angling his head so he can deepen the kiss.

This one is nothing like his greeting kiss. *This one* is a claiming kiss.

"I'm going to throw up in about 0.3 seconds if you two don't cut that shit out right now," an annoyed voice snaps, successfully ripping Jax and I from the haze we had sunken into.

I pull away from Jax, suddenly embarrassed. I was never huge on affection before, so PDA was never an issue, but something about Jax makes me eager for all the attention he wants to give me.

Jax takes his time turning back to the group. He presses his forehead to mine, his eyes closed, as he savors our moment for a little longer. Then he places a kiss against my forehead and turns us toward the group, his arm wrapping around my shoulders and keeping me close.

Everyone in the group is staring at us. Aiden is grinning, Max and Lucy look stunned, and Remy just looks uncomfortable.

My whole face heats at the thought that everyone just witnessed what we did. I can't bring myself to look at Remy except for a quick glance. "Sorry," I mumble awkwardly. "I didn't mean to force that in your face."

She softens at that and sighs. She doesn't look annoyed or like she hates Jax and I together, she just seems uncomfortable watching someone maul her little sister. Which, I can't really blame her for.

"So it *is* true," Lucy says with a grin. "I always knew you scaring the guys away from her was a little suspect. Guess now we know why."

Jax just glares at her. "Tell me you'd want your sister dating any of the assholes at the gym."

That makes Lucy wince. "Okay, fair point."

"Hey, we're not assholes," Aiden argues. "We're gentlemen of the highest caliber." He throws his arm around Max, who just rolls his eyes at his best friend's antics.

Someone snorts, and Jax and I turn to the girl standing behind Aiden with surprise. I hadn't realized she was with our group.

"I'm not sure the word 'gentleman' could apply to any part of your life," she says with a laugh. "I could pick some other words, but not that one."

I see Jax's eyebrows shoot to his hairline out of the corner of my eye.

I've only ever really been close with Jax and Lucy, so the rest of the fighters' group is a little unknown to me. The only thing I know about Aiden is that he's an even bigger ladies' man than even Tristan was, because he's all charm and good humor. Women fall all over themselves to get to him, sucked in by his smile and eager to seduce him in any way they can. I've never heard anyone tease him.

"Sorry, I didn't realize you were with our group," Jax finally says when his shock wears off. It's not uncommon for women or girlfriends to be brought into the group, but it is odd to see someone that's not the typical wannabe-WAG that is just trying to worm her way into the gym with fake words and plastic tits. "I'm Jax. This is Hailey, and that's her sister Remy."

The girl steps around Aiden and makes her appearance. She's beautiful, with long, dark brown hair that resembles a mane more than anything else, and her eyes look like emeralds. They're brought out by the green flannel that she's wearing over a simple black crop top and shredded black jeans. She's also got an incredible sleeve of black ink running down one arm and over her hand.

She reaches out her knuckles for a fist bump. "I'm Danielle. Just call me Dani."

Jax's lip twitches in an almost-smile at the greeting. He gives her a fist bump and nods his approval. "Nice to meet you, Dani. I assume you're here with the dimpled asshole?" He jerks his chin toward Aiden.

Dani just sighs, as if she's begrudgingly accepted her current situation. "Yup. Not sure how I got roped into his orbit, but here we are."

Aiden just smirks from his place behind her. "You weren't sad about our situation last night, sweetheart."

Again, Jax's eyebrows shoot to his hairline. It's not odd to meet Aiden's conquests, but it is odd to see him bring them himself and then brag about them to the group.

"How did you two meet?" Remy asks, sounding just as curious as the rest of us are about this mystery girl.

At that, Dani grins. "I met him on Temple's campus when he helped me run from a security guard. We ended up having to—"

Aiden shoots forward to cut her off by slapping his hand over her mouth. "Aaaand that's enough story time," he growls. "That big mouth of yours is going to get both our asses in trouble."

Dani tugs his hand from her mouth and turns to smirk at him over her shoulder. "Oh please. You love my big mouth." Her grin widens as she wiggles against where Aiden is pressed to her back. "And my ass."

Aiden's eyes widen, Remy barks a startled laugh, and Jax grins. "I like her," Remy chuckles. "We need more women to keep these guys in line." She grins at Dani, the two women bonding instantly with a single, unspoken conversation. "It's about time this asshole found a Daddy."

Dani just winks at her in answer.

New Girl has definitely made an impression.

Aiden immediately jumps to distract Dani by ordering another round of drinks, and I'm not at all surprised to see that she's a whiskey drinker, or that she's bonding with Max over whatever quality whiskey they both order on Aiden's tab.

Finally, Aiden turns back to Jax and I. "It's good to have you back, Little Porter," he says. "Glad you finally got the shithead off your back."

I offer a small smile, even though I'm trying to never hear about Steve ever again. "Me, too."

He grins, his eyes twinkling. "Heard you got a good punch in."

Now it's my turn to grin. "Damn right, I did. I can't be a Porter without having a good right hook." I see Remy out of the corner of my eye, smiling proudly into her beer.

Jax chuckles next to me. "She insulted his dick, too. I'd be surprised if he ever finds his ego again."

Aiden's eyes sparkle with amusement. "You did? Damn, girl. You took that man down in every way that counts, huh?"

I shrug. "He seemed to be under the wrong impression that his lap pinky was something to be proud of. I was just trying to help the guy out."

My words are met with an uproar of laughter.

Aiden seems delighted, Max and Lucy both crack up, and even Dani chuckles. Jax grins and I can *see* the pride glowing in his eyes.

It's Remy that's left staring at me in shock, with a look of *who are you and what have you done with my innocent sister?*

Aiden's laughter is the last to die off. "That's fucking amazing," he says on a final chuckle. His eyes rake over me, taking in my short red dress and the happy smile that seems to have taken over my face. "You look better now too. More alive. More womanly."

Remy rolls her eyes, sensing her idiot teammate's taunt, but Jax growls and tightens his grip around my shoulders. But before anyone can say anything, Aiden just starts laughing.

"Jesus Christ, bro. I wasn't hitting on her. I was just saying she looks… let's go with happier. Does that satisfy your protective instincts?" He rolls his eyes at Jax, but his satisfied smirk is still in place.

"If you thought I was protective before, I can assure you,

it's about to get a whole lot worse," Jax threatens in a deep voice. A shiver runs through me, just as it always does when he gets like this.

His words heal something in me in that moment. It's always been obvious that Jax cared about me, but I never really thought about what it means to have it be so intrinsic. With Steve I had his words, all the time and whenever I asked. He was quick to tell me he loved me and to remind me of the things he did that "proved" that love. But I was never actually convinced of it.

Not like I've always been about Jax.

I don't know if he's "in love" with me, but there has never in my life been a doubt in my mind that Jax shows me the kind of unconditional love that people rarely experience from people other than their parents. Even with friends, this kind of love is rare. But with Jax, with his declaration of *it's Hailey*, I've never been so sure of being loved in my entire life.

And even though I'm mortified at the feel of them, I know tears are burning at the back of my eyes, simply because I feel grateful.

I don't let them fall, though. I blink them away and turn my face into Jax's chest. And when I feel him press a kiss to the top of my head, I feel even more loved.

"You two are so adorable," Lucy sighs. "I always thought you'd be good together but I didn't know it would be like this. Fuck, I'm jealous."

I turn back to my friend with a smile. But in that glance, I see Dani listening to our conversation with a sad look on her face. When she sees me looking, sees me frowning in confusion about what part of my love for Jax could mean anything less than incandescent happiness, she just gives me an even sadder smile before turning back to her conversation with Max.

I throw myself down on the couch with a happy sigh. "That was so much fun. I feel like I haven't been out with you guys in forever."

Remy plops down on the loveseat with a grin. "That's because you haven't. Steve loved to steal you away from us."

The smile slips from my face. "Yeah..." I breathe a heavy sigh. "I can't get over how different it feels being free of him. It's like an actual chain is gone from around my neck, like I can finally breathe, and live my life without looking over my shoulder."

Remy's quiet for a moment. Then she says in a small voice, "I'm glad you got away from him. I didn't like what he was doing to you. And I didn't know how to fix it."

I lie on my back and stare ahead of me, watching the lights of the city dance across the walls of the apartment. "I wasn't always sure I'd get away from him. For a while, I really didn't know how it was going to end." I sigh, the sound of defeat heavy. "I don't like what he made me become. I'm still messed up over a lot of stuff that he planted in my head. Honestly, watching you and Tristan has been helpful because I feel like I'm re-learning how men should act with their women. It sounds ridiculous, but it's true."

Remy can't help the smile that my words bring to her

face—just as any reminder of her man does. But then she looks at me with a carefully guarded expression, seeming like she's hesitating saying something.

"How does Jax play into everything?" she finally asks.

I cringe, knowing I should've brought him up before this, and feeling guilty that I didn't. "He *is* everything," I admit on a breath. "It feels like he's the one bringing me out of the hole that Steve for me and buried me in." I sit up and nervously fold my hands into my lap, unable to look at my sister as I mumble, "I'm sorry I didn't tell you about him. He was helping me so much and we were spending so much time together that when our chemistry became this tangible thing, we just gave into it. It felt like the most natural thing in the world."

I peek up at Remy from beneath lowered lashes and find her giving me a blank stare that Tristan would be proud of. It's calculating, and gives me no insight into what she's thinking. I take a deep breath and say the hardest part. "I don't think I can apologize for dating him—he's too important for there to be even an ounce of me that could've stopped from starting this up with him. In the past few weeks he's helped me in ways that I didn't even realize I needed help with. He's always been invaluable, but now especially. But… I'm sorry I didn't tell you. I shouldn't have hidden it from you, and I regret that you found out in a way that wasn't us telling you." I swallow roughly. "I hope you know that we both love you very much. The last thing we wanted to do is hurt you."

Remy visibly softens on a heavy sigh. "I know that," she says. "I could never doubt that. And I can't say you two don't deserve all the happiness in the world, or that you're not a good match for each other. Anyone with eyes can see how smitten you are with him, and how obsessed he is with you. Plus, there's obviously no way for me to be upset about anything without being a massive hypocrite since Jax was so good about Tristan and I getting together." She pauses, and for the first time she seems nervous. I knew from the moment she found out that there was a *but* coming—this is the moment I've been bracing for. I just wish I had an inkling about what she might be worried about. "But..."

There it is.

"...I'm worried that it's too soon. I know you don't want to see Jax as a rebound but if you lean on him too much and he becomes a crutch, that's kind of what he becomes. It's not sustainable."

I stare at my sister, stunned. The idea that Jax—caring, selfless, protective Jax—could be anyone's rebound is insane. It's more like he's the kind of guy every girl dreams of meeting.

Remy looks guilty as she continues. "I love you both. So much. But I think you're still healing, and even though Jax is helping you with things that I'll admit I have no experience with, there are things that you need to figure out on your own, without his help. Without him being so close and so eager to pick you up and put you back together."

I finally find my voice. "Remy, that's insane. There's no such thing as too much help. Plus, I'm not a broken little doll that needs to be glued back together." I can't help the hurt that finds its way into my voice. I love my sister, but she has no idea who I am or what I need—and to hear that she thinks I'm broken hurts.

"Of course I don't think you're broken," she hurries to assure me. "I'm just saying you're healing from your relationship. And even though Jax can help with things, I just don't want you to lean so heavily on him." She sighs. "Just… try not to get too serious too fast, okay? It's the same thing I told him. I just want to make sure you get over Steve's bullshit in a way that doesn't hurt you worse in the end. And that doesn't hurt Jax…"

My eyes widen. "I would never hurt Jax. That man is a saint and deserves only the best things in the world."

Remy's smile is sad. "I know you wouldn't. He would never hurt you either. I just love you both so much and… I hate the idea of it not working out between you two because you both deserve the fucking world." She swallows roughly and I'm startled to see her gaze turns pleading. "Just… promise me you'll try to take it slow. Don't get too serious too fast. It can only help things to take it easy, right? There's no reason to rush into anything deep."

She sounds like she's trying to convince herself more than me. And while I appreciate the sentiment, I don't think I agree with it. Jax can only be a positive in my life right now so distancing myself from him could only hurt me.

I give Remy a sad smile anyway. "I'll try. But I can't make any promises, because Jax is ten times greater than even you realize."

Remy's smile is sad, too. She stares down at her hands and breathes, "Yeah, he is."

After a silent, contemplative moment and in an uncharacteristic show of affection, she stands and walks over to me so she can lean down and wrap me in a hug. It's even more surprising when she tightens her arms and doesn't pull away right away.

"I love you both. I could only ever wish for happiness for both of you, because you both deserve it more than anyone else I know." Then, she presses a kiss to my head and pulls away without looking at me. She just walks to the bathroom and starts to get ready for bed.

I stare after her in confusion. I don't sense that she's angry, just sad. She really is worried about us. And while part of me loves her for caring, another part of me is still frustrated that she sees me as something broken that I can't fix myself even with the right tools.

I sigh and rub my temples.

When she comes out of the bathroom a few minutes later, I'm still lost in her words. "Night, Hailes," she says quietly.

I sigh. "Goodnight, Remy."

Her bedroom door closes, and I lie on my makeshift bed, watching the city lights cast shadows across the room as Remy's comments tumble around in my brain.

Is she right? Am I using Jax as a crutch? Am I too invested too soon?

I close my eyes and pinch the bridge of my nose—my head hurts just thinking about it.

I sigh again and drop my hand to the sheets. When it lands on my phone, I automatically grab it and lift it to my face.

And smile when I notice I have a text from Jax.

12:32 AM JAX

> I miss you already. Hope you and Remy are having fun together.

All thoughts of my conversation with Remy eddies from my mind—instead, I'm left with only the euphoria that now fills me at the thought of Jax.

I start to text back but then I feel the sudden need to talk to him instead of just exchanging a few words.

He picks up on the second ring and I can practically hear the smile in his voice. "Hey, baby girl."

I sink deeper into the cushions with a happy sigh, immediately feeling the tension drain from my body. "Hi," I say quietly.

"Everything okay? I thought you'd be hanging out with Remy."

"I was. She just went to bed. And I felt like hearing your voice, so I thought I'd just call you. Are you busy?"

I hear a door shut in the background. "No, I'm not busy. I was just about to get into bed. Where are you right now?"

"I'm lying on the pullout couch, I just laid down too."

I'm sure he's got a devilish grin on his face when he asks, "And what are you wearing?"

I look down at my outfit. "I haven't changed yet. I'm still wearing my red dress."

His groan sounds across the line. "You looked so hot tonight, baby. I could barely keep my hands off you. I wanted to devour you all night.'"

"You *didn't* keep your hands off me tonight," I say with a laugh. "You were all over me."

He chuckles. "Guilty. You might just have to get used to it, then. That was about as much as I could hold back." My chest warms because I could easily get used to that. I loved every minute of his roaming touches and random kisses throughout the night, regardless of who was watching.

"I wish I was with you right now," I admit. "I wish I was in your bed."

"Yeah?" he asks. "Feeling needy, baby girl?"

I shiver at his deep timber. "I always need you."

My answer causes a pleased sound to rumble through his chest. "Are you sure Remy's gone to bed? She won't come out of her room?"

I glance at my sister's bedroom door. When I see the lights are off and hear the fan is on, I murmur, "She's out for the night."

"Good," he growls. "Because I want you to touch yourself."

Even though he can't see me, my lips part in shock. "Right now? While we're talking?"

"Yes, right now while we're talking," he says in that deep voice that sounds ten times deeper over the phone. "I'm going to tell you exactly what I want you to do, and you're going to do it and come quietly like a good girl."

I shiver again at the commanding tone that brokers no argument. I don't even have to say anything—he knows I'll do whatever he asks of me like this.

"I want you to tug down your dress and expose those beautiful breasts of yours," he starts, the seduction dripping from his words. I'm almost certain I could come from his voice alone.

I do as he says, pulling my dress down so my breasts are perched on the neckline. With one hand, I automatically reach to cup one, kneading the flesh and plucking my nipple.

"I'll bet you went straight for those rosy nipples, didn't you?" Jax growls in my ear. "Are you pinching them between your fingers right now? Remembering how it feels when I touch them? When I suck on them?"

I can't stop the moan that flows out of me at the vivid memory. I've barely even done anything, and I'm already drenched, captivated by Jax's words and wanting to come for him.

"Quiet," he commands in a quiet but stern voice. "You have to be quiet, Hailey. Don't make me put an end to our game before we've even started."

That shuts me up. My mouth snaps closed, the action an audible one that makes Jax chuckle.

"Good girl. Now, I want you to run your hand down your body and pull your dress up, just enough to expose that sexy thong."

Again, I do as he says, tugging my dress until it's high enough that I can reach into my panties.

"Don't even think about touching yourself before I say so," Jax growls. At those words I pause, my fingers inches from sliding underneath the satin. "I want you to take your panties off completely right now. But *don't* touch."

Again, I do as he says. Before I can tell him it's done, his voice comes across the line again. "Now spread your legs and feel yourself. Tell me how wet you are, baby girl."

A breath stutters out of me as I slowly open my legs—and I whimper when the cool breeze from the fan hits the heat of my soaking wet center. With one hand holding my phone, I slide the other down my body to glide over my aching heat.

"Jax," I gasp. "I'm so wet. I want to come already."

"You'll come when I say you can and not a second sooner," he scolds. I swallow a moan in response, my fingers gliding up and down my center.

"I want you to touch your clit now, baby girl. Touch it like I like to touch it, in soft, quick circles."

I comply right away, trying desperately to contain my moans.

"You're already so hot for this, aren't you?" Jax's teasing voice says. "I can hear it in your breathing. You could come right now if I let you, couldn't you?"

"Yes," I gasp. "Jax, please."

I hear a groan rumble through his throat at that. "That fucking word. You're lucky I can't see you writhing the way you usually are when you say that word, or this game would be over very quickly." There's a pause, and I hear some faint rustling in the background. But then he seems to compose himself because in the next second, his voice is just as serious and deep as it was before. "Now take those same fingers and slide one inside you. Just one."

The feeling when I comply is a total tease. "Jax, it's not enough," I whine. "I need more."

The bastard actually laughs; his chuckle rolls across the line and sinks directly into my aching body. "Slide another one in, baby girl." I do, and whimper quietly as I thrust my fingers in and out of myself in a sad effort at replicating how Jax feels. "How about that, is that enough?" It's impossible to miss the teasing in his tone, even though his voice sounds a little rougher.

"No," I whine. "Jax, please, I need you. It's not—I can't—"

"Quiet," he interrupts. And after my pleading, his voice definitely sounds strained now. "I don't want to hear another word until I let you come. Now, I want you to take the heel of your hand and start rubbing your clit again."

With my fingers still inside me, I do as he says and begin to grind the heel of my hand against my clit. It's barely enough and definitely doesn't feel the way it does with Jax, but I'm still immediately overwhelmed by the dual sensations. I can't stop the whimper that escapes my lips.

"I bet you're imagining how much better it feels when it's my hands on you, aren't you?" Jax says in a rough voice. "When it's my fingers inside you? My tongue on you? God, what I wouldn't give to have my face between your legs right now. Do you know what I would do?"

He doesn't wait to see if I'll disobey him and answer. He just continues on, weaving the fantasy between us. "I would lie down on the couch and drag you over to sit on my face. I've been thinking about it for days now. You'd look so pretty above me like that, watching me as I lick your pretty pussy. Would you like that? Would you like riding my face?"

I can't help it—I let out a moan. The combination of my fingers on my body and Jax's erotic words are ratcheting the pleasure higher and higher. My fingers start to move faster, my breath coming quicker.

"I'd tease you with my fingers too. I'd slide them in and start fucking you as you rode my tongue. Maybe I'd even play with your tight little ass. Has anyone ever done that?"

"Jax," I gasp. I'm so close, *God*, I'm so close.

He ignores or doesn't notice the fact that I spoke. He's too caught up in the fantasy, and it vaguely registers that I hear the sounds of him jerking off on the other end of the line.

"I'd make you come on my tongue at least twice before putting you face down on the couch and sliding inside you from behind. Then I'd make you come on my cock until you couldn't anymore, until you were limp and shaking in my arms."

I turn my face into the couch cushions to muffle my moans. They're too loud, the sensations too strong, and my orgasm is bearing down on me with a frightening intensity.

"Jax," I groan helplessly.

"That's right, baby, say my name when you come. I want to hear you fall apart from just the thought of my cock inside you."

And that does it. With a final gasp of his name before again burying my face in the pillows and muffling my cries for him, my release crashes over me.

"*Fuck*, Hailey," I hear him groan. The sounds of his fist moving over his cock are clear, and I shiver in the aftershocks of my orgasm at the vision of him jerking off. And then the primal, and very *male*, sound of his groan as he explodes on my name is enough to make me hot all over again.

The only sounds we're left with are those of our heavy breathing. After a moment, I hear Jax say, "*Goddamn.* The sounds you make are so beautiful. Even when you're not in the same room as me, you make me lose my fucking mind, baby girl."

A warmth—completely separate from the one caused by my mind-numbing orgasm—rushes through me at the awe in Jax's voice. I've started to notice that Jax is always full of praises after sex, and that in itself is enough to give me a rush of happiness that rivals that of the orgasm he just gave me.

It's yet another difference between Jax and what I'm used to, yet another reminder that this man is better to me than I could have ever imagined I would deserve.

CHAPTER TWENT-FOUR
Hailey

"Hailey, do you have a minute to talk?"

I look up from where I'm checking vendor deliveries on my tablet and make eye contact with Stacey. "Yeah, of course." I hand the tablet over to the on-staff manager, telling him, "Double check that what's coming in is what I ordered. Let me know if there are any discrepancies." When he nods and starts his count, I turn back toward my boss the café owner.

"Here, let's go into the back room." She ushers me past the kitchen and into the room that everybody uses for breaks. By the time we're both inside and she's shut the door, I'm looking around with a raised eyebrow, trying to figure out what's going on. If I wasn't curious before, I definitely am now.

"I'm sure you're wondering what's going on, so I'll cut right to the chase," Stacey starts. "You've been here for almost three years now, and a staff supervisor for almost two. Have you thought about where you want to go from here? What's next for you career-wise?"

I blink. "Career-wise?" I echo, trying to wrap my brain around her question and somehow come up with a logical answer. "Honestly, I haven't really thought about progression much. I'm pretty busy with school. Plus, I wasn't aware there was anything to advance to after my position now."

Stacey nods, as if she was expecting that answer. "Usually, there's not. Staff supervisor in any restaurant is as high up as you can get without being an owner." She pauses in wait, but when I can only blink again, she continues. "How long do you have left before you get your bachelor's?"

"A year, maybe year and a half, depending on how I can fit my classes into my schedule."

She just nods again. "Do you like working in this industry?"

I startle at the repeated change in topics. She's bouncing around something, which isn't like her. I feel like she's trying to lead me to something and I'm not picking up on it. "In this type of restaurant, yes. I wouldn't want to work in a bar, and I'm fairly certain a lot of dinner restaurants wouldn't be the right fit for me. But in a brunch or café spot, absolutely."

And just like that, she stops dancing around and instead shoves me face-first into her point.

"How would you like to take over the café for me?"

That actually manages to shock me into taking a step back. "What? Now?"

A slight smile twitches on her lips—part of her is enjoying throwing me off like this. "Not now. Not anytime soon. But I want to retire within the next couple of years, and I'd rather pass this place off than shut it down or sell it to a stranger. You're the perfect choice."

My eyes widen even further. "I'm twenty-one and I don't have a business degree, how could I take over an entire restaurant?"

Her face sobers as my voice starts to take on a hysterical pitch. "Hailey, you don't need a degree to run a restaurant. You already have more knowledge and experience than most people do when they open a restaurant. And I wouldn't just drop it in your lap, I would help you transition into it. We could take a year or even two, whatever you felt comfortable with. I could train you on everything you need to know—although, you know way more than you think you do. You could probably take over in six months and be totally fine."

"Six months?" I squeak. *Am I really having this conversation right now? What the hell is happening?*

"Like I said, I don't want to just drop it in your lap. But Hailey, this has your name written all over it. I've known you're the right person for this for longer than you probably want to hear. And you yourself just admitted that your ultimate dream is to open a café like this."

My mouth snaps shut at that. She's not wrong, that *has* always been my dream. I just didn't expect a golden opportunity to pop up for it at twenty-one.

"I don't have that kind of money," I say quietly, grappling for some kind of argument that she can't shoot down. Because this is insane.

That particular point seems to hold the most water because she nods in agreement. "I kind of assumed that. I won't lie and say it wouldn't require a bit of an initial payment, but it's not nearly as much as you're worried it is. We could work something out where I get a cut of profits over the next few months or years, so you pay it off that way. We could make it work."

I have no more words left. No more questions or rebuttals. I'm at a total loss for words.

Stacey studies me for a moment, waiting for either my agreement or some more issues, and when she gets neither, she just sighs and rubs the back of her neck. "Look, I'm not expecting an answer right now. I don't even need one next week. But I wanted to put the idea in your head and let you deal with it however you need to, because I really do think this is a great solution not just for me, but for you. I think this is where you always pictured yourself ending up—you probably just didn't think it would happen like this."

I'm struck mute, so all I can do is stand there with wide eyes and no words. Stacey actually looks amused at my speechlessness, and eventually she chuckles and pats my shoulder. Then she opens the door and ushers us both out of the room.

"Just think about it," she finishes. "Take a week, take a month, but let's figure out if this is something you want to do. I'm getting too old for this life—I'd like to retire and leave my baby in the hands of someone that I know will love and take care of it."

I nod dumbly and continue onto the restaurant floor. My shift supervisor quirks his eyebrow in question but I just shake my head in disbelief and gesture for him to continue his inventory task.

Stacey leaves soon after our conversation and I finish up my last few tasks of the day, moving around the restaurant in a daze as I replay our conversation in my head and try to make sense of it.

When I've finally kicked out my last few servers and locked the café, I grapple for my phone so I can call Jax. He picks up on the first ring.

"Hey, baby girl." It's impossible not to hear the smile in his voice. "What's going on? Are you done work?"

"Yeah, that's why I'm calling," I say on a rushed breath. "The owners just dropped a bomb on me."

"What do you mean? What happened?"

"They want me to buy it," I blurt out.

Yup, sounds just as crazy out loud.

"Buy it? They offered you the café?"

"Yeah." I pause, nibbling on my lip. "That's crazy, right?"

There's a pause on the other end of the line now. Then… "Hailey, that's incredible! Holy shit!"

My jaw drops. "Incredible? It's not incredible, it's crazy! I can't run a café, I'm twenty-one and still in college!"

Jax chuckles in my ear, which only sparks my frustration. This is funny to him? "Hailey, you're a 21-year-old college student now and you're running the café. You just told me the other day that the owners barely do anything. That's all you. Why wouldn't you want to take it over?" He pauses to consider something, then asks, "Is it the price? Is it something outrageous?"

I rub my temple, a headache starting to set in. "We didn't talk price. She said we could work something out where she gets a cut of the profits for a year or two and I pay her that way, but I'd still need to get a loan for the initial buyout."

Another hesitation. "So she wants to make it easy on you. That… sounds like a really good deal." My anger rises at his tone, like he specifically softened it because he thinks I'm being ridiculous. "Isn't this what you've always wanted? I thought you were going for a business degree so that you could open your own business one day. Isn't this what that is? Why do you sound so put-off by it?"

"Because it's insane!" I burst out, losing all sense of calm. "Because it's unheard-of. No restaurant owner sells their baby to a 21-year-old with barely any experience and barely any money. She doesn't know what she's asking for." I rush through more of my complaints before he can interrupt to contradict me. "And even if she's serious, I can't do this. It's too soon. I don't even know what I want to do with my life so why would I tie myself down like that? And I'm in school, so I don't have the time or the money for it right now anyway. And running the day-to-day like I do now is not the same as owning, so I'd have no idea what I'm doing. And…" I swallow roughly and drop my voice to a cracked whisper. "And I just couldn't do it."

"Hailey…" Jax murmurs soothingly. "You could do anything you set your mind to, but especially this. You've been doing it for two years already. And you've always wanted to open one. You would kill it."

I shake my head even though he can't see me. "I can't. I just… can't."

A sigh sounds over the line, and it sounds sad. Resigned. "I wish you could see yourself the way that I do. I wish you could see how strong and capable and incredible you are."

Hearing that just makes me even more uncomfortable than I already am, and suddenly, I just want to be off the phone. I can't listen to how great Jax *thinks* I am.

"I have to go," I say quickly. "I have homework to do tonight, I'll just call you later."

No sound is heard over the line, but I can sense his heavy exhale. "Okay, baby girl. We'll talk later."

I hang up and start to busy myself around the café. I could go through the closing tasks in my sleep, which is unfortunate because right now I could use the distraction.

I can't get Jax's words out of my head. I hear his voice, on repeat, telling me all these wonderful things that once I was dying to hear. I *wanted* to hear that I should go after my dreams, that I could do anything I set my mind to.

That I was good enough.

For the longest time, I didn't hear any of that. All I heard were comments that slowly cut me down and made me think I wasn't anything special.

Over the past few weeks, I thought I had started to see myself as better than that, as worth more. I've been dressing more like myself, feeling more beautiful in my own skin, doing things that make me happy. I've been feeling like I'm finally growing into the woman I always wanted to be.

So then why did I just freak out on Jax?

I collapse onto a chair and drop my head into my hands, groaning in frustration. I feel immediate regret for how that phone call just went. Jax has only ever been a light in my life, and the last person that should deserve anything less than my total gratitude. He's been a cheerleader, a listening ear, a shoulder to cry on—he's only ever shown me support and unfailing loyalty.

I wince as I play back the conversation in my head. *God, I was a total bitch.* Being shocked and nervous about Stacey's offer is no excuse to bite off Jax's head, no matter how automatic the reaction was. I was completely in the wrong.

I feel the familiar sensation of shame and guilt slither through my veins. And suddenly, I become singularly-focused on apologizing, on making this right between us.

I hop off the chair, an idea already forming in my head.

My arms are exhausted from carrying the grocery bags by the time I reach Jax's house. I knock on the front door, willing my physical and mental tiredness from the day away. I manage an exhausted smile when the door opens and a confused-looking Tristan appears.

"Hi," I greet him with forced excitement. "I came to make you dinner. Can you grab the bag from my hand? My fingers are about to fall off."

He shoots forward without hesitation and grabs every bag from my hand. I exhale a shaky breath of relief and flash him a grateful smile. "Thanks," I mumble. He just nudges the door open wider and gestures for me to come inside.

Tristan places the bags of groceries on the kitchen island. "Jax isn't home yet," he offers. "Does he know you're coming? He didn't mention dinner plans when I saw him at the gym earlier."

I just shake my head and begin unpacking the bags. "He doesn't know. I wanted to surprise him, and I figured food is a good way to make him happy." Tristan nods in understanding—

it's common knowledge how much Jax likes to eat. "I have plenty of food, so if you're hungry, you're more than welcome to join us. It should only take me about forty minutes to whip this up."

Tristan stands leaning against the fridge, watching me with that expressionless, see-all gaze of his. I fidget awkwardly with the bags, not wanting to make eye contact with him lest he see the turmoil and guilt inside of me right now.

"I'd love that, thank you," he says. And then, taking pity on me, he lightens the mood. "Any way you could teach your sister some of your tricks? Last week, she almost killed me with some weird chicken recipe that she found on Pinterest. I thought she was kidding when she said she royally sucked at cooking."

I let out a loud laugh, the tension dissipating from the air as I relax into Tristan's company. It occurs to me that this is the first time it's been just the two of us. "She's not kidding," I say with a chuckle. "She actually burned water one time. I didn't even know that was possible."

He shakes his head with an affectionate smile, and I can't help thinking about how much he clearly loves my sister. Theirs is the kind of relationship anyone would strive for—the kind where both people are so deeply smitten with the other that they only really come alive when they're together or at least thinking about the other.

I grin and ask, "Did she ever tell you about the time she…"

By the time Jax walks into the house thirty minutes later, Tristan and I are crying laughing after exchanging half a dozen Remy stories. He freezes in the doorway, glancing between us with a confused look on his face.

"What… is happening right now?"

I grin at him. "We're telling Remy stories. Remember the time she woke the entire cabin up at 4am because she was drunk and wanted mac and cheese but forgot to put water in the little Kraft cup?"

At that, Jax chuckles and relaxes his stance. "I forgot about that. Dad wanted to kill her." He looks over at Tristan and asks, "Where is she, anyway? I didn't realize we were throwing a party tonight."

"She's at home, writing," Tristan answers. "She got on a roll and didn't want to be distracted." He tips his chin in my direction. "I didn't know we were having a party tonight, either. Hailey just had the sudden, overwhelming urge to cook for you, I guess. Hence the Remy cooking nightmare stories."

Jax turns his attention back to me. He's not tense, necessarily, and he does have a smile on his face, but there's a sliver of unease in the air from earlier, and from the unexpectedness of my visit. He drops his bags in the living room and walks the rest of the way into the kitchen, stopping beside me to lean down and kiss my cheek.

"Hi," he murmurs against my skin.

I peek at him shyly. "Hi," I whisper back.

Tristan quickly interrupts our private moment by excusing himself upstairs. "I'm going up to shower. Food's done in fifteen?" he asks.

I nod. "Ten or fifteen, yeah."

He nods and disappears from the room, leaving me awkwardly fussing with the salad in front of me in order to avoid eye contact.

"Hey," Jax says quietly, nudging my hips. "Everything okay? I'll never say no to you cooking for me, but I am surprised to see you here." He hesitates, looking unsure for a moment. "I didn't think you'd want to see me after this afternoon."

I wince at the memory of my freakout and force myself to turn to face him. "I'm sorry about earlier. I shouldn't have yelled. You were just trying to help, and I acted like a total bitch to you. I'm sorry. I'll make it up to you, I swear."

Jax frowns and reaches up to brush his knuckles against my cheek. "There's nothing to apologize for. You're allowed to have a stressful day. I'll always be here to help you navigate anything—I always have been."

And he has. Always, without any hesitation. Shame washes over me all over again for the way I spoke to him—he deserves so much better.

My face flushes crimson, and I duck into Jax's shoulder to try to hide my embarrassment at my selfishness and immaturity. "I'm so sorry," I whisper into his shirt. "You didn't deserve what I said today."

Before he can respond, a sense of desperation rushes through me—a need to show him my apology. I step away from his embrace and turn to gesture toward the oven. "I thought I'd make you dinner to apologize. The casserole is almost done, and I just need to finish the salad while we wait for it, but I can always make you something else if you're not in the mood for what I made—"

"Hailey," Jax says, trying to interrupt me.

I don't even hear him, I just continue babbling. "Or, um, if you're sore I can give you a massage while we wait. It's whatever you want, really. You tell me."

"Hailey," he says, stronger this time.

"Or if you'd rather I just leave, I can do that too. I probably shouldn't have showed up and inserted myself into your night anyway, so I'll just leave as soon as the food is—"

"Hailey." He stops my word vomit with a tone that brokers no argument, at the same time that he grabs my arms and turns me to face him. "Please, just… shut up for a second, would you?"

I swallow thickly and force myself to look up at him. He doesn't look angry, just slightly frustrated.

"You're not going anywhere," he starts. "We're going to eat and then you're going to stay in my bed tonight if that's what *you* want, because that's where I want you. And not because you did something that you need to apologize for, but because that's where you belong. I love that you showed up to make me dinner, but you didn't need to do that just because things got a little heated today. When that happens we just talk through it, deal with it, and move on. None of this is necessary. Got it?"

I'm not entirely sure I got it, but I nod anyway. I want to be what he says but I still feel this intense, inherent need to make up for the way I acted.

He studies my expression, looking skeptical that I believe him, but he doesn't say anything else. He just pulls me into a hug.

"You're a queen, remember?" he murmurs into my hair. "I never want to see you beg or plead." A pause. "Unless you're on your knees for me, of course."

That finally causes me to relax. I bury my nose in Jax's chest and tighten my arms around his waist, unable to hold my smile back. I hear him sigh in relief and hug me closer.

"So what did you say you made for dinner?" he eventually asks, pulling us out of the tense bubble.

Dinner is a fun, easy time. I've never hung out with Tristan without Remy, so it takes me a few minutes to get to know him as a person instead of a couple, but by the time Jax is cleaning his plate of the last piece of meat, I've become increasingly familiar with Tristan's dry humor and expressionless gaze.

We even decide to watch some TV together after Jax clears the dishes off the table—without prompting, of course. It actually took me a moment to shake my shocked and unblinking stare from him when he started reaching for the plates.

We've barely started the first *Criminal Minds* episode when Tristan starts yawning and decides to call it a night, leaving Jax and I alone on the couch.

I'm curled up under his arm, sunk deep into my thoughts about everything that's happened today—about Stacey's offer, about my conversation with Jax, about how differently the *make-up* conversation with Jax went.

It's that last one that keeps me stuck in my thoughts. I don't want to compare the two men, but Steve is so deep in my brain that it almost feels like he's the only experience I have. Where Steve would've wanted to sweep the fight under the rug and ignore me for two days, Jax wants to get it out in the open. He wants to talk it out. And where Steve would've played the passive aggressive, unspoken blame game, Jax honestly doesn't seem to judge me for my freakout. It's almost like it never happened.

Yet, I still can't shake my guilt. If he would just let me make it up to him, I would feel better about myself and could move on.

I peek at him from under lowered lashes. My eyes rake over his languid body, sprawled lazily as he watches TV with a content smile on his face. He changed into joggers and a T-shirt after the gym, and because both are thin enough that they're plastered to his body in this position, I can see every bump and ridge of his muscles. I drop my gaze to his lap, finding the outline of what I'm looking for.

I only debate my actions for a moment. Then, I'm sliding off the couch and kneeling between Jax's legs, my hands running up his dense thighs until I'm bracketing his hips.

Steve wasn't a sex fiend by any means, but he loved making me pay penance by giving him head. It was an easy power play for a few reasons, namely because vanilla blow jobs gave him pleasure but not me, and because it put us in a physical hierarchy of power—he loved looking down when I was on my knees. And then when he was done, the issue would never be apologized for or spoken of again.

And while I know Jax would never do any of that, I'm desperate to right the power dynamic between us in a way that I know and feel comfortable with.

"Hailey," Jax murmurs, sounding unsure.

I tug on the waistband of his joggers and motion for him to lift his hips. He does, but I can feel him watching me closely. He doesn't say anything else, he just tenses his muscles when I fist his hardening cock in my hand and begin to stroke.

Barely a few breaths later, Jax is rock-hard in my hand. I waste no time taking him into my mouth and working him over with my tongue and lips.

"Fuck," he mutters. But he doesn't touch me or take over the way I thought he would.

I peer up at him through my lashes.

He doesn't look pained like he usually does when he's trying not to come; he's frowning. I close my eyes to avoid his gaze, even as I double down on my efforts to make him feel good.

"Hailey," he says softly. "Hailey, look at me."

I don't. I just continue working his dick as deep into my throat as I can get him, trying to suck the pleasure out of him.

"Hailey," he says, even softer than the last. He gently tugs me off of him using my hair and tilts my chin to look up at him. "Hailey, you don't need to do this."

I frown. "I want to. I like going down on you."

He shakes his head, looking almost sad. "I know you do, but not like this. I feel like you're doing it now because you think you need to."

I don't respond because I don't know how to. I just stare at him with what I'm sure is a confused look on my face.

He lets out a heavy exhale before he tugs his pants back up, then just as quickly he reaches down to lift me onto his lap. He nuzzles into my neck for a moment, as if he needs the comfort of our closeness to reassure him. I let the tension in my shoulders begin to relax. I reach up to run my fingers through his hair in an effort to soothe us both.

"I never want you to do something you don't want to do,

just because you think I want it," he says eventually. "I don't want to be anyone who, consciously or not, coerces you into doing things you don't want to do. I don't want you to do things because you feel like you need to, or because you think I won't want to be with you if you're honest with me." He finally pulls his head away to look at me. "Do you understand why I wouldn't want that? Do you understand why I would rather we be honest with each other and talk about things?"

My feelings morph from shame, to surprise, to embarrassment. I drop my hands to my lap and lower my gaze so I don't have to look at him.

The truth is… I *don't* understand. How can he say he'll still want to be with me if we're talking about a hypothetical disagreement? I don't know which of my preferences or thoughts might upset Jax. The whole thing I want to avoid is having an issue in the first place. No issue, no problem. No risk of me saying something wrong. My entire relationship with Steve was spent trying to avoid or minimize confrontation because I never knew which issue would set him off. If he didn't enjoy having control over me, any one of our arguments could've been a relationship-ender. And the thought of this ending with Jax is… soul-crushing. The only way to minimize the chance of that happening is to avoid the confrontation altogether.

"I want to understand," I mumble. "I just feel like my instincts are all messed up. All I know is that I want to make you happy." I look into his eyes. "Is that so wrong? To want to make you happy?"

A heavy exhale whooshes from his chest, and he wraps his arms tight around my body. "Of course not. I want to make you happy too. But I don't want you to do things for me out of guilt. I want you to start focusing on your happiness a little bit more, okay? *That* would make me happy."

I take a deep breath as I think about that for a moment. It feels backwards, but if me being happy makes Jax happy then the guilt does seem to loosen a little bit. "Okay, I'll try."

He nuzzles into my neck again, all remaining tension sagging from his body. We just sit there, hugging for several long minutes, content just to hold each other and breathe in the other's presence.

CHAPTER TWENTY-FIVE
Jax

"Motherfucker," Hailey mutters.

My head pops up at hearing her curse. We're currently sitting on the couch in Remy's apartment, both of us with our computers in our laps, even as Hailey's stretched the length of the couch with her feet pressed against me. Where I'm catching up on some work, she's doing homework for one of her classes.

Or trying to, apparently.

"What's wrong?" I ask her, rubbing her calf where her feet are pressed under my thighs.

She lets out a frustrated sigh as she rubs the heels of her palms into her eyes. "It's this statistics homework. It's driving me out of my mind."

I knead her calf muscle to try to soothe the tension in her body. "Want some help? It's been a while since I've taken a statistics class, but I can take a stab at it. Maybe we can work through it together."

She shakes her head with a frown. "No, I need to work through this myself. I've already reviewed it with a study group and with the professor, so at this point, it's just my brain. I just can't wrap my head around it."

I set my laptop on the coffee table and pull her feet into my lap so I can focus all my attention on her. "Is this the same class you struggled with last semester?"

Her frown intensifies. "Yeah. I failed this one and another business class. That set me behind schedule, so I definitely can't afford for that to happen again. And they're both required, so I need to pass this course."

Something occurs to me that makes my thumbs pause in their massage on the balls of her feet. "If you take over the café, do you even need a degree?"

She tenses, and I mentally curse myself for not thinking that thought through. We haven't talked about her freakout over the café owner's offer the other day, but I've had a feeling it's been simmering below the surface in the back of her mind. I probably should've broached the subject a little better—or at least not piled it on top of an already-frustrating topic.

"I should get a degree regardless," she says stiffly. "You can't get any job worth having without a bachelor's, and a business degree specifically would be helpful for most opportunities."

I start rubbing circles on her feet again, willing the tension to melt from her body. "Is that why you enrolled in the first place? To get a degree so you can list it on your resume?"

I don't say it in an accusing way, but the way she narrows her eyes at me makes it apparent that's how she took it. "One of the reasons, yes," she bites out.

I try to soften my tone even further. "That's... new. You used to say college isn't necessary—that real-life experience is more valuable than a piece of paper. What changed?"

Her jaw clenches, the mounting frustration clearly apparent on her face. Part of me wants to drop the subject and sweep her away in a night of mind-numbing orgasms, but another, bigger part wants to push this a little. Not just because we've been doing a lot of the orgasm thing lately and I want to prove to her that's not all this relationship is, but also because it's clear she needs to get better at communicating about difficult topics. I can only guess at the horrific communication Steve pushed on her—likely either none at all, or simply forcing her to accept his opinion—so this is exactly one of those things she needs to recalibrate for a healthy relationship.

So as much as I want to take back my question and borderline accusation, I don't. I just hold her gaze and wait for her answer.

When she realizes I'm ready to wait for a real answer, she clenches her jaw and says stiffly, "I grew up, that's what changed." Then she narrows her eyes at me. "You went to college for the same reason. You know you couldn't have gotten your current job without your business degree, so why are you picking on me?"

I never stop massaging her foot as I hold eye contact and say gently, "I would never pick on you, Hailes. I just want to have a conversation. And you're right, I did go to college to get a degree so I could get a job. But I knew the job I wanted, and I knew I needed a degree to get it. So there was a clear purpose. The reason I'm asking about school for you is because the job that you want was placed in front of you on a silver platter, and nowhere does it require a college degree. So, I'm wondering, why stay in school? Why not drop out?"

Her eyes widen at that. "Drop out?" she squeaks. "That's insane! I've already put in two years, I can't stop now. Plus, it can only be a good thing to have a bachelor's degree on my resume."

"That's true," I agree on a nod. "But not only is that degree not necessary for the career you want, but it might actually be stopping you from accepting your dream job. You know you wouldn't be able to spend enough time on school if you took over for Stacey; you'd have to focus all of your energy on the café. So why not do that? Why hold so steadfast to this college idea that never seemed like your thing anyway?"

She glares at me and pulls her feet off my lap. "Sorry we can't all have our career plans laid out perfectly in front of us. Some of us have to fumble through our choices and hope that we end up on the right one before the age of forty."

I ignore the distance she's trying to put between us and grab her around the waist so I can lift her into my lap. She doesn't try to pull away, but she continues to sit stiffly.

"I'm not judging you for fumbling through anything," I murmur as I brush her hair over her shoulder and press a kiss to her collarbone. "We all fumble, there's nothing wrong with that. I'm just trying to point out that for whatever reason, you're so hell-bent on college that you're not looking at the big picture—or mainly, the major opportunity in front of you." I tighten my arms around her waist and pause to kiss along her shoulder. "I just want you to be happy doing whatever it is you want to spend your day doing. I think that means running your own café, but if I'm wrong and it's actually getting your degree so you can go after something else, then I'll support that too.

I'm just trying to push you a little."

She relaxes slightly in my arms, and I breathe a sigh of relief. Part of me was expecting her to pull away from me again. And because we seem to be making progress with this conversation, I take a chance and push a little bit further.

"Did Steve tell you that you needed a degree?" I ask quietly.

She stiffens. And then pulls away, just like I was scared she would.

She unwinds my grip from around her and stands to put some distance between us.

"I *am* capable of doing things without a man's input, you know," she says coldly. "I know you and Remy think Steve had some kind of hold on me and influenced every decision I made, but I'm actually intelligent enough to be independent."

"I know that," I say softly. But, sensing I've pushed her too far, I don't mention the fact that I think she still has way more bits of Steve's influence woven into her psyche than she even realizes. That I think Steve had her so fucked up, that I'm pretty sure she does subconsciously need a man's input for big decisions. That that's the reason I'm pushing her to justify staying in college when the opportunity she wants is staring her in the face, even though I know she just wants to play it safe by continuing to do what she's doing—what she was told to do.

"I don't think you do," she snaps. "I think that's exactly what you're implying. And I don't appreciate it. Just because Steve was a manipulative asshole doesn't mean I somehow became a meek woman who can't make her own decisions anymore. And I resent the idea that my own boyfriend thinks that of me."

"Hailey, I would never—"

"I thought you of all people would understand," she rasps.

I shoot to my feet in a panic. I'm on her in an instant, cupping her face in my big hands and murmuring, "Fuck, baby, I'm sorry. I wasn't trying to hurt you. I would never think that of you. I…" I hesitate and swallow roughly. "I think the world of you. You're the strongest person I know. I'm sorry I suggested Steve is the reason you're in school, that was out of line. I was just trying to understand."

She deflates in my arms, leaning into my chest and wrapping her arms around my waist. She just feels tired.

"I don't want to talk about this anymore," she whispers. "I don't like fighting with you."

"Okay, baby, we don't have to," I murmur, stroking her hair in what I hope is a soothing caress. Despite wanting to push her past her comfort zone, I hate upsetting her—I always have. Even when she was a kid, Hailey stressed out made me stressed out.

She tightens her hold on my waist and burrows her face into my chest. "Let's just watch a movie or something."

I smatter kisses across her hair. "Whatever you want to do, baby girl."

So we spend the rest of the night watching movies, curled up in each other as if we're both desperate for the closeness to fix the space that our argument put between us.

And all night long, I can't shake the dread that Remy may have been right.

I'm stretching on the mats, lost in my own thoughts when I hear, "Hey, man, wanna do a few rounds in the cage?"

I snap out of my daze and turn toward Aiden. "What? Yeah, sure, let's go." I grab my sparring gloves out of my bag and step into the cage, ignoring the look Tristan shoots me. I wrap up my hands and take the center of the space.

"Ready?" Aiden asks before we start. I nod.

We start slow, even though we've both been working out for over an hour. I'm typically the one to charge out like a bull, so Aiden looks understandably confused. He's still an amateur fighter and used to getting his ass kicked by Tristan and I. But, sensing that I'm not in my usual *bull-in-a-china-shop* mode, he starts forward with a flurry of punches.

I parry them easily, but I don't see the body kick coming. I grunt at the impact when it lands clean.

"Jax, get your shit together," Tristan barks.

I roll my shoulders in an effort to shake the mental fog I seem to be in. I step forward with a boxing combination of my own.

Which Aiden easily deflects.

I grunt and shoot forward again. I manage to land a punch at the end of my combination, but Aiden takes advantage of my overextended position and ducks down to wrap his arms around my legs for a takedown.

Which he gets.

We wrestle for positioning on the ground but it takes me way longer than usual to dislodge him enough to get back to my feet. And once we're standing, Aiden doesn't give me a second to breathe before he's on me with strikes again.

We go back and forth for the rest of the round but I get caught with a big hook to the chin right before the bell sounds.

"Fuck," I mutter to myself, stretching my jaw.

"What the fuck is wrong with you today?" Tristan snaps. "You're normally all over Aiden. You barely got a shot in that entire round."

"I take offense to that," Aiden mumbles from the other side of the cage.

"What's going on?" Tristan presses.

"It's just an off day, calm the fuck down," I grit out. "You've had your ass handed to you plenty of times."

He stares at me from where he's holding onto the outside of the cage. He doesn't say anything, but his glare speaks volumes in a way that only Tristan's can.

The bell signals the start of the second round. This time, Aiden doesn't wait to see if I'm going to charge at him, he just shoots forward for another takedown. I manage to defend the first one, but now that he's sensed I'm not as much of a threat as I usually am, he's not letting up on his attacks. He faints another takedown and when I defend it, he hooks my leg and takes us to the mat.

I grunt as I land on my back. I try to get out from under him, but he manages to trap my arm during the scramble and, without any hesitation, falls immediately into an armbar.

I scowl as I hold onto my hand to keep him from being able to straighten my arm completely. And as much as I hate doing it, I use sheer strength instead of technique to get out of it. I shove my shoulders through where Aiden's legs are holding me in place, and press all my weight down on top of him. He's gritting his teeth and scrambling to finish me with something.

But the bell rings and he lets go of me with a scowl. I stand up with a frown of my own, only to come face to face with an angry Tristan.

"Breathe," he growls, pouring water on top of my head. I do as he says, even though bringing my heartrate down at the end of a round is as natural as breathing itself. I glance across the cage to where Max is now standing in front of Aiden and giving him the same treatment.

"Whatever is going on in your head, figure out how to get rid of that shit," Tristan snaps. "I'm not saying you can't have a bad day, but use this as a training exercise—you're bound to have a fight where you feel just as bad, so practice today how to let that shit go so it doesn't affect your fighting."

I glare at him even though I know he's right. This isn't my first rodeo, with a head that's not in it or with getting my ass handed to me, but it's still annoying to hear him say it.

"I got it," I grit out. I open my mouth to swallow some of the water Tristan pours for me. And when the bell rings and the third five-minute round starts, I bite down on my mouthpiece and start forward immediately.

"Be smart," Tristan barks.

But I'm way beyond that. I'm fueled by frustration, annoyance, and my own confusion over the mess of this entire day. This entire week, really.

I shove all of that away and fall on Aiden with a flurry of punches. I catch him with one shot at the end that forces him back, and I follow him eagerly. I step up the pace even though I'm running out of steam fast—off days always feel ten times more exhausting.

My anger at this day makes my punches wild. I'm not pressuring in a smart way, even though Tristan is screaming the same command at me over and over again. But I'm in such a frustrated state of mind that I ignore him completely and press forward, throwing as many punches as I can and hoping that one of them connects.

Aiden's not an idiot, though. He went into this sparring session expecting me to pressure forward, so he's probably been set to throw a specific technique since the very beginning. And when he throws it now, it lands flush.

I crumble when his left kick smashes into my liver. It's like an automatic off-button, no matter how tough you are. I immediately drop to my knees and curl into myself.

"You're done," Tristan barks. "Aiden, finish up with three blitz rounds on the heavy bag. I don't care what you throw, but go as hard as you can for three rounds. I want you burnt out." He jerks his head toward the bag room. "Max, you too. Coach is trying to get you on the January card so I need you ready."

I fall back against the cage and watch the guys leave the room. Tristan takes a seat across from me, both of us leaning against the padded posts and not saying a word for a minute while we just stare at each other.

"It's Hailey," I grumble, breaking the silence.

Tristan just nods in understanding and waits for me to continue.

I look down at my feet, unable to meet his eyes for this part. "I think Remy was right, man. I think it was too soon." I wince. "She... she doesn't even know how to talk to me if it's not sunshine and rainbows. It's like the only relationship she knows how to be in is a toxic one."

Tristan looks thoughtful for a moment. "You must've known that going in, though. That you'd have to hold her hand a little bit in the beginning."

I look up with a pained expression. "I knew. I just didn't expect her to fight me on it. I thought—fuck, I thought... it's *us*. We're Jax and Hailey. We've been able to communicate on the same wavelength since she was a kid. And now... now she either wants to fight me if I disagree with her, or just shove the whole argument under the rug. It's just not what I thought we'd struggle with." I let out a heavy exhale. "Sometimes I think I'm thinking too much into it, since it only really happens when we're talking about school or work, but then other times I get this feeling that she's holding her tongue with me. Like, she's too scared to tell me how she really feels because she's that uncomfortable with arguments or with making me unhappy. I just don't know how to make her understand that disagreements aren't the end of the world. That I won't love her any less if she talks to me about these things."

Tristan looks thoughtful. "It sounds like you need to show her how to communicate. We forget that she's young but she is—she probably doesn't know how to be a part of a healthy couple. Just be patient with her.

I groan and drop my head back against the post. "I'm trying, but I'm worried she's going to start resenting me. We've had a couple of arguments that stuck with me because we weren't able to work through them because she panics and then shuts down on me. And every time she makes a comment about me talking down to her. Which, I guess I can understand why she feels that way, but I can't figure out how to talk to her about things without her interpreting it as condescending." I swallow roughly and choke out, "I couldn't handle it if she started hating me."

"She could never hate you, you know that," Tristan soothes me. "Just give her time. You guys will work through this."

"What if I'm making it worse by being with her?" I ask quietly. Brokenly. "What if she has to work through this on her own? I'm worried that Remy was right—that Hailey needs space to figure things out by herself before she can be with someone again."

I pause, letting the worries of the past few days overcome me for a moment. "And it's freaking me the fuck out because if I let her go now she might never take me back," I choke out.

Tristan doesn't say anything. He just lets me sit there, staring blankly at the far wall as I let my mess of thoughts swirl over and over in my brain. I'm suddenly overrun by nerves, worry, hope, fear, everything. I feel everything. Because I have no idea what to do about Hailey or how this is going to work out.

I'm left with only panic.

Which Tristan sees immediately. "Go hit the bag," he orders, standing up from the mat. He walks over to me and reaches a hand down to pull me up. "Go burn off your nerves and then go talk to your girl."

Five rounds of bag work aren't enough to clear my head—I'm still stuck in a downward spiral of fear and confusion by the time I walk out of the gym.

I can't shake the feeling that this isn't leading to a good place.

That thought leads to even more panic, as well as the need to see Hailey right away. I check the time and realize she's probably finishing up work now, so I head straight for Remy's apartment.

She's already home by the time I knock on the door.

"Hey," she says, sounding surprised. "I didn't know you were coming over."

I push into the apartment so I can close the door and gather her in my arms. "I missed you," I murmur into her neck, taking a deep breath and inhaling as much of Hailey's essence as I can get.

"I missed you too," she says softly, wrapping her arms around me in return. "I was just about to call you to see what you wanted to do this weekend."

"I don't care, I just want to spend time with you." I squeeze her tighter, that nagging feeling of worry tightening its grip on my heart.

She giggles into my chest. "I love when you miss me like this."

I loosen my hold on her and start to pull away, murmuring, "Sorry. It's been a weird day."

She doesn't let me go far, though, because she traps my arms where they hold her waist. "I didn't say I minded it," she says with a smile. But then she notices something on my face and frowns. "You have a black eye. Were you sparring today?"

I nod glumly. "Aiden and I went a few rounds."

"Aiden?" she asks in surprise. "But you always beat him. What happened? Lucky shot?"

I shake my head. "Off day," I grunt.

She cocks her head as she looks at me. She doesn't ask anything else but she must come to a conclusion because she nods and turns to pull me into the living room. "Let's hang out here tonight. We can watch a movie or something?"

I nod and let her pull me down to the couch. I don't give her any space, I just wrap immediately around her, which causes her to giggle again.

I love the sound more than anything.

We spend the next few hours curled into each other watching TV and talking about everything and nothing. It's the kind of easy night that—minus the touching—Hailey and I have enjoyed for years throughout our friendship.

I slowly manage to let go of my nerves. My conversation with Tristan is still sitting in the back of my mind, but instead of waiting for the shoe to drop, I now find myself focusing on his words to *be patient with her, she'll figure it out.*

I sneak a glance at Hailey as she's tucked under my arm. She's happy, and laughing at something on the TV. My heart wants to burst at the sight of her looking so content.

"You're not working tomorrow, right?" I ask her, suddenly overcome with the need to keep her by my side for as long as possible.

She shakes her head. "I'm off tomorrow and Monday." She turns to look at me. "Why? Wanna do something?"

I can't help reaching forward with a finger to trace her nose, her eyebrows, the angles of her face. I feel so enamored with her, it's insane.

"I have to teach two private lessons tomorrow but why don't you come with me and then I'll take you out on a date at night? Whatever you want to do, I'm down. We can even hit repeats on your *Carpe Noctem List* if you want."

I'm smiling at my joke, but I feel her stiffen against me. My finger pauses on its trail, and I frown in confusion.

"You don't want to wait for me at the gym?" I ask her.

She sees my smile dropping and immediately tries to plaster one on her face. It would fool me except I know every expression she has, and I know this one doesn't reach her eyes.

"Of course, I'll come with you," she says, but it sounds forced. "That sounds fun."

My frown deepens. "You don't have to come, Hailes. The only reason I suggested it is because I'm selfish and want you by my side for as long as we're both off work. But I understand if you don't want to come. I'll just pick you up after."

She shakes her head before I'm even finished talking. "No, it's okay, I want to come. I'll come."

She's lying, I know it. I know this girl better than she knows herself some days, and I know she doesn't want to come with me tomorrow.

I study her profile as she watches the TV and avoids meeting my eyes. She probably knows I'm reading her lie. But why? Why is she lying about something little like this?

And suddenly, a boulder drops into my stomach. The feeling that's been sitting with me all day, about something bad happening… this is it. This is what I knew was coming.

My whole body goes cold with realization.

Not just about the reason for her lie, but about what that lie means.

She doesn't want to say no to me. Even about something like this, she can't bring herself to tell me no.

I try again, this time with desperation lacing my words. "Hailey, I promise it's fine if you don't want to go. I completely understand. It's boring, and the only reason you'd be going is because I'm a selfish bastard. Just stay at home, I'll pick you up after."

"I said I want to go," she says tightly, her body stiff in my arms. She's annoyed.

I swallow roughly, my palms going clammy with nerves. "Tell me no," I whisper brokenly. "Just tell me no, Hailes."

I need her to say no. I *need* her to say no.

I need her to stand up for herself. I need her to show me that she *can*.

Her gaze shoots to me in confusion and annoyance. "What? No, I said I'd go. I'm going." Then she turns back to the TV, effectively ending our conversation.

I close my eyes, the pain of our current reality washing through me like a tidal wave. A wave that sees only destruction in its path and that can't be derailed, no matter how badly I wish I could change things.

It just… is.

She can't even tell me no. Even if I tell her to, even if I give her an environment where she feels safe enough to, she can't do it.

And in this moment, I realize that in order to save her, I need to do exactly the thing that might drive her away from me forever.

"Hailey," I croak, the pain rushing through me. "We need to take a break."

CHAPTER TWENTY-SIX
Jax

Her head snaps to face me. "What?!"

The look on her face shreds my heart. *Fuck, I don't want to do this.*

I try to get my words out, but they get stuck in my throat. I swallow roughly and try again. "Your sister was right. We rushed into this too quickly."

She quickly shuffles away from me to create some distance between us. "You're breaking up with me?" she whispers in disbelief.

"No," I say hurriedly. "I could never—I don't want..." Fuck. This is the hardest thing I've ever had to say. "I just think we need a little bit of space. I was wrong to jump on you right after yourbreakup, I should've given you space then to clear your head after that piece of shit—"

"*You* help me clear my head!" she interrupts angrily. "You're exactly what I need right now. Why are you trying to push me away? What happened?"

I mutter a curse and look to the ceiling for patience and a way to explain this without sounding condescending. "I...

I just think you're leaning on me too heavily," I say without looking at her. "I think Steve made you dependent on him and now that's the only kind of relationship you know. It's how you're treating us." I drop my gaze to my lap and admit quietly, "I don't even think you realize you're doing it."

She jumps up from the couch, the anger evident on her face. "Stop it," she hisses. "You don't get to tell me how I feel, Jax. You have no idea what I went through or how I feel being with you."

I hold my hands up in surrender. "You're right, I don't—"

"You don't get to make a decision for me," she continues angrily. "You don't get to be noble Jax and save poor little Hailey from herself."

"Hailey, I would never—" I say in a panic.

"That's exactly what you're doing!" she exclaims, throwing her hands in the air. "You're making a decision for me without me."

She's right. I know she's right. But that doesn't mean I'm wrong about this. She needs to become her own person again, and she can't do that when I'm this close to her.

That thought hardens my resolve and convinces me that I'm doing the right thing. I take a deep breath and stand from the couch, keeping my movements slow so as to not make her any more panicked. She watches me with a wary glare, the anger still radiating from her body.

I step in front of her and cup her face, my thumb lovingly rubbing her cheek. "Hailey," I murmur softly. "I don't know anything about what you went through, you're right. All I know is you… I know you. And I'm not looking at the same

Hailey that I know is deep inside you. I just want to give you some space to find her again because I think being with me is giving you a crutch and an excuse to not deal with all the shit in your head. I think if we just took a break for a little—"

She knocks my hand away from her face. "There's no such thing as a break, Jax," she cuts me off angrily. "We're either together or we're not. There's no in between."

I swallow roughly, even though I knew there was a possibility she'd say that. The Porter sisters have always had this thing about being treated as second-best, so I'm not surprised she's giving me an ultimatum.

"If that's what you want, then I understand," I mumble, even though saying the words feels like driving nails into my own goddamn heart. "I still stand by needing some space."

She stares at me in disbelief, and I can practically feel the realization start to hit her that I'm being serious about this.

"So if I started fucking someone else, you would be fine with it," she says in a flat tone.

I flinch. No, I wouldn't be fine with it. Even thinking about it makes me want to take back everything I just said and lock her into my bedroom so no man can ever look at, let alone touch, her ever again.

But I grit my teeth and remind myself that this is for the greater good. That Hailey just needs a little space to heal on her own, and then we can try this again, for real. This is just the necessary painful part.

"I wouldn't be fine with it, but it would be your decision and I would understand," I somehow manage to say. I take a breath and add, "But I would hope you would try to understand why I'm doing this and take the space to heal instead of trying to fill the void with another guy. Which is exactly what I'm trying to fix, by the way."

Her face falls. "Fix?" she whispers brokenly. "You want to fix me?"

Fuck. "That was a poor choice of words."

The anger returns to her face in the blink of an eye. "No it wasn't. That's exactly what you meant." She crosses her arms over her chest, waiting expectantly. "Go on, then. Tell me what you think I need to fix. If we're going to have this conversation let's at least be honest about it."

I hesitate, sensing the trap but not knowing how to deal with it.

"Go on," she pushes. "Tell me."

I deflate, resigning myself to my fate. And instead of trying to take it all back and beg for her to forget everything I just said, I tell her the truth.

"You're too used to being in a toxic relationship," I admit, dejected. "You don't know how to exist in a relationship when it's not perfect all the time, because you're so used to your concerns being either ignored or treated like they're invalid." I inhale a stuttering breath, searching for the courage to go on.

Hailey just stands there, frozen.

"I could get through all that with you, if that's all it was. I could show you healthy communication. But it's not just that." I can't help but wince at the next part. "Steve manipulated you so badly that he crushed your will and made you dependent on him for any kind of self-confidence. And now you're leaning on me the same way. You can't make a decision on your own because you're too scared you're not good enough, and it's holding you back." I meet her gaze, resigning myself to the sadness that's slowly starting to overwhelm my system. "You can't even tell me you don't want to go to the gym because you don't want to tell me no."

Her eyes widen at that. "You're breaking up with me because I didn't want to hurt your feelings?"

I hesitate, but then nod. "When was the last time you said no to someone?"

Her lips part in surprise. "I say no at work all the time!"

I nod again. "Yes, but only because you've somehow managed to compartmentalize your work-self away from everything else. You've been in the restaurant industry long enough that work-Hailey managed to not change, even as real-life Hailey became less and less like herself." I pause, my resolve hardening. "When was the last time you said no to someone?" I repeat.

She looks lost for a moment. "I... I... there's been plenty of times that I—" But then the anger returns and her face clouds over. "That's not fair. It's not a crime to be a people-pleaser."

"It is if it's at the cost of your own mental health. You deserve to do what makes *you* happy just as much as anyone that you make happy by compromising when you don't want to," I say quietly.

Her eyes widen. I brace myself for another outburst, which means I'm caught off-guard when I get the opposite.

Just a flat statement, a cold dismissal.

"Fuck you, Jax. Fuck everything you just said."

I flinch. Hailey cursing—especially aimed at *me*—is like a

knife through the heart.

"Fine, let's break up, then. If that's what you want."

I've never heard her voice so cold.

I hesitantly raise my gaze to meet hers. Her arms are still crossed and she's staring at me with a level of hate and anger that I never thought I'd see from the sweet little girl that used to follow me around when she was a kid.

It breaks my fucking heart.

"I'm sorry," I choke out. "I hope you can understand why I'm doing this."

"I don't," she says coldly. "All I see is you giving up on us."

I shake my head, dropping my gaze. "I could never do that. I'm just trying to do what's best for us." I swallow roughly before looking at her again. "I just don't want to be a rebound."

And just like that, all the anger and coldness leaves her body like a breath leaving her lungs.

"You could never be a rebound," she says in a shell-shocked voice. She swallows, looking slightly panicked now. "You're Jax," she whispers brokenly.

Fuck, what that does to me. I never thought it would hurt to hear someone say Jax and Hailey in the inevitable kind of way it's always been said.

But this… hearing her say my name like that? It *hurts*.

Her panic escalates. She starts to shuffle her feet where she stands, the emotion building behind her eyes. "You're not a rebound, I swear. You're…" She looks away, her fidgeting increasing. "You're *everything*."

When she turns back to me I almost crumple to my knees from the sight of the pain in her eyes. "Just tell me what you want, and I'll fix it. Tell me what you need from me." Her voice cracks when she adds, "Please."

"I can't, baby," I whisper. "I need you to do this for yourself."

Her panic intensifies and her breaths start to come quicker. "Don't do this," she begs. "Please, don't leave me. Just... let's try again. I'll be stronger, I promise."

I give up on trying to keep distance between us and step up to stand in front of her. I hesitate for a moment but then when I realize she's not pulling away from me, I cup her cheek again, with both hands this time. "I need you to be stronger without me," I whisper.

A tear rolls down her cheek, and I swear I can hear my heart crack down the middle at the sight.

And fuck, I just want the anger back. I can deal with the anger.

I can't deal with the sadness.

"I can't do this without you," she sobs, her tears coming faster now. "You're the only thing holding me together. I—I can't—" She buries her face in my chest, clutching me tightly.

I wrap my arms around her, wanting to shield her from the pain and the hurt even as I know I'm the one inflicting it.

"I promise I'm not abandoning you," I murmur into her hair. "This doesn't mean you'll never see me again. I'm still here, I still care about you just as much as I always have. That will never, ever change. I promise you that."

She pulls back to look at me, her expression turned to pleading.

Shock. Anger. Panic. Sadness. Desperation.

I can't handle any of it. I'm dying inside.

"Please, don't do this," she begs, her face damp and her nose pink. "Please." Her gaze darts over my face, looking for any sign of help. I don't know if she can see the pain that it feels like is etched all over it, but whatever she sees doesn't reassure her at all. In fact, she seems to become more desperate, because she turns to the one thing that she knows threatens my resolve the most.

"Jax, please," she whispers.

My eyes close, a single tear rolling down my cheek at the sound of my name as a plea on her lips.

"I'm sorry," I choke out. I lean forward to press a kiss to her forehead, lingering with the contact because I know it'll be the last for a while. "I'm so sorry. I never meant to hurt you."

I try to step back, but I can't bring myself to move away from her. I can't stop holding her.

I press my forehead to hers and take a deep, stuttering breath. "I want you to find that little girl that I first met when I moved into the neighborhood, the one who demanded I take her to the movies. The teenage girl who danced because it made her happy. The woman that you grew into who embodied kindness while still living her life and doing what she wanted. That's the Hailey I want you to find again. And as much as I want to do it for you, I think you have to do that on your own."

She cries silent tears, clutching my shirt in her hands. And when I gently peel her hands away, it hits me that even crying, she's the most devastatingly beautiful woman I've ever seen.

It doesn't take much for me to nudge her to let go. When she does, she just looks resigned—she looks tired, like she doesn't have it in her to fight me anymore.

I walk toward the door before my heart can win the battle of calling the whole thing off. Every step is a struggle, and it's most likely a testament to my training that my mental fortitude pushes me forward.

Even still, I can't stop myself from looking back at her when I get to the door. She hasn't moved an inch, just continues to stare at me with a look of sad resignation.

I try to speak but the words won't come. I clear my throat and try again. "I meant what I said about not expecting you to wait for me. I want you to do whatever feels right, whatever makes you that Hailey I've always loved. But... I want you to know that I'll be waiting. I'll never want anyone but you. And even if it takes you years..." My eyes fill with more tears, and I struggle to blink them away. But my voice still cracks when I say, "I hope one day you'll come back to me."

She curls into her stomach with a sob. And at the sight of her fresh tears, the knife that I've been slowly cutting us with settles into my heart and bleeds me dry.

I don't look back again as I leave the apartment and shut the door behind me.

I watch the door shut with a horrible feeling of finality. Not just because Jax isn't one to joke about something like this or change his mind, but because it *feels* final. I can feel the pain in my bones. I can feel the loneliness in every breath I suck into my lungs.

At the thought, I actually start to hyperventilate. I struggle to pull enough air in, taking short breaths that quickly turn into wheezing. I curl over my stomach as I drop to the couch, my head automatically dropping between my knees.

Fuck. What just happened?

I struggle to wrap my brain around the fact that Jax, one of my best friends, just broke up with me. After barely a few weeks and with no warning.

At that thought, I feel a flicker of anger. It's lost in the fire of hurt but immediately I realize it's easier to deal with.

I latch onto it.

I feel angry that he abandoned me. Angry that he made this decision without talking to me.

Angry that he thinks he knows what's best for me.

My resentment grows. How dare he assume he knows what I went through? Who is he to make decisions for me? He doesn't know what he's talking about. He has *no idea* what I need.

How *dare* he tell me that I'm broken and in need of fixing? And that he knows how to *fix me?*

I let the anger grow and grow until my tears turn into tears of rage. I'm trembling with fury, clenching and unclenching my fists as I try to remind myself to breathe.

But when the door opens and Remy and Tristan walk in, the walls of anger prove to be completely useless against the river of pain. The second I make eye contact with a shocked Remy, I double over and let the tears run free.

I don't comprehend Tristan's muttered curse or the way he whispers something to his girlfriend before rushing out the door. I don't even register Remy as she approaches me with cautious steps, because I'm crying too hard to notice anything beyond the bone-deep pain.

God, it hurts. How could he do this to me? How could he leave me like this?

"Hailey," my sister says as she moves to sit next to me on the couch. "What happened? What's going on?"

It takes me a few minutes to be able to even attempt talking. Remy just stays by my side, stroking my arm in an effort to comfort me.

"He—I—" I start, but I'm still crying too hard and trying to talk just makes me gasp for air.

"Take a deep breath," Remy murmurs.

It takes me a minute to breathe without feeling like I'm

hyperventilating but eventually I'm calm enough to choke out, "He left me."

Remy freezes. "Jax?"

I nod, unable to say his name out loud. "He broke it off. He said he wanted space."

She doesn't say anything but I can sense the tension in her stance. Suddenly I'm reminded of something that Jax said earlier, and then my body freezes, too.

"You told him to do it," I breathe. I stare at her in shock, the details of Jax's comment crystallizing in my head. "He did it because of you."

She jerks back in surprise. "I would never tell him to do that."

"Not directly, but he did it because of what you said to him." I jump to my feet and stare down at her, my anger returning. "You're the reason he just dumped me."

And still, the anger is ten times easier to deal with than the pain. So I embrace it. I embrace it and aim it at my sister, ignoring my subconscious that's whispering that nothing my sister could ever do would be deserving of my rage.

"Why couldn't you just let us be happy? Did it bother you that much that your best friend could like your little sister? Or was it the fact that he didn't ask your permission before fucking me?"

Remy flinches at my crude words. "Hailey, I would never want—"

"You told him it was too soon. You told him to give me space. How did you think he would take that? He probably thinks that was your way of not giving your approval."

She can't quite make eye contact with me as her hands fidget in her lap. "I can talk to him, I never meant for him to—"

I laugh, the sound cruel and harsh. I feel like I'm losing my mind. I don't even recognize myself right now, but the pain in my chest is turning me into someone else entirely.

"Go talk to him, go let him know he did the right thing. I don't need someone that's too scared of my sister to be with me."

At that, she frowns and finally meets my eyes. "Jax would never hurt you because he's scared of me. You trump me every time when it comes to that man. How don't you know that?"

I stumble in my anger. A part of me does know that he's always been more protective of me, but I'm having a hard time reconciling that side of him with the one that just walked out the door.

"That's hard to believe when he would never leave you behind," I snap.

She drags a hand down her face in frustration. "He loves you, Hailey. I'm sure he thought he had a good reason—"

At that one word, all the fight goes out of me. And I'm just left exhausted. "I don't want to talk about this anymore," I interrupt. "I just want to go to bed."

For a moment, it looks like she's going to fight me on this and attempt to force me to talk more about it, but she must see something on my face that lets her know it would be a fruitless battle. She nods and stands up off the couch.

"I'll leave you alone. Just… let me know when you want to talk about it." She grabs the bag that she dropped at the door when she came in and makes her way toward her bedroom. But before she walks through the doorway, she pauses and lifts her gaze to mine, guilt shining clear as day in her eyes.

"I'm sorry," she whispers brokenly. "I never want you to be unhappy. If this is my fault, I'm so sorry." There are tears shining in her eyes when she looks away, but I can't bring myself to reassure her right now. I just stare after her sullenly.

Realizing I'm not going to say anything, she walks into her bedroom. At the sound of her door shutting a breath whooshes out of me, as if I can finally let some of the pressure in my chest ease.

But it doesn't do anything for the pain. I feel like I can finally let myself go, to do whatever feels natural now that I'm by myself, but it doesn't lessen the feel of my soul bleeding out on every breath.

I curl up on the couch and succumb to my thoughts and feelings. I let every confused, frustrated, angry thought blow through my mind.

For the rest of the night, I lay curled in a ball on my makeshift bed, and let myself get dragged down into the pain.

Although my rare two-day break from work does end up being beneficial, it's not nearly as enjoyable as I was anticipating. Instead of spending it with Jax—cooking together, laughing about childhood memories and making new ones, getting lost in each other between the sheets—it's spent on shitty food and trash TV used only to distract me.

I don't speak a word. Remy tries to get me to engage with

her, but I barely give her more than a grunt of acknowledgement. Even those are scarce. I'm wallowing and I know it, but I'm feeling betrayed by the two most important people in my life and I can't dredge up the energy to even attempt to fix it.

By the time I go back to work on Tuesday, I have a stoic face that even Tristan would be proud of.

And I realize that Jax may have been onto something when he said I'm able to compartmentalize my work self from the rest of my life—because despite the hurt still festering inside me, you would never be able to tell by looking at me.

I plaster my customer service mask on and go through the motions. For days. I give my employees and my customers the same level of attention that they would've received on any other week. And when Stacey pulls me aside on Friday and asks if I've thought any more about her offer, I tell her the truth: that I'm in the middle of an existential crisis that only a 21-year-old could go through and still trying to figure out what I want to do with my life, with both school and the café.

"Keep thinking," she tells me. "I wouldn't have offered it if I didn't think you were both ready and meant for this."

Her honesty is what leads me back to the conversation I had with Jax about it. I turn his words over and over in my brain as I finish out my shift, to the point that I'm so distracted by my own thoughts, I don't even notice Remy walk into the café.

"We're closed," I call over my shoulder, lifting the last chair onto the table.

When I don't hear anything in response, I turn toward the door, ready to take out my frustration on whatever idiot customer can't read a goddamn sign.

But when I see my sister standing by the host stand, hands clasped nervously and her expression pleading, my anger deflates.

I don't say anything, I just wait for her to tell me why she's here. We've barely spoken all week. On the nights that she's not at the gym, I bury my nose in my computer and ignore every attempt at conversation that she throws at me.

But I'm tired of fighting with my sister. We've never gone through something like this and the distance is starting to wear on me. Subconsciously, I know the breakup isn't her fault, but it was hard to look at her and know that her comment to Jax played a part in his leaving me.

I miss my sister. My resolve has already weakened enough this week, so when she asks if I want to get a drink and talk, I nod without a second thought.

"Just let me finish closing. I'll be done in ten minutes."

She nods and lets me continue working. By the time I've got the key in my hand ready to lock up, the silence has grown to an uncomfortable level. Which is saying something because I've never been a big talker.

"Let's just go down the street," she says, breaking the silence. "It'll still be slow enough for us to find someplace to sit."

I nod and follow her into the restaurant.

Remy leads us straight to the bar, where she orders a sour IPA, just like I knew she would.

"I'll have a loaded Corona," I answer automatically.

Then cringe when the memory comes rushing back.

"You'll have to tell me what's in that," the bartender says with a bored look.

"It's just a Corona and a shot of tequila," I answer simply. I see Remy watching me out of the corner of my eye, and I know she's wondering why I'm drinking straight liquor. But she won't comment on it, of course. And if she knows that loaded Coronas are Jax's thing, she doesn't mention it.

"Have you seen him?" I ask without looking directly at her.

She winces at my blunt question but nods anyway. "Yeah."

"How is he?" I try to make my voice as flat as possible but I'm not sure how much I'm succeeding. I'm hanging onto her answer way more than a self-respecting, recently-dumped woman should be.

"Not great," she mumbles. "He looks about as frozen as you do. Which is saying something about his mental state because that man is more expressive than any other man I've ever met. He just seems like he's going through the motions."

A flicker of relief wars with a stab of pain at hearing that he's struggling. I would never, ever wish hurt onto any of my friends, but it's helping to know I'm not the only one affected by this.

"What happened, Hailey?" she asks quietly. "Jax won't talk to me either. I have no idea what happened or how to fix it. You two went from disgustingly perfect to... this. Help me understand." She swallows roughly and doesn't look at me as she whispers, "And if it was my fault, let me fix it."

I exhale a heavy, tired breath. I don't want to blame her anymore. I don't want this distance between us anymore. I miss my sister.

Before I can launch into the sordid tale, the bartender slides our drinks over to us. Remy takes her IPA but before I can think better of it, I throw back the shot of tequila on its own. I still wince and chase it with the Corona, but it's way better than the heartbreakless-Hailey would've done.

"Can I get another shot?" I croak at the bartender. He just nods and pours me another. But instead of downing this one too, I pour it into the beer and swirl the concoction around. It's only after I've taken a big swig that I start talking.

"He said he wanted to give me space," I start. "He said he thinks we jumped into this too fast and that he doesn't want to just be a rebound for me."

Remy looks down at the beer in her hand but not quick enough to hide the flash of guilt on her face. I obviously know those were her words to Jax, so it wasn't exactly a surprise to hear him use them as an excuse, or to see her feel guilty about them.

I just feel tired.

"He said I'm leaning on him too heavily. That I'm too self-conscious because of Steve and too unsure of myself to exist without a relationship." I continue on despite seeing Remy's wince out of the corner of my eye.

Great, even my sister thinks I'm pathetic.

"And the icing on the cake was my supposed inability to communicate effectively in a relationship. Again, the fault lying with Steve. He said I'm too used to either ignoring it or getting irrationally upset about it when we do try to work it out." I laugh, the sound jarring and pitiful. "So basically, I'm dependent on a relationship, but at the same time, I'm not actually able to function within it. All I hear is a lose/lose scenario. Either way, I end up looking like the weak, pathetic idiot."

"Don't," Remy barks suddenly. I turn to her in surprise. Her eyes are locked on mine and she's glaring daggers at me, clearly pissed off.

"Don't you dare play the woe-is-me game right now," she says sharply. "I know you're sad, but you don't get to sink into that bullshit hole that we just dragged you out of. You're better than that."

I can only blink in shock. My sister is never harsh with me, and right now she looks downright angry.

She must feel that she's coming on too strong because she sighs and releases the tension from her shoulders. "Hailey, we know what Steve did to you. We all saw it. That man picked at your self-esteem until it was in tatters just because he wanted the challenge of trying to bring down a strong woman." Her gaze hardens again. "Don't let him win. Right now, tomorrow, ten years from now, don't let anything turn you back into what Steve manipulated you into believing. You're strong, and kind, and capable, and intelligent, and nothing that anyone will ever say, including Jax, including me, should ever make you think otherwise."

I swallow roughly, suddenly overwhelmed by my sister's words. She's right, of course. Jax's words have let me fall back into my old habit of believing anything that the man in my life tells me, including going a step further by myself in order to beat him to the punch. It's easier to hear it from my head rather than his lips.

I sigh in defeat and turn back to my beer. "I'll cut the self-deprecating part, but it doesn't change the fact that that's basically the message I got from Jax. He gave me 'space' because he thinks I'm too dependent on him. He doesn't think I can heal from Steve's bullshit if he's close enough to use as a crutch."

I twirl my beer on the bar top as I allow myself to consider Jax's words for the first time since he said them. *Was I leaning too heavily on him? Have I been dragging too much of my baggage into my relationship with Jax?*

Remy echoes my thoughts as she quietly asks, "Can you think of why he'd say you're too dependent on him? Did anything happen?"

I sigh again, heavier this time. *I'm so tired of being in pain.* "I mean, the whole thing started because I wouldn't tell him that I didn't want to go to the gym. He was trying really hard to get me to admit that I didn't want to go."

"So why didn't you say no?"

"Because clearly, Jax wanted me to go or he wouldn't have offered. So why would I say no to him? I like making him happy."

Remy just watches me for a moment, clearly trying to be careful about what she wants to say. "Because what about making you happy?" she finally asks softly. "When was the last time you did something that made you happy?"

I glare at my sister. "I do that plenty of times," I snap. "*Jax* makes me happy. Spending time with *you* makes me happy. You guys are acting like I'm a miserable yes-man that follows everyone around like a sad puppy."

She shakes her head, the sadness apparent in her eyes. "First of all, no one thinks that. Second of all, I'm not just asking about things that make you happy, I'm asking when you *prioritized* your happiness. When was the last time you chose yourself even though it inconvenienced or bothered someone else?"

I roll my eyes and open my mouth to answer, but... "Oh," I breathe.

Remy just gives me a sad nod.

I shake out of my daze and try again. "But it's not like I've ever been a selfish person. I mean, you know me, I've always been the people-pleaser. Why is it a problem now?"

"Because it's at a level where it's hurting you now. Because you don't even think you can say no since Steve convinced you that you don't deserve to stand up for yourself. And Jax probably saw that, and cared about you enough to want that for you."

I twirl my beer again, feeling uncomfortable with this revelation. "But why did he have to dump me for that to happen? Why not just *help* me become a stronger person? It's not like he wasn't already doing that. So why now? Why like this?"

"Because you can't really embrace it while he's close enough to hold your hand. He probably wants you to discover that level of self-confidence on your own." She hesitates, then asks, "A couple of weeks ago you said something about not being able to make a decision on something until you talked to Jax. Did that have anything to do with this?"

I open my mouth to tell her about Stacey's offer. But when

I realize I haven't considered it seriously enough to even tell Remy about it, I drop my head in shame.

"Stacey offered me the café," I mumble, my face heating.

"*WHAT?!*" she shouts. "When did this happen? Why didn't you tell me?!"

I wince. "I'm sorry. I should've told you. I don't actually want to take it and Jax and I got into a weird fight about it so I didn't really want to talk about it anymore."

"Why wouldn't you take it?" Remy asks with a shell-shocked expression. "That's insane. That's your whole dream!"

For some reason, when Remy's the one thatlays it out like that, it seems ridiculous.

But I try to defend my reasoning anyway. I stutter through my defense, trying to remember why I felt so adamant about it with Jax. "Because I'm in school right now! Because I'm too young, I'm not ready."

Remy just continues to stare at me as if I have three heads. Or rather, like I have none, since she's looking at me like I'm an idiot.

"What are you talking about? Stacey's name might be on the café, but you've been running that thing pretty much since you moved to the city. It has your name written all over it. To be honest, I'm surprised it's taken her this long to offer it to you."

I can only blink at my sister in disbelief and panic. "What about school? I still have two more years left!"

Remy just waves a hand in the air as if that doesn't matter. "You don't need a degree if you're offered your dream job without it. I'm not saying you haven't learned valuable business skills in the past two years—okay, maybe only one, everyone knows freshman year is a joke—but you can learn *way* more from real-life experience. You can probably run circles around graduates of the business program even now." She narrows her eyes at me in accusation. "Plus, tell me that Stacey didn't offer to show you the ropes first."

I duck my head so she can't meet my eyes.

"Yeah, that's what I thought. So what's your hold-up?" I start to answer but she cuts me off with a firm, "What's your hold-up *really?*"

My immediate reaction is to defend myself and continue arguing that I'm not ready for this kind of responsibility. But Remy's staring at me with such an intense glare that I force myself to think about it for a minute first.

"I—I don't know," I finally admit. "I do think both of those things are still true, but I guess part of me is just scared that I wouldn't be able to handle it. I mean, *fuck*, it's a huge responsibility to own your own business."

A wry grin stretches across Remy's face. "When did you start cursing, little sister?"

My smile feels tight and unused on my face, but genuine nonetheless. "It's a new thing for when I'm dealing with intense emotions."

She just laughs. "I like it." But then she sobers and turns her attention back to me. "It's okay to be afraid. But more often than not it's worth doing things *despite* being afraid. This is one of them."

I don't respond, I just take another swig of my beer and mull over her words.

"Okay, what about school, then? Why is it so important to finish your bachelor's? Even though you clearly don't need it to land your dream job."

I had started to answer but snap my mouth closed and glare at her for that last jab. She just chuckles and raises her hands in surrender.

"I guess I just thought you couldn't get any job worth having without a bachelor's. It goes without saying that your resume is ten times stronger with a degree on it, so starting school seemed like the obvious thing to do. And obviously finishing it felt even more obvious, since I've already wasted two years of time and money."

"But why would you think it's so important? Mom and dad *never* pushed college on us. They always told us there were plenty of other things that could be more important to our careers. Where would you get the idea that college is the end-all be-all?"

My eyes lock with hers, the answer lying unspoken between us. We both know exactly why I suddenly thought a degree was so important. I'm just sick of saying it out loud.

I'm sick of admitting that one person had so much fucking control over my mind and my emotions.

"It just seemed like the right thing to do," I murmur. "I felt like such a loser skipping a year after high school. All I did was work."

"And move to the city and get a job and make friends and learn a shit ton about life. That's *all* you did. And that's not even talking about the fact that you set down roots to find a place that is now offering you *your dream on a platter*."

I start to pick at the label on my beer bottle. "So what am I supposed to do, just drop out? After I already spent two years of my time and money?"

"You can always go back if you really want to, it's not like it's a total waste. If you decide a year from now that it was a mistake to stop, you can go right back. No harm no foul." She looks at me with an almost pleading expression. Like she's begging me to understand what she's saying. "But the alternative if you don't do it is losing out on your dream."

I wince and drop my head into my hands. "This whole thing is crazy. I mean, we're talking about me *buying a café*. What 21-year-old does that?"

Remy just shrugs. "If you were like other 21-year-olds, you wouldn't give a shit about wasting away your college years because you'd be more worried about getting drunk and laid. So I wouldn't put too much stock in that."

"But what if I fail?" I ask. "What if this turns out to be a huge mistake?"

She shrugs again. "It's a possibility. But it's even more likely that you'll rock it, just like you already are. Most of the pressure is in your head. But honestly, Hailes, it really just comes down to taking a chance. And as cliché as it sounds, you'll end up regretting the things you didn't do more than the things you did do. So it kinda feels like a no-brainer, although obviously you're the only one that can make that decision."

"Alright," I say softly. "You're right, it's worth thinking about, at least."

"Attagirl," Remy smiles. "And if you decide to not go through with it, I'll support you in that too. I still want you to do what feels right. I just don't want you to make any decision based on the wrong reasons."

I nod sullenly. "I know. I can understand that." I peer nervously at her, hesitating before I voice my next thought. "I'm sorry I freaked out on you after Jax. I'm sorry I've been a total bitch this week."

She waves me off again. And I'm once again reminded how much I appreciate my sister and my bond with her.

"You were upset, I can understand that. Nothing to apologize for." But then the easy expression on her face drops. "I'd be sad without Jax, too."

"Do you—" I swallow nervously and try again. "Do you think we're really over? Should I even think about what it would take to change his mind and get back together?"

Remy's smile is sad. "I wouldn't worry about anyone else for a little while, Hailes. You should focus on controlling your own happiness, by your own power. When you're ready, if you two still want to be together, you'll make it happen. I promise."

I choke back the tears that are threatening to overflow at the thought that it really is over with Jax. Maybe not forever, but for the first time in over a decade, I am truly without my best friend.

And it hurts so fucking bad.

But then I think about what Remy said, about taking some time to find my own happiness.

And suddenly, that doesn't sound like the worst idea anymore.

For the next week, I can't stop replaying both Remy's and Jax's words in my head. I've talked myself down from the defensive and furious reactions that come automatically, and instead have forced myself to think about why my two best friends—and the people that I admire the most in the world—seem to think that I need to be more selfish about my happiness.

I work at the café with my usual level of energetic professionalism. I have never wavered at my job, and over the course of these few days it becomes apparent just how good I am at it.

I handle the vendors and deliveries without issue, I have total control over my employees and everything that comes with managing people, and I easily handle customers with grace. Even Stacey compliments my iron control.

"Have you thought any more about my offer?" she asks me during one particularly challenging shift.

I swallow nervously. I *have* been thinking about it. Pretty much constantly. Not just about the café, but also about how school ties into this.

"I have," I answer. "And I have a few questions, if you have some time to talk today."

Stacey looks at her phone. "Not today, but I'm glad you're taking my offer seriously. By your deer-in-the-headlights look, I thought I'd scared you away for good. Can we chat on Monday? I'd like to make sure I have plenty of time to have this conversation with you."

I nod. "Monday is perfect. Thank you."

She smiles at me and turns away to finish her final tasks of the day. "Monday, then. It's a date."

By the time my shift ends, I'm ready to kiss this week goodbye. I'm exhausted, from both the challenges at work and the repeat thoughts rolling around my head like pinballs. I need to clear my brain.

It's November in Philadelphia which means it's chilly, but not quite cold yet—we won't get snow until after the new year. And there's just something about walking through Rittenhouse Square on a crisp fall day that makes me perk up a little bit. A walk should clear my head.

I start toward the park and take a deep breath, slowing my heart and trying to pause my thoughts. I think back to the breathing exercises I learned when I used to dance and incorporate them now.

Right as the memory of my dancing exercises surfaces, a business catches my eye at the end of the block. I quicken my pace, feeling drawn to the space even before my brain comprehends what I'm looking at.

It's a dance studio. I peer inside and see a hip-hop dance class going on, about a dozen dancers counting out steps and practicing a routine in sections. It looks like an intermediate class, not quite as intimidating as the famous dance company on the other side of the city, and as I look around the studio, I notice the pictures on the walls of many different dance styles. I see some of a jazz class, lyrical, modern—there are even ballet classes offered. It looks like a regular studio, meant for anyone that wants to try a dance class.

It's exactly the kind of studio I used to love. The kind of dancing I did in my spare time, that made me happy and that introduced me to friends I haven't talked to in way too long.

And I *miss* it. I miss it because I stopped going to classes when Steve and I moved in together. He made me quit with his looks of disappointment and his silence. When really, I needed encouragement.

I freeze when my brain catches up to the thoughts in my head.

And just like the moment that I realized Steve was a narcissist, I now realize how wrong he was about so many things that became ingrained in my head. About school, about jobs, my hobbies, all of it. And even though I already knew his main goal was to alienate me from the things that brought me happiness outside of him, I feel like I'm only now understanding how deep into my psyche that actually went.

And in this moment, I decide that I'm going to burn every bit of Steve's bullshit toxicity out of my brain. I'm going to force myself to acknowledge my insecurities and self-doubt, and I'm going to look them in the face as I shoot them down. Every day. I know now it's the little things that built up to form these blanket misconceptions, which means it'll be the little victories every day that will tear them down. But every day, I will take one step closer to taking back my life. Taking back *myself*.

A wave of empowerment rolls through my chest and straightens my spine. A huge grin splits my face. I open the door to the dance studio.

Starting with something that makes me happy.

Two months later

I collapse onto my couch with a groan of exhaustion.

"Did we get everything?" Aiden calls from where he disappeared into my bedroom with the last of my moving boxes.

"There's nothing else in the truck," Max answers as he walks through the door.

"Yeah, I think that was the last of it," Tristan confirms as he places my air fryer on the kitchen counter and looks around the apartment.

I take in the sheer chaos of boxes, bubble wrap, and dirt from the guys' shoes. It only took the three of them an hour and a half—commute to Fishtown included—to move me out of Remy's apartment and into my own little one-bedroom apartment. And even though I know it's going to take me forever to unpack my clothes and organize my million kitchen items, I feel nothing but pride and contentment at the sight of my new home.

"Do you need help with anything else?" Remy offers as she aims a wary look at the overwhelming amount of boxes in the kitchen—no doubt trying to figure out how anyone could need anything more than an air fryer and a grilled cheese maker.

I shake my head. "That was everything. All that's left is unpacking, but I'm going to do that this week. The jet lag is killing me too much to start it tonight."

Tristan shakes his head as he throws an arm around Remy. "I still can't believe you scheduled a trip to Europe *and* a move to a new apartment in the same week. You're insane."

I let out what can only be called a tired grunt of agreement. He's not wrong.

"You'll have to tell us what Rome was like," Max says, leaning against the front door. "Remy said you got to see the locals' Rome, party scene and everything. I'd love to hear about it. Maybe Aiden and I will plan a trip."

"Sounds good to me," Aiden grins in response. "Italian chicks are hot. I wouldn't mind putting in some work on my *European countries I've hit* list."

Max rolls his eyes. "Yeah? And what about Dani? I thought she would've put a stop to any of your *lists*."

Aiden waves him off. "You act like we're dating. There's nothing exclusive about us. She's just as likely to sleep with an Italian girl of her own." He shoves his hands in his sweatpants and studies his best friend. "Don't act like you don't know me. Or *her*, for that matter." He cocks an eyebrow pointedly.

Max grins, while Tristan smothers his own smile with a cough. Remy just rolls her eyes in a way that can only convey the message *you guys are such pigs.*

I have no idea what secret conversation they're having right now. "I don't think you could handle Italian girls either way," I tell Aiden and Max. "They eat American men for breakfast, and then their men drink you under the table at night."

Aiden's eyes narrow in disbelief. "Bullshit," he argues.

I shake my head with a chuckle. "I'll give you my cousin's number if you actually want to plan a trip. He'd be happy to show you guys around." I push to my feet and face Tristan to try one more time to offer them money. "Are you sure I can't pay you? You guys had no reason to help. I feel like I'm taking advantage of you."

But before the question is even out of my mouth, Tristan is shaking his head.

"This one's on the house, Little Porter," Aiden agrees. "Plus, Jax would kill us if—"

He cuts himself off, his eyes widening as he realizes what he just let slip.

At the mention of his name, my throat immediately closes up. I try to swallow against the dryness but it's no use—the reminder is already there. And it's just as painful today as it was on the day he walked out.

"Fuck, sorry," Aiden mumbles sheepishly.

I clear my throat and push past the awkwardness. "At least let me buy you guys a round of drinks," I offer. "Next week, maybe? Once I can stay up past 8pm again."

Max and Aiden both give a jerky nod, clearly uncomfortable with the tension.

"Are you sure you don't need anything else?" Remy asks. "The guys have to get over to the gym but I can help you start to unpack. Or we could just hang out?"

I shake my head. "No, it's okay, I have to head over to the café to let Stacey know that I'm back and to check the schedule. Then I'm going to pass out for about fourteen hours."

Remy sighs. "Okay. Then we'll leave you to it. Let me know if you need anything?"

I smile at my sister and nod. "I will. Thank you guys so much for helping today, I really appreciate it."

They all file out of the apartment, Remy giving me a smile and affectionate shove and whispering *proud of you* before she leaves.

Once I've locked the front door behind them, I collapse on the couch again. I groan at the knowledge that I really do need to get up and over to the café before they close. *Maybe a week-long trip to Italy wasn't the best idea when I have so much going on.*

But I shut that thought down as quickly as it comes. I'm sick of putting things on the back burner. I did it for too long, and I'm not doing it anymore.

It's been two months of living with this new *do what makes you happy* mentality, and so far it's served me well—to say the least. It's gotten me to drop out of a college program that made me miserable, motivated me to make my dream of owning a café a reality, to take a trip that I've been putting off for years, and helped me to rediscover my individuality by finding my own space and pursuing my own hobbies. It's been a busy two months, but also the most incredible.

And just like it always does when I think about how much I've done recently, my mind wanders back to the turning point where it all started.

To Jax.

I drop my head back on the couch with a heavy exhale. It never hurts any less to think about him. I'm still just as in love with him as I was the day he walked out. No amount of time will ever lessen that.

I've only seen him twice since that night, once because I had something important I needed to give Remy at the gym, and once when the fighters all showed up at the bar that I was at. That time sucked the most because we both tried to make small-talk with each other before I ran out of the bar when I couldn't go another minute without crying. It hurt even worse because I could see *his* hurt as I turned away.

And as much as I'm dying every day to go back to him, something is stopping me. It just doesn't feel… right.

Not because I don't think Jax and I are meant to be together. But because he was right to end us.

I shake the ugly thought from my head. *He didn't end it. He put us on pause. He would* never *end us.*

But every day, it's a little harder to convince myself of that. *What if he was telling the truth at the time, about wanting to take a break, but now too much time has passed? What if I took too long to figure my shit out and now he doesn't want me anymore?*

It's an ugly cycle of thoughts. On good days, I can believe that Jax meant it when he said he would wait for me, but on bad days, I can almost convince myself that I'm too messed up and took too long.

Another heavy breath escapes my lungs. I take a deep breath, and then exhale again.

Every time I get caught up in this chaotic cyclone of worries, I have to remind myself that as much as I love Jax, as much as I'm dying to show up on his doorstep and beg him to take me back, part of me would be lying. Because I'm not ready yet. I still need some time to settle into my new life, into my new career goals and hobbies, with my rekindled friendships. And whether Jax and I end up together or not, he still saved me when he let me go.

I let myself meditate for a few more breaths before pushing to my feet and getting ready to walk down to the café. But before I close the door, I take a moment to look around my new apartment. At my new home.

And I allow myself to feel grateful. Not just for the good things that exist in my life right now, but for the power I found in myself to *create* these things. Because *I* brought this to fruition. *I* found the strength to go after what makes me happy, and to create this space and this amazing life for myself. And whatever happens next, I'm still winning at the game of life.

I step into the hallway and close the door behind me.

I just have to hope Jax can wait a little longer before I'm ready to win him as the final prize.

CHAPTER TWENTY-EIGHT
Jax

"You sure you don't want to come with us to grab food?" Tristan asks as he packs up the rest of his gym bag.

I shake my head. "I'm good. Thanks. I'm just going to hit a few more rounds and then I'm going home to get some work done for this week."

Tristan sighs, and I know what he's going to say before he even opens his mouth. He's a good friend, and he hasn't pushed me—even when I know he really wants to—but I know him better than I know myself. And I know what he's going to tell me. I know he's reached his limit.

"You can't do this for much longer, man," he says quietly. Sadly. "It's been three months. All you do is train and work. You don't even eat like you used to. How much longer are you going to live this empty life?"

I shrug. "However long I feel like it. I feel fine this way."

"Feeling fine isn't a victory. You need to figure out how to get back to being yourself, because this is not the answer. You're killing yourself, Jax." He shakes his head. "You didn't give Hailey her life back just so you could throw yours away."

I have no response to that.

He's right, of course. I'm not doing anything but hurting myself by living like this. I should be happy that Hailey took what I said and figured out how to move on, not depressed that she didn't try to force herself back into my life to try to convince me I made a mistake. I should be looking at those few weeks as a gift, and should be living my life like I'm better for it.

But I can't. No matter what I do, I can't stop feeling like I'm missing an entire piece of myself. I feel shredded, and lifeless, and I've felt this way since the moment I walked out of Remy's apartment three months ago.

Tristan leaves the gym without waiting for me to respond. He knows I won't. He knows what I'm dealing with, since he just went through it not long ago with Remy. The difference is, he didn't lose a friend too. A friend that he could talk to, that he could count on. That he'd already loved for years. And his heartache didn't last long enough for him to have to figure out who he is without his girl.

I shake my head to clear it of the increasingly spiraling thoughts. I tighten the wraps on my hands and pull my gloves on, then head over to the bag room to hit the heavy bags.

Every punch loosens the grip around my heart a little more. It's only in these moments that I feel like I can breathe, and even though the squeeze returns immediately after I stop moving, I relish these workouts as a momentary reprieve from the pain.

It's also the only time I can think about Hailey without

getting sucked into a vortex of heartache. With my mind focused mostly on my body not killing itself, it allows me to think of her almost objectively for just a little bit.

For the longest time, I wrestled with the question of *did I make the right decision?* For weeks, I thought about how Hailey must've thought I abandoned her, or I didn't think she was worth it, or God forbid that she was just another girl to me. I asked her for a *break*, for fuck's sake. Could I have sounded like a more stereotypical douchebag?

Why didn't I stay by her side and just hold her hand through everything? Why did I think leaving her was the answer?

But then one afternoon a few weeks after that horrible day, I overheard Remy telling Tristan that Hailey had decided to quit college and buy the café—that she was ridiculously happy about the decision and so proud of herself, it was all she could talk about.

And that in itself cemented my choice for me. If Hailey could find the kind of confidence again to make a decision of that size on her own, then hopefully it was my push that started the dominoes falling. And even without the minor tidbits that I picked up from eavesdropping for the weeks after that—that she started dancing again, that she found her own apartment, that she took a trip by herself—I knew I did the right thing.

Even if it felt like I was slowly dying from the effects of it.

It doesn't matter that she's forgotten about me. It doesn't matter that I'm in the same hollow state of alternating pain and nothingness that I fell into the day I walked out of her life. If she's happy, it was worth it. That's all I've ever wanted for Hailey. And if it took me being a rebound for her to make that step, then so be it. I would bear that cross.

I would just have to figure out how to live with it. Even if I was doing a shit job of that at the moment.

My punches never slow, even as my lungs burn and my muscles begin to scream at me. I push through all of it. I even pick up my speed and continue to throw every remaining ounce of energy into my strikes.

If I don't collapse into a heap on the ground, I'm not numb enough.

Just when I think that particular goal might get met, I hear the squeak of a door. It doesn't register enough for me to stop my assault on the bag, since there are plenty of people always walking around here off-hours. But when the door to the bag room swings open, I finally glance at the stairs.

And promptly go cold all over when I see Hailey standing on the landing.

I stop the heavy bag in place right before it swings back and almost knocks me off my feet.

I can't take my eyes off her.

Part of me is worried that I've either lost my mind or finally worked my body to exhaustion enough that I'm hallucinating. Because it doesn't make sense that she's here. And it doesn't *look* like Hailey.

She's still beautiful, just as beautiful as she's always been. Her blue eyes are shining, never moving away from me as she tucks a strand of hair behind her ear and steps forward to lean on the railing overlooking this room. Physically, she looks like herself.

It's her aura that's different.

Those same blue eyes now hold an unwavering sense of confidence. Those pink lips that I've kissed senseless and fantasized about every day are surrounded by smile lines. And that body that I've worshipped with awe and devotion, now exudes a sense of self-assured grace that Princess Diana would be proud of.

She's fucking breathtaking.

Between my workout and Hailey's appearance, I'm literally breathless. My chest is heaving with the effort to take in the oxygen that I desperately need right now.

She just stares at me, not quite smiling, but definitely not looking sad either. Just... thoughtful.

After a few moments—and after I've somehow managed to catch my breath—her lip finally lifts into a tiny smile.

"Hi," she whispers.

My heart goes from a thousand miles per hour to flatline with just that one word.

"Hi," I manage to reply.

Without taking her eyes off me, she pushes off the railing and starts down the stairs. I don't think I breathe the entire time. When she finally stops in front of me, I have to remind myself to take a breath so I don't pass out before I figure out what she's doing here.

I haven't seen her in three months—other than that one time at the bar and my occasional stalking outside the café—and I can't bring myself to guess why she's here. Over the weeks, I convinced myself that she would've come back to me already if she wanted to, and since she hasn't, that obviously means she's gotten over me. That what we had wasn't as important to her as it was to me. So right now, it definitely feels like too much to hope for that she's here for me. It's more likely she wants closure between us.

She just watches me as these thoughts flit through my head, and I swear she can actually hear them. Her eyes begin to shine with a hint of sadness. And when she starts talking, there's sadness laced in her words.

"I hated you at first," she says quietly. "I didn't understand why you had left me, or how it could've been so easy for you."

My eyes widen, and I open my mouth to refute that any of this was *easy*. But she stops me by placing a hand on my arm. And that small contact is enough to make my heart stutter, enough to make me have to fight dropping to my knees and begging her forgiveness.

She keeps talking.

"I was mad at Remy too. I was mad at everyone. I felt ganged up on and like I was being treated like I was this broken, fragile child. I felt worse than I did with Steve."

A pained sound breaks out of my chest at that. I open my mouth to try again to interrupt her, but this time she steps closer and puts her hand on my chest. She's so close to me that I could lean forward slightly and brush my lips across her forehead, just like I've done thousands of times before and like I'm practically shaking to do now.

I know she's trying to tell me something but I can't let her go on without saying, "I never meant to hurt you. You have to believe me, Hailey. I've only ever wanted—"

She cuts me off with a whispered, "Jax, please."

I swallow the whimper that wants to slip out when she

utters those words. My heart feels like it's being shredded in the face of her admission of pain, and it takes everything in me not to start talking again. But I take a deep, trembling breath and nod for her to continue.

She waits until she knows I'm ready to listen before she starts again. "It killed me when you left. Not just because you left me but because I hated being without you. You weren't just my best friend, you were *Jax*." For the first time since she walked in, her composure seems to stumble, and her voice cracks when she says, "A part of me died inside when you left."

I choke on a cry and lean forward to press my forehead against hers. I can only whisper *I'm sorry* over and over again as we stand there, leaning on each other in our vulnerability.

She moves her hand from where it never strayed off my chest, to cup my face in her palm, pulling back slightly so she can look at me. Tears glisten in her eyes, but they never fall, and then I see her shield of strength snap back into place.

"But then I realized you never would've done it without a good reason," she starts again, her gaze never leaving mine. "My whole life, you've always been my protector. You shielded me from every harm, big or small, because that's who you are. You never would have hurt me unless it was to keep me from an even bigger hurt."

I can only nod, my throat too thick with emotion to answer.

"So I started thinking about what you said when you left. I tried to put myself in your shoes so I could understand why you did it. And I realized that everything you said that night was right, even if I didn't want to hear it. Even though it killed me to hear that I was broken and needed to heal, you told me anyway. Because you knew I needed to heal, and to do it myself." She hesitates for a moment. And her voice cracks when she asks, "You did it because you love me, didn't you?"

My gaze darts across her face, searching for her reaction to those words. But she doesn't give me anything, just watches me and waits.

I can only nod mutely.

A heavy exhale rushes out of her, as if she was waiting with bated breath for me to confirm what she suspected. Then one corner of her lips lifts into a small smile, though it looks sad.

"I know it hurt you to do that," she finally whispers. "But I want you to know that you were right. About everything. You were right about me, and you were right to make me deal with it on my own. I may have never dealt with my problems if I had you there to lean on. So I wanted to thank you. Because without that wake-up call, I might still be broken."

When she leans forward to press a kiss to my cheek, my eyes close and my heart splinters into unfixable pieces. This feels like closure.

This feels like goodbye.

She pulls back. "You saved me," she admits softly. "You forced me to deal with the pieces of me that I wanted to bury deep and forget about. I had to take those pieces and figure out why they were hurting me, and then make changes so they wouldn't hurt me again. I started saying no to people. I started dancing again. I even took a trip by myself. I learned how to make my happiness a priority." She cups my cheek in her hand, her eyes searching mine. "But I never would've done that without you. And I don't think I can ever thank you enough for that. But—" Her shield drops and raw vulnerability shines through her bright blue eyes. "I'd like to spend the rest of our lives trying." Her voice cracks when she says, "If you'll have me."

My eyes widen. I thought this was her way of getting closure and officially breaking things off with me, but those words make it sound like—

"You want to be with me?" I manage to choke out. I clear my throat and try again. "I mean, do we go back to being friends or—"

She's shaking her head before I've even finished. "I can't be your friend anymore, Jax." She trains her honest gaze on me again. "I love you too much to settle for just friends."

A breath whooshes out of me, and I can't go another second without touching her. I barely manage to get out a whispered *Hailey* before I'm cupping her face in my hands and pulling her to me.

The second our lips touch, it feels like my very soul has been brought back to life. Her whimper only feeds the sparks in my chest, her hands making me *feel* again as she clings to me, completely uncaring about the fact that my shirt is drenched from my workout. She presses against me like she can't bear even an inch of space between us, like she can't go another second without recapturing the intimacy that was always so fucking easy between us.

I wrap an arm around her waist, my other hand still woven into her hair, and I lift her off her feet to bring her even closer. I deepen the kiss in borderline-frenzy—I can't get enough of her, can't get close enough. Can't quite convince myself that this is real, that she's here in my arms and wanting me back.

After what feels like forever, but at the same time not long enough, I force myself to pull away, but only far enough to separate our lips. I lean my forehead against hers, my eyes closing as I struggle to catch my breath.

"I'm sorry," I whisper. She opens her mouth to interrupt but I cut her off, desperate to get the words out. "I know you'll tell me I don't need to be, but I just need to say it. I'm sorry I hurt you. *God,* I'm so sorry. It killed me to do it. But you have to know that I'll never hurt you, ever again. I swear. I'd rather cut my own arm off than be the cause of even one more tear in your eye." I pull back farther to study her expression, and to make sure that she's hearing my words. "Tell me you believe me. Please."

For a moment she just looks at me, and I can't help but be mesmerized by the change in her. There's not a shred of insecurity in her gaze right now. She's just standing here, sure of herself, sure of her decision. A decision that she made on her own based on her own needs.

"I believe you," she says quietly. "Of course I believe you. You're my Jax."

And *fuck,* what hearing my name on her lips does to me.

With a groan, I fall onto her with my kiss again. After three months, I can't get enough of her scent, of her taste, of the feel of her in my arms. I'm obsessed.

"I love you," I whisper against her lips. "I love you so much…"

I feel her smile against my mouth, and the knowledge that she's happy is enough to send me into a frenzy again. And in this moment, I vow to only ever make her smile again.

I force myself to pull away and put a little distance between us, although I can't bring myself to actually let go of her. "Let's get out of here. The next time you tell me you love me, I want to be inside you immediately. I'm not exactly keen on the idea of fucking you against a heavy bag."

She laughs, and I swear to God I missed that sound more than anything in the world. But she also has a twinkle in her eye because she looks at me and whispers, "I do love you, you know." She says it with a grin, seeing if I'll go against what I just said and take her right here, right now.

I growl and reach under her thighs to wrap her legs around my body. And as tempted as I am to actually fuck her against a heavy bag, I'm more interested in getting her home.

"Naughty," I murmur as I nip at her neck. "You've become more mischievous." Without setting her down, I start to make my way up the stairs and through the gym.

"A few things have changed," she admits softly.

I just look up at her with a smile, silently letting her know that I'm excited to navigate those new waters with her—that I'll take her however she is, now and forever.

"I'm taking you home," I tell Hailey as I set her down to change my shirt and grab my gym bag.

I've just pulled my sweaty shirt over my head when she says simply, "No."

I look at her in surprise. "No?"

And again, there's that mischievous smile. She's looking at me like she's proud of herself and excited about her secret, all at once. She nods and says again, "No. We're not going to your house."

Finally, understanding dawns. A grin slowly slides across my face even as pure joy spreads through my chest. "Yes, ma'am."

She gestures at the clean shirt in my hand as if to say *hurry up*. I just shake my head, feeling both amused and proud of this bossy side of her. "We're going to my place," she declares. "I haven't christened my new apartment yet."

The comment is immediately sobering. I swallow roughly, forcing myself to meet her eyes, even though I'm nervous as fuck about what I want to ask.

"You weren't, uh… with anyone else?" I ask quietly.

The smile drops from her face as quickly as it did mine, though where mine was replaced by what I'm sure looks like terror, Hailey's morphs into tender affection.

She doesn't even hesitate before she steps up to me and wraps her arms around my waist, her chin tilting up so I can see the truth in her expression. I hesitantly place my hands on her waist, waiting with bated breath for her answer.

"There wasn't, and will never be, anyone else," she tells me. "You and I have been soulmates since I was a teenager, even before we could've ever been romantic. Our hearts match— they always have." Uncertainty enters her gaze, but still, she doesn't look away from my eyes. Still, she stays strong. "I got a little lost along the way, but I've known you were it for me since the night you walked away from me. When it felt like… like a part of my heart walked out the door. I knew then that I was right about what I felt when we were kids. That you and I were meant to be together. I haven't even *thought* of anyone else since that moment. Everything I've done since then has been to find myself, yes, but also to get back to you. Because you and I are it, Jax. There's no one else."

The tension leaves my body in a whoosh. It would've been her right to date if she wanted to, of course, but I didn't realize how badly I needed to hear from her that she's been just as caught up with me as I've been with her. The immense relief almost knocks me off my feet.

"*Fuck,* I love you," I murmur as I fall onto her with another kiss. She's already wrapped around my waist, so all it takes is dropping my head to press my lips against hers. She meets me with the same eagerness that I feel, that same desperation to connect again in any way possible. And it takes me several long seconds to pull back enough to drag some air into my lungs and respond to her declaration—and even still, I can only go so far as to put a few inches between our lips.

"I feel it too," I say quietly. "You're it for me. Of course you're it. I've been dying thinking I wasn't going to get to be with you, and that's because I knew there would never be another person more right for me than you. I'm yours, Hailey. Yesterday, today, ten years from now. However long you'll have me, I'm yours."

Her eyes close, and she drops her forehead against mine. I watch as a look of peace washes over her, and I wonder if she's feeling the same weight lifted off her chest that was just lifted off mine.

"Take me home, Jax," she whispers, tightening her hold on me in a way that makes me think she'll never want to let go.

I nod and press a kiss to her forehead, murmuring, "Yes, my queen."

EPILOGUE

"Fuck, Hailey, you feel so good," Jax groans.

I lean back to brace myself on his thighs, giving him a better view of not only the length of my body but also of where he's disappearing into me as I grind on him.

"Oh *fuck*," I moan when he hits a spot deep inside me that immediately sets off sparks. My eyes close and my head drops back with a whimper as I'm swept up in the sensation.

"Jesus *Christ*, you're hot," he gasps in a pained voice. I feel his grip tighten on my hips. "Do you have any idea how hot you look right now? Riding my cock like this? I could come from just the sight of you."

I'm too wrapped up in the tsunami of pleasure that's rolling toward me to answer with words. I just increase the pace of my hips, desperation leading my movements.

He pushes up into a sitting position so he can pull me closer and suck a nipple into his mouth. I moan at the feeling, but the new position and Jax's closeness aren't letting me move as quickly or as deeply as I want to. So I place a hand on his chest and shove him back to the bed, leaning my weight forward now and increasing the pace of my hips.

I can feel the orgasm bearing down on me, and I *need* it.

Jax's eyes go wide with surprise at the aggressive move but then his expression quickly becomes heated.

"That's my girl," he whispers. "Take what you need from me. Ride my cock just like that. I want to feel you make yourself come."

And just like they always do, his filthy words tip me over the edge.

"Fuck *yes*," Jax growls, his grip on my hips continuing to move me through the climax. But before it's even really finished, he slides his hands under my ass cheeks and shifts me in one motion to straddle his face.

I yelp at the sudden change in position, but he's already lost in eating me out, so the sound falls on deaf ears. He's so hungry for my pleasure that one orgasm immediately catapults into another.

I slump sideways onto the bed as my muscles all go limp.

"My turn, baby girl," he murmurs, pushing up onto his knees and running a hand along my back. I mumble something incoherent.

He pulls my ass into the air and takes his place behind me. He's gentle when he slides into me, though even with his slow thrusts, it doesn't take long for my pleasure to spike and my moans to start up again.

"Quiet, baby, or my parents will hear you," he rasps.

My mouth slams shut at the reminder. It's so easy to get lost in Jax when he's like this. I completely forgot that we're currently fucking in his childhood bedroom at his parents' house.

I manage to stifle my sounds for a little bit. But when he starts thrusting harder, *deeper*, it's pretty much impossible to stay quiet.

"Do I need to keep you quiet?" he growls. It would sound annoyed if I didn't know Jax as well as I do. He's not annoyed, he's *excited*. At the idea of busying my mouth with something.

I love him when he's like this, all alpha and dirty. In the past few months, he's made every single fantasy I've ever had a reality. He flinches at nothing, wants what I want, and will do anything to please me. My pleasure brings *him* pleasure. And if that means degrading me a little bit… then that's what he's going to do.

Just to taunt him, I don't stifle my moans. They're not loud enough to actually alert his parents downstairs, but they're enough to force Jax into action.

I feel the bed shift as he slides out of me and moves off the bed. Curious, I push onto my hands and peek over my shoulder, straining to see what he has planned.

Watching as he bends over to dig through our pile of clothes on the floor, I suck in a breath when I see him pull his belt out of the loops on his pants.

He smirks when he sees me biting my lip through a smile. "I love how much you love my belts," he says with a grin. I don't take my eyes off him, my body dripping with anticipation as he walks toward my head, his belt held like an offering in his hand.

"Open," he orders.

I open my mouth obediently, my gaze locked onto his eager expression.

He pushes the folded-in-half belt between my lips and waits until I bite down on the leather before letting it go. The weight of the buckle pulls it down just enough that I have to force myself to keep my teeth clamped so I don't drop it.

Jax brushes the back of his hand along my cheek, the contrast between his gentle touch and dirty action making me even hotter than I already am.

His voice is just as gentle. "If you drop it, I'll spank you and won't let you come until we're back home."

My eyes narrow in confusion. *The whole point of this is to keep me quiet. How are you going to spank me quietly?*

He reads my thoughts in a way that only Jax can. Like he knows my reactions, feelings, musings, before I'm even aware of them myself.

He grins. "Where I'll be spanking, I won't need to go hard or be loud."

A shiver runs through my whole body at the thought of him spanking my pussy. I have no doubt he would do it in a way that I would enjoy, but I'm not exactly keen to try it out right now. All it does is convince me I shouldn't drop the belt.

Jax sees the decision in my eyes. With a nod of approval, he moves out of my sight until I feel the bed dip behind me again. A hand caresses the length of my spine down to my waist. I can practically feel his hot gaze traveling over my body, and it's enough to make my heartrate spike with anticipation.

He slides inside me and starts moving at a rough pace. He's not taking his time or easing me into it, he's just going right back to chasing his pleasure. No more teasing.

It doesn't take me long to start panting around the leather in my mouth. And then to start groaning. By the time a few whimpers slip out, I'm fairly concerned I'm going to lose this game.

"Don't you dare drop it," Jax growls behind me. I clamp my teeth down harder, saliva starting to drip from the corners of my mouth as I struggle to keep my bite. But my jaw is aching and the pleasure is starting to make my body shake with the need to keep it at bay so I don't lose control.

I squeeze my muscles in an effort to keep the sensations at bay. I hear Jax's breath hitch when I tighten around him, his movements getting harder, more carnal.

"Don't drop it, Hailey," he rasps, his words taking on a desperate tone.

I squeeze my eyes shut, focused solely on obeying. Saliva drips from my mouth and coats the leather. The ache in my jaw is enough to muffle my moans and keep my orgasm from completely taking over. I feel Jax's thrusts become frenzied but it's a distant sensation, second to my singular focus on the belt in my mouth.

"Fuck, fuck, *fuck*," Jax starts to chant under his breath, his grip on my hips adding another tinge of pain to the overwhelming sensations.

He lets go with a groan, shoving deep, and I whimper at the feeling of him coming inside me.

He slumps over me, his hands landing next to mine to catch his weight. "Fuck," he rasps.

I'm too wired from the unreleased pleasure, too focused

on the damn belt to relax. All I can do is hold my stance and continue panting around the mouthful.

"Good girl," Jax whispers in my ear, pressing a kiss to the spot right underneath that always makes me shiver. He takes the belt from my mouth and guides me onto my back, his touch soothing. Loving.

"Do you want to come now?" he asks me. "I know you're hurting. But you did so good, baby girl." He brushes my hair away from my face and leans in to kiss me, completely unaffected by my spit-soaked lips and chin. The action being both tender and dirty is enough to make my heart start pounding at a rapid pace all over again.

He stretches out beside me on the bed, propped up on one elbow, laying kisses along my neck and shoulder as his hand traces along my body. His fingers make their path between my breasts, circling around my nipples, giving a quick pinch to make me gasp, and then traveling down my stomach and around my navel. By the time he moves farther south and veers off to trail his fingers along my inner thigh, I'm breathing so hard a whimper slips out.

"Have I ever told you how much I enjoy coming inside you?" he whispers in my ear, his touch moving so close to my center that now I'm definitely whimpering, trying to arch into his touch. "I've never done it before, never wanted to. Never needed to claim someone so badly." His fingers finally reach their destination, but he doesn't give me what I'm so desperate for that I'm shaking. He just feels along my lips, my inner thighs, everywhere he just left his mark on me.

"Because this?" he continues in a deep voice. "Feeling my

cum leaking out of you, knowing it's my touch that you want? I've never felt more like a man than I do right now."

I don't know if he still wants me to be quiet, but I can't go any longer without begging. "Jax, please," I gasp, arching my hips, trying to force his fingers inside me.

"*Fuck*, that word," he growls as he breaks.

His fingers slam inside me, and I can't tell if he's working to give me the orgasm of all orgasms or trying to push all of his cum back inside me. Right now, I don't care. All I know is he just lit a fuse with his words and is coaxing the explosion with his fingers.

My pleasure climbs higher and higher, my breath coming in gasps and my fingers gripping the sheets in an effort to stay tethered to this world.

"Jax, I'm—" I gasp.

"That's my girl," he growls as he finally curls his fingers and rubs the spot that is about to send me flying. "Come all over my hand like a good little whore."

His words set me off. A scream tears from my throat, smothered by Jax's hand when he covers my mouth at the same time that he doubles down on his efforts to prolong my orgasm.

"*Fuck*, yes," he groans, watching my face as it crumples in pleasure. His fingers slow as I come down, leaving me panting and twitching with aftershocks.

"You're so fucking beautiful," he murmurs as he leans down to kiss me. I wind my arms around his neck and return the kiss eagerly. I always feel particularly affectionate after he shakes up my world.

He smiles down at me after he pulls away, taking a moment

just to look at me. I give him a happy smile in return.

He chuckles at that. "You're going to have to wipe that sex-drunk look off your face before we go downstairs, though. I don't exactly need my mother knowing I made my girlfriend come hard enough to see stars."

I roll my eyes, but I can't fake my annoyance enough to actually let go of him. "So cocky," I murmur as I pull his mouth down to mine.

It doesn't take long for the kiss to escalate again. Just as I slide my tongue across Jax's, pulling a groan from his throat, a voice calls from downstairs that dinner is ready.

Another groan, this time clearly frustrated about the interruption.

"Later," he says, nipping at my lip before he rolls off of me.

I grin. I hope he never gets tired of me, never loses the hunger that always shines in his eyes when he looks at me—regardless of if it's been a week since he's touched me or five minutes.

For some reason, the thought sobers me. I'm quiet as I clean myself up and pull on my clothes.

Jax notices, of course. He always notices.

He pulls me into his arms before I can walk through the door.

"Hey," he says quietly. "Where'd I lose you? What's wrong?"

I wrap my arms around his waist and bury my face in his chest, taking a deep breath and soaking up the essence that is Jax. Warm, comforting, stable. Loves me.

Six months ago, I would've swept my worry under the rug

and told myself it was a ridiculous thought. Too stupid to share.

But I'm not that person anymore.

So I pull back and look Jax in the eye as I confess, "Sometimes I worry that this much happiness isn't sustainable. That we're in the honeymoon phase right now but that it's not always going to feel like this, that you won't always look at me like you want to devour me, and… I don't know, I'm just worried it's too good to be true."

Jax doesn't brush off my concern. He nods, as if he completely understands, and tightens his arms around me.

"I know why you're worried, but do you ever think that it *is* sustainable? That maybe the honeymoon phase is for couples that aren't 100% right for each other the way that we are?" He pauses to actually let me think about it. "Because if I think about it, I can't picture a day where I love you even an ounce less than I do right now. And I *definitely* love you more today than I did yesterday. Or six months ago. Don't you?"

I nod my head immediately—of course I feel the same way. Every day, I think I can't love him more, and every day, I fall more in love with him. Of course I can't picture a day where I love him any less.

He tightens his hug again. "This isn't a honeymoon phase, baby girl. This is our new normal. It's okay to get used to it."

I nod again, this time in agreement. Though my days of worry are few and far between, he always knows exactly what to say to make me feel better—knows exactly how to put my mind at ease.

He presses a kiss to my hair. "Trust me enough to love you just as much today as I did yesterday."

Any remaining worry leaves my body in a whoosh. Then I'm weaving my arms behind Jax's neck and pushing up on my toes so I can better kiss him with all the love I can muster in a kiss.

"I love you," I whisper against his lips, my kiss becoming urgent. Urgently trying to express just how big my feelings for him are. "Today, tomorrow, and every day after that."

His mouth curves against mine in a smile. His arms tighten around my waist, and I know he loves these moments when I'm overwhelmed with affection for him. "I love you too, baby girl," he murmurs against my eager lips. "Always. Forever."

When I finally pull back, it's just in time, because another call comes for us from downstairs. I untangle my arms from around Jax and step back, though he only lets me go so far since he keeps a hold of my hand. "We should go before she sends Grandma Birdie to come looking for us," I say with a chuckle.

Jax smiles, and with that one smile, I wonder how I ever thought my love for this man could fade. He squeezes my hand and checks in with me one last time. "Good?" he murmurs.

I smile and nod. "I'm good," I whisper.

Mrs. Turner is pulling a casserole out of the oven when we finally walk into the kitchen.

"Oh, there you two are," she says with a big smile. "Did you have fun looking through high school yearbooks? He and Remy were a terror during those years. But I could've sworn there were a few with Hailey in them too. Did you find them?"

Jax's lips twitch as he fights a smile. "Yeah, we had fun looking through the yearbooks." He ignores my pinch to his side. "Do you need help with anything, Mom?"

She gives him a grateful smile. "If you could set the table, that would be great."

Jax nods and makes his way toward the cabinets. But as he walks by her, he pauses to give her a peck on the cheek. She smiles at him in return.

"So, Hailey, how are you?" she asks me as she pulls off her oven mitts and gives me her full attention. "What's new in your life? Are you still living with Remy?"

I shake my head. "No, I found my own place a few months ago. I'm still in South Philly, but I live on my own now."

Mrs. Turner twists to look at Jax where he's counting out utensils. "That reminds me, are you and Tristan going to renew your lease? It's up soon, isn't it?"

Jax and I exchange a look, a smile tugging at his lips. "We're not going to renew. I'm sick of living with men."

I look down with a smile, feeling my face flame with warmth. Even the thought of living with Jax makes me deliriously happy.

Mrs. Turner nods solemnly. "I can appreciate that concern."

"Oh, please," sounds Mr. Turner as he walks into the kitchen. "If it wasn't for me, you would have overgrown grass, spiders would be running rampant in the house, and you'd have no one to make fun of those horrible reality TV shows with that you refuse to admit you like." I practically melt when he kisses his blushing wife and chuckles.

She swats at his chest, a smile creeping onto her face.

"They're *not* horrible," she murmurs.

Jax claps his dad on the shoulder as he passes him to grab glassware. "Ask Hailey how work's been going, Mom."

Mrs. Turner turns her attention back to me. "How's work? Are you still at that lovely little café?"

I nod. "I am. I'm actually in the process of buying it."

Mrs. Turner's eyes go wide in shock. "You are? That's incredible, honey! Congratulations!"

I couldn't help the smile on my face if I tried. "Thanks. It's kind of been a lifelong dream, so I'm pretty excited about it."

"Oh, that's right!" Mrs. Turner exclaims, clapping her hands together. "You always loved baking when you were little. You used to make those delicious double chocolate cupcakes, if I remember correctly."

I nod again. "I won't actually be doing the baking like I wanted to when I was a kid, but it'll be fun to be in charge of the menu. I have some great recipes that I think people will love."

"I would say being able to make a good dessert is the best way to make a man fall in love with you, but it looks like you've already learned that lesson."

We all turn to watch as Grandma Birdie walks into the kitchen. And true to form, she has an obnoxiously large bird pin clipped to her hair.

She levels her gaze at me, and I suck in a breath. I've met Jax's grandmother before, but never in any setting that wasn't as Remy's little sister; it's common knowledge that she's been trying to set Jax and Remy up for years, so I was never really worth paying attention to in her eyes.

Now, she's giving me her full attention.

I don't breathe the entire time she looks me up and down. I'm pretty sure no one else is breathing, either. I feel like I'm waiting for a verdict that will either free me or send me to the electric chair.

"Is that why my grandson likes you?" she asks with a quirked brow. "Because of your... cupcakes?"

Mrs. Turner gasps. "Mom!"

Birdie shoots an innocent look at her daughter. "Get your mind out of the gutter, Emily. I'm just asking about her skills in the kitchen. It's important for a woman to be able to feed her man."

"I'm actually more than capable of feeding myself, Grandma, believe it or not," Jax quips.

She flaps a hand at him without even taking her eyes off me. Like his efforts to save me from her inquisition are in vain.

She just waits and stares.

"He loves me for a number of reasons," I say in a steady voice. "I'm sure my baking and cooking skills are among them."

She tilts her head, studying me. "You know, the reason I liked Remy for Jax is because she was a strong, take-no-shit kind of girl."

"Who can't cook," I interrupt.

She ignores me. "You've always been the sweet, quiet girl in the background. How do you know you're a good match for my grandson?"

I quirk an eyebrow, never once looking away from her staredown. "Just because I'm not as loud as my crazy sister doesn't mean I'm weak. Or incapable of matching wits with an old lady." I end my parting shot with a wink.

Mrs. Turner sucks in a startled breath.

Mr. Turner sighs and shakes his head.

Jax just grins.

"You think you could take me, huh?" Birdie asks in a curious tone.

I give a stiff nod. "If you try to push Jax toward my sister again, I can guarantee it."

She continues to stare at me. For a breath. And then two.

I never break eye contact.

Then… she grins.

A wide grin that lights up her whole face, and I swear even the bird in her hair looks happier.

"Good," she says with a nod. "I've been waiting for the day that someone stands up to me. I knew that would be the kind of woman my Jaxon deserved. Even Remy never did that. Well done, girl."

The tension in the room deflates like a balloon. Everyone heaves an audible sigh of relief, myself included—though I wait until Birdie turns toward the wine rack before I let it out. God knows I'm never letting that woman get even a whiff of fear.

"And you're right about the cupcakes," she says as an afterthought. "They really are the way to a man's... heart. I could tell you a story or two about my cupcakes that had Jax's grandfather begging for—"

"Birdie!" shrieks Mrs. Turner.

Mr. Turner winces.

Jax groans and drags a hand down his face.

I just laugh. Loudly.

"Congratulations, you've officially defeated the final obstacle," Jax murmurs in my ear. "Everything after this is a cakewalk. Or a cupcake-walk, apparently." I snort at the pun and bring my hand to my mouth, shaking with silent laughter.

As always, he looks downright giddy at the sight.

He wraps an arm around my shoulders, and asks, "So what's next? Our options are limitless. We can do anything you want."

I wrap my arms around his waist and gaze up at him with what I'm sure is hearts in my eyes. "Anything?" I whisper with a smile.

The smile he shines at me lights up my world the same way it's been doing since I was ten years old. The same way it always will.

"Anything, baby girl," he answers.

BONUS CHAPTER

I wake up to a feeling of bliss.

I cling to sleep, wanting to stay enveloped in this wonderful dream forever, but the harder I try to keep my eyes closed, the more I start to realize this feeling isn't actually a dream.

I let out a moan and spread my legs wider, arching into the incredible sensations that only Jax has ever been able to evoke in me.

"Jax, please," I whisper, my hands fisting beside me in the sheets.

An answering groan sounds beneath the covers. And just as predicted, the words result in a frenzy of activity.

His tongue continues swirling over my clit, but now it's joined by the feeling of two fingers sliding inside me. I let out another moan as the wave of my orgasm starts to bear down on me.

"Yes, right there," I whisper. "Jax, *fuck*, oh my God…"

And when the wave finally breaks over me, pleasure spreading like water through my body, I have a fleeting thought that my reality lately is so much better than any dream state.

Eventually the pleasure fades and I sag back into the bed, sighing in contentment. I blink my eyes open as Jax starts to crawl up my body and I chuckle when his head pops up from under the covers.

"Good morning, baby girl," he purrs, leaning down to press a sweet kiss against my lips. I smile into it, then smile wider when he starts to trail kisses along my jaw and down my neck.

"Good morning to you, too," I respond, lifting my arms to wrap around his broad shoulders and trail my fingers through his blonde hair. "That was a nice surprise."

Jax nips at my neck and somehow the throbbing in my core begins again. I have no idea how, since we spent two hours in this bed last night doing anything and everything.

"Well, today is a special occasion," Jax murmurs, pulling my attention away from the memories of last night. "I wanted to start the day off right."

I frown. "What's today?"

At that, his head finally pops up so he can look down at me. A tiny smile pulls at his lips—the one that always stops my heart in its tracks because he looks *so happy* when he aims it at me. With just that smile I can *feel* how much he loves me.

"It's your birthday," he answers simply.

I can only blink at him for a moment. I completely forgot I turn twenty-two today. "Oh," I manage to say.

Then... a huge smile breaks across my face. I tighten my grip around Jax's neck and ask, "So, does that mean you have big plans to celebrate me? I'll have you know I expect undivided attention and lots of orgasms and to be generally treated like a queen today."

I say it in a joking tone but Jax's expression is anything-but. He brushes the back of his knuckles against my cheek and says quietly, "I want to do that for you every day."

My expression morphs from joking to a genuine smile. I lift up slightly to kiss him. "I know," I murmur against his lips. "And every day you do."

He lets out a relieved breath, and then his smile is back to being happy and in love. "I do have plans for us today, though. Would you like breakfast in bed or do you want to come out to the kitchen?"

"In a minute," I murmur, too turned on by his care for me to focus on food right now. I pull him back down for another kiss. "First I want you to finish what you started."

He chuckles against my lips. "Hailey, that was supposed to be for your pleasure, not mine. I'm okay without it."

"I'm happy to hear it," I say into a kiss. "I, on the other hand, am not." I wrap my legs around his waist and pull him down so his hard cock is pressed against my aching center. He groans at the sensation and drops his forehead to mine. "It's my birthday, isn't it? Didn't you say you'd give me what I want? Well, I want you to fuck me."

His lips start to twitch with a smile that he's trying not to show. "Yes, ma'am," he finally answers when he loses the battle and a grin spreads across his face.

Then he reaches down to guide himself inside me.

It doesn't take long for both of us to start moaning and writhing in pleasure. By the time I start scratching at his back and gasping his name, Jax is already burying his face in my neck and letting out a string of curses.

"Jax," I gasp. "Please, make me come…"

I feel him lift his head just enough that he can breathe his command directly into his ear.

"Let go, Hailey. Come for me like my good little whore."

Pleasure sparks in me like fireworks in the sky. I'm vaguely aware of Jax groaning into my skin, his hips jerking as he finds his release, but I'm so far gone in my own orgasm that it barely registers.

"Fuck, you always feel so good," Jax gasps as he sags into my body. "It almost feels like *my* birthday today."

I let out a weak giggle at that. He lifts his head, looking just as pleased that he made me laugh as he always does, and drops a quick kiss to my lips.

"Ready for food now?" he asks.

I let out a groan and throw my arm over my face. "How is it possible for you to be ready for food at any point in the day? I can't even think about breakfast right now. I'm going to need about an hour to recover from that dicking."

He chuckles and pulls away from me. I peek out from under my arm so I can not-so-secretly drool over his massive muscular body. I watch as he pulls on shorts and a T-shirt, then let out an exaggerated huff when he tosses another one of his shirts at me to put on.

"Let's go, baby girl. You'll love it, I promise."

I reluctantly sit up in bed so I can pull his shirt over my head. When he tugs me to my feet and the hem reaches my mid-thigh, I can't help but chuckle at the size difference between us.

"I need to pee and brush my teeth," I tell him. "I'll meet

you downstairs in five minutes?"

He nods with a grin and practically prances out of the bedroom. I can't help but chuckle at the childlike excitement my boyfriend has anytime he does something for me.

But when I make my way downstairs and see what he set up for me, I can't even blame him for it. I'd be excited, too.

Jax is standing behind the kitchen island, smiling proudly at the breakfast buffet he has laid out in front of him. There are waffles piled high on one plate and bananas foster simmering in a skillet beside them, plus glasses of orange juice and a bowl of chopped fruit. There's even a vase of fresh flowers.

"How did you… when did you…?" I trail off in a shell-shocked voice.

His grin widens. "I got up early to get everything set up. Do you like it? I tried a new recipe for the bananas foster, I'm really hoping it's as good as it smells."

"It's amazing," I say in a daze. "How did you time this so perfectly? I mean, this is… perfect."

He walks around the island so he can step behind me, wrapping his arms around my waist and nuzzling into my neck. "I was pretty confident you'd sleep in this morning. It was one of the reasons I kept you under me for two hours last night."

I smother a whimper at the deep, sexy timber of his voice. And at the memories of the things he had done to my body, the pleasure he had wrung from me…

"Your heart is racing, baby girl," he teases, and I can feel him smile against my skin.

"I'm trying really hard to focus on this breakfast instead of how badly I want you to bend me over again," I murmur.

He chuckles. "Such a dirty mind."

I shake my head to try to clear the sudden lust-drunk haze. And when I notice the gift bag at the end of the counter, it becomes a little easier to do just that.

"You got me a present, too?" I ask. Although I don't know why I'm surprised—*of course* Jax thought of everything.

"I did," he says, nudging me in the direction of the gift. "Open it, then we'll eat."

When I reach the gift bag it takes me a minute to dig through the insane amount of tissue paper inside. I look at him in confusion, which only makes him grin.

"Keep looking," he encourages.

I pull everything out of the bag and roll my eyes when I realize the only thing inside is an envelope at the very bottom. I slide my finger under the flap and pull out a folded piece of paper.

And then yelp in excitement when I see what it is.

"You got me tickets to see Odesza?!" I shriek. I take a closer look at the paper. "Wait, this is in Miami." I look up at him in confusion.

Jax just shrugs and explains, "I bought plane tickets and booked a hotel room for you and Remy to go down for the weekend. Figured you'd enjoy a few days away with just the two of you."

I gawk at my boyfriend, completely stunned into speechlessness.

After a moment, I manage to make my mouth work. "So let me get this straight," I start. "Not only did you buy tickets to an event for me to take *someone else*, but you also planned a whole weekend around it?" I gape at him. "Are you even real?"

He shrugs again, looking a little bashful this time. "Well, I know you like going to shows, but since it's not really my kind of music I thought you'd have more fun with Remy." He hesitates for a second, looking slightly confused as he asks, "Would you rather I go with you? Because I can do that."

I walk back to him so I can wrap my arms around his waist and smile up at him. "You're amazing," I whisper. "And I love you more today than I did yesterday. Thank you for making this the best birthday ever."

The concern melts from his face, to be replaced by a pleased smile. He leans down to kiss me, then whispers, "Anything for you, baby girl."

Eventually I manage to pull away from him just enough that I can reach the skillet of bananas. I dip a spoon into the mixture and bring it to Jax's lips in offering, but he just shakes his head and nudges it toward me, saying, "You first."

I take the spoon in my mouth and almost immediately, my eyelids flutter shut. "Oh my God," I moan in pleasure. The bananas are warm and the mixture is delicious, the flavors mixing into the perfect sweet mouthful. "It's like an orgasm in my mouth." My eyes pop open so I can look at Jax when I praise his cooking skills.

But I never get that far because his eyes are black with desire, and he's looking down at my lips as his grip tightens on my waist.

"Moan like that one more time and we'll have to skip breakfast entirely," he growls.

I grin and dip the spoon in the skillet again, this time

bringing it to Jax's lips. Reluctantly, he tears his gaze away from me and takes the spoon in his mouth.

And sure enough, he groans when the flavors explode on his tongue.

"Okay, yeah, you're right, that's delicious," he admits. Only now I'm the one that's distracted by *his* sounds, because all I can think about is seeing what it tastes like on him.

"Before I capitalize on that look and bend you over this counter, let's talk about one thing first," he says in a strained voice. "What do you want to do after breakfast?"

"I don't care," I admit in a distracted tone, pushing up on my toes so I can leave kisses along his jaw.

His chuckle vibrates against my lips. "That's not an answer, Hailes. We have dinner with Tristan and Remy tonight because I knew you'd want to see them, but other than that we have the whole day to ourselves. So what do you want to do?"

I lean my forehead against his cheek and think for a minute. *If I can spend the day doing anything today, what do I want to do?*

I pull back and give Jax an honest answer. "I just want to spend it with you. Here. Maybe we can hang out and watch movies? If we're going out tonight then I don't really want to do anything big today." I tighten my arms around his waist. "Spend the day with me here, please?"

He smiles and presses a kiss to my forehead. "Anything for you, my queen."

Then he reaches for the banana mixture. I open my mouth for another bite, taking my time pulling my lips off of the offered spoon.

"Now that that's settled, I really want to see what these

bananas taste like from your mouth," he growls, backing me against the counter.

And when he leans down to do just that, I forget about everything except the way he feels against my body.

To read the rest of this bonus chapter, visit
Nikki's official website!

ACKNOWLEDGEMENTS

This book was a labor of love, to say the least. I wanted so badly to do this story justice, so I put my heart and soul (and the sweat of many others) into these pages.

I have so many people to thank. The first one is always my husband, who has not only supported my dream to be a writer but also tirelessly volunteered to test out certain scenes with me. I appreciate your sacrifice, babe.

To my sister, who was my sounding board throughout this entire process and who never complained about my million phone calls when I absolutely needed to know if an idea was shit or a scene was cringe-worthy.

To Amanda and Nicole, who are my beta readers, graphic designers, therapists, and friends all rolled into one. This book would have looked very, *very* different without you two being a part of this entire crazy process. I can't thank you enough for all your help, not just with this book, but with so many other things that I never anticipated needing a support system for. I'm so grateful for you both.

To Dora, Krista, and Maria, my wonderful beta readers and friends who helped shape this book into what it is today. And an extra shoutout to Dora for proofreading for me at the 11th hour because she's just that kind of friend that drops everything for you when you ask.

To my wonderful, amazing, brilliant editor Kenzie: you're a genius. To say this book would not have been half as good without your help is an understatement. I'm constantly in awe of the way you're able to shape a story to be exactly what it needs to be. Thank you for helping me to tell this story in the way it deserved to be told.

To my family, friends, readers, *everyone* that has supported me throughout this writing journey, all I can say is *THANK YOU!* Without you, a book is just some ink on a dead tree. Thank you for taking a chance on this book and for helping to share Hailey and Jax's story. I love you all more than words can describe.

ALSO BY NIKKI CASTLE

More in the **Fight Game** Series:

Book One: 5 Rounds
Book Three: 3 Count
Book Four: 1 Last Shot

Or if you want some fun, quick spice, check out the **Just Tonight** novella series!

The Stranger in Seat 8B

ABOUT THE AUTHOR

Nikki Castle is a wife and dog mom from Philadelphia who writes spicy love stories about alpha MMA fighters and the women that melt their badass, playboy hearts. She's a full-time romance author during the day and spends her evenings running a Mixed Martial Arts (MMA) gym with her husband, who is also a retired fighter.

Nikki has been writing in one way or another since she was a teenager. She pursued an English and Philosophy degree in college, and finally decided to sit down and fulfill her longtime dream of writing an entire novel when quarantine began in 2020.

Made in the USA
Las Vegas, NV
21 April 2024